SMILER's

By

George Donald

Also By George Donald

Billy's Run
Charlie's Promise
A Question of Balance
Natural Justice
Logan
A Ripple of Murder
A Forgotten Murder
The Seed of Fear
The Knicker-knocker
The Cornishman
A Presumption of Murder
A Straight Forward Theft
The Medal
A Decent Wee Man
Charlie's Dilemma
The Second Agenda
Though the Brightest Fell
The ADAT
A Loan with Patsy
A Thread of Murder
Harry's Back
Charlie's Recall
The Broken Woman
Mavisbank Quay
Maggie Brogan
Malinky
The Privileged Daughter
A Conflicted Revenge
Charlie's Swansong
The Rookie Suspect
No Sad Loss
Maitland
The Rule Of The Six 'P's'
The Dragon's Breath
The Murder Suspect List
The Convicted Woman
The Honest Policeman
The Man With Inner Rage
DCI Wells
Malice by Mail
The Murderous Route To Peace

This work is mine and mine alone and all characters and events mentioned, other than those clearly in the public domain, are fictitious (apart from those characters who have asked to be part of the story).

And so any resemblance to any *other* individual is purely coincidental.

As I likely have previously mentioned, writing crime fiction is not my profession, but my hobby and so while I recognise that it is not ideal to self-edit and self-publish one's own work, I accept that any spelling, grammatical or other mistakes are mine and mine alone.

If you should come across some errors, hopefully you'll cut me some slack, forgive such mistakes and fingers crossed, they do not interfere with the storyline.

George Donald

PROLOGUE

The rain dribbled down the front of the windscreen as he sat staring into nothing.

He had been lucky, of that there was no doubt in his mind, but then again, he inwardly sighed; that depends on how you viewed being lucky.

Lucky that he still had a job maybe, but that luck was down to the lawyer representing him and contracted by the Police Federation, Mr Crossan, an old style lawyer, dressed a suit that was older than his client and who when close by, gave off a definite whiff of stale perspiration and ruddy cheeks and an even ruddier nose that was a clear indication of his fondness for whisky.

However, whereas a younger or more inexperienced brief might immediately throw in the towel, the wily old Crossan had argued his case against what should have been an instant dismissal.

Lucky, again, but tempered with a boot in the balls because of course it also meant the end of what had promised to be a successful career; a career that just seven months previously had seemed so bright and worthwhile.

Crossan's defence of him had fully blamed and maligned Janice and at the outset caused him some discomfort and even had him contemplating interrupting the old lawyer, but the more details the Crossan disclosed, the more he reasoned that the white-haired older man was correct to vilify her as she *bloody* deserved!

He grimly smiled, inwardly regretting that she had not been present at the Disciplinary Hearing to hear her character torn apart and defamed, just as she had abused and completely disregarded her wedding vows.

His brow furrowed when he recalled some of the details Crossan had revealed, details that he had not known and their disclosure must have shown on his face when he felt his body become rigid and his face turn white with shock, for he could see the sympathy written on the face of the Deputy Chief Constable and who had avoided his eyes, her pity expressed in the tightening of her lips and her downward glance.

He had not expected that reaction from her.

With eloquence and dignity, the white-haired lawyer had abridged those four months of his marriage, relating how their whirlwind romance of just three months had concluded with a civil marriage ceremony after Janice had wept, then declared herself pregnant. God, what a fool, what a *complete* and naive idiot he had been! Sitting there silently, his hands clenched in his lap, he had listened to Crossan's slow and laconic voice while the lawyer continued to address the Hearing, a rasping voice that echoed the countless years of nicotine intake.

"And let us also consider that my client," the old man had said, "till the time of the incident was a much-respected officer of this Force. A young man of impeccable character who with just under eight years' service had already achieved the rank of sergeant and of whom great things were expected. A young man who, when informed by his then girlfriend that she was pregnant, did not hesitate, but did the honourable thing by offering marriage, only for his new wife to reveal just three weeks later she had lost the baby." He had theatrically paused after that statement, then with a forthright stare directly at the Chief Constable, he posed the question "The question must be considered; had there in fact *been* a baby? Or is more than likely my client had in fact been duped?"

Seconds passed to permit the Hearing to consider this thought, then he sighed, "But the young woman, Janice, now his wife and living in idyllic comfort with my client in his flat where unemployed, she was not only accessing his salary and yes," he raised a forefinger to the ceiling, "squandering his savings too, for it now transpires she was *not* the woman she pretended to be."

He had slowly turned to stare narrow eyed at his client when he softly added, "These details I have retained till now, fearful that my client might refuse me the opportunity to apprise this Hearing of the sordid details, but in truth and though it will pain him deeply, I must now disclose the shocking facts."

Once more, he paused to shake his head, then turning to stare into his client's eyes, Crossan took a slow breath before he began, "The woman who deliberately manipulated herself into your life is in fact a liar, a philanderess, but more importantly, I regret having to inform you, was a *viper* in your nest."

He had felt himself tensing, his body bristling, yet some instinct told him to refrain from reacting, which was just as well, for Crossan again gently sighed, "My client, good man and good husband that he intended to be, was completely taken in by this woman."

The Chief and his Deputy watched as the old lawyer reached into his briefcase to withdraw a sheet of paper that he dramatically flourished in the air, then said, "I can now disclose to this Hearing that my inquiries have discovered this duplicitous bride was *not* as my client and the officials at Martha Street Registry Office had been affirmed by her to be, an unmarried woman, but in fact prior to their wedding ceremony, was already divorced once," his voce raised a pitch, "that we *know* of and had prior to meeting my client, re-married to another man! In truth, a woman who I can only describe as a serial bride!"

The revelation, kept from him by Crossan, had taken him completely by surprise and the shame of being so deceived had burned at his cheeks.

Now sitting in the parked car, he recalled how under the table he'd been seated at, his legs had shaken, his throat too dry to respond and when he reached for it, spilling the glass of water across the table where he sat.

The silence in the room had been broken when the Chief Constable beckoned the uniformed Administration Inspector to fetch the sheet of paper to him.

He'd watched the Chief place his reading glasses on his nose, then hand the paper to his Deputy, who studiously scanned the document before she carefully said, "I must ask, Mr Crossan, how did you come about this information?"

The old lawyer smiled when he replied, "My informant, my dear Ms Clarke, must at this time remain anonymous, though if required, I can produce a notarised statement declaring the copied document you hold in your hand to be true."

The tense silence that followed with all eyes in the room now on the Deputy Chief, who like all present, realised that to enable Crossan to complete a background check on Janice, he must have had someone enter her details into the Police National Computer, the PNC.

But who that individual might be, they also knew, would remain secret for the wily old lawyer would never reveal his source.

And so, rather unveil a probable misuse of the PNC system and cause a data protection investigation, the Deputy Chief wisely ignored pressing the issue and simply nodded when she replied, "You understand, Mr Crossan, that by disclosing this information, you have libelled an accusation of bigamy against your client's wife, a contravention of the Marriage (Scotland) Act of 1977. An accusation that must be investigated by officers under the Chief Constable's command."

"Indeed I do, Ma'am," the portly Crossan had drawn himself up to his full height of five feet and four inches, then added, "And of course of behalf of the Police Federation, I will represent my client in any action that might entail to extract him from this dastardly, bigamous marriage he had unwittingly entered into."

Seconds passed before the assembled Hearing watched as the Deputy Chief Constable leaned across to whisper into the Chief's ear and by his expression, seemed to have surprised him.

After she sat back and upright in her chair, it was then the Chief Constable had turned to solemnly stare at him when he said, "Sergeant Devlin, you of course will not be involved in such an investigation other than as a possible witness against your wife. Or rather," he deeply inhaled, then blew out through pursed cheeks, "the woman, Janice Goodwin, who has, eh, falsely entered into a dishonest marriage with you. Do you understand?"

"Yes, sir, of course," he had muttered, his mouth dry and surprised that he was able to even speak.

"Now," the Chief had straightened in his own chair, then continued, "to business. As to the common law charge of assault that was initially laid against you, Sergeant Devlin, though of course the complaint was later withdrawn, you did bring the Force into disrepute and thus contravene the Police (Scotland) Act of 1967 and so on that charge, I find you guilty."

The Chief had stared steely eyed at him before he added, "It is within my power to exercise such punishment as I see fit and in normal circumstances, you would be dismissed without reference and that would also mean the forfeiture of all pension rights. Do you understand?"

It was the phrase 'under normal circumstances' that caused his eyes to flicker and to cause him the slightest of hope.

The Chief paused and drew a short breath before he continued, "However, I take advice from my Deputy and I also I take note of your Counsel's very persuasive defence of your state of mind at the time of the alleged assault and it does somewhat tend to mitigate your reaction when discovering the circumstances of your wife's, eh," he grimaced, "behaviour."

He paused for breath, then continued, "That all said, your conduct on the night in question was less than that expected for a police officer of your rank and so, it is my finding that you be stripped of the rank of sergeant, returned to the rank of constable and transferred from your current post to…"

He turned to glance at the Deputy Chief who quietly prompted him with, "F Division, sir. Craigie Street."

"Well," the Chief turned back to him, then nodding, said, "there we have it. You are transferred to F Division at Craigie Street, *Constable* Devlin. This Hearing," he rose from his chair at which all seated present did likewise, "is now concluded."

In the corridor outside and standing with the uniformed Administration Inspector and unable to believe his good fortune, Devlin turned to Crossan to thank him, but his thanks were waved away when the old lawyer laid a hand on is arm, then smiled, "If there is any issue about an annulment from that wretched woman, Mathew, first inform the Federation office in Merrylee Road, who will make an appointment for you to come and see me. Oh, and if you have any notion of thanking me," the old lawyer outrageously winked, "my preferred tipple is a bottle of that rich, golden liquid from the Campbeltown distillery, Glen Scotia."

CHAPTER ONE: Thursday, 1pm, the same day 8 March 1979.

Devlin glanced at the black bin bag in the rear seat of his Mark 3 Ford Cortina and sighed.

The Administration Inspector, though not known to Devlin, had seemed a decent enough sort and accompanied him to the stores department on the first floor of Pitt Street, where the former sergeant had exchanged his tunics with the three stripes on the arms for constable tunics, then informed him, "The Chief Inspector at Craigie Street will be contacted by the Personnel Department and will expect you to arrive straight from here."

Shrugging, the Inspector quietly added, "I can't imagine how you must be feeling, but can I suggest you attend there right away. Bad enough what's happened to you, Mathew, and what you had to endure in the Chief's office, but you'll not want to piss off your new boss by having him wait for you to arrive."

"Sound advice, sir, thanks," he'd nodded, then made his way out of the building to his car parked at the bay in Elmbank Street.

Now sitting in the navy-blue coloured Mark III Cortina, parked in Craigie Street outside the F Divisional headquarters, he turned to stare at the old Victorian building, seeing two uniformed cops in their nylon raincoats depart the front entrance, their heads down and one hand on their caps to foil the sudden gust of rainy wind.

His stomach unaccountably churning, he reached behind him to withdrew a tunic and his uniform cap from the black plastic bin bag, then taking a deep breath, got out of the car.

****

Seated behind the desk in her office, Chief Inspector Lizzie Whitmore replaced the handset into its cradle, then sighed.

The Superintendent from the Personnel Department at Pitt Street had unknowingly landed another problem in her lap, as if she didn't have enough going on with her lack of personnel and particularly, junior supervisors.

What made it worse was his supercilious response when she asked why a demoted sergeant was being landed on her.

"Because he has to go somewhere, Chief Inspector, so deal with it!"

Wanker, she had thought, but like it or not, she now had a demoted sergeant on her hands who she rightly guessed, would be bitter at being reduced in rank to constable.

This on top of her acrimonious divorce action was the last thing she needed right now.

Sitting upright in her swivel chair, she arched her back to reduce the ache in her neck and idly speculated who she'd unwittingly pissed off to land her with this new problem.

Her thoughts turned to her pending divorce, the date for the hearing set just one week away and speculated that her husband, Martin, dirty rotten *bastard* that he is, would fight tooth and nail to get his share of her pension and commutation, due her when she retired, though he'd another eleven years to wait for it.

If he were to be successful and even if it did cost her financially, if nothing else she would be free of him; free to be the woman she really was and, she smiled, with the loving support of her twin daughters too.

And that, she knew, was worth more than any sum of money.

They had met as most couple did back then, at a city centre dance hall; the Locarno in Sauchiehall Street, then following a year's courtship, marriage had naturally followed.

On hindsight, she recognised now that theirs had never really been a contented affair; she a rookie cop and he just completing his accountancy training.

From the outset, he'd constantly complained about her shift work, then the arrival of the twins disclosed he was not only hopeless at rearing children, but took little part in the domestic duties, as well as preferring the golf course to family outings.

As the years passed by, so did the stress within their relationship. Yet somehow they'd muddled through those early years together, though by their fifteenth anniversary, it was clear that all love was lost and clearly, Martin was not cut out to be a father.

Then there was his affair, albeit a brief liaison with one of the staff from his firm; an affair she forgave, but didn't forget and reconciled with simply for the sake of the girls.

It had finally come to an end the previous year on the Spanish trip. The supposed celebration of her fortieth birthday and their first time on holiday without the twins.

The week in Majorca at the luxury hotel in Cala D'or was, she had vainly hoped, an opportunity to rekindle some of their relationship, but when he had returned home a week prior to their flight with a brand-new driver and putter, she realised then that it was Martin's intention to spend the holiday golfing.

Yet pissed at him though she were, with the hotel and flights already booked and prepaid, she decided to travel to Majorca and though she hadn't known it at the time, the trip was to change her life.

It happened on their third night.

Martin, returning tipsy and sunburned from an excursion to an exclusive golf course, decided to booze the rest of the night away and staggered off to their room a little after ten o'clock.

Bored and extremely irate, she had engaged in conversation with Melanie, an attractive divorcee holidaying from Aberdeen and younger than Lizzie by just three years.

One drink led to another and before she knew it, they were in Mel's room and where she awoke in the morning in bed naked, the daylight streaming through the balconied window with a similarly naked Mel asleep and her arm carelessly flung across Lizzie's shoulders.

Confused and more than a little embarrassed, she quietly slipped from the bed and dressed, then when trying to creep from the room, stopped and turned to thoughtfully stare at the sleeping woman.

It was, she later explained to her daughters, as though she had some sort of awakening; a realisation that she had become the woman she really was meant to be.

What made her strip off and return to the bed, she never knew, but when she did, Mel awoke and there she remained for the next hour.

Smiling at the memory of that time, her head snapped up when her door was knocked.

****

The youngish, fair-haired man with the clear complexion, standing a little over five ten, she thought, but difficult to be sure with his cap on, entered at her call, then approaching her desk, stood beside the chair opposite, then shuffled to a form of attention before he said, "Constable Mathew Devlin reporting, Ma'am."

Staring over her head at the window behind, she guessed Devlin to be the demoted sergeant, confirmed when he quietly replied to her question, "Yes, Ma'am. I've just come down from Pitt Street and I was instructed to report directly to the sub-Divisional officer."

She sensed he was nervous and though unaware of the circumstances of his demotion and rather than craning her neck to stare up at him, politely told him, "Please, Constable Devlin, take a seat."

"Ma'am," he removed his cap and sat down and that's when at last, he met her stare.

A police officer for nineteen years, Lizzie had seen the best and the worst of people and that included the police officers she worked with.

So, while she couldn't explain it, some inner instinct told her that Devlin wasn't as bitter as she might have expected him to be and so she admitted, "I haven't been informed why you are here at Craigie Street…"

She hesitated, then asked, "Can I call you Mathew?"

"Yes, of course, Ma'am," he nodded, though she saw still remained tense.

"Anyway, Mathew," she hesitantly smiled at him, "for what it's worth, I'm pleased you are here for right now, underpaid and understaffed as Strathclyde Police currently is, you're a welcome addition to the Division and particularly with your experience as a sergeant under your belt."

He didn't respond, so she slowly continued, "No matter what occurred that brings you here, as far as I am concerned, you have arrived with a clean slate. All I ask from you is that you give me an honest day's work, that whatever baggage brought you here in the first place is left at your previous office. Oh, where was that, anyway?"

His eyes narrowed in suspicion, when he said, "If I might ask, Ma'am, are you telling me that you have no idea why I was demoted and sent here?"

"I neither know nor have any interest in why," she glibly lied, though of course her curiosity was killing her and felt certain she'd find out in due course.

However, that answer seemed to satisfy him and taking a slow breath, he said, "I was previously stationed at Clydebank office, Ma'am, though I started my service in the former Dunbartonshire Constabulary."

She smiled when she said, "Well, we're all Strathclyde officers now, Mathew."

Pulling open a desk drawer, she reached in and fetched out a small, brown envelope, then handing them across the desk, said, "These are your Divisional Numerals. Now," she rose from her chair, "the late shift is mustering downstairs, so let me take you down there and introduce you to your new Inspector, Iain Cowan."

****

Just at that moment, Cowan, a fifty-one years old former City of Glasgow police officer, was shaking his head, his tunic hanging on the chair behind him and bemoaning to his sergeant, Lucy Chalmers, about the lack of officers on his shift.

"I mean, Lucy," he grumbled while seated at the spare desk in the Sergeants Room, "how the hell am I to police half the southside of the city with just seven cops, three of who are probationers and hardly have enough experience to wipe their own arses? That and those bloody Burndept radios are well past their sell-by date. I mean, the batteries don't last a shift and after what happened last month," his brow knitted when he sighed.

Chalmers, a thirty-five years old former detective constable, promoted back to uniform two years previously, wisely let Cowan grumble, yet couldn't disagree with him either.

The previous month during a late shift, a variable rest day for the shift which meant they were even more understaffed with two officers off duty, one of the probationers patrolling without a neighbour had been assaulted outside a pub on Cathcart Road when trying to break up a fight between some local neds.
Attempting to call for assistance, the young cop discovered the radio was dead and but for the bar staff dialling nine-nine-nine, the cop might have suffered worse than bruises and a blackened eye.
What riled the rest of the shift was the cop, Lesley Mirren, was a twenty-two-years old female with just nine months service.
Unfortunately for two of her assailants, they were caught running off and according to the police report to the Procurator Fiscal, both resisted arrest and that accounted for their baton injuries.
However, the incident not only left Cowan with a disillusioned officer off on sick leave and the suggestion she might not return, but he now had to deal with the Complaints & Discipline investigating four of his shift after both arrestees complained of being severely beaten.
"And all because of those damned radios," he had fumed at the time.
Seeing how irate he was, Chalmers refrained from smiling, though at the time had thought if the young lassie had been sensible enough to find a phone and call the rammy in before rushing in to tackle the drunken bastards on her own, she might have saved herself a beating and we'd have one more cop out on the street.
But that said, she had to admit, give young Lesley her due; she was no shrinking violet, though hopefully the incident would cause her to think twice at any future brawl.
With a sigh, she was about to suggest a coffee before they went out to read the Daily Briefing Register to their cops, due to commence their shift in fifteen minutes, when the door was pushed open by the Chief Inspector with a constable in tow.
Nodding at Chalmers she turned to address Cowan.
"Inspector Cowan, this is Constable Mathew Devlin, who has just been assigned to the Division from, eh, Clydebank," Lizzie forced a smile. "I know that your shift is desperately short, as are the other three," she sighed, "but Mathew here might at least make up part of the shortfall."
"Right, Iain," she took a breath, "let's have a word about resources before you read the DBR to your shift, so we'll leave Mathew here

in the capable hands of Sergeant Chalmers."
With that Lizzie turned away and out of the door in the sure knowledge that Cowan would follow.
When they were alone, Chalmers stared curiously up at Devlin before she bluntly asked, "You volunteer to come into the city or did you fall foul of someone?"
Realising the word would soon get out anyway, he shrugged when he responded with, "I was up in front of the Chief earlier on today and he demoted me from sergeant to constable."
Now that, I did *not* expect, she inwardly startled, then replied, "Anything you can share or will we all find out in due course?"
He stared down at her, seeing a woman to be in her mid-thirties, he guessed, his own height with collar-length blonde hair and…his eyes narrowed when he realised he was thinking, muscular looking as though she worked out.
He could not know that Chalmers was a fitness fanatic who regardless of her shift, spent at least an hour each day at a private gym, both strenuously exercising and boxing training.
He humourlessly smiled when he replied, "It was a domestic incident gone wrong. I broke the nose of a man who was shagging the woman I thought was my wife."
He saw Chalmers face crease when she hesitantly said, "Wait, you *thought* was your wife?"
"Long story, Sergeant, but if you don't mind, I've just had a kicking at the Chief's Disciplinary Hearing, so right now, I'd rather not go into it all again."
"Fair enough," she turned back to her desk to stare down at the duty roster, then said, "I'll neighbour you with Smiler. He can show you the ropes and introduce you to the beat he works."
"Smiler?"
"Don't ask," she held up her hand with a pretend grimace.
"That's his nickname that as far as I'm aware, he's been called since he started here in F Division, though God knows how many years ago that was," she grinned, then added, "The word is when Smiler started here, the vehicles were still horse drawn. Anyway, Stuart McGarry is his real name. He's known as Smiler because in my time on the shift and as far as anyone recalls, he's never been known to do anything else, but smile. That said, Mathew," she frowned, surprising him by using his forename, "don't be taken in by him.

He's as sharp as they come and smart too, but let's just say he hasn't yet got used to this new way of thinking; this political correctness that the Force and the media are all on about. He's what we younger polis fondly refer to as an old-fashioned cop."

"I'm sorry, Sarge," his eyes narrowed, "how do you mean?"

"Well," she grimaced again when she slowly drawled, "you know the old saying, call a spade a spade? Smiler's stuck somewhere in the nineteen-fifties and so is his attitude. Anyway, he's old school, smart as a whip," she resignedly shook her head, "and knows this area like no one else does and with a who's who encyclopaedic knowledge of its residents. A walking collator, so he is."

She stopped and stared for a few seconds at him before she added, "One thing about Smiler you should know. He's been around the dance floor more than a few times and he's rock solid. I know from experience," her voice lowered, "if you share something with him, it's like talking to a priest."

"I'll bear that in mind," he nodded, but curiously keen to meet this man who had so impressed Chalmers.

She was interrupted from saying more by the Inspector returning to the room, who surprised Devlin by extending his hand and shaking the younger man's, telling him, "I'm hearing you've just been demoted, Mathew, but I'm not interested in what you've done, only what you can do for me. From what the Chief Inspector just told me, you're sitting with almost eight years' service, so that makes you one of my more senior constables."

"Now, so that we get started on the right foot, I've only three rules. If you get into trouble with the bevy, I'll stick by you as long as you don't try to blame anyone else for your problem. If you get into bother because of a woman, I'll stick by you. However," he stared meaningfully at Devlin when he added, "If you get caught thieving, I'll be the first to fire you into the PF. Is that clear?"

Devlin had been in the job long enough to know that with the ridiculously poor salaries the police across the UK were currently being handed, it wasn't uncommon for some officers to take bribes or, what was common, dip the pockets of drunks they arrested. He had even heard of one officer in the Baird Street Division who had been tasked with guarding the house of an elderly woman found dead in her bed, but caught by his sergeant rifling the house and stealing a sum of money from a wardrobe drawer.

And so, pokerfaced, he calmly replied, "Clearly understood, sir."
"Good," Cowan visibly relaxed, then said, "Look, Mathew, that's the talk I give all my new cops, regardless of whether they come from the training college at Tulliallan or elsewhere."
He hesitated, then said, "Right now, after what happened this morning at Pitt Street, you'll be feeling a bit raw, but we both know that times are rough out there in civvy street, so at least the Chief's kept you on in the job. I don't know if that's what you want," he shook his head, "after being demoted and maybe you're staying on just until you decide what you really want to do. But as long as you're here on my shift, I'll be looking for your experience and commitment. Is that also clearly understood?"
"Yes, sir, you'll have no trouble from me," he formally replied.
"Good, right then," Cowan took a deep breath, glad that was out of the way, then said, "Away out to the muster room along the corridor there, Mathew, and meet some of your new colleagues. I'll formally introduce you when Sergeant Chalmers and I get there and oh," he grimaced and held up his hand, "I'll leave you to explain if you wish, how you come to be working here."
"Yes, sir and thank you," Devlin nodded then left the room.
In the corridor outside, he took a sharp breath, then made his way to the muster room along the corridor.
****

Unlike his former station at Clydebank, built in the nineteen-sixties, with its many office and corridor windows that permitted fresh air to filter throughout, the Victorian building housing Craigie Street office, with its decades old painted walls and décor, had a curious intermingling smell of dampness and stale fried food. Even worse was the dank, cellblock corridor, each cell with its antiquated steel toilet embedded in concrete and regardless of the strong disinfectant used by the station's cleaners, still faintly smelling of urine and vomit that permeated the very air.
On the occasion a football match was played at Hampden Park, the smell of drink, vomit and other bodily wastes was so strong that officers on turnkey duty quite literally had to bind handkerchiefs around their noses to prevent them gagging.
And so it was to this office that the newly demoted sergeant, Constable Mathew Devlin, found himself warily striding into the muster room, conscious that the grapevine must already have beaten

the drums as the room fell silent and six pairs of eyes turned towards him.

A little embarrassed he forced a smile and made towards a chair in the second of the two rows, only to be stopped by a large man who stood at six feet three inches of what seemed to be solid muscle and who said with a huge smile, "Hello, you'll be Mathew Devlin? I'm Smiler."

Staring at the large man, Devlin could see why rowdy neds might be intimidated by Stuart McGarry. Sporting a full head of neatly cut, dark brown hair with flecks of grey, a battered face and a nose that looked like it had been broken more than a few times, he was closely shaved and his face wore a ready smile. Above his left brow was a two-inch horizontal scar, now faded white against his skin. Nor did it miss Devlin's attention that Smiler's shirt, brilliantly white, was starched at the collar, his police tie old style and tightly knotted rather than the more modern clip-tie, his tunic sharply creased, but all four pockets with the buttons fastened, though bulging with heavens knew what and the police issue whistle chain correctly worn on the tunic and undoubtedly with the whistle tucked into his left breast pocket.

Above that same breast pocket were three medal ribbons. Devlin recognised the police Long Service and Good Conduct medal, awarded to officers who had completed twenty-two or more years' service, though he did not recognise the other two ribbon.

His trousers too were sharply creased and as for his size fourteen boots, they gleamed as though spit polished.

Devlin took the extended hand and immediately regretted that decision, for Smiler's grasp was like a vice and he involuntarily winced.

"Oops, sorry, pal, that's me all over," he continued to smile at Devlin. "I just don't know my own strength."

"So," a woman's voice called from the end of the front row of chair, "you the guy that broke your wife and her boyfriend's noses?"

He glanced along the row to see the older of the two female cops staring at him, her red hair piled up into a tight bun, though with several loose strands needing attention and her tunic straining at the buttons due to her large bosom. His first impression was that she might have been pretty, but for the make-up that was pancaked to her face.

His brow knitted and he almost retorted with a rude reply, but staring at her, he could see no guile in her face and wondered; was she simply being curious?

And so, conscious at the speed of the police rumour machine that easily outdid the red Indians smoke signals, he took a breath and nodded before he replied, "That's me."

"Harry," the big cop turned to face the female cop. "That's too personal, hen. Give the lad a chance to get to know us before asking about his darkest secrets, eh?"

Blushing, the woman called Harry turned sharply away and head down, concentrated on her notebook lying in her lap.

Turning, Devlin sat down on the wooden chair, feeling it give slightly as though one leg was about to collapse and staring around the room, he saw the dull green paint flaking from the walls and strips of old sellotape where posters had once hung. A tattered notice board hung precariously at a slight angle as though the weight of the few items thumbtacked to it would pull it from the wall.

Aware that Smiler had slumped into the chair beside him, he leaned towards Devlin, then whispered in a stage voice, "Don't mind, Harry, she's all right most of the time."

"Harry?"

"Harriet," Smiler smiled, only to hear Harry calling out, "What do you mean most of the time?"

But before he could respond, the door opened to admit the Inspector and Sergeant Chalmers.

Making his way to the chipped and unsteady wooden dais, Cowan began, "As you will have noticed, we have a new shift member joining us. Constable Mathew Devlin, who has arrived from Clydebank."

"Smiler?" he directed his attention to the large man, "your usual beat and you'll be conducting Mathew around for the next week or so to let him get a feel of the place."

"Sir," the large man acknowledged with a nod.

"Right then," the Inspector continued by allocating the beats to the rest of the shift, then over the next ten minutes, proceeded to read from the DBR points on interest that occurred during the preceding twenty-four hours. Items that included lookouts for persons or vehicles, extra attention to areas of disorder or properties at risk to housebreakings or vandalism and anything that directly required individual beat officers to be aware of.

He slowly wheezed when he concluded with, "I know it's a lot for you guys to take on and particularly as we're so short of bodies, but don't forget we have the response car, Foxtrot Mike Two, with Drew and young Roz on patrol, as well as Sergeant Chalmers and I here in the office with the supervisory vehicle."

He paused and his face creased when he stared around the room, then added, "I regret that I have been informed by the bar officer that only five of the radios are in working conditions, so those of you who are to be neighboured, you will take one radio between you. Try not to get separated from your neighbour."

He let the muttered complaints die away before he raised a hand to say, "Do not get yourselves in a tizzy if you're overloaded with calls. If you feel you're under stress, radio in and yes," he held up a hand to stem protests, "I know the bloody radios are crap, but we have to work with what we've got. Right now, you all have a neighbour, so be safe and no heroics. Got that?"

A muttering of "Yes, sir," and nodding of heads didn't suffice for Cowan, who loudly repeated, "Got that?"

A more positive response satisfied him, then he called out, "To your duties."

Shuffling to their feet, the shift began to make their way to the door, but Devlin was stopped by Smiler, who grinned, "Where's your raincoat?"

"In my car. I didn't have time to bring in my bits and pieces."

"Right, let's see about getting you a locker first, so away and get your gear and I'll meet you in the locker room. That's just a wee bit down the corridor," he waved a meaty hand.

When Smiler left him, Devlin was touched on the arm and turned to see the cop, Harry, at his elbow.

"Sorry if I was a bit forward," though her smile didn't rise to her eyes and unaware that some of her bright red lipstick was adhering to her teeth, "I'm just a nosey cow."

"No problem," he faked a smile in return.

"Right," she drawled, her eyes boring into him. "I'll be away then," and turned to join her neighbour, a tall, skinny man with greying hair, who leaned towards her to engage her in a whispered conversation.

Whatever was said, she turned to glance back at Devlin and he knew he was the subject of the conversation.
"You okay, Mathew?"
He turned to see Sergeant Chalmers staring at him, then nodding, replied, "Just about to grab my raincoat from the car, Sarge. Smiler's away finding me a locker."
"A locker? You'll be lucky," she scoffed. "I've been here two years and I'm still using my desk drawers to keep my stuff in. Right, off you go then, and I'll see you when you're out and about."

CHAPTER TWO.

It was when they were walking in Alison Street that Smiler's brow creased when he asked, "What was wrong with Lucy Chalmers? She didn't seem too happy when I said I'd got you a locker?"
Devlin smiled when he replied, "I think she's been after a locker since she got here, but hasn't had any luck."
"Should have mentioned it to me," Smiler shook his head, then said, "So, what do I call you? Mathew or Matt?"
Devlin shrugged before he replied, "Since I was a wee boy at school, most people have called me Mattie."
"Then Mattie it is," Smiler grinned at him before he continued, "Have you worked in the city at all?"
"No," Devlin shook his head. "Only ever visited to Pitt Street and of course, Oxford Street for courses. My service has always been over in Argyle. I was prom…"
He stopped, his mouth suddenly dry, then instead, said, "I started my time in Dunbartonshire Constabulary at Dumbarton office, then after the amalgamation, I went to Clydebank."
Smiler stopped walking and turning to Devlin, frowned before he asked, "What really brings you here, then Mattie? And before you go off on one as to why I'm prying, we both know the polis leaks like a sieve, so no doubt the word is already out. I mean, take Harry in the muster room. She's already heard you broke your wife's and some guy's nose. Is that right enough?"
"Not my wife's nose, no," he grimaced, "but her boyfriend's nose."

"Shall we move on," Devlin gestured with his hand, then nodding, dryly admitted, "I was demoted earlier today from sergeant."
That stopped Smiler in his tracks and rubbing at his square jaw, he said, "Not a lot surprises me, these days, but aye, you've definitely surprised me there, Mattie. Want to talk about it or shall I just shut up?"
He wryly smiled when he replied, "Not a lot to tell, Smiler. I was married a matter of months to a woman who completely deceived me. When I came home early one evening to our house in Old Kilpatrick and…"
"Old Kilpatrick? That's out Dumbarton way, is it?"
"It is," he sighed. "It's a mid-terraced police authority house just off the Old Dumbarton Road. Nice wee place and to be honest, if I'd been sacked as well as demoted, I'd be homeless right now."
"Sorry to hear about your troubles, Mattie, and while you're not looking particularly upbeat, at least you're not crying like a wean either."
Continuing along Alison Street, Smiler said, "No wish to offend or anything, but you said you came home early one evening. Am I to assume you found your missus, ah, *In flagrante delicto*, so to speak?"
"If you're asking if I caught her shagging somebody else, yes; spot on, big man."
"Hence the broken nose for the villain of the piece?"
"Exactly," Devlin sighed.
"And your wife?"
Devlin stopped and glancing around at the busy street, asked, "A man of your undoubtable service, I'm assuming you have somewhere you can park your backside with a cuppa?"
"Oh, I've one or two wee howffs where I'm welcome," Smiler tapped at the side of his nose with a stubby finger.
"Then if we've no immediate calls to attend to, why don't we retire to one of them and I'll bare my soul," Devlin softly smiled.
****

Seated in two folding chairs in the rear of the City Bakeries shop in Allison Street, their caps on a third chair, a mug of tea in one hand and a jam doughnut in the other, Smiler and Devlin continued their conversation.

His face heavyset at the sad tale of woe, Smiler learned of the woman Janice Goodwin, who had not only completely deceived Devlin, but squandered his savings that were destined to be the lump sum to enable him to obtain a mortgage and free him from the police authority tied house.

Devlin couldn't quite believe he was baring his soul to Smiler, yet some inner sense told him the older cop wasn't looking for salacious information, that he was simply getting to know his neighbour.

"And it was that old rogue, Crossan, who represented you at the Hearing?"

"You know him?"

"Oh, aye, a good man, for a lawyer I mean. I've crossed swords with Mark many a time in the low court's and the high court's when he was into defence work, but these days," he sighed, "like the rest of us, he's slowing down and a bit too fed-up with the cut and thrust of the justice system, though still maintains a good relationship with the Federation. You were lucky it was him, Mattie. He'll have gone all out to get you kept in the job."

Till that moment, Devlin had been angry with the old lawyer for keeping Janice's bigamy from him, but slowly was coming to realise that had he known about her deceit prior to the Hearing, his pride might have caused him to instruct Crossan not to make it publicly known.

And that decision, he now knew, would most certainly have lost him his job.

"Dearie me," Smiler broke into his thoughts when he shook his head, then licked the jam from his lower lip. "You've had a bit of bad luck with that woman, Mattie. I take it you threw her out on her ear?"

"Aye," he sighed, "she's away to God alone knows where. Fortunately, the marriage being bigamous, I'm not liable for her financially or otherwise so frankly, I couldn't care less where she is right now."

"And you, Smiler," he sipped at his tea. "You have family?"

He watched a slow smile cross the big man's face before he replied, "A boy and a lassie. I say boy, but Adam's thirty and married with two of his own weans. Jean, she's twenty-five and was living at home until last year, but she's out now in a shared flat. As for the wife," he sighed and took a deep breath, "the love of my life and always in my thoughts."

Surprised at Smiler's admission his wife was 'always in my thoughts,' Devlin realised Smiler had used the past tense and was about to ask if the big man was widowed, but just then, a voice distracted him and turning, he saw a woman standing in the doorway of the rear shop, an overcoat over what clearly was the company uniform.

"Hi, Smiler," she grinned at him. "Our telephone's gubbed, so I was away out phoning the head office," the woman continued, then hanging up her coat, glanced at Devlin when she asked, "Who's this, then?"

"Sally, this is Mattie Devlin," Smiler waved a hand at her, then added, "Mattie, Sally is the boss in here and suffers me to come in for my tea and a doughnut."

Slim and standing just about an inch short of Devlin's height with cropped blonde hair, he saw Sally Rodgers to be an attractive woman with an easy smile, guessing her to be in her early to mid-thirties and who smiled at him, then said, "You're Smiler's new neighbour?"

"For the time being, yes," he nodded.

"And will that include the early shift," her eyes narrowing, she directed her question to Smiler.

"Should do," he too nodded.

"Then things will go that little bit faster, eh?"

Bemused, Devlin asked, "Faster for what?"

"Eh," Smiler's face contorted as though embarrassed, "on the early shift, if I don't have any calls to attend right away, I usually come in to earn my breakfast by helping out."

"Helping out?" Devlin's eyes narrowed.

"Aye, I butter the rolls for the takeaway counter," he explained.

Devlin stared at him, half thinking he was joking, but from his expression, clearly he wasn't.

"You *butter* the rolls?"

"Aye, but like I said, I get my breakfast for it."

There was nothing else to do but smile at the thought of him and Smiler, tunics off, sleeves rolled up and buttering the rolls for the busy takeaway counter in the front shop.

What the hell have I got myself into, he wondered, just as Sally asked, "What you grinning at, Mattie?"

"My change in fortune," he grinned at her, a genuine grin that somehow felt so relaxed after the day he'd had so far.

"Right," Smiler licked the last of the jam from his fingers, then standing, grabbed at the caps on the chair and handed Devlin his. "Late shift till Tuesday, Sally, then back on earlies on the Friday, but we'll pop in now and again between then, just to say hello."

"I look forward to it," she smiled, then outrageously winked at Devlin.

****

As they patrolled along the busy Allison Street, with its numerous shops on either side of the road, it seemed to Devlin that Smiler stopped to briefly speak with and call many passers-by, by name. Giving a cheery 'Hello' or nodding at every second person, Devlin saw that most of them returned his greeting with an acknowledgement of, "Hi, Smiler," or more formally, "Constable McGarry."

Chalmers was right, thought Devlin. Smiler seems to have a right good knowledge of his beat's residents.

In addition, the older man continued with a running commentary of the area; which shops were worth visiting, pointing out those who illegally sold alcohol and fags to underage kids.

The corners from where the junkies congregated or watched for their victims they intended mugging.

The pubs that were well-run and refused to serve customers who were already drunk and seldom had any cause to call the police; then the pubs where the staff were not so observant or compliant with the Licensing Laws and where alcohol related trouble could usually be found.

"And don't get me started on the parking," Smiler slowly shook his head. "The double parking is a constant complaint by the local community council and the bus companies, that can't safely get by. Most of the double parking is vans loading or unloading, so I try to give them a bit of time to get it done, even sometimes directing the traffic round the vans, if it helps."

He stared at Devlin when he asked, "I take it you've done points before?"

"You mean, directing traffic? Yes, of course."

"Good. I ask because when this road," he nodded at Allison Street, "gets really busy and any of the traffic lights are buggered, it's a hell of a job keeping the traffic moving."

He saw Devlin staring at his face then grinned when he asked, "You're wondering about my Duke of Montrose? How it come to be so battered?"

His face flushed, Devlin replied, "It did cross my mind. Happen in the job, did it?"

"Actually, no," Smiler sighed. "I did my National Service out in Korea in '51. Took an enemy's rifle butt right smack on the face, so I did. Hasn't affected my good looks though, has it?" he pretended to glower at Devlin, who hastily shook his head and replied, "No, not at all…" before realised the big man was joking.

It was then that Smiler's radio burst into life with a message requesting he attend at a house in the nearby Annette Street and respond to the report of a disturbance.

The controller, a woman's voice, Devlin heard, added, "It's her again, Smiler, the woman in the flat below the McDonald's. Says the wife is screaming and she can hear the kids crying."

Surprised, Devlin saw Smiler's face pale and heard him acknowledge with, "Got that, Mary. Tell Eric to have the van ready." Turning to Devlin, he broodily remarked, "Now we'll see what kind of neighbour you are, Mattie, my boy."

****

Arriving outside the blonde sandstone tenement building in Annette Street, they began to make their way up the stairs inside the building, with Smiler telling Devlin, "The McDonald's live on the second floor. The old biddy on the first floor directly below them has phoned in several times about the husband, John McDonald. Forty-three, he's an unemployed drunk not beyond punching his wife around the house. I say unemployed, but the bugger has no interest in getting a job. The money from the Social might as well be paid directly to his local pub and the bookies and heaven alone knows how his wife manages to feed and clothe the weans," he shook his head and sighed heavily.

"I've warned him in the past about his behaviour," he continued, "but his wife, Jessie, she refuses to speak up against him."

"Right then," both breathless, they arrived at the unpainted wooden door. "Let's see what's going on this time," Smiler glanced at him, then quietly added, "Let me handle this, Mattie, eh?"

Devlin stood behind Smiler who knocking on the door, widely smiled when the door was pulled open by a woman in her early thirties, Devlin thought.

Thin and pale faced, her long brown hair in disarray and her eyes red from crying, she wore a crossover apron over a stained light blue sweatshirt and navy-blue tracksuit trousers.

Devlin could see a visible red mark on the left side of her jaw, the swollen lips and her left eye too was beginning to swell. That and there was blood caked on her nostrils and a faint smear on her cheek where she had wiped the blood away.

From inside the house they could hear the sound of young children wailing.

Seeing the two officers, the woman startled, her head bowing and her eyes avoiding looking at them when she forced a smile and muttered, "Mr McGarry. Can I help you?"

Almost jovially, Smiler replied, "Just attending a complaint of noise coming from the house, Mrs McDonald. Everything okay here?"

Devlin, his eyes widening, stared at the big man, his mouth opening as if to protest and thinking; my God, Smiler, can you not see she's just taken a bleaching?

But before he could react to the woman's condition, he saw the husband, John McDonald, walk from a room at the bottom of the hallway, then stop to stare at the officers.

"What's going on?" they heard McDonald call out as he strode towards them.

Devlin saw the unshaven McDonald to be about five feet seven inches tall with greasy collar length hair, bare footed and wearing a stained, once white tee shirt with a heavy beer gut hanging over the waistband on his trousers.

Standing behind his wife, he lifted his hand and placing it on her shoulder, Devlin saw her flinch as though fearing she was about to again be struck.

"What's going on?" McDonald repeated, his voice rasping and even from where Devlin stood, he could detect the smell of alcohol.

"I was just telling your wife, Mr McDonald," Smiler began in a pleasant voice, "that we've received an anonymous phone call about noise coming from your flat. I take it everything's okay now?"

Drawing himself up to his full height, Devlin saw McDonald's fingers tighten on his wife's shoulder, seeing the knuckles whiten and hearing the woman softly gasp, before he replied, "No noise here, Smiler. Some old busybody," he spat out the word, "is wasting your time."

He glanced down at his wife, the warning in his voice evident when he added, "Everything's grand, isn't it, hen?"

As if eager to get away, Smiler interrupted with a nod when he said, "Look, you know how some people overreact when they hear weans playing and anyway, I'll need to result this call with my controller." Winking at McDonald, he added, "Maybe we can have a private word?"

Devlin could feel his face pale, angry that for all his apparent experience, Smiler was ignoring the obvious fact Mrs McDonald had been clearly been subjected to a beating by her husband.

Leaning past McDonald, Smiler gently took the woman by the arm and guided her back through the door, then grabbing at the handle, pulled the door closed with a quiet click.

"So, what happened then, sir?"

Suspecting that the big cop was a kindred spirit, he breezily grinned, "Ach, you know what women are like, Smiler," he breezed, believing himself to be confiding in a kindred spirit. "She wouldn't stop nagging and I only slapped her a couple of times anyway. I mean, it's not as if I've given her a right doing, is it?" he shrugged.

Stepping back to face McDonald, Smiler nodded at him then taking a breath, softly exhaled before he quietly said, "So, you fat bastard, you're a hard man with the women, are you?"

Surprised at Smiler's sudden change of attitude, McDonald's eyes widened and his mouth opened as if to respond, but then to Devlin's astonishment, in one swift movement Smiler used the flat of his hand to shove McDonald squarely on the chest, propelling him backwards.

Stunned as he lost his balance, in those few heartbeats they watched as McDonald's arms flailed, then shrieking in panic, he fell backwards down the flight of the stone stairs, his back first landing heavily on the stone stairs and driving the breath from his lungs, then continuing down the stairs, saw him crashing noisily against the side wall as he grunted then open-mouthed, Devlin saw him land heavily in a heap on the half-landing.

Clearly winded and gasping for air, McDonald moaned in pain as he slowly curled into a foetal position.

With a resigned sigh, Smiler glanced at his neighbour, then almost casually nodded that they make their way down the stairs to stand over the now weeping McDonald.

Still shocked at the big man's unexpected assault upon the unfortunate McDonald, he turned when Smiler said, "This excuse for a man has bullied his poor wife for years and she's been too terrified to make any complaint, not that it would do much good with the law as it stands at the minute," he sighed, then shook his head.

Turning to stare at his neighbour, his voice no more than a whisper, he continued, "Women like Jessie McDonald have nobody to protect them, Mattie, so that's our job. Yours and mine and all like-minded polis. So, this is where you make your mind up. Did you or did you not see this man attempt to assault me and try to wrestle me down the stairs?"

In his eight years of service, Devlin had attended more domestic abuse situations than he could recall and on each occasion because the law, as Smiler rightly pointed out, was weak on domestic abuse, little or nothing was done. Most if not all police officers hated the inevitable resolution to such calls, the standard and accepted procedure being to remove the abuser from the dwelling for that night to permit the victim, commonly the spouse, to seek shelter or help elsewhere.

And again of course while the majority of officers disagreed with the practice, without the legal authority to do otherwise and unless the spouse or partner made a complaint of assault, which was almost never, the attending officer's hands were tied.

In those few seconds that passed, Devlin knew he had a decision to make.

Tell the truth and have Smiler charged with assault and McDonald, wife-beater that he was, treated as a complainer and likely returned to the house that very evening to continue thrashing his wife.

Or corroborate the big man's lie; the lie that would see McDonald locked up and as the charge would be one of police assault, very likely detained for court the following morning.

Staring at the rugged and expressionless face of the big cop, in those brief heartbeats that passed, it also occurred to Devlin that if he didn't make the correct choice, he might find himself also hurtling down the next flight of stairs and so, he made his decision primarily based on what an old and seasoned cop had taught him during his probationary period.

The law and justice are not the same thing.

Turning to stare up at his neighbour, he sombrely replied, "Call for the van, Smiler."

****

While Smiler roughly manhandled the shaking and subdued McDonald down the stars, Devlin returned to flat where knocking on the door, it was almost a full minute before it was slowly opened by Jesse McDonald, who stared fearfully at him.

"Just me," he tightly smiled, then lowing his voice, he softly said, "Your husband's being arrested for assaulting a police officer and he'll be taken to Craigie Street to be charged. The likelihood is he'll be detained for court tomorrow morning, Mrs McDonald, so for his appearance before the court, if you could provide me with some footwear, a shirt and maybe a jacket too?"

Her lip trembling and visibly close to tears, she hesitantly asked, "Will he get out in the morning?"

There was no option other than to tell her the truth, so nodding, he replied, "Yes, I'm afraid he probably will. Do you have anywhere to go to with your children?"

Her head dipped when she shook it, then muttered, "No. My parents, they washed their hands of me when I married him. You know the old saying," she grimaced. "You've made your bed and all that." Raising her head, her eyes now brimming with tears, she resignedly shrugged when she said, "I made my choice falling pregnant to him, so I suppose I'll just have to take what comes, eh?"

Before he could respond, she'd turned away to fetch the clothes, then returning a moment later, handed him a plastic bin bag with a clean dress shirt, unpolished black shoes and a thin, nylon waterproof jacket.

Almost in desperation, she asked. "I don't suppose if he gets found guilty, he'll get the jail for a while?"

"It'll be a pleading diet tomorrow," he replied. "If he pleads guilty he'll be dealt with, but whether that means jail or not will depend on his previous convictions if he has any. Has he been convicted before?"

"You don't know him, then?"

"No, I've just arrived in this area."

"John, he's been in trouble with you lot plenty of times. Stealing and being drunk."

"Hitting you?"

"No," she vigorously shook her head, regret in her face when she added, "I've never had the nerve to complain about him. He told me if I ever did tell anyone, he'd hurt me and hurt the weans too."

"You can complain now, particularly as you've obvious injuries," he quickly said and pointed at her face.

She stared at him before she quietly sneered, "And you think me complaining about him, you polis would be able to do something to stop him again using me like a punchbag?"

She closed the door before he could respond, then bag in hand, he turned and made his way downstairs.

****

On his break, the bald-headed man stood in the dark shadow with his back against the tenement building, watching them standing at the corner, sharing the cheap bottle of fortified wine, guessing it to be Lanliq or El Dorado, both locally referred to as 'electric soup.' Concentrating on them both and not wishing to be seen, he resisted the temptation to have a fag.

What, he wondered, could Moxy, now leaning down and almost head to head with her, have to tell wee Jeannie that was so interesting?

The bald man's blood run cold when he remembered those days, what they had done and knew too that there was a real chance he could still do time for it, no matter it was so long ago.

Cutting ties didn't erase memories and the more he thought about it, the more he worried that Moxy's mouth and his insufferable urge to prove himself as a big man, no matter that it was to a dirty wee harlot like Jeannie, it might still cause him problems.

Even after all those years.

His mouth tightened and his hands clenched when he realised the only solution, the only way to be sure he could not be suspected and have the cops on him, like it or not, was to deal with them both. Permanently.

CHAPTER THREE.

The Duty Officer standing behind the charge bar at Craigie Street police office, a young-looking female Inspector with fair hair bundled up into a bun, stared with narrowed eyes at Devlin before she bluntly said, "You'll be the one that was demoted and sent here?"

"Yes, Inspector, that's me," he wearily sighed.

Standing beside her, the turnkey, a balding constable in his mid-forties, rolled his eyes in disapproval at her harsh remark, then made his way out from behind the bar to search the prisoner.

Stood between Smiler and Devlin, John McDonald at last found his voice when he snivelled, "I want to make a complaint."

The Inspector stared at him when she coolly asked, "And that is?"

"Him there, Smiler," McDonald nodded at him. "I didn't assault him. He's arrested me for nothing because I haven't done anything. He just pushed me down the stairs and I banged by head and my back. I'm charging *him*, so I am."

Seconds passed before the Inspector, leaning forward onto the large, black bound register, sighed, then said, "Tell you what, Mr McDonald, let's just note all your details here then after you've been charged, I'll hear what you have to say? Is that okay with you?" sarcasm oozed from her voice.

Not recognising her sarcasm, his eyes narrowed, uncertain whether she was taking the mickey or what, then he nodded.

His details noted, Smiler formally cautioned McDonald before charging him with police assault."

"I didn't do it!" he hissed at the Inspector. "I admit slapping my wife, but I'm not charged with that, so you can't do me for it! He just used that as an excuse to assault me! He's making it all up, him and his wee pal here," he nodded with a sneer at Devlin, "because he's lying too!"

Pokerfaced, the Inspector turned towards Smiler to tell him, "I hope that you noted that reply, Constable McGarry, that while Mr McDonald admits assaulting his wife, he denies assaulting you."

"I did indeed, Inspector," Smiler nodded, "and it occurs to me that when he appears at court, should Mr McDonald decide to plead his innocence," he turned to meaningfully stare at the angry man, "I'm certain when I present my evidence the judge will take cognisance of that admission of domestic abuse."

"In the meantime, Mr McDonald," the Inspector addressed the open-mouthed prisoner, "you will be detained in custody till your appearance tomorrow afternoon at the District Court."

****

Ten minutes later, both seated in the muster room while Devlin completed a crime/offence report, the younger man smiled when he said, "Nicely done, Smiler."

"Aye, but at what cost, Mattie. You said you have eight years in, so during that time I'm certain you must have encountered a number of domestic abuse cases and it's the same old story," he sighed. "We lock them up for a night at best, then they're out the next day to continue their abuse."

Shaking his head, he added, "It's not a fair world, is it?"

"But things are getting better, Smiler. I'm hearing there are women's rights groups springing up here in Glasgow. Hopefully before long, the law will catch up too."

"And not before time," Smiler agreed.

"That Inspector, the Duty Officer. I thought she was going to record his complaint against you."

"Inspector Bruce," Smiler nodded. "Aye, our Marion's a bit dour, but she's no fool. She arrived about a year ago after being promoted from Mill Street over in Paisley. Frankly, I think she's bored being the indoor Inspector, while Iain Cowan gets to have all the fun, running around in the supervisory car," he smiled. "It's only when our Iain is off on rest days that Marion sometimes gets out to play."

"Right, that's me," Devlin returned his pen to his tunic pocket, then rising from the chair, carried the completed report through to the bar officer for typing the case to the Fiscal's.

Minutes later found the pair, the rain now a little heavier and wearing their nylon raincoats, returned to their beat.

****

In the Sergeants Room, while sipping at a now cold cup of coffee, Lucy Chalmers was engaged in the boring task of outstanding paperwork.

She turned when Inspector Iain Cowan said, "I'm taking a turn out in the car to check on the troops, Lucy, if you're wanting to come along."

"Anything to get away from my desk," she sighed, then grabbed at her tunic and her cap.

Minutes later, with Chalmers driving, found them in the marked police Ford Escort and patrolling in Dixon Avenue.

"Marion Bruce was telling me that Smiler and his neighbour brought in a wife beater," he said. "Some guy that Smiler charged with assaulting him."

"Assaulting Smiler?" she grinned. "What, did the muppet have a death wish or something?"

He returned her grin when he said, "I suspect the wife was too frightened to make a complaint, so Smiler's evidently practised the law as only he does."

"Aye, all well and good, Iain, but his neighbour," her face displayed her concern. "I mean, he doesn't know this guy Devlin. I hope Smiler trusts him to corroborate him if the case goes to court."

His face creased when he said, "I've a wee confession to make, between you and me only, of course."

He took a short breath, then began, "Jimmy Faulkner is the Chief Inspector over in Clydebank and I know him from when we were cops together in the old Tobago Street office. Anyway. I gave him phone earlier on and asked about Devlin."

"And?" she snatched a glance at him.

"According to Jimmy, Devlin is one of the good guys. Run his shift well, keen and tenacious and Jimmy thought he had the makings of a good career in front of him, even though he's only got just eight years in."

He paused while reflecting on the phone call, then continued, "His downfall was his wife. Met this good-looking lassie who within a couple of months told him she was pregnant then apparently," he made italics with his fingers, "lost the baby. But that's not the worst of it," he grimaced.

"Jimmy's received a phone call from the Complaints and Discipline requesting he provide them with a statement regarding what he knows about Devlin's marriage. It seems they've been tasked with tracking down his wife and charging her with bigamy, that she was divorced, then remarried and separated from her second husband. Then, meeting Devlin, told him she was single and married him too."

"What! You're at the madam!" she turned wide-eyed to glance at him.

"Nope," he drawled when he shook his head. "That's what Jimmy says and before you ask, the poor guy didn't have a clue and only learned about her bigamy at his Hearing this morning."

"My God, what a bitch."

"Aye, but it doesn't end there, Lucy. The woman, Janice something, she's not only skedaddled, but rooked him as well. She's away with his savings."

"Jesus!" she exhaled with a mirthless laugh. "He's not only demoted, but on the same day he finds that out as well? I'm surprised he's not away looking for a tall building," she softly exhaled.

Her brow furrowed when she asked, "But why are the rubber heels wanting a statement from his former Chief Inspector?"

"Jimmy says he'd met the lassie and thought there was something not quite right about her, then tried to have a fatherly word with Devlin before he jumped into marriage with her, but says that Devlin, who he considers to be quite an honest and upright young guy, believed he was doing the honourable thing. As for the statement, Jimmy thinks the instruction has come from the Deputy Chief, that it's to protect Devlin from any allegation she might make when they arrest her that he was complicit in her bigamy."

"Fair play to the Paula Clarke. I've heard good things about her," her brow furrowed, Chalmers nodded.

Then she added, "But look what Devlin's honour has done for him," then slowly shook her head.

"Anyway, the reason I'm telling you, Lucy, is that maybe we should keep an eye on young Devlin and you're right," his eyes narrowed. "Smiler has trusted him to corroborate the arrest, so fingers crossed if it does go to trial, Devlin speaks up in favour of Smiler's evidence."

****

Meandering along Victoria Road, the rain now eased, Devlin did not immediately realise that he was becoming distracted and inwardly smiled, for his thoughts were taken up by his new his neighbour's courteous smile or greeting to each and every man or woman they passed.

Now just gone four o'clock, many of the passers-by were schoolchildren, most of whom grinned at Smiler's cheery nod or wink, though too there were some teenagers who predictably were too cool to engage with them and sullenly ignored the police officers.

At the junction of Prince Edward Street, Devlin saw a woman who he thought to be in her sixties, no more than five feet two or three inches tall and shabbily dressed in an old and torn parka coat, her matted shoulder length, dark greying hair, shiny wet through from the rain and watched as she shuffled towards them.

But then she stopped when he heard Smiler greet her with, "Hello, Jeannie. Have you had any dinner today, hen?"

Jeannie, her shoulders slumped and head bowed as she stared at her feet, they saw her shake her head and mutter, "I'm not really hungry, Smiler."

"Well, hungry or not, you need to eat something, hen, so here's what you're going to do. You're going to walk round to the chippy in Allison Street and tell Marco that he's to give you a pie supper and that I'll square up with him later. Now," he ignored the curious glances of passers-by when he waggled a finger at her, "I'll be checking that you've been there, so don't be letting me down, okay?"

Jeannie shuffled her feet and head still bowed, nodded before wordlessly shuffling off.

Smiler stood watching for almost a minute, then when they'd continued walking, he sadly shook his head and said, "She's a poor soul, is wee Jeannie. How old do you think she is, Mattie?"

"In her sixties maybe?" he shrugged.

Smiler sadly sighed before he replied, "She's not long turned forty-five and I know that to be true because she's a regular visitor to our cells."

Stunned, all Devlin could think to reply was, "You're kidding!"

Smiler grimaced when he explained, "Jeannie was married to a nice man with whom she has two kids, both grown up now. She used to be a nurse, but about ten years ago, for whatever reason that I don't know, she took to the drink. However, as you'll be aware from your own experience in the job, there are happy drunks, fall-down-unconscious drunks, moody drunks, selfish and violent drunks and all sorts of ways the alcohol affects the individual. As for Jeannie?" He gently sighed when he added, "She becomes a violent drunk." Continuing seconds later, he wryly smiled when he added, "Seeing the size of her, you wouldn't think it, would you?"

"Anyway, to continue the story, after a couple of years of attending her flat over in Coplaw Street for reports of her attacking her husband, he finally had enough and threw her out of the house.

Needless to say, time and time again she was getting the jail for being drunk and incapable or committing a breach of the peace because just like female spouses, her husband never complained about her assaulting him, though he got a few sore faces from her. Of course, by that time and due to her drinking, she'd also been dismissed from her job and quickly became homeless because frankly, the Social Work could no longer place her anywhere else for she was too disruptive when she was on the bevy."

He softly exhaled as though the telling of the tale was painful, then added, "Sorry to say too, as far as I'm aware, neither of her children will have anything more to do with her."

He paused, then began again, "For the last five or six years, she's been sleeping rough, up tenement closes or empty properties and though she draws unemployment benefit, spends it all on the bevy; doesn't feed or properly care for herself and as you can see, when she's sober she's as timid as a mouse."

His brow creased when he quietly continued, "Sad thing too is that looking at her, you'd think no man would want anything to do with Jeannie, but she also earns some money prostituting herself at the end of the night, around some of the not so reputable pubs, though not for money; no, Jeannie will provide her favours or *other* services for a couple of cans of super lager or even a half bottle of cheap wine. In fact," he drew a breath, then slowly exhaled, "I'm surprised that she's still alive, given what she has been through."

"But you keep your eye on her?" Devlin grimly smiled.

"If I don't," he grimaced, "who else will? But that said, some of the charity shops provide her with clothes that are too old or unsellable, so if nothing else, she has some sort of wardrobe, though where she keeps it I don't know. Probably wears most of it," he added with a soft smile.

Continuing their talk, once more Devin gave some thought to his neighbour, unaware that thinking about Smiler for the moment distracted him from his own problems.
****

Chief Inspector Lizzie Whitmore glanced up when her door was knocked, then opened by the bar officer who said, "Mail in from Pitt Street, Ma'am, and there's a package for you."

Taking it from him, she smiled her dismissal, then tore open the bulky wrapped envelope to discover it was Mathew Devlin's file forwarded from the Personnel Department.

Normally she would give such a file no more than a cursory glance to ensure it was correctly addressed, but curiosity go the better of her and she sat back to read it.

Winner of the prestigious Baton of Honour at Tulliallan Police Training College, she read Devlin had shone throughout his probationary period, then passed both his elementary and advanced examination in consecutive years.

He had so impressed his supervisors that with just five years' service, he'd been promoted from Dumbarton to Clydebank where again his enthusiasm and commitment had promised great things.

Then came his fall from grace; the assault upon the man that led to his demotion.

Laying the file down onto her desk, her eyes narrowed in thought as she contemplated the file and its contents.

Devlin, for all his lack of service was, according to his annual appraisals, a fine police officer and keenly motivated too.

Her problem was, if she were to take her idea to the Divisional Commander, Jimmy Thompson, unpredictable and crusty old bugger that he is and with just his few months left to serve, it was odds against that he'd support her.

Then again, she sighed, fair heart and all that nonsense, so glancing at her watch, she decided by now Thompson would have left his office downstairs, so tomorrow was another day and it would give her time to plan her move.

Locking Devlin's file and her other paperwork in her desk drawer, she glanced again at her wristwatch and decided that was time enough to head home.

****

Turning to her neighbour, Willie Strathmore, Constable Harry Dawson said, "Are we going in for the same piece break or what?"

"You heard the Inspector," he glanced right then left, before beginning to make his way across Florida Avenue, "he wants us neighboured after the piece breaks are finished, so I'm down for first break and I'll meet you before you go for yours, to hand over the radio."

"Bloody nonsense that we have to share radio's," she predictably moaned.

"It is what it is," he carefully replied, knowing that the wrong word would have her sulking for the rest of the shift.

A former police cadet with Lanarkshire Constabulary, Strathmore, now thirty-eight years of age, had never previously sought nor pursued promotion, but now, at the urging of his wife, he was studying for his elementary examination, colloquially known as the sergeant's exam, while the advanced examination was known as the Inspectors exam.

Right now, if he didn't have Harry trailing alongside him, he'd be in a howf somewhere, reading up on the notes in his tunic pocket and preparing for the exam due to take place next Wednesday, the fourteenth, in the Glasgow University hall over in the city's west end.

"That new guy."

"What of him," he replied.

"Well, I heard he beat up his wife and her lover. That's what got him demoted."

"Is that what you heard?" he couldn't help his tight-lipped retort.

The sarcasm was lost on Harry, who continued, "Aye, and why do you think they sent him to us?"

"I really don't know and care even less," he sighed, his attention taken by a couple of young males, mid-teens both of them he thought as watching them, they suddenly took off running down the lane at the bottom of the road.

As if seeing them for the first time, Harry called out, "They're getting away!" and began to run towards the lane, her skirt tight around her heavy thighs and her police issue handbag slapping against her raincoated back.

Raising his eyes to heaven, Strathmore called back, "Stop!"

Confused and breathless, even though she had run just thirty yards, she turned to stare at him.

Slowly walking towards her, he calmly asked, "Why did you decide to chase them?"

Whether red-faced from her short spurt or embarrassment, he wasn't certain, when she replied, "They were running away, so they must have been up to something," she huffily added.

He forced himself not to smile when he shook his head and said, "Running away from the polis isn't a crime, Harry, so think in future before you wear yourself out chasing after them."

Now at the spot where they had seen the teenagers make off from, Strathmore glanced at the cigarette butts littering the ground, guessing why the kids had been loitering there, then continued, "They're either away into the Cathkin Park or down the lane. Either way, there's nothing here to indicate what they were doing other than maybe having a fly fag because they're underage, so let's me and you stroll back towards Cathcart Road and I'll head off for my break."

****

Glancing at his wristwatch, Smiler said, "Sergeant Chalmers suggested we take first break, Mattie, and that as you're not familiar with the area yet, we take it together while Foxtrot Mike Two covers any calls on our beat."

He turned to stare at Devlin when he asked, "I'm thinking that you'll not have had time to bring some food with you?"

"No," he shook his head. "I came here directly from Pitt Street, but if there's a chippy nearby?"

"We'll pop along and see Marco in Allison Street. I owe him anyway for Jeannie's pie supper."

Ten minutes later, Devlin, carrying his hot food in a plastic carrier bag, they were making their way towards the office when the Burndept radio in the breast pocket of Smiler's tunic crackled with a message that any station near Bowman Street attend regarding a disturbance.

"Is that near?" asked Devlin.

"Around the corner," replied Smiler, "but the van crew will deal with that, Mattie. If they need help, they'll call us, but in the meantime, your foods getting cold," then added, "Don't be worrying. There will be plenty of opportunity for us to attend calls when we get back out onto the street after our break."

CHAPTER FOUR.

Driving the marked Transit van with the designated call-sign, Foxtrot Mike Two, Constable Andrew 'Drew' Taylor sneaked a glance at his neighbour, Rosalind 'Roz' Begley.

Taylor, twenty-eight and five years a cop, was currently dating a woman, Sharon, who at thirty-one was a receptionist in a city centre hotel and making overtures that after eight months together and now spending more and more nights at his West End flat, they should consider formalising their relationship with an engagement ring. Strikingly good looking though Sharon was - the good looks go with the job, she was fond of telling people - and admittedly while she was good company, Taylor had reservations about spending the rest of his life with her.

His first problem was though, how to break off with her for knowing her as he did to be petulant at best and at worst, believed that Sharon could be a vindictive and resentful individual who would go all out to make life difficult for him.

It came to him then like a bolt that if he was even *thinking* like that, then Sharon definitely wasn't the woman for him.

Inwardly sighing, his second problem, though he dare not confess it or even hint at it, was that he found himself attracted to his neighbour, Roz, who with just over six weeks passed since the completion of her statutory two-year probationary period, was unlike any woman he had previously dated or had a relationship with.

With her auburn hair cut pageboy style and four inches short of his five feet eleven, the former primary school teacher did not have Sharon's model figure, but more of an hourglass shape. Not that she was unattractive, for Roz drew more attention from men than she realised, but what drew him to her was her smile, her undoubted intelligence and, in the three months they had worked together, saw her confidently handle stressful and confrontational situations with aplomb and a beguiling smile.

His first indication of feelings for her was when just three weeks into being neighbours, an incident occurred tasking them to a report of a woman brandishing a four-inch, black handled Kitchen Devil knife at a group of children, who reportedly had been teasing the woman, constantly ringing her ground floor tenement building doorbell or banging on her windows before running off.

The woman, frustrated and at the end of her tether, had chased the terrified kids into the rear court, then cornered the five of them, the oldest being just eleven years of age.

Taylor and Begley had arrived to find the woman completely distraught, screaming and waving the knife at them.

Fearing the woman might turn upon them, his initial reaction had been to draw his baton to protect himself and his neighbour from the knife-wielding woman.
However, raising a cautionary hand towards him and indicating that he stand back, his neighbour had calmly approached the agitated woman and in an even voice, talked her down from her anger, then disarmed her.
While he later admitted he had favoured putting the woman in handcuffs and arresting her, Roz had requested he stand down and helped the weeping, shaking woman back to her flat, made her a cup of tea, then phoned her doctor.
When the angry parents had arrived at the tenement, demanding the woman be arrested, Roz had turned on them for their lack of parental control of their children, threatening that she'd have the Social Work on them and her voice icy cold, completely routed them.
The incident ended with the three ringleaders, two boys aged eleven and a girl aged ten, being dragged off by their ears and the parents apologising for their kids' behaviour.
It was when the woman's doctor arrived to sedate his patient, they learned not only had the woman just four months previously been widowed, but to add to her misery, was recently diagnosed with ovarian cancer.
Sneaking another glance at Roz, he realised then that as good looking as his girlfriend Sharon was, she could never compete with his neighbour's composure and common sense, a quality that would last far longer than looks.
His guts twisting, he exhaled when he thought; more's the pity that she's already got a steady boyfriend.
"Ah, there we are," he slowed the vehicle to stop alongside Willie Strathmore and his neighbour, then joked out of the window, "Taxi for Craigie Street."
Watching Strathmore hand the radio to Harry Dawson, he waited till the older cop climbed in the back of the van, then when hearing the rear door slam closed, waved cheerio to Dawson.
"Do you think she'll be okay on her own?" he called out to Strathmore.
"When you drop me off, Drew, and I know you're supposed to be covering Smiler's beat when he is on his break, try and stay handy around this area if you can," he drily called back. "If I know Harry,"

he added, "give her fifteen minutes and she'll be getting herself into trouble somewhere."
Taylor grinned at Roz before he replied, "We'll listen in for her calling out, Willie, but as we're an All Stations vehicle, we could be anywhere in the sub-Division, so maybe remind the Inspector and Sergeant Chalmers that she's out and been let loose on her own?"
Roz fought her smile, for though the red-haired and stoutly built Dawson had almost four years' service, the shift as a whole continued to treat her like a newly arrived probationer simply because there weren't many calls she attended where she ably handled the situation on her own. On the contrary, she was known for overreacting or requesting immediate back-up after some stupid or inane comment that invariably turned the complainer against her. In short, the shift was becoming intolerant of her and Roz had quickly realised that Dawson was an unpopular choice as a neighbour. Unfortunately, she was also acutely are that Dawson was jealous of the younger woman, though Roz had never given any cause for such a feeling, she believed that the jealousy had arisen from a shift night out, some months previously.
Dawson, who though in her mid-twenties, continued to suffer from a skin condition, likely brought on by teenage acne and daily, used a pan stick to conceal her spots but then, Roz suspected, overlaid it with another conditioner.
In the female toilets that evening, Dawson, tipsy and embarrassed after being rebuffed by the admittedly handsome barman, had criticised Roz's unblemished skin only for Roz, believing she was being helpful, foolishly suggested that if Dawson cut back on the pan stick and used pure natural soap, remarking that it might make a difference.
Taken aback, she had not expected the gutter language that followed and the slamming of the door as Dawson stormed out.
She turned when she sensed Taylor staring at her and who grinned, "I know what you're thinking. Maybe we should run a sweep on how long it takes for Harry to call for assistance."
She blushed, for he was entirely correct, though her brow creased when she thought that in fairness, Harry would get stuck in when there was a scrap, even if *she* had started the brawl.
She involuntarily scowled when she further thought, unlike that plonker, Telford.

****

The man in Roz's thoughts, Constable Keith Telford, was at that time handing his police radio to his own neighbour, Constable Ian Parker, a twenty-three years old former police cadet with just under four years' service and who accepted the radio with no more than a grunt.

Parker didn't like Telford and worst, didn't trust him, particularly if they were to become involved in any kind of fracas.

As far as Parker and, he presumed from their conversation when Telford's name was mentioned, as far as the rest of the shift were concerned, Telford should never have qualified as a police officer. It was commonly known the twenty-eight years old, five feet nine inch, stick thin constable with bad teeth and more than a hint of halitosis and who considered himself to be a tough man, beneath his bragging exterior, was in actual fact a coward who went to great lengths to try and win his colleagues acceptance. Had he known of his colleague's opinion of him, that included the story he wore hobnailed boots on nightshift to warn off any lurking neds of his approach rather than surprise them, he might not have been so voluble trying to win over his shift members.

His frequent attempt to ingratiate himself was his imprudent boast telling all and sundry who would listen that he would "…speak to anything," a foolish assertion that he was more than willing to perjure himself at any court to back up his colleagues.

Fortunately, none of his colleagues would ever dream of taking up his offer, for it was widely known that in the few court appearances anyone could recall Telford giving evidence, he was easy meat for the defence lawyers and during not just the Fiscal's examination, was a bumbling wreck when cross-examined.

And so, though it was never openly discussed, when Telford's colleagues submitted report cases to the Procurator Fiscal's office, more than a few deleted or forgot to include his name as a witness in the case and the reason was commonplace.

Stories about Telford's avoidance to engage in any kind of confrontation had circulated for years, but it seemed the management neither wished to believe nor consider such stories to be worthy of challenging him and so he continued to be a member of the shift. Were the bosses, Iain Cowan and Lucy Chalmers, aware of Telford's shortcomings?

Undoubtedly they were, Parker reasoned, but being so short of patrol officers, they probably couldn't afford to have him transferred or whatever.

In short, Telford was a uniform carrier; a physical presence on the street only.

Watching Telford strutting off towards Craigie Street to take his break, Parker frowned, recalling the latest incident some weeks previously when the probationer, Roz Begley, and her neighbour, Drew Taylor, had pursued suspected car thieves who after colliding with a parked car, abandoned their stolen Ford Cortina in Butterbiggins Road.

It being an early shift and with Begley wearing her police issue skirt and like all female colleagues, issued with the pathetically small wooden baton that just about fitted into their issued handbag, both officers had independently pursued the two suspects who'd decanted from the stolen Cortina and made off through the adjoining tenements to the rear courtyards.

The call for assistance had echoed throughout the Division and beyond and was immediately acknowledged by the shift's foot patrols as well as a passing Traffic vehicle and some patrolling nine-nine-nine response vehicles in the nearby vicinity.

Several anxious minutes passed with a breathless Taylor declaring he had arrested his suspect and was returning to the police van, but there had been no response from Begley, who was known also to be carrying a Burndept radio.

Frantic calls were made to elicit her whereabouts, but still nothing came back.

So concerned was the extremely competent civilian controller, Mary Wiseman, she had issued an emergency alert, a code twenty-one, to find the young policewoman and was gratified to hear further patrolling Traffic vehicles and most of the beat officers respond. But not all of them.

What later angered the shift was the pursuit had occurred in the beat at that time being patrolled by Telford, who not only failed to attend to acknowledge the call to assist in the search for Begley, but later claimed that his radio had failed and he was unaware of the situation. Fortunately, Willie Strathmore and Harry Dawson, having hijacked a passing car and its willing driver to attend the search, discovered Begley in a rear court, her uniform and her hair dishevelled, but

otherwise uninjured and in the act of handcuffing her suspect, her knee in the car thieves back as he lay prone on the ground.
Parker's brow furrowed when he remembered back at the office, Telford being challenged at the time by an angry Drew Taylor who with his fist bunching the front of Telford's tunic, had snarled, "Weren't the blue's and two's of the responding Traffic and response cars a hint?"
Once more it was Smiler who had intervened and grabbing at Taylor, instructed him to cool down.
Later that morning and without Telford's knowledge, the shifts' father, as Smiler McGarry was jokingly referred to, subtly swapped radios during their mutual break and discovered there did not appear to be anything wrong with Telford's Burndept.
However, rather than challenging him, Smiler insisted that no one made Telford aware of Smiler's ruse, that the big man would deal with him in his own good time.
But that didn't prevent the shift as a whole from mistrusting Telford, who seemingly oblivious to his colleagues' anger, continued as though nothing had occurred.
But now those same colleagues would no sooner trust Telford to have their back than the criminals and offenders they arrested, let alone have him corroborate their evidence in a trial.
With a sigh, Parker turned away, dismissing his neighbour from his thoughts, then glancing at his watch, continued his foot patrol, already imagining the taste of the pasta dish his mother had prepared for his break.
****

Seated at the old and scarred wooden table in what served as a refreshment room, Mattie Devlin finished his chip supper just as Smiler stooped to hand him a mug of tea.
"Just milk, you said?"
"Aye, thanks," Devlin nodded.
Seating himself opposite, Smiler turned as the door opened to admit Keith Telford, who nodding to them both, said, "Anything doing, guys?"
With a fixed smile, Smiler responded for them both when he replied, "All quiet on our beat, Keith. But what about you and young Ian?"
"The same," Telford took off his wet raincoat and cap to hang on the pegs driven into the wall, then sitting beside Devlin, said, "The word

is you were a sergeant before you came here."

Catching the merest hint of a raised eyebrow from Smiler, he calmly replied, "Don't be shy and withdrawn, just ask away."

Blushing, Telford stuttered, "That was the word anyway, and I hear that you came from the sticks, out in Clydebank?"

With an amused glance at him, Devlin repeated, "The sticks? Oh, you mean that quiet wee hamlet where nothing ever happens, and you're suggesting that now I'm in the big city I'll maybe see some action?"

Uncertain if he was being teased, Telford squinted at Devlin before he replied, "Well, yeah. I mean," he shrugged, "Clydebank. It's not exactly the centre of the universe, is it?"

"True, but there are bad people living there, just as presumably there is bad people living here in the city, wouldn't you say?"

In an obvious attempt to impress him, Telford glanced at Strathmore coming through the door, then turning back to Devlin said, "Aye, but here in the big city, I'm guessing we're a lot busier than you guys were out in Clydebank."

"Have you ever been to Clydebank, eh, Constable Telford, is it?"

Unaware of the silence in the room, with Smiler and Strathmore pretending to ignore the conversation, Telford replied, "Well, I've passed through it, but I can't say I've ever stopped there."

"So," he pursed his lips, "you won't know there's over twenty-five thousand people living in Clydebank, that the local football team play in the First Division alongside Celtic and Rangers and the rest, so that means every home game, we're invaded by thousands of supporters that often include your Weegies, drunk and fighting and we lock up dozens of them for the courts at Dumbarton and I suppose you are unaware that historically, Clydebank is the heartland of the ship building industry on the River Clyde? And, believe it or not, we've even got electricity and the television down there now."

He watched Telford blush, then try to joke, "Maybe not a wee hamlet after all?"

"No," Devlin lifted his mug and turned to stare at the wall opposite, "not a hamlet."

The door opened to admit Lucy Chalmers, who called to Smiler, "See me before you go back out, big man."

"Will do, Sarge," he toasted her with his mug, then when she closed the door behind her, he grinned, "That woman just can't get enough of me."

"In your dreams, Smiler," Strathmore smiled. "Our Lucy is to good looking for an old guy like you."

Listening to the banter, Keith Telford forced a smile, but didn't join in and head bowed, munched at his Chinese takeaway.

He'd never really felt he was a part of the shift; never felt he was a part of anything, if truth be told.

Friendless and never having had a girlfriend, something he'd dare not admit, he'd joined the police almost three years previously to escape the misery of working in a Safeway Supermarket where he knew the women and his male colleagues were always talking and sneering behind his back.

The police, he had thought at the time, would provide him with the respect of the public and the comradeship he so craved, but quickly became disillusioned at the training college when he discovered it was more of a boy's club than he'd reckoned.

As for the public, he'd quickly realised they really didn't give a shit about their police.

Initially, the legal training and classroom work at the college hadn't troubled him too much, but the self-defence lessons had shown him what he'd always known.

He was a feartie, a coward and within days of working the streets, soon came to dread any kind of confrontation.

Not just the physical side of the job either, but dealing with the great unwashed he was often tongue-tied and more often than not when attending calls, relied on his neighbour to deal with the public.

How he managed to survive not just the training, but his two years probationary period was still a wonder to him.

Stirring the rice with his fork, his face burned with shame when he recalled that night just three months into his probation.

He'd been neighboured with Smiler and while patrolling the Dixon Blazes industrial estate in Lawmoor Street, encountered a gang of three youths who were in the process of breaking into a warehouse. Surprising the youths, Smiler quickly had two by the scruff of their necks, then when the third bolted, the big man shouted that he pursue the suspect.

Chasing after the youth in the dark, he'd managed to corner him in the flats in Caledonia Road, some distance away, finding the youth who was aged about seventeen, standing in the back of the close by the rear door that was bolted.

But the youth had screamed abuse at him, then raised his fists to fight.

Shocked and, yes, frightened, he'd stood back against the wall as the youth, recognising his fear, sneered when he raced past him and escaped.

For several minutes he'd stood there in the darkness of the close, his legs shaking and catching his breath until at last, hearing his call sign on the radio, he'd replied that he'd lost the suspect in the darkness.

With Smiler's two in custody, nobody questioned him losing the third youth, but that incident was to haunt him to this day and set the tone for the rest of his service.

Again, if he was honest with himself, he should have resigned from the police and found something that was not a confrontational occupation, yet some part of him liked being a cop.

His mistake and conscious of it too, was he persistently boasted of his prowess in dealings with offenders and in an effort to impress his fellow cops, set himself up as a man who could be trusted to back them in any situation, whether that be in a fight or giving evidence in court.

Court, he inwardly shuddered.

While most officers accepted their appearance in the witness box to be just another facet of the job, on the few occasions he found himself cited to appear at court he worried himself sick and in the days prior to his appearance, suffered sleepless nights.

Snatching a glance at the jovial Smiler who was engaged in telling another raucous and funny story, he suspected the big man disliked him and knew his secret, yet had never even alluded to calling him out.

That in turn caused him to consider the easy-going, older man; a man he secretly despised for his popularity amongst the shift.

One day though, he unconsciously gritted his teeth, he'd show them all what he was really like, what he was capable of.

Drunks.

He liked arresting the drunks. The drunker they were, the easier to handle and he'd threatened then slapped more than a few around when he found them on his beat.

There was something immensely satisfying about being able to rough them up, jailing them for being drunk and incapable, the charge known throughout the Force as the D&I, and to date, not one had been sober enough to complain.

It was then his thoughts turned to his admiration and unrequited desire for the shift's probationer, Roz Begley, a young woman who constantly filled his thoughts.

Yet no matter what he said or did, it seemed that she hardly acknowledged him, almost as if she was ignoring him, though for the life of him he couldn't understand why.

He glanced up, his face beetroot to see Willie Strathmore staring at him and who repeated, "I said, Keith, we're talking about having a wee lock-in at the Georgian tomorrow night after the shift. Are you up for it?"

Much as it pained Strathmore to extend the invitation for Telford to join the rest of the shift for a drink at the King George's Rest on Pollokshaws Road, known throughout the Division as a polis pub and where the owner was himself a former sergeant, Smiler's subtle but meaningful glance had indicated it wasn't proper to exclude the unpopular Telford.

Taken aback, he replied, "Eh, aye, sounds like a plan," and already envisioned himself cornering Roz with a line of patter.

"Right then," Strathmore nodded, "time I was back on the street or Harry will be going nuts. Anyway," he nodded at Telford, "with you that makes us four and I'll pass the word to the Inspector and Lucy Chalmers and the rest of the guys about the lock-in.

Glancing at his watch, he nodded to Devlin when he asked, "You live local, Mattie?"

"No," he shook his head, then said, "I'm over in Old Kilpatrick. I'm in a police authority house there, but if I'm travelling every day to Craigie Street, I think I'll be looking for somewhere closer."

"Now, if nothing else," Smiler rose to his feet and grabbed at his tunic, "that would save you a fortune on petrol. Ready to go?"

Also on his feet, Devlin smiled as he nodded, but the thought of a lock-in and the drink induced questions that his new colleagues would invariably ask of him, decided him he'd find some excuse not to attend.

****

When Smiler and Devlin left the police office, they found the rain had returned and darkness was falling throughout Glasgow and beyond.

Less than a mile from where the pair stepped into the street was located the small and well-tended Govanhill Park. Almost perfectly square in shape the Park was bordered on four sides by red sandstone tenement buildings and during the daylight hours, the Park was popular with local residents and their families, with a playpark for the younger children and a basketball court, admittedly a little run-down, located in the corner of the Park at the junction of Govanhill Street and Langlefield Street.

Easily accessed through a gate on each of the four sides of the Park, its one downfall was that the overhead lighting on the paths through the Park were either broken or had through the years been vandalised, thus in the darkness creating shadowed areas within the thick shrubbery of the Park that made it popular with underage drinkers and, on occasion, women plying sexual favours for money.

It was on this rainy, dark evening, within one of these shadowed areas, the shrubbery so thick it created a canopy over a concealed space littered with empty beer cans, bottles and other debris, where Jeannie Mason, her head befuddled by the cheap bottle of wine she had earlier consumed, led the punter. Within a minute of arriving at the space, Jeannie, well used to the ways of the men who manhandled her, found herself forced to her knees on the rough ground while the man, his hands encased in brown leather driving gloves, grabbed her by her hair.

Accepting of her unhappy life and prepared to offer any sexual service in exchange for the means to obtain more alcohol and in particular, the half-bottle of whisky he'd promised that lay in the plastic carried bag he carried, Jeannie was no stranger to a man's particular desire, but weakly protested at this punter's tight grip of her hair as his hand.

Reaching up to grab at his wrists, pleading that he relax his grip a little, he hissed at her in the most coarse and obscene language, then tightening his gloved hand in her hair even more, hissed at her, "You think I'd let a dirty flea ridden cow like you touch my dick?"

With his other hand the man viciously slapped Jeannie on the side of the head.

Shocked and stunned, then as if in a sudden realisation she become aware of the dangerous circumstances she found herself in, that the man never intended having any sexual intention, Jeannie tried to pull herself away from him, muttering she didn't want to go through with this, but he was now beyond all reasoning and ignoring her pleas, angrily made a fist with his free hand.

It was then in a mindless rage and still retaining a hold of her hair, he began with his free gloved fist to rain blows down onto Jeannie's head and face.

Stunned, blood pouring from her nose, mouth and her ears, he suddenly let go of her hair, causing Jeannie to fall backwards in a daze onto the well-trodden ground.

But he wasn't finished.

His teeth gritted, he stared down at her lying prone beneath him, he lifted his booted foot and stamped it down, again and again onto her unprotected face, her neck and her head and chest.

His rampaging attack lasted for almost a minute, then breathless, he turned to guiltily stare into the darkness about him before quickly making off.

Lying on her back, Jeannie stared up at the dark, cloudy sky, the falling rain on her face diluting the blood that continued to pour from her facial wounds, gasping for breath through her shattered jaw and broken teeth.

Then, with a soft gurgle as the blood seeping from her broken mouth subsided, Jeannie Mason, former Staff Nurse, once loving wife and mother, with a gentle sigh succumbed to the murderous beating.

CHAPTER FIVE: Friday, 8.25am, 9 March 1979.

During the night, the rain had reduced to a drizzle, then at last gave way to a bright, if chilly morning.

His eyes fluttering open, Mattie Devlin stared at the sliver of light peeking through the curtains to reflect on the wall opposite the window.

He'd enjoyed the craic at the previous night's shift lock-in, albeit he was only there an hour, reminding one and all he had too far to travel for alcohol and joking there was just so much squash a man could drink before his bladder exploded.

Being the only non-alcohol drinker in the pub gave him the opportunity to weigh-up his new colleagues and other than the tall, skinny cop called Telford, thought them to be a decent enough bunch.

Certainly, the Inspector and his sergeant, Lucy Chalmers, had a good time and he was astute enough to realise that though they freely mixed and joked with the cops, there remained that respect and civility for their rank.

That and it was evident that his new neighbour, Smiler, and Iain Cowan shared more than just being cop and Inspector.

He frowned when he recalled the redhaired female, Harry something, obviously having partaken too much swally, winking at him in what he thought was a highly suggestive come-on, but having just discovered Janice was a lying, cheating scrubber, he completely blanked her.

Minutes later he knew that to be a mistake for he caught her scowling at him and inwardly grinned when the old adage of a woman scorned had crossed his mind.

When bidding his farewell, he hadn't then noticed that Smiler too was leaving and it was only when Devlin was making his way to his car, he saw the big man. In that instance, he had been about to call out to the big man, but then saw him getting into the front passenger seat of a dark coloured Vauxhall Viva, though he didn't get a look at the driver.

When the car drove off, Devlin hadn't bothered giving the issue a second thought.

With groan, he sat up in bed and almost immediately, reflected on the previous day.

Unconsciously shaking his head, he wondered how he'd survived the day, the day in which so much had occurred; so many revelations that even now, shocked him to his very core.

First demoted, then learning his wife was not, as he'd believed, the woman he'd married.

Married?

He softly snorted at the idiocy of it all and how easily he'd been taken for a fool by Janice.

It no longer mattered, for when driving home he'd made up his mind that meantime, while he continued to work as a cop, he'd be looking for something else for it was unlikely he'd ever progress in the police after all that had occurred and didn't relish the thought of spending the next twenty-two years walking the beat.

His bladder reminded him it was time he was up and rising from the bed and so gingerly stepped around the broken glass and wooden frame that lay on the bedroom floor with the wedding photograph that displayed a smiling Janice and he grinning like the idiot he now knew himself to be.

He wasn't by nature a violent man, but getting ready for bed the previous evening, he had unaccountably swept the frame from the bedside table, leaving himself now with a clean-up job.

With a regretful sigh, he strode through to the bathroom in the hallway where after making his toilet, he showered.

Dressed in a cotton robe, he made his way downstairs to the kitchen in time to catch the nine o'clock news on Radio Clyde.

There was nothing new to attract his interest and his brain in neutral, went through the process of making his breakfast of tea, scrambled egg and toast.

Sitting at the small, gateleg table, he glanced around the kitchen and decided there really was no point in continuing with his plan to renovate the place, that it was unlikely he'd be occupying the police authority house for many more weeks and certainly not if a better job opportunity was to come his way.

Which, his brow furrowing, decided him that when he'd dressed and prior to commencing his late shift, he'd visit an employment office to determine what was currently available.

It wouldn't do any harm either, he thought, to take his Glasgow Uni Degree with him to support his applications, then idly wondered where it might be. Perhaps something else that Janice had stolen from him, beside his savings and his dignity.

His decision made, he finished his breakfast, tidied the dishes away, then returned upstairs with a small brush and pan to clean up the damage.

****

As was usual for her, Chief Inspector Lizzie Whitmore was early in to work that morning, believing it to be better prepared to meet with the Divisional Commander, Chief Superintendent Jimmy Thompson, when she presented her case for Mattie Devlin.

Knowing the pernickety old bugger like she did, Whitmore reckoned he'd protest and refuse, but decided she'd remind him that he had not many months to serve and why would it matter to him anyway? Glancing at her wristwatch, she lifted her desk phone, then called down to Thompson's secretary to learn he had not yet arrived at his desk; another indication that he was beginning to relax from his duties and in her mind, strengthened her case.

"Tell him I'll be popping down to see him when he gets in," she told the secretary, "and if you will, please, phone me at my office to let me know when he's there. Oh," she grinned, "and don't forget to let me know what kind of mood he's in."

****

It was just after nine that morning when a dog walker, a middle-aged resident who resided in in one of the tenement flats in Govanhill Street, led her collie into the Park, cheerfully waving or nodding to the other dog owners she either knew by name or sight.

Letting the collie off the lead, the woman kept a weather eye on her dog, a bitch and by far *too* friendly with some of the neighbour's dogs when she had the opportunity. Unusually, the collie seemed to be ignoring the other dogs in the Park and instead made a beeline for a thick cluster of shrubbery near to the metal fencing. Quickly following the dog or as fast as her seventeen stone permitted, the now red-faced woman saw the yapping dog hesitate as it approached the shrubbery located at the boundary fence.

Continuously calling to the dog, she frustratedly watched it disappear into the undergrowth, aware from local gossip it to be a well-known hide for the wayward teenagers and the glue-sniffers and almost immediately realised that there was a real likelihood of broken glass, maybe even junkies' needles, within the cramped space.

Ignoring her calls to return, the worried woman, now bent almost double, followed the dog into the undergrowth, using the trodden path to enter the enclosed space.

Her anorak catching on the overgrown shrubbery, her eyes narrowed to widened as she peered into the dimly lit space within, then to her horror saw the dog standing over the bloodstained body of a woman. Her loud scream attracted the attention of some passing workmen and so, Jeannie Mason was at last discovered.

****

Laura Gemmill was at her desk when the control room phoned upstairs to inform her that uniformed officers were on their way to

Govanhill Park in response to a report of a dead woman being found there.

At thirty-seven, Gemmill was considered to be young for the rank of Detective Chief Inspector and particularly in a Department that until just a few years previously, was male dominated.

Collar length fair hair and standing at five feet seven inches, Gemmill had joined Lanarkshire Constabulary seventeen years previously and been a CID officer for eleven of those years, four of which had been served with the Scottish Crime Squad.

It was rumoured that she was considered a candidate for the vacant post of Detective Superintendent in charge of the Serious Crime Squad, a post that had to date never been held by a woman, but her recent divorce from her husband with the very public scurrilous stories of his infidelity had put a dampener of her hopes of being appointed.

Now, slowly exhaling, she decided that if indeed it was a dead body, she'd not wait for the beat cops to trample all over what might be a suspicious death and taking a note of the phone call, left her desk to grab at her raincoat hanging from a peg on the wall.

Making her way through to the DI's room, she saw Sammy Pollock, bent over his desk, his tie as usual unknotted and a pencil behind his right ear while he scratched at his balding head as he pored over a report.

"Sammy," she saw his head jerk up, "that's the report of a woman's body over in Govanhill Park. I'll grab some car keys and I'll meet you in the yard."

"Okay, boss. Suspicious?" he asked when he rose from his desk.

"Don't know yet, but I'd like to get there before we have our unformed colleagues tramping all over the locus."

Grinning and collecting his own waterproof jacket from the peg on his wall, Pollock inwardly sighed at Gemmill's hurry, correctly guessing she was too impatient to wait for the uniform guys to confirm it was a body and not some tailor's dummy discarded in the Park.

Pulling on his jacket, Pollock grabbed his cigarettes and lighter from his desk then made his way into the corridor, once more inwardly shaking his head at his boss's decision to check out the report rather than tasking one of the DS's or even a DC to confirm the nature of the report.

Younger than Gemmill by a decade, Pollock had been a CID officer for nigh on twenty-two years, five as a DI and had never previously worked for anyone like Laura Gemmill, but believed she still had a lot to learn about handling her staff, himself included, and was apt to run off at the mouth without thinking first or fly off the handle at the most trivial issues.

That said, he liked Laura Gemmill and considered her to be very competent, mostly from what he'd heard and experienced since she'd arrived at the Department, but if she had a fault it was her impatience.

But maybe it's a woman thing, he smiled to himself as making his way downstairs, he decided no, it was probably more to do with her recent divorce from her ratbag of a husband.

A defence lawyer working for a prestigious Glasgow firm, Mark Gemmill was no stranger to Pollock and many a time they'd crossed swords in the low and high courts.

It had always been common knowledge that her husband was a bit of a player with the women, though why a bright and highly educated woman like Laura had wound up with him was anyone's guess.

Fortunately, there were no children involved in the divorce action, so that was likely a blessing, thought Pollock, himself happily married with three adult children.

Upstairs, Gemmill had made her way to the general office where she collected a Burndept radio. Turning, she informed the uniformed CID clerk, Bobby Davies, where she and Pollock were going and instructed that he keep what detectives were in the office to remain there till Davies heard from her.

Acknowledging with a nod, Davies watched her leave the room and slowly exhaled, for he had learned in the nine months he'd been doing the job that when she'd the bit between her teeth, Laura Gemmill, good boss that she was, was like a whirlwind and no wonder, he wryly smiled.

She was like a mad woman when she got going and it was no surprise most of the Department couldn't keep up with her.

****

In the bedroom of his three-bedroom, semi-detached home in Tweedsmuir Road in the Hillington area of the city, Stuart 'Smiler' McGarry rapidly shook the quilt cover to air it, then flapping it over the bed, let it drop to cover the sheet. Puffing the four pillows, he slowly inhaled and even though she'd been gone now for more than a couple of hours, he could still smell the perfume she knew he favoured.

How he'd landed a good-looking woman like her at his age remained a mystery, but there was no denying they were good for each other or rather, he could not help but smile, she was very good to him.

He sat down heavily onto the bed and his brow furrowed when he once more wondered, how and more importantly, when could he introduce her to his children. Adam, married with two kids of his own and Jean, not resembling her mother in looks, but as fiercely independent as Jean had been, now sharing a west end flat with her boyfriend and both about to complete their final year in medicine at Glasgow University.

It was an issue that had troubled him since some six months previously, they had got together.

He idly thought of that day, the morning when he had joked that she nagged him like a wife and that before he knew it, she'd be straightening his tie and making his dinner.

If that was an offer, she had coyly replied, gently tugging him towards her as her hand remained on his tie, then she'd be round to his place that night to cook him a meal.

He recalled he'd been wide-eyed and dumbstruck and for once in his life, did not know how to respond when she had softly added, "Stew, tatties and peas do you, then?"

Returning home from the early shift, he'd hurriedly straightened the house, not that it took much for he was a tidy man, and still believing she was at the madam, that she had been joking.

But then, his heart hammering in his chest, almost to the minute she arrived at the door with a carrier bag over her arm and marching past him, said, "Set the table. Dinner will be twenty minutes."

She hadn't stayed that night; in fact it was almost a month before she stayed over and he found himself blushing as he recalled their first, tentative night together.

But since that time they had been inseparable, though both had agreed that their relationship for now, remain private.

His brow knitted when he recalled that both Adam and Jean, as well as Adam's wife, Grace, had almost a year after Cheryl died, encouraged him to move on. However, as the years passed, almost four now, he'd resigned himself to being alone.

Well, not really alone, he smiled, for the kids had been and continued to be supportive as were his close-knit family and wide circle of friends.

But even though the time had passed since Cheryl had succumbed to the kidney disease, if he were to disclose he was now in a relationship, would the kids be as supportive and particularly when they discovered the age difference.

Glancing at the digital clock on the bedside cabinet, he sighed that his decision whether to tell or not would keep for another day, then rose to make his way into the kitchen to prepare his breakfast and organise food for his break on that evening's late shift.

As he worked, he whistled along to the popular song playing on Radio Clyde, then when the ten o'clock news commenced, his eyes narrowed at the bulletin reporting the discovery of a woman's body in the southside of the city, in Govanhill Park.

According to the report, the police had issued a statement regarding the discovery, but refused to admit if the circumstances were suspicious.

It briefly occurred to him to phone his pal, the CID clerk, Bobby Davies, and inquire what the story was, but glancing at the wall clock and seeing it now to be a little after eleven o'clock, he decided he'd wait till he commenced duty and probably get the full story then.

When the news concluded, his thoughts turned to the new guy on the shift, Mattie Devlin, and if his initial assessment was correct, he thought Mattie to be a nice guy and smart too.

That and if his story about the unfaithful and deceitful wife was correct and he'd no reason to doubt it, then punching the boyfriend in the face was a natural reaction and Smiler was the last man in the world to condemn Mattie for it.

His eyes narrowed when he considered that maybe the Chief Constable was a bit hard on him, demoting Mattie, when he could have dealt with it by a heavy fine, particularly as the boyfriend had withdrawn his complaint of assault.

His breakfast finished, he sat sipping at his tea and wondered if young Mattie would remain in the job, but though he couldn't know it, his thoughts paralleled those of Devlin when Smiler thought it was likely he'd leave and look elsewhere for employment.

Pity, though, for he thought Mattie would be a definite asset to the shift, undermanned as they were.

****

Minutes after the Divisional Commander's phone call to Chief Inspector Lizzie Whitmore, there she was at his door, a personnel file under her arm and with her free hand, pulling down the hem of her tunic then using the same hand to sweep back a loose strand of hair from her eyes.

"Come in," the gruff voice called.

Closing the door behind her, Whitmore strolled across the floor to the chair opposite the desk, then uninvited, sat down and stared pokerfaced at her boss, Chief Superintendent Jimmy Thompson. Though they'd had their differences in the past and he wasn't beyond bawling at her, Whitmore actually like the old bugger, a former City of Glasgow officer who was outdated and knew no boundaries when making his views known about things that annoyed him. One of those reasons she liked Thompson was when he believed himself to be correct he was not afraid to argue with the top tier at Pitt Street, or as he called them, the shiny-arses at police headquarters who, he was frequently heard to growl, "…had never seen an angry man in their lives."

From her tunic pocket, she fetched out an unopened packet of Polo mints, then handing them across the desk, said, "You know you're reeking of the bevy?"

Cupping his hand, he breathed into it, then cautiously asked, "You can smell it?"

"If I can, then so can everyone else," she sighed, aware like the rest of the Division knew, Thompson was a functioning alcoholic and though he'd always been a man who liked a swally, his drinking had got worse eleven months previously when his wife of thirty years succumbed to the Big C.

But alcohol wasn't the real problem, because Thompson, a forty to fifty cigarettes a day man, had in the preceding year developed a hacking cough that though he confided in no one, was of real concern to his GP who had arranged for Thompson's visit to an oncologist.

The bad news resulting from his visit diagnosed inoperable lung cancer with at best, six to nine months left to him, but only if he gave up the fags.

Watching him tear three or four mints from the roll, he popped them into his mouth, then opening a desk drawer, placed the pack inside before he said, "So, apart from looking out for me like I know you do," he stared meaningfully at her, "why are you really here, Lizzie?"

This is it, she thought, gambling that old Jimmy, as he was known by his staff throughout the Division, would agree to her idea and see it as one last poke at the hierarchy in Pitt Street.

Not only that, but Thompson was very much behind his officers and at the forefront of righteous complaints to the Chief about his Division being badly undermanned.

"Well," she took an inward breath, "you know that Iain Cowan's shift is not only six constables short of a full shift, but he's a sergeant down as well?"

"I do," his eyes narrowed when he stared suspiciously at her.

She placed the file in front of him and slowly said, "This young fellow, Mathew Devlin, was demoted yesterday from sergeant to constable, then sent to us."

Continuing, she watched as he leafed through the file, then explained the reason for his demotion and said, "As you can see from his personnel file, he's a smart young guy and I've spoken with someone I know over in Clydebank. Frankly, sir, they're sorry to lose him. He's keen, eager and until yesterday, had the makings of a good career."

Thompson sighed heavily when his face creased and he said, "I'm guessing where this is going, Lizzie. But if we appoint him as an acting sergeant with Iain Cowan's shift, you lose a constable and really, gain nothing. That and if the Chief finds out what I've done, he'll have my head on a platter."

She had come prepared for the argument and so replied, "Two things, sir. One, with the time you've left to serve, when did you worry about the Chief falling out with you?"

That, she was relieved to see, provoked a grin.

"And secondly," she hurried on before he could interrupt, "Cowan's sergeant, Lucy Chalmers. You'll recall she's a former DC and she's now got two years back in uniform under her belt. Frankly," she pursed her lips, "I'm expecting a call any day from the Personnel Department to inform me that she's being transferred back to the CID as a DS. If that should happen, Cowan would be on his own, left without any supervisor, so all I'm trying to do is get ahead of the game."

He sat back in his chair, then arched his nicotine stained fingers arched in front of his nose and stared at her before he said, "Lizzie, you're wasted at your rank. In fact, no, you're wasted in the polis. You should be a bloody politician."

He shook his head, then grinned evilly when he added, "Can you imagine the Chief's face when one minute he's demoted this young guy, then the next minute I'm appointing him as an acting sergeant?"

"Well," she frowned, "the easy answer to that, sir, is you *are* the Divisional Commander. If the Chief trusts you to run F Division with the limited resources you have, he's hardly able to criticise you if you make a decision based upon your requirements and regardless of whether or not he approves. I mean, you have to utilise your staff as *you* see fit. Isn't that right?"

His brow furrowed before he broke into a slow grin, then replied, "I suppose that's my defence when I get a phone call from Pitt Street demanding to know what I'm up to, is it? Anyway," he continued to smile when he said, "Lucy Chalmers. You'll know her better than I do, Lizzie. Smart young woman, as I recall from her last annual appraisal that crossed my desk."

"Oh, aye, she is that, and she's bound for better things than continuing as a supervisory sergeant here at Craigie Street," Whitmore nodded.

He changed tact when he said, "This body that's been discovered in Govanhill Park. I'm hearing it's a murder, that the CID haven't had the woman identified yet."

"So I'm hearing, sir, aye. I heard on the network the SOCO have been tasked to attend and the Park's been cordoned off."

He sat for several seconds in silence, then thoughtfully said, "Likely Laura Gemmill will be in to see me soon to confirm the details of it being a murder. Did you know she's been bleating to me like everyone else about her lack of resources and needing an extra DS, as if I've got one hiding under my desk," his voice dripped with sarcasm.

He suddenly sat forward, his hands flat on the desk when he said, "You're right, as you usually are, about the time I've got left. So, here's what we're going to do, Lizzie."

He licked at his lips, then unconsciously fetching the pack from his drawer, snapped two more polo mints from the packet and into his mouth when he said, "Head back to your office and phone young Chalmers to tell her to come in to work in civvies, that I'm appointing her as acting DS and *post haste*, she's to be seconded to the CID, at least for the duration of the murder investigation. If nothing else that will get the DCI off my back for a while."

His face creased when he added, "It won't do her file any harm either to have it recorded she's already served as an acting DS. Now, this young man, Devlin. He's the problem, as you already know he will be," he pretended to scowl at her.

But Whitmore was nobody's fool and saw through the scowl when he added, "Iain Cowan's shift are late shift today, so when Devlin arrives for work, bring them both to me and Lizzie, make sure you give Iain a heads-up. He's a good man and it's not fair that this be sprung on him, okay? In fact, when you get back to your office, I suggest you call him at home to give him time to take it in."

"Of course, sir," she nodded with some inward relief.

His thoughts turned to the logistics of his decision when he said, "There must be spare tunics kicking about the office somewhere with sergeants' stripes, so try and track one down for Devlin and have it ready for him."

He stared at her, then sighed when he said, "We both know there will be grief about this decision, Lizzie, and I'm too long in the tooth for it to bother or hurt me. Frankly," he sighed, "there's nothing the Chief or the Deputy can do to me now with the time I've got left, but if word gets out it's your idea or even that you are complicit in this…"

He didn't finish, but simply stared at her, the clear implication that it could finish her career.

She smiled at him, a sorrowful smile before she informally said, "Jimmy, I'm a divorced woman who took up with and is now living with another woman. Far from it for me to accuse the police of being intolerant of those sort of things, but we both know it's unlikely that I'll progress beyond my current rank. So," she took a deep breath and to Thompson, she seemed to sit a little straighter in her chair when she continued, "my priority right now is to do my job to the best of my ability and to *my* own standards. As you well know, there are some decent cops out there on the streets, performing their duties

beyond what is expected of them and if I can help them in any way *and*," she leaned forward in her chair when she stressed, "if that puts noses out of joint, then sod it to anyone who wants to complain."
He slowly smiled when he quietly said, "One day, Lizzie, and hopefully not too far off, the glass ceiling *will* shatter."
****

Laura Gemmill, unconsciously shivering in the claustrophobic shrubbery that she saw was littered with empty bottles, beer cans, glue tubes and cigarette butts, stared down at the body as the duty casualty surgeon, a man who she privately thought should have retired a decade ago, but likely was earning more money now on police callouts than he ever did as a GP, shook his head.

"My initial diagnosis, DCI Gemmill," he began, "is she was beaten to death. The obvious damage to her face and her jaw likely contributed to her death because I can only assume, prior to a post-mortem of course, that the damage to her throat has blocked her air passageway, thereby in layman terms, causing her to suffocate by the lack of oxygen."

His brow furrowed when he stared down at the body, then slowly shaking his head, added, "Whoever killed this poor woman did so in such a violent rage that, well, to be frank," he grimaced, "I don't think I've ever attended any victim with such ghastly injuries. Might I suggest too that if bare hands were used, there is every likelihood the killer with have at the very least, bruised knuckles. That and," he pointed to her torso, "as is plainly visible, the mud stained imprint of a boot or a shoe suggests she was stomped upon, so the PM will no doubt determine that her breastbone and ribs are likely broken."

Aged or not, Gemmill had to inwardly admit at least the old duffer seemed to know what he was about.

Closing his bag, the doctor added, "I'm of the opinion that with the weather as it is, she's been dead maybe twelve hours, perhaps a little longer, and while I cannot rule out sexual activity, as you can plainly see, her undergarments are in order and from the smell of her breath, I'd suggest she's been heavily intoxicated."

He seemed a little embarrassed, causing Gemmill to ask, "What? Is there something else?"

His face creased when he replied in a low voice, "I know she's wet from lying here and the rain dripping through the bushes," he glanced upwards, "but the poor woman."

The doctor sighed deeply before he quietly continued, "I fear she might be a down and out. She's wearing a man's briefs and, well, she's not *particularly* clean," he frowned before he added, "but unusually, her hands. Well," he shook his head as though in surprise, "her hands are very well tended. Surprisingly clean and the fingernails are neatly trimmed too."
Then he asked, "Have you identified her yet?"
"No, not yet, but the scene of crime officers are already in possession of her fingerprints, so if she's known to us, I hope to have a result by this afternoon, unless of course someone comes forward with a name."
"Is that likely? Someone coming forward to report her missing, I mean."
Gemmill shrugged when she replied, "If as you suspect she has been living rough, then no. I don't suppose anyone has missed her yet."
The doctor, a deeply religious man, briefly bowed his head in silent prayer, then with a sigh, bid Gemmill a cheerless goodbye.

CHAPTER SIX.

Living in the west end of the city had always been an ambition for Constable Drew Taylor, achieved some years previously when he managed to save up his deposit of eight hundred pounds, then with some real and cautious hesitation, took on his mortgage at a crippling thirteen percent.
The first year of his occupancy had been particularly difficult, but he quickly learned to adapt his income to making ends meet, for as well as calling in favours from family and friends to assist with décor and plumbing and some electrical issues, he'd also learned not just to budget shop, but to cook cheap and cheerful meals.
And daily he come to realise it had all been worth it, for in the three years he had occupied the first-floor tenement flat in Chancellor Street, just off the main thoroughfare of Byres Road, the value of the property had greatly appreciated and was now far in excess of the price he had paid for it.
Of course at the time, his parents had argued why he needed a three-bedroom flat, but his original idea of renting out a room to assist

with the mortgage payments had fallen by the wayside, for he soon discovered he not only enjoyed his own space but could *just* survive on his income without a lodger. Besides, he had told them with a wide grin, should the time come when he decided to settle down with a wife, he'd get more profit from selling a family flat towards purchasing a house, than a single bedroom flat.

One benefit of living in Chancellor Street, he had come to realise, was the vibrant social life around the corner in Byres Road, where everything he needed was a short walk away.

Just out of the shower, he stood staring at his uniform lying on his bed when his brow furrowed as his thoughts turned to Sharon.

It was a pub in Byres Road where he had met the vibrant and outgoing Sharon.

At the time, meeting her seemed to be a good thing and he had thought his life then was on the up.

He had a career he loved, good friends around him, a home to call his own and a beautiful girlfriend who he thought, adored him.

Never at that time would he have believed how quickly she come to bore him.

Neither would he have guessed that Sharon was so egotistical nor so controlling and, he hated even the thought of it, so manipulative.

When he'd first brought her to the flat, he had been pleased at her enthusiasm for the place, admiring what he had achieved and cheerfully clapping her hands together, already envisioning herself living there.

So taken with her was he, he had not at first realised that the spendthrift Sharon, who lived with her parents, expected him to wine and dine her nor suspected her long-term plan; to move in with him while expecting he not only shoulder all the bills, but contribute to her lifestyle as well.

That and to his knowledge and though he pointedly complained whenever she stayed over, which was becoming increasingly more often, he spent an hour cleaning up after her for Sharon was, he now realised, a very spoiled and selfish woman.

A good hardworking and tenacious cop, nevertheless Taylor was not good at confrontation in his personal life and while he continuously practised in his mind how he would break up with Sharon, when it came to actually confronting her, he always backed off.

However, since being neighboured with Roz Begley, that he determinedly decided was about to change.

Yet, he began to dress in his uniform, there was the slight problem of Roz having a current boyfriend, Derek, but from her recent comment, though he would never admit to it, he was heartened to learn that they were having their own difficulties.

His thoughts turned to Roz and he smiled.

Being neighbours in the job and living not too far from each other, they had quickly agreed to car-share, cutting down on the petrol cost and today it was his turn to pick Roz up from her parents ground floor flat in Partick's Caird Drive.

He'd enjoyed the short car-share ride with her to and from work, for it gave them both an opportunity to be relaxed without the necessity of listening for or attending to calls and it was during their recent journeys to and from work, they had each been more open about their respective relationships.

Quite apart from her being in a relationship and he about to end his, his real problem was not knowing whether her close friendship was anything more than that.

His brow furrowed in thought, he finished dressing and decided on a cuppa before he left to pick her up.

****

As was his usual routine and being the old-fashioned cop he was, Smiler arrived almost thirty minutes prior to commencing his shift, giving him time for a once-over uniform check in the stained and cracked mirror attached to the wall in the men's toilet and a mug of tea before the Inspector read the daily briefing register to the shift. He liked being early for work for it also gave him time to catch up with what had occurred since his preceding shift, prior to going out on the beat, as well as the opportunity to chat with the constable who that morning, covered the beat area he was to patrol and learn if there was anything Smiler should know.

However, that Friday afternoon, what he didn't expect was the Inspector to be in the office before him and who said, "You'll have heard on the news about the body being discovered?"

"I did, yes."

"The CID have no ID for the victim and while the Fingerprints Department are already working to identify her, with your extensive local knowledge of the area, DCI Gemmill has requested you attend at the mortuary to see if the woman is known to you. So, if you're happy to take your own car over to the mortuary in the Saltmarket, the DCI is already there and waiting for you."

"No problem, Inspector," he nodded, then eyes narrowing, softly asked, "All I heard, Iain, was that a body was discovered. Can I assume it's a murder investigation?"

"I don't have all the details, Smiler," Cowan grimaced, "but the word is the victim was terribly beaten and it resulted in her death."

"And it was in the Govanhill Park?"

"Yes, it was. Why?"

Smiler, inwardly hoping he was wrong, already had a bad feeling about this and so replied, "Some of the local down and outs and women prostituting themselves have been using the Park after dark. You'll likely have read about it in the collators weekly report."

Nodding, Cowan peered at him when he asked, "You have a woman in particular in mind?"

"Sadly, I do," he nodded, then added, "but whether I'm correct or not, no matter who it is…"

Smiler didn't finish the sentence, but drawing himself up and taking a breath, simply said, "Right, Inspector, I'd better not keep the DCI waiting, so I'll head over there the now."

****

Arriving outside Craigie Street police office, Mattie Devlin reflected on his decision to leave the job, deciding on the drive over that he'd give it a month to find something else, then irrespective if he did find employment, he'd leave anyway. Not only was Janice the architect of his downfall, but his pride had taken such a knock he believed the stigma of being the cop cuckolded by someone he'd once called a friend would follow him wherever he was posted.

Finding a bay some hundred yards from the office, he made his way to the archway that led to the rear yard, then entering the building via the back door, saw Inspector Cowan standing by the charge bar and in conversation with Lucy Chalmers.

Curiously, Sergeant Chalmers was not in uniform, but dressed in a white blouse and navy-blue skirted suit, her collar-length blonde hair tied up into a fierce bun.

Both turned to him when the Inspector said, "Ah, Mattie, good. You're here. Follow me, please."

Without waiting for an acknowledgement, the Inspector turned away and began to head for the door that led towards the corridor where both the administration offices and Divisional Commanders office were located on the ground floor, but not before Devlin saw Chalmers smile and wink at him.

Confused, Devlin hurried after the Inspector and his heart sinking, wondered; what the hell have I done now?

Leading him to the Chief Superintendent's office, then stopping outside the closed door, he heard the Inspector tell the secretary, "I think he's expecting us."

It occurred then to Devlin that not only was he still wearing his anorak, not having had time to grab his tunic and cap from his new locker, but he also carried his Tupperware container with his evening food in his hand.

He watched as the Inspector pushed open the door to the Divisional Commander's office then with an apologetic grimace, Devlin hastily placed his food container onto the secretary's desk and followed Cowan through the door, seeing the wooden nameplate screwed to the door that proclaimed, 'Chief Superintendent James Thompson.'

Seated behind his desk, the wizened man with the ring of grey fluffy hair surrounding a bald crown, glanced up to wave Cowan and Devlin into the room, then coarsely asked, "This is him, then?"

Devlin's nose twitched, for his first impression was that the room stank of tobacco and…again, curiously, peppermint?

"It is, yes sir," Cowan agreed with a nod.

Glancing at the desk in front of the Chief Superintendent, Devlin saw what seemed suspiciously like his own personnel file and inwardly sighed, then heard Thompson address him with, "It's no secret, Constable Devlin, that my Division is grossly understaffed, but we in the police are grateful that the first implementation of Lord Edmund Davies pay reform has already taken effect and by the second implementation this year, our resources should hopefully match our requirements. In the meantime," he took a slow breath, "and regardless of the circumstances that brought you to the constable rank, I cannot afford to have an experienced supervisor walking the beat. With Sergeant Chalmers now seconded to the CID for the duration of the ongoing murder investigation…"

And that explains her being in civilian clothes, thought Devlin.

"… it leaves Inspector Cowan with no supervisory officer. Therefore, Constable Devlin, I am appointing you acting sergeant for the duration of Sergeant Chalmers placement."

The shock of his words left Devlin stunned, but then Thompson, who almost growled, carried on, "But be in no doubt your temporary appointment will not sit well with those who are aware you have so recently been demoted and will likely cause issues for not only me, but Chief Inspector Whitmore, who has assured me that you seem to be a resilient officer and who will likely perform your duty to the best of your ability."

Thompson paused for a few seconds, then his voice a little softer, said, "However, I am certain you will feel a sense of betrayal, if not actual bitterness towards the Force, so I will provide you with this opportunity that will *not* reflect badly on you. Do you accept or reject the acting rank of sergeant?"

Swallowing hard through a tight throat, Devlin heard himself stutter, "I accept, sir, and thank you. Both of you."

"Well, then *Sergeant* Devlin," he replied pokerfaced, "I believe Inspector Cowan has sorted out a tunic with stripes, so be off with you and do not give me caused to regret my decision."

Bowing his head towards his desk, Cowan took that as their dismissal, then nodding at Devlin, they left the office.

In the outer office, standing by the secretary's desk, Cowan nodded at her then smiling, from a chair beside her, she handed Devlin a tunic bearing sergeant's stripes on both arms.

"Okay, Mattie," Cowan smiled at him, "we'll see the shift out, then you and I will have a private word."

That said, he turned on his heel and followed by Devlin, clutching both the tunic and his Tupperware box, they made their way back towards the muster room.

****

With their two DC's outside the mortuary enjoying a cigarette, they sat in the relatives' room; DI Sammy Pollock, a white china mug of coffee in his hand and DCI Laura Gemmill, who glanced at her wristwatch, then said, "This guy, Constable McGarry. You really think he might recognise our victim?"

"Smiler," Pollock reminded her when he nodded and continued, "He's got what you might call a comprehensive knowledge of everyone in the central residential area of the office, boss. If she's known to anyone, it'll be to him. He's not what you'd expect, though," his brow furrowed in thought, then explained. "This is my second appointment to the Division. I was here as a young cop, then into the CID as a DC and as you know, returned as a DI. I'm thinking Smiler must be near his retirement time, but he was here when I started the job and has always been here, or so it seems," he grinned. "A big, amicable guy with a very moral outlook and courteous to everyone, regardless of rank or situation, even believe it or not, to the neds he arrests. Well," he scowled, "unless they're wife-beaters or hurt kids. That type is open season for the big man."

"But he's never progressed from being a constable?"

He couldn't explain why, but that remark stung and more irately than he intended, he defensively replied, "Not everyone is career conscious, boss. There's a lot of good, hardworking cops out there who remain at the honourable rank of constable and without them, quite frankly, the job would be twice as hard as it already is."

Realising she had somehow offended him, she was thinking about how she might placate him, but he quickly added, "Look at us two sitting here, for example. Two senior CID ranks and we've the pathologist and our two DC's waiting to commence the post-mortem on an unidentified female victim. Yes," he nodded, "the fingerprints will likely come up with a name in due course and that's only *if* she's on the system. But right now, for all you're a DCI and I'm a DI, we're relying on an *experienced* beat officer with good local knowledge to identify our victim. What does that say about the honourable rank of constable?"

Seconds passed before she smiled, then humbly said, "And that, Sammy, puts me firmly in my place."

They both glanced up as the door opened to admit Smiler, who wearing his tunic, but carrying his cap in his hand, hesitantly greeted them with, "Ma'am, DI Pollock. I understand you're looking for me?"

Gemmill recognised the big man from seeing him about the office, though had never exchanged a word nor, she inwardly admitted, even acknowledged him with nothing more than a cursory nod as he passed her by.

Her first impression then and taking notice of him now was that Constable McGarry seemed to be a smartly turned out individual, but recalling Pollock's admiration of his attitude to police work and though a little dubious of his reputation, she decided to give him the benefit of her doubt and replied, "Thank you for coming. Eh, Smiler is it?"

He almost dazzled her with his grin, then nodded and replied, "That's me, Ma'am. Now, I understand you have a victim you believe I might be able to identify?"

Now on her feet as was Pollock, she grimly said, "Please, follow me."

She led the way into the corridor and then to the examination room, where the DC's, alerted by Smiler's arrival, patiently waited with the SOCO photographer, the mortuary assistant and the elderly pathologist, who was at that time holding court with his captive audience and relating a macabre tale of a previous post-mortem.

On the stainless-steel examination table lay the body of the deceased, photographed numerous times, stripped of her clothing, her body carefully washed by the assistant prior to the physical examination and now covered to the neck by a brilliantly white sheet with only her head in view.

It had been after the body had been washed that the true extent of the horrific injuries became clear, the footprint injuries stamped into her body by her killer that were themselves photographed and revealed the tread of the killer's footwear in minute detail; detail that if the footwear was to be discovered would indicate the guilt of the wearer.

It was not the first time that Smiler had seen anyone or even a dead body with severe wounds, yet the very sight of her injuries caused him to baulk and the big man felt his body tense and turn cold with rage.

Stepping closer to the examination table, he laid his cap down onto the surgical instrument table and to those watching, it seemed that the big man was no longer conscious of anyone else being present, for to Gemmill and Pollock's surprise, Smiler reached out to raise one edge of the sheet.

Reaching out, he took the deceased's cold, right hand in his, then gently massaged it between his own hands.

The silence in the room was palpable when they all heard him quietly say, "Albeit she was living rough, she always kept her hands scrupulously clean and her fingernails neatly trimmed. Habit, I suppose, from her time working in the theatre."

As he leaned down to stare at her injured face, they then heard him softly mutter, "Jeannie, lass, you poor wee soul. I'm so sorry that this happened to you, but believe me. We will find him. I promise you. We'll get him."

Straightening up, Smiler, his face chalk-white, turned to Gemmill, then seeing the grave expressions and as though now realising that he was not alone, he took a soft breath before he softly said, "Jeannie Mason is her name, Ma'am. No fixed abode. Jeannie is, was," he corrected himself with a frown, "forty-five years of age. She was an alcoholic, but prior to her fall from grace, she was an operating theatre Staff Nurse and worked at the Victoria Infirmary."

He paused to draw breath, then continued, "Jeannie was known to us at Craigie Street, but as I recall, nothing criminal, so it's unlikely she'll have been fingerprinted. Offences only, such as being drunk and incapable and breach of the peace. That said, when she was drunk she took it out on her husband, punching him and generally being violent, but to my knowledge Archie, that's his name, he never retaliated," he added with a shake of his head. "The marriage ended in divorce, of course, and Archie was awarded the kids. Two of them and they'll be grown up now."

His eyes narrowed when he continued, "I can't exactly recall Archie's current address," he shook his head, "but I will find it for you. I'm sorry to say," he took a sharp breath, hating himself for having to share her terrible secret, "Jeannie had fallen as low as any woman might find herself and I'm aware that in the recent past, she would hang around some of the less salubrious pubs in the Division, particularly around closing time, then offer sexual favour in exchange for drink."

He paused, his face still pale, and stared into Gemmill's eyes when he asked, "Do you have a suspect?"

"Not at the minute, Smiler," she replied, then dismissively added, "but thank you for coming today and assisting us with identifying our victim."

He didn't immediately respond, but then his face frozen and more curtly than he intended, he said, "Jeannie Mason, Ma'am. Her *name* was Jeannie Mason."

Unaccountably embarrassed and unable to break eye contact, Gemmill found herself blushing when she replied, "Yes, of course, Smiler. Mrs Mason."

With a satisfied nod, he turned and lifting his cap, left the examination room just as Sammy Pollock had the uneasy thought that the CID had better catch the killer before Smiler did.
****

Feeling a little self-conscious in his ill-fitting tunic with the sergeant's stripes, Mattie Devlin stood beside Inspector Cowan who explained to the bemused shift of Sergeant Chalmers temporary secondment to the CID and the Divisional Commander's decision to temporarily appoint Devlin as the new supervisor.

"And I know," he glanced meaningfully at the six constables, "you will support Mr Thompson's decision and provide Sergeant Devlin with the same support and courtesy due his rank. Any questions?"

The silence and shaking of heads was followed by Cowan reading the notes in the daily briefing registrar, then a short summary of what was known about the discovery of the woman's body.

"Do we know who she is yet, sir?" asked Willie Strathmore.

"No," Cowan shook his head, "but Smiler's away over to the mortuary to have a look at the deceased and if anyone will recognise her…"

"It'll be our Smiler," Drew Taylor finished for him with a grin and a sly glance at Roz Begley.

"Aye, very good, young Taylor," Cowan was not amused at being interrupted, then there being no more questions, dismissed the shift to their beat duties.

"Mattie?" he indicated Devlin follow him and nodded towards his office.

In the office, he gestured Devlin sit then closing the door behind them, said, "How you feeling about working with the shift, them knowing you were demoted, I mean."

"I don't foresee any problems, Inspector. They don't know me and I don't know them and to be frank, I was young when I was promoted to sergeant. I had to quickly learn that there are those cops who tried to take advantage of my relative inexperience and my age, so you might say I've had a steep learning curve on how to handle the bolshie ones."

"Good to hear," Cowan smiled, then opening a locker, fetched out two tunics with sergeants' stripes.

"Rather than have you attend at the stores department for a new tunic where someone in Pitt Street might recognise you, can I suggest you take five minutes to unpick the stripes from these tunics, then take your own tunic down to Allison Street. There's a wee tailor shop down there and Smiler knows where it is, so if you mention I sent you," he quickly added, "they'll sew the stripes on for a couple of quid and you should have them back by tomorrow at the latest."

"I'll do that, sir, and thank you."

Cowan returned his smile when he asked, "Must have been quite a shock, getting the temporary appointment."

Blowing out through pursed lips, Devlin softly laughed when he replied, "Shock doesn't begin to describe it."

He got no further, for the door was knocked, then opened by Smiler who grim faced, said, "Inspector, a wee word, please."

Then seeing Devlin, added, "Mattie, I mean, Sergeant Devlin. Congratulations are in order, I'm hearing."

"It's temporary, Smiler, but thanks anyway. Ah, is it a private word you want with the Inspector?" he began to rise from his chair, but stopped when Smiler held up the flat of his hand.

"No, you're alright. I've just come from the mortuary," he exhaled as he addressed Cowan. "It's wee Jeannie Mason, sir."

They saw the Cowan's shoulder's slump when he gasped, "Oh, for God's sake. Not wee Jeannie."

Shaking his head, he added, "Sober, that wee woman was such a poor soul, but with a drink in her," he shook his head, his lips tight but his meaning clear.

"That's the woman you pointed out to me yesterday, Smiler?" Devlin glanced from one to the other.

"That's her." he agreed with a nod.

It was Cowan who asked, "Any suspects, Smiler?"

"The DCI, she says no," he shook his head. "No suspects."

"And you? Do you have any thoughts on who might have murdered her?"

"Not yet," he frowned.

"Okay, then. Now, on other issues," the Inspector returned to the locker and fetched out a frayed sports bag that he handed to Devlin. "Sergeant Devlin here needs to take a tunic down to Joshua's wee shop over in Daisy Street to get stripes sewn on, Smiler, so while he's doing his own bit of tailoring," he grinned at his own joke, "have yourself a coffee and take him down there when he's ready."

"Mattie," he turned to Devlin, "if you're up for it, can you neighbour

Smiler for the rest of the shift. I know you're now a supervisor, but with us being so short-staffed it won't do you any harm to have a look around the office beat and get your bearings, as it were."

"Fine by me, sir," Devlin nodded, inwardly pleased that he was spending his first shift as the acting sergeant with the big man.

****

It was Roz Begley's suggestion that they take a turn past the Govanhill Park, where the four entrances on each side of the squarish Park were taped across the wrought iron gates, each gate guarded by an early shift uniformed constable earning some valuable overtime.

Inside the Park at the corner where the body had been discovered, they could see two more officers standing smoking and who would remain there until the SOCO team were satisfied that there was nothing more they could collect that might be of evidential value.

Turning to Taylor, she asked, "What do you think the chances are of the CID catching the guy?"

"Do we know it's a guy?" he teased.

Frowning, she replied, "You think it might be a woman that took the victim into the Park, then murdered her?"

"No, I don't," he sighed, "but it's a mistake to make an assumption the killer *is* a man."

"To *assume* is to make an *ass* of *u* and *me*," she quietly repeated, then added, "That's what they taught us at Tulliallan."

"And they were correct, Roz. Couple of years ago while I was still in my probation, I attended a report one night of a man attacking a woman at the building site in Pleasance Street over in Shawlands. When I got there, I saw this woman on the ground; well, actually on her hands and knees and a big lump of a guy standing over her. I was on him before he knew I was there and wrestled him to the ground," he slowly exhaled.

"And?' she stared curiously at him.

"Turned out he was her boyfriend and she'd taken an asthmatic attack and he was trying to calm her down."

She smiled when she asked, "What was the outcome then?"

"Naturally, he fought back and she's gasping for breath and trying to explain he was only helping her. Anyway, I ended up with a sore jaw before the rest of the shift arrived to get him off me. Fortunately, she quickly recovered and he saw the funny side of it and there was no complaint, but…"

"Never assume," she finished for him.

"Correct," he turned to smile at her.

The next couple of minutes passed in silence before he said, "So, how are you and your boyfriend, eh…"

"Derek."

"Yeah, Derek. So, how you guys doing?"

Her face creased before she replied, "Well, that's nearly eight months, now, but," she hesitated, then slowly drawled, "I'm not really sure."

He felt his stomach tense when he asked, "You having second thoughts?"

"No," she shook her head, "not me. Him, I think."

"Oh," he mentally crossed his fingers when he asked, "Am I being too forward. I mean, do you want to talk about it?"

But she didn't get the opportunity to respond, for the All Stations radio set, colloquially known as the AS and installed in the Force's emergency response vehicles, interrupted with a broadcast, a lookout for a vehicle stolen within the preceding five minutes from a street in the city centre.

Within seconds, the same broadcast was repeated on the Divisional personal radios, the almost obsolete Burndept radios.

The vehicle, described as a blue coloured XR3i Ford Escort, was last seen travelling at speed towards the Glasgow Bridge and thereafter probably headed into the F Divisional area.

Grinning, Taylor gunned the engine towards Pollokshaws Road, then risking a glance at Begley, said, "Seems like the chase is on."

****

On foot towards the tailors' shop in Daisy Street, both Devlin and Smiler, each carried their nylon rainproof coats folded across their arms, or rather rainproof coats that in reality were hardly shower proof let alone any use against the Scottish weather.

Smiler and Devlin, with the sports bag in his other hand, listened to the general broadcast on the personal radio they each carried.

It was Smiler whose expression suddenly grim, nodded that they quicken their step, and who suggested they carry on towards Calder Street, then explained, "Young Drew and his neighbour, Roz, will likely head towards Pollokshaws Road, which is the main arterial road through to the south, but if experience has taught me anything, the car will likely turn east onto Calder Street and weave its way through the side streets towards *chateau lait*. I heard from the collator the other day that there's a team operating out of there and stealing Ford vehicles to order, which they're stripping for the parts."

"*Chateau lait?*"

"Castlemilk," Smiler grinned. "You'll have heard of it, I'm sure. It's the big, sprawling council housing estate south of here and where more than a few worthies are domiciled."

Devlin couldn't help but smile at Smiler's descriptions for both Castlemilk and worthies; an old-fashioned term, he'd heard used by senior cops to describe criminals and for the life of him, could not recall any officer ever using the word, 'domiciled.'

Hurriedly making their way through the tenemented streets, they were striding along Daisy Street and more than one hundred and fifty yards from the junction with Calder Street when to their consternation, they saw a navy-blue coloured Ford Escort race eastwards at speed through the junction.

"That'll be it," Smiler grimly remarked, then breathlessly using his radio, reported the sighting.

"Nothing more we can do now," he shrugged at Devlin, then added, "Perhaps we should visit Joshua and you can drop that sports bag into him."

They had barely walked thirty yards when in the far distance, they heard the sound of police sirens, causing Smiler to grin and remark, "Seems our stolen car has grown a tail."

****

Returning from the post-mortem examination at the mortuary to Craigie Street office, they were stopped at a red light when DI Sammy Pollock sensed that his boss, Laura Gemmill, was more than a little peeved at her dressing down by Smiler McGarry.

The silence was broken when to his surprise, she sighed, "I made a mistake back there, Sammy, didn't I?"

"A mistake?"

"The big cop, Smiler. A lack of judgement on my part. I forgot I was dealing with a victim and not a human being. He was correct when he put me in my place; put me right, he did," she nodded at her own embarrassment.

Pollock risked a glance at her before he replied, "Aye, he *was* correct, boss. But sometimes as you know, we tend to forget the bodies we're actually dealing with have once been vibrant, living people with families who loved them or in turn, who they loved. Yes," he nodded with a shrug, "I know we also deal with our fair share of arses who frankly, won't be a sad loss to society, but on this occasion our victim, Jeannie Mason," he deliberately stressed the name, "before she fell afoul of the alcohol, seems to have been a decent member of society; a Staff Nurse with a husband and two children, albeit as Smiler said, she's apparently estranged from them."

He stopped speaking, then slowly continued as the memory came flooding back like a stabbing pain to his chest.

His mouth suddenly dry, he said, "Before I was appointed as DI here at Craigie Street, I was a DS over in Govan CID. Do you know Paisley Road Toll?"

"Yeah, I know it. Why?"

"Well, a couple of years ago, in nineteen-seventy-seven, the Glasgow Council handed over and old municipal building to the Talbot Association; the Kingston Halls they're called and located on the Paisley Road. You know, the charity that looks after homeless men?"

"I've heard of it, yes," she nodded, her eyes betraying her curiosity.

He took a deep breath as the telling of the story came flooding back. "Well, as likely you might be aware, most of the men who were taken in by the charity were alcoholics. They'd be given a night's shelter, hot food, then each morning after a cuppa and a roll and sausage, turned out to fend for themselves. Not that the charity workers liked doing that," he grimaced, "but there was only so much they could do for those guys."

He pulled the car to a stop at a red light on Pollokshaws Road, then continued, "On the day of the ceremony and once the official palaver and speeches were done and the Halls handed over to the Association and the so-called *dignitaries*," his voice was full of scorn at the word, "had gone after they'd had their finger buffet, the problem of the down and outs was left to the locals and to us at Govan. Almost within days there were reports of begging outside shops, drunks being mugged, women being accosted in the street for loose change and the local pubs in the area having problems keeping the down and outs from entering and frankly, they were a bloody nuisance."

His brow furrowed when he reflected on that day, then said, "About a fortnight after they'd moved into the area, I got a telephone call from the control room telling me that the young cop who was the Toll beat man for that morning, required the CID at his locus, some waste ground behind Stanley Street it was. When I got there, he'd already called an ambulance for this old guy whose name was Dutch Holland or rather, on account of his surname, that's what he was known as; Dutch."

His face creased when he described Holland as, "Maybe in his early to mid-sixties, it was hard to tell because of the state of him. Grimy, unkept grey hair and straggly beard and wearing clothes or what had been clothes that he simply piled on top of the next jacket or jersey or trousers. Again, as I recall the cop later telling me, when the old guy was admitted to the casualty ward at the Southern General Hospital, they undressed him to find he was wearing three pairs of socks and he'd foot rot so bad that the first pair had actually dissolved into his skin. I won't even try to describe how dirty he was or how soiled his trousers were."

She shuddered at the thought, then asked, "But why did the cop call for you?"

"Ah, well, the cop had discovered Dutch lying on his back on the waste ground muttering and obviously on his last legs, as it were, with his trousers pulled down to his knees and though the old guy couldn't explain what had happened, the cop suspected he might have been mugged."

"Was it a street robbery then?"

He didn't immediately respond, but then said, "At that time there was a couple of teenage tearaways mugging the elderly around the area of the Toll, but catching them or obtaining statements from their victims, most of whom were half blind, wasn't enough to put a case together. Anyway," he sighed as the light turned to green and rolled the car forward, "and to my everlasting shame and because of the nuisance these guys were, my judgement was impaired and I had already made my mind up that it wasn't worth investigating, that the old guy had likely taken down his own trousers to have a crap or something and so, to my regret, I left it with the cop to deal with."

The traffic light turned to green and he slowly accelerated away from the junction, then said, "Would you believe it when I tell you the cop travelled in the ambulance to the casualty with the old guy and was actually berated by the Nursing Sister for bringing the dirty old guy into her Ward?"

Surprised, her eyes fluttered when she asked, "Did he survive?"

"No," Pollock shook his head, "he died within twenty minutes of arriving at the hospital and while the young cop was still at the casualty ward."

"I'm guessing there's a postscript to this story?" she slowly drawled.

He slowed to permit a bus to re-join the line of traffic, then nodding, said, "The young cop, I forget his name," he shrugged, "he was instructed by the sergeant running the Divisional Enquiry Department to complete the Sudden Death Report for Dutch and as I recall, he was unable to trace any next of kin. As you'll know, that meant Dutch went into a council paupers grave. However," he took a sharp breath and his brow furrowed, "just over a week I think it was, after I'd dismissed the incident as of no interest to the CID, this young cop who I don't believe had even completed his probationary training, arrived at my desk and right in front of the rest of the Department, went off on one and verbally gutted me."

He paused again as the memory rolled back, then said, "It seems, and I'm not certain how he found out, the cop discovered Dutch had been a merchant seaman during the war and *twice* been torpedoed in the Atlantic. It also seems that on the second occasion, he had been in the water lying on a wooden life raft for three days before being rescued."

He paused once more when he said, "The young cop, no more than twenty-three or twenty-four he was and I recall he was ex-military, he was so bloody angry at me for dismissing old Dutch as of no interest to the CID and to be honest, I just sat there and took it," he bit at his lower lip.

Then glancing at Gemmill, he said, "I deserved every name that cop called me because I knew then that I had been too busy and too disgusted by the appearance of this old man to even consider he was worthy of *my* precious time investigating the possibility he might have been mugged. An old man who was a war hero."

He was turning into Craigie Street, before she replied, "That's a lot of baggage you've been carrying around, Sammy, and I get why you told me. Yes, you're right. It's a hard fact that sometimes we…me, on this occasion," she frowned, "forget that we're dealing with our victims who regardless of their backgrounds, have meant something to someone."

She softly smiled when she added, "I think the next time I bump into Smiler, I'll have to work at being a little less arrogant."

"Oh," he grinned at her, "Smiler won't hold a grudge, boss. He's too civil for that sort of thing."

"Good man, is he?"

"Well, since I've been a DI at Craigie Street, Smiler has been a regular visitor to the CID suite. Not that he's interested in joining the Department, it's just that with his knowledge of the area and the worthies who live there, he's always bringing in bits and pieces for the DC's; you know, who's doing what and where. That said, he's also a regular contributor to the collator's intelligence bulletins. Smart man, is our Smiler, though some of the younger DC's have quickly learned not to underestimate him."

"How so?" she turned to glance at him.

"Well, one example about a year back and no names, no pack drill," he stressed, "is that one of our young guys, a bit flashy and not long appointed to the Department, brought in a suspect for a knife robbery in a Paki shop on Calder Street. Then, as quickly as he locked up the suspect, almost run into your predecessors office to boast about it while completely ignoring Smiler's warning, he'd arrested the wrong man."

"And was it the wrong man?"

He sighed at the memory when he replied, "Later that afternoon, Smiler brought in the actual culprit who had confessed to the big man it was him and not the DC's suspect."

"Ouch," she frowned. "Red faces all round, then?"

"What made it worse for the DC concerned was that after Smiler had a word in the cells with the wrongfully arrested man, he then spoke up for the DC, telling the DCI that there would be no complaint, that the matter was dealt with. Needless to say, the DCI breathed with relief that the rubber heels would *not* be involved."

"And do you happen to know how that matter was dealt with by Smiler?"

"Not *officially*," he grimaced, "but it seems that Smiler also has contacts in the PF's office and I heard on the grapevine that a pending case against the wrong man, where he expected to receive at least six months in HMP Longriggend, was dealt with by a heavy fine."

"And if I can ask," she coyly smiled, "what about the DC?"

He smiled when he said, "Lesson learned, bollocked by the DCI and now one of your hardest working officers."

CHAPTER SEVEN.

When Smiler pushed open the door to the tailor's shop in Daisy Street, Devlin beamed when the bell above the door tinkled to announce their arrival and he saw a small man pushing through the flowery curtain to emerge from the rear of the shop, who aged about sixty, wore a brilliantly white dress shirt and pale blue and white striped tie with a black coloured yarmulke cap on the back of his head.

Hands on the counter, the man greeted them with, "And what can I do for you today, Smiler?"

"Joshua, this is Sergeant Devlin who needs stripes sewn onto his tunic," Smiler replied, then asked, "Any likelihood it can be done by tomorrow afternoon?"

Peering at Devlin, Joshua frowned when he said, "Not *that* tunic, I hope? It'll take me more than a day to make that fit."

Devlin smiled when he placed the sports bag onto the counter, then said, "No, this tunic's borrowed. My tunic's in here and I'll leave the bag with you in the meantime, Joshua, if that's okay?"

"No problem and for Smiler," he nodded towards the big man, "I'll have the tunic ready by late this afternoon, say five-thirty?"

Impressed, Devlin nodded and turned to leave, but then heard Joshua ask, "Is it true, Smiler? The body in Govanhill Park? Is it wee Jeannie?"

Smiler sighed, then nodding, he replied, "Afraid so, Joshua. Needless to say, anything you hear?"

"Of course," Joshua nodded, then with a bow of his head, he added, "She was a harmless woman, was Jeannie, may Yahweh watch over her and forgive her sins. I will recite El Malei Rachamim for her soul."

He slowly exhaled, then added, "Oh, and call back in a couple of hours," he addressed Devlin, "and your tunic will be ready."

"Good man, Joshua," Smiler gave him a wave as he left the shop.

On the pavement outside, Devlin asked, "What was that about, the El something?"

When they began to stroll along Daisy Street, Smiler's brow creased when he replied, "As far as I'm aware, Mattie, oh," he stopped and stared, then asked, "Can I still call you Mattie or will you prefer Sergeant?"

"It's me and you here, Smiler, so what do you think?" he grinned at the big man.

"Aye, right enough," Smiler returned his grin, then said, "Anyway, as far as I'm aware, El Malei Rachamim is the Jewish prayer for the dead and Yahweh is their name for God."

"My, but you're a mine of information, big man," Devlin teased him.

Before Smiler could respond, their radios activated with a transmission, requesting they attend the report of loud music coming from a tenement flat in Coplaw Street.

Devlin imagined he could hear the controller, Mary Wiseman, sigh when she added, "It's the woman downstairs again, Smiler, says that old Dennis is at it again."

"On our way," Smiler shook his head, then ending the call, turned to Devlin to tell him, "Now, Mattie, here's the story before we get there."

****

Acting DS Lucy Chalmers was sitting in the general office speaking with the CID Clerk, Bobby Davies, when Gemmill and Pollock arrived back in the CID suite.

Courteously rising to her feet when the DCI entered the room, Chalmers introduced herself.

"Good to have you on board," Gemmill nodded with a smile, then said, "DI Pollock will sort you out with a desk, Lucy. Now," she turned to Davies, "Anything for me, Bobby?"

"Just two things, Ma'am. The Fingerprints Department have already been on the phone to say they've no trace of the deceased's prints."

"Just like Smiler said," seemingly impressed, Gemmill nodded at Pollock, then asked, "And the second thing?"

"Well, now you mention him, Ma'am, Smiler left an address for you. The victim's former husband, Archie Mason, now apparently lives over in Renfrew," he bowed his head to read from the note, "Kinloch Road."

Gemmill frowned when she turned to stare at Pollock, then said, "Might as well get it over with, Sammy. I'll take Lucy with me to break the news to the ex, if in the meantime you manage the incident room and sort out the teams."

"Will do, boss," he replied and handed the CID car keys to Chalmers.

"Ma'am?"

She turned to see Davies handing her an A to Z map book, who then said, "I had a wee look in the book here for Kinloch Road. It seems to back on to the Glynhill Hotel and that's on the main thoroughfare, Renfrew Road, but you'd better take this anyway."

"Good call, Bobby," she smiled at him, then nodding at Chalmers, said, "Ready?"

****

Trudging towards the tenement building in Coplaw Street, Devlin said, "So, let me get this straight. The neighbour downstairs, this Mrs Morrison, is a frequent complainer about her neighbour upstairs, this man McGregor, because he plays his classical music too loud and you're telling me he's also an invalid who smokes the wacky-baccy?"

"Ah, aye, that's about the sum of it, Mattie," he nodded.

"But when we're there, you're asking me to ignore the fact that when McGregor opens his door, I'm bound to get a lungful of cannabis?"

"Aye, again, you've got it in one," Smiler cheerfully nodded.

His features twisting, Devlin couldn't help but ask, "Smiler, you do know that cannabis is a Class B drug that is illegal under the Misuse of Drugs Act?"

"Oh, aye, Mattie," he half turned towards Devlin, then with a nod, added, "I'm more than aware of that, yes."

"Which begs the question, why haven't you arrested this man McGregor for possession of cannabis?"

"Ah, well, there's a very good reason for that, Mattie. You see, old Callum, I say old because he must be in his mid-seventies by now, is a retired music teacher who some years ago was with his wife in a horrific car accident down in the borders somewhere."

His face creased almost in pain as he related, "She was killed and Callum suffered a severe spinal injury that no orthopaedic surgeon could repair. Through the years the medication prescribed to him has had little effect in easing his pain and it's only in the last couple of years that he's discovered though cannabis won't fix his condition, it does lessen the pain; enough to permit him to get through the day."

"And how did *you* come by all this information?"

"Ah," he grimaced, "that's a bit of a sad tale. It was about three years ago now, that I attended a call where Callum's friends had called at his flat, but informed Craigie Street they were unable to contact him nor have him come to the door, so I was sent along to try and find out if he was okay. Getting no response at the door, as you'll have guessed, I used my size twelve door key and discovered," he frowned, "well, he'd tried to kill himself."

He paused at the close entrance to the tenement building, then continued, "Cutting a long story short, the ambulance crew revived him, but because of the continuous pain he's suffered, there was a real danger he might again attempt suicide. As it happened, somehow he discovered that cannabis, taken as a medicine you understand," he stared meaningfully at Devlin, "would alleviate the pain and so as the last couple of years has passed, there has been no further attempts at suicide."

"Where does he obtain his cannabis? From a dealer?"

"I've always thought it prudent not to ask," Smiler dourly replied.

Almost with disbelief, Devlin then asked, "What about these complaints from the neighbour downstairs, this Mrs Morrison? Is it about McGregor smoking cannabis?"

"Eh, no, *not* exactly," he drawled. "Mrs Morrison is a widow of a similar age to Callum and, well," to Devlin's surprise, Smiler blushed, "she has a wee fancy for Callum and because he's rejected her, she likes us going to knock on his door now and then to remind him she'd still downstairs, alive and kicking, as it were."

Suppressing his grin, Devlin asked, "You mean, you act like a Cupid between the two of them?"

"Maybe," he slowly drawled, "but a Cupid going one way, not both."

Oh, this I've got to see, Devlin inwardly thought and nodding into the close, said, "Right, then, Smiler, lead on and I'll try to refrain from breathing in."

****

DCI Gemmill turned to her driver, Lucy Chalmers, to ask, "Where did you serve as a DC?"

"Started in P Division in Wishaw, boss, then DC there before being promoted to Craigie Street."

"Wishaw? I heard they eat their children out in Wishaw," Gemmill joked.

So, she has a sense of humour after all, thought Chalmers, who replied, "Only when they've exceeded the allotted ten kids, boss."

Gemmill smiled, then said, "I'm presuming you'll have delivered more than a few death messages?"

"As you say, boss," Chalmers sighed, "more than a few."

"Our victim, Jeannie Mason. Was she known to you?"

Chalmers brow furrowed at the memory of the wee, drunken and abusive woman being dragged through the doors to the charge bar, then said, "I recall seeing her being brought in occasionally, usually for being steaming drunk and on those occasions she was very belligerent. On the odd occasion I was out walking one of the beats with a cop, I'd sometimes see her then and sober, she was," she shrugged, "I suppose the words I'd use is timid looking."

"Any opinion as to why she might have been murdered?"

Chalmers snatched a glance at her before she replied, "Did you manage to speak with Smiler? I mean, Constable McGarry?"

"Oh, aye," Gemmill nodded. "put me right in my place, he did."

"Oh?"

"Simply put, Lucy, I'd forgot our victim was a human being and not just a dead body to be investigated."

Chalmers huffed when she replied, "Sounds like our Smiler. He's a big man with a big heart too. You know," she began with a smile, "I've watched him arrest fighting, cheeky drunks, then quietly speak to them to calm them down and believe it or not, I've even heard them apologising to him for their behaviour. Everyone seems to have a good word about Smiler, even the neds," she shook her head as though hardly believing what she was saying.

"Sounds like you admire him," Gemmill stared curiously at her.

"Truth is," her eyes narrowed, aware her face was suddenly flushed, "I suppose I do. With his lengthy service, to me he personifies the old-fashioned cop, a kind of Dixon of Dock Green polis, if you know what I mean. A real old sweat who's seen it and done it. I remember the first time I neighboured him," she smiled at the memory. "There was me, the brand-new Sergeant Chalmers and back in uniform for the first time in six years. The Inspector had put me out walking with Smiler to get to know the beat areas. Everybody and I mean, *everybody* we passed by, Smiler had a nod or a wink or a wee chat with them and what surprised me was they all knew him."

She paused, recalling those few days they'd neighboured, then continued, "He was like a village cop, but in the middle of a big city, if that makes any kind of sense. What surprised me even more was *he* knew them all. The local residents, I mean."

But she got no further for Gemmill, the A to Z resting on her lap, pointed, then said, "Next right should take us into Kinloch Road."

Almost as though a switch had been pulled, both Gemmill and Chalmers settled into a professional mode, preparing themselves to deliver the worse of news.

****

At her desk, Chief Inspector Lizzie Whitmore answered the persistent ringing phone, then heard the Superintendent at Personnel in Pitt Street go off on one.

Holding the receiver a few inches from her ear, she waited till he'd finished his tirade then teeth gritted, said, "Well, sir, if you give me the opportunity to explain," but that only set him off again.

Another minute passed with the Superintendent repeating himself, demanding to know why his Department had just that morning received a notification that the previously demoted Constable Devlin, demoted just the previous day, he raged, was now to be accorded the increase in salary commensurate with him being an acting sergeant.

Whitmore sighed, then deciding she'd had enough, politely replied, "Tell me, sir, are you on your speaker phone?"

She could almost imagine his surprise at her question when he snapped, "Of course not. Why would I be?"

She smiled at the thought of his outrage when she sourly said, "Well, listen to me, you jumped up smart arse! This is an *operational* Division with *real* staffing issues and problems! Office wankers like you, you smarmy tosser, have no idea what managers like me have to deal with and if *my* Divisional Commander has to utilise Devlin to supplement the lack of supervisors because *you* lot in Personnel can't do your job and *properly* allocate staff, then you can bugger off with your petty complaint!"

A few seconds of stunned silence was followed by the noise of the Superintendent's phone being slammed down.

With a resigned sigh, Whitmore dialled the internal number for Chief Superintendent Thompson to give him the heads-up that he was about to receive a phone call from headquarters.

****

Knocking on the brown painted door, Smiler cast a glance at Devlin when he said, "Can I just ask, Mattie, are we on the same page about Callum and his, eh, wee habit?"

"Let's just have word with him first and let me make my mind up," Devlin tactfully replied.

It was then the door was pulled open by a clean-shaven and handsome man of his own height and about seventy-something, thought Devlin, with a full head of grey hair that was collar length and wearing a striped, collarless shirt with the sleeves rolled back to the elbow, a brown waistcoat and brown coloured corduroy trousers. But it was the crutch under McGregor's right arm that took his attention, a wooden crutch festooned with small metal badges of the type usually found on walking sticks.

"Smiler," he greeted the big cop with a grin and extended his free hand.

"And who is this gentleman?" McGregor asked with a soft Lewis brogue.

"Callum, this is Sergeant Mattie Devlin, my neighbour for the day," Smiler replied as they followed the limping man along the hallway, with Devlin closing the door behind them.

His nose twitched at the smell of cannabis, recognising the thick, woody scent, but he decided this was not the moment to bring it to anyone's attention.

Led through to a brightly lit and comfortably furnished front room, a record player in the corner was quietly playing a Frank Sinatra song and not, as Devlin had expected, the loud music of the complaint by the neighbour downstairs.

"Sit, sit," McGregor urged them both, then added, "I'll just get the kettle on."

Removing their caps, both men sat together on the three-seater couch and it was then that Smiler whispered, "As you can hear, Mattie, the music is not loud enough to be a nuisance, but like I said, just an excuse for Elsie downstairs to remind Callum she's there."

"So," he pretended to frown, "what you're telling me is that she's making a false accusation?"

Smiler sighed before he nodded, then said, "The problem is that she's a lady who's getting older, on her own and frankly, I suspect she's just lonely. Hardly a crime, is it?"

"Maybe not, Smiler, but we're not social workers," he replied, then pointedly added, "and not paid to play Cupid either."

Further conversation ended when McGregor re-entered the room, carrying a tray supported by brown string attached to the four corners that he held with his free hand and upon which were balanced three mugs, a milk jug and sugar bowl and a plate of biscuits.

Springing to his feet with a quickness that belied his size, Smiler took the tray from McGregor and laid it down onto a coffee table.

Nodding his appreciation at the older man's initiative, Devlin remarked, "That's a smart way for a man with only one free hand to carry a tray, Mr McGregor."

"Needs must, Sergeant Devlin," he smiled appreciatively, then settling himself down into an armchair, he glanced at them in turn before he asked, "The music's not too loud for you, is it gentlemen?"

"It's fine, Callum." Smiler raised a hand, then handed out the mugs.

With a sigh, McGregor asked him, "Is this Elsie again?"

"It is," Smiler nodded.

McGregor glanced at Devlin before he asked, "Did Smiler mention her downstairs?"

"That she might have a crush on you, yes," Devlin fought hard to control his urge to smile.

"Woman's a bloody pest," he sighed, but without any rancour.

To Devlin's surprise, Smiler said, "I recall you telling me a while back that you're fond of Chinese food, are you not, Callum?"

"I am, but why do you ask?"

"Oh," his brow creased, "it's just that when I last spoke with Elsie down stairs, she happened to mention she's a regular visitor to the takeaway in Victoria Road. Do you know the one?"

"I know *of* it," he replied, "but of course, I don't get out and about as much as I used to."

"Hmm, never mind, Smiler," shrugged. "It was just that on the way up to your flat, she popped her head out of her door and in conversation, happened to mention she was thinking of having herself some takeaway noodles this very evening."

Devlin said nothing, for they hadn't spoken with the woman at all, yet couldn't help but notice that McGregor's eyes narrowed thoughtfully.

"Noodles, you say?"

"That's what she said, wasn't it, Sergeant?" he turned to Devlin.

"Noodles, yes," Devlin nodded in agreement to the lie.

Conversation lasted as long as it took to drink their tea, then getting to his feet, an indication they should take their leave, Smiler said, "I'm sorry, Callum, I should have asked how you're coping with your back?"

With a resigned smile, he said, "It won't get better, Smiler, and we both know that, and thanks to you I can manage the pain far better than what those quacks at the surgery prescribe me."

Devlin glanced sharply at Smiler who he saw, had the good grace to blush.

Leaving the flat, they descended in silence to the ground floor where Smiler knocked upon the door of the flat directly beneath McGregor's.

The woman who answered his knock, Elsie Morrison was, thought Devlin, to be in her early seventies and still an attractive lady.

Her once blonde hair had now faded to a carefully tended white and it was clear she was still a sharp dresser.

Her eyes widened at the sight of Smiler, then she dolefully said, "Smiler. You've come to tell me off, haven't you?"

"Yes and no, Elsie," he replied. "We'll not come in, but you must know you can't have us continually calling on Callum for playing loud music just because you want to go and knock on his door yourself."

Tight-lipped, she blushed, but before she could apologise, he held up his hand then said, "Do you happen to like Chinese food?"

Confused, she nodded, "Yes, I do. Why?"

Offhandedly, he said, "Are you aware that Callum is fond of Chinese noodles and that he'd dearly love some from the takeaway in Victoria Road?"

"Eh, no I didn't know that," she hesitantly said.

"So," he shrugged, "perhaps to make amends, you might consider that a peace offering could be you taking him some noodles to take up to him and maybe even getting something for yourself and we'll say no more about your calls regarding his loud music. How does that sound?"

Glancing at him, Devlin wondered at this big man who just the previous day almost casually arrested a wife-beater on a trumped-up charge of assault, yet today was openly lying to bring two elderly people together.

It was clear that Elsie Morrison recognised Smiler's ploy and with a wide grin, said, "I'll do that, yes, and thank you, Smiler."

When they'd stepped back out into the street, Devlin remarked back to McGregor's slip of the tongue and said, "It was you, wasn't it? You who suggested to Callum that cannabis might ease the pain in his back."

There seemed little point in denying it, so Smiler nodded when he replied, "I read an article in a magazine some time ago and told him about it. And yes," he exhaled, "there's a wee story about how he came to meet the man who provides the cannabis."

"And that story is?"

"Well," Smiler drawled, "a few years ago I was filling in on one the Divisional response vehicles for the regular officer who was on holiday. A wee break from the routine of the beat, you might say. So, one fine afternoon, me and my neighbour get a call to attend at a house in Kings Park Avenue, a nice area it is too and it was about an attempted break-in to the garage at the house. When we got there, there was no reply at the front door, so I took it upon myself to check around the back of the house and there I found the owner, we'll not bother with his name," his face creased, "pottering away in his greenhouse."

"I think I know where this is going," sighed Devlin.

"Anyway, the poor man almost died with shock to see me striding into his greenhouse while he was attending to his, what we might call, his exotic plants."

"You mean his cannabis plants?"

"A wee bit pedantic there, Mattie, but aye, right enough, you're a sharp one, Mattie," he smiled with a nod. "When I pointed out to him that the plants were *not* strictly legal, he explained that he only grew them because his wife, lovely woman that she is, suffered from that horrible disease, multiple sclerosis, and a wee smoke of the cannabis relieved her pain. Well, he was such a nice man, never been in trouble with the law and what was I to do? I mean," he extended his hands in explanation, "I didn't think it was fair to bring him before a court, Mattie, when all he was doing was relieving his wife's agonising pain and after all, it wasn't as if he was dealing the stuff."

"So, you happened to mention this man to Callum McGregor?"

"Ah, yes, I did," he softly exhaled.

"Bloody hell, Smiler," he shook his head, "if the bosses found out about that, you could lose your job, your pension, maybe even earn yourself a conviction."

Smiler stopped walking and turning, stared pokerfaced at Devlin when he replied, "I won't defend what I did, Mattie, but when I made that visit to his flat and discovered Callum had tried to kill himself because the doctors were unable to help with his pain relief, I had a choice to make. Let him know about cannabis and where he might obtain it or wait for the call back to his flat where undoubtedly, I'd find him dead. Yes," he exhaled when he slowly nodded, "I knew if the word got out my decision would have consequences for me, but ask yourself this. You've just met a man who though infirm, continues to have a quality of life, who can still enjoy his music and fingers crossed, might even make a friend with Elsie, who clearly is keen to be friends with him. Now, just as yesterday you agreed that John McDonald deserved the jail for beating his wife, we both know that what I did, what *we* did wasn't strictly within the parameters of the law, but it *was* the right thing to do. So, again, sorry though I am to put you in the position of knowing what I've done is not strictly legal, but I won't apologise for doing it. Yes," he held up his hand, "there might come a day when *prescribed* pain relief is available for Callum, but that day is yet to arrive. Unfortunately, that now leaves you with a decision to make; either ignore what you *suspect* you heard or report me and for what it's worth," he solemnly shook his head, "I won't hold it against you for doing your job as you perceive it to be."

A short pause ensued as Devlin stared at him.

"The problem we have, Smiler," sighed Devlin, "is that the Scottish criminal law code is set and very precise about what crime and offences are. It's written down in black and white and you know, given your vast experience that you're breaking those laws and you, a police officer?" his face reflected his dismay when he added, "I bloody hope you know what you're doing.".

"Of course I know what I'm doing, Mattie," he quickly nodded, "but that's the problem, isn't it? The law *is* black and white with no room for flexibility."

"Flexibility? Now wait a minute, Smiler…"

"Look," he interrupted and raised his hands in explanation, "there's no *grey* area in law, but there is in society. Point in case, the abuse of women. We know that there's a type of man who is an abuser and the law *should* protect vulnerable women," he stared meaningfully at Devlin, "but it doesn't, does it?"

Devlin sighed heavily, unable to argue the point.

"So," Smiler earnestly continued, "just as we did with John McDonald, we *bent* the law to save his wife from further beating. At least for those twenty-four hours he was in custody, though not long enough," he added with a sigh. "Now, as far as Callum McGregor is concerned and the man who provides him and his own wife with pain relief, our NHS, wonderful though it is, is currently unable to assist those individuals who are in constant pain, pain so dreadful it almost cost McGregor his life. So, either sticking rigidly to the law or acting as my conscience dictates, I'll go to bed each night knowing that I've done the right thing."

Seconds passed before Devlin, his shoulders slumped, grittily replied, "Smiler's Law, eh?"

He paused, then with a slow shake of his head, he added, "Do me a favour, Smiler. I've known you for just two days, yet while I can't explain it even to myself, I find I'm implicitly trusting you and your judgment."

He gave the big man a weak smile when he continued, "After the day I had yesterday, I was considering leaving the polis, but now find I've another chance of staying in the job. Do you think that when we're working together, you might try to avoid getting *me* the jail?"

Returning his own wide smile, the big man patted Devlin on the shoulder and said, "You've the makings of a right good police officer, Mattie, and in my book, that's an officer who knows the difference between right and wrong, which really has nothing to do with the law."

CHAPTER EIGHT.

When DCI Laura Gemmill knocked on the door to the detached bungalow, it was a young woman in her early twenties who greeted them.
"Can I help you?" she glanced from Gemmill to Chalmers.
Suspecting her to be a daughter, Gemmill displayed her warrant card, then asked, "Is Mr Mason at home?"
"No, he's at work. I'm his daughter, Susan. What's this about?"
But before Gemmill could, explain, the girl turned pale then in a low voice, asked, "Is it about my mother?"
Pokerfaced, Gemmill replied, "Perhaps we can speak inside?"
"Yes, of course," Susan stepped aside to permit them to enter, then led the way through to a neat and comfortably furnished front room. After inviting the detectives to sit, Gemmill asked Susan, "Your father. Can he be contacted by phone?"
"Yes, he's at work in Renfrew, that's why we moved here," she explained. "At the town hall. "He's a what-do-you-call-it, a planner. A town planner."
"And do you have a contact number for him?" Gemmill saw Chalmers fetching her notebook from her handbag.
Rubbing furiously at her forehead, Susan recited the telephone number, then Chalmers stood up from the chair and said, "Your telephone?"
"Eh, it's in the hallway," she stammered, then as Chalmers left the room, she turned to Gemmill to again ask, "Is this about my mother?"
"Yes, Susan, I regret it is, but perhaps we should wait for your father to return home."
"I'm twenty-two, not a child," she snapped, then almost immediately, raised a hand in apology and added "I'm sorry. That was uncalled for."
"Perhaps you should sit down," Gemmill gently urged her.
"She's dead, isn't she?"
"Yes, Susan, I'm sorry to have to break this news, but your mother is dead."

Seconds passed before the younger woman quietly said, "There was a story on the radio about a woman's body being discovered in a park in Glasgow. Was that her?"

"It was. Govanhill Park."

"I had this feeling, you know. Something I couldn't explain. That's over where we used to live before she…"

Then she began to sob, her shoulders quivering, her head bowed and her body wracked with pain at the news.

Though Gemmill's inward desire was to sit beside the young woman and comfort her, she knew she must maintain her professional stance for experience had taught her when delivering such news that not all bereaved family members appreciated being comforted by a police officer.

Chalmers returned to the room and seeing the young girl now distraught, quietly informed Gemmill, "Mr Mason will be here in about ten minutes, boss. He asked if it is about his wife and I told him it is, but not anymore than that."

"Some water?" Gemmill suggested with a nod to Susan and Chalmers left the room to find the kitchen.

"When was the last time you saw your mother?" she gently asked the younger woman.

Sniffing, Susan wiped at her nose with the sleeve of her multi coloured cardigan before she replied, "God, it must be years. Maybe two, two and a half? I'd went to find her to tell her I'd obtained my degree," her face turned scarlet at the admission. "Took me a while searching the pubs, but I found her in the end standing in the doorway of some scabby pub in Allison Street," she paused, then her voice registered her disgust when she added, "With a man."

She took a deep breath before she added, "I couldn't even bring myself to speak with her. Just walked away," then the tears rolled down her cheeks.

"And your father? Was he in contact with her?"

Susan's head jerked up, then she stared quizzingly at Gemmill before she replied, "You think that after the way she treated him, my dad would have anything to do with her?"

"I'm sorry, but I have to ask the hard questions. I understand it might have been an acrimonious divorce; my information is that when she'd been drinking, your mother physically abused your father. A condition of her alcoholism, I presume?"

But Susan was prevented from replying, for Chalmers re-entered the room with a glass of water in her hand and with an apologetic squint at the younger woman, said, "I hope you don't mind. I've put the kettle on and prepared some mugs. I expect you and your dad will want a cuppa when he gets here."

They both saw Susan's eyes narrow and her expression change to one of confusion when she glanced at them in turn and hesitantly asked, "You're the CID. If my mother was found dead, I'd have thought it might be a uniformed police officer who would come to inform us. Why are you here?"

This time it was Gemmill who hadn't time to respond, for they heard the hurried crunch of tyres on the stone chips in the driveway outside as a car came to a halt.

Getting to her feet, Susan glanced through the window to announce, "That's dad. I'll get the door."

When she'd left the room, Gemmill quietly said, "I haven't disclosed her mother was murdered. I decided I'd wait till her father got here."

A minute later, Susan's eyes now red from weeping, led her father into the front room where both officers were standing to greet him. Mason, a thin man of around five feet ten inches, with thick grey collar length hair, wore thick lensed spectacles and a three-piece, grey coloured business suit.

In a surprisingly deep voice, he greeted them with, "Susan has just told me that Jeannie's body was discovered in a Glasgow park. The very fact that a senior CID officer, eh…"

"I'm Detective Chief Inspector Gemmill and this is Detective Sergeant Chalmers," she formally introduced them both.

"Yes, of course," he nodded at them in turn, then added, "please, sit down."

When all four were seated, he said again, "The fact that a senior CID officer has arrived to break the sad news, DCI Gemmill, suggests that there is more to Jeannie's body being found than it being her lifestyle that's responsible for her death."

"I didn't want to say to your daughter prior to you arriving, Mr Mason, but you are correct," she nodded. "I regret to inform you that subsequent to a post-mortem that was carried out earlier today, I can confirm that your former wife was indeed murdered."

Susan, hand to her mouth, took a sharp intake of breath as Gemmill watched her father tightly close his eyes and heard him mutter, "My God, poor Jeannie."

She waited for almost a full minute to permit them to get over their shock, watching as Susan leaned into her father who placed a comforting arm around her shoulder before she quietly asked, "When was the last time you saw Jeannie, Mr Mason?"

Neither Gemmill nor Chalmers failed to notice him darting a glance to his daughter before he replied, "Eh, just a few weeks ago."

"Dad!" Susan was clearly shocked.

He half turned in his chair to stare at her when he said, "I didn't want to tell you and Ian in case it upset you both, sweetheart."

He sighed when he turned back to face Gemmill, then with a slow shake of his head, continued, "Every few weeks, nothing regular, I'd take a wee turn down into the southside where we used to live and have a look to see if I could find her."

He raised his hand as if in explanation when he said, "I know the state she'd got herself into, living rough and the clothes she wore," he sadly shook his head. "Anyway, if she was sober when I found her, I'd give her some money to try and help her out though of course I knew she'd spend it on drink. If she was drunk, I'd not approach her because…"

He stopped and stared at Gemmill, his lips quivering and his eyes tearing up when he said, "I suppose you already know what Jeannie was like when she had a drink in her?"

"One of our officers," she softly replied, "Constable McGarry. He positively identified her at the mortuary and was able to provide some information about Jeannie that included her, eh, behaviour when she'd been drinking."

"Smiler," he nodded, then added with a soft smile, "He was always very kind when he came to our flat."

Seeing how upset he was, she continued, "At the minute, Mr Mason, we are in the early stages of a murder investigation, so I have nothing to tell you that will offer any explanation as to who might be responsible for Jeannie's death. I am of course aware you were divorced from her, but in the absence of any details regarding any other relative or next of kin, are you happy that you and your children," she nodded towards Susan, "be the point of contact for me during the investigation?"

"Of course," he stuttered, then drew a drew a deep breath to compose himself.

"Just one final question for now, sir. On the last occasion you saw Jeannie, did she give any indication that she might have been seeing anyone in particular? I mean, romantically?"

Again, he drew a deep breath before he said, "DCI Gemmill, I loved my wife very much and it broke my heart when she turned to drink and we ended up divorced, but in these last years," he bowed his head, unable to stop the tears from trickling down his cheeks. "You must have seen her at the mortuary. I mean no disrespect to her when I say that Jeannie was, I don't know how else to put it, no longer a desirable woman. So no, she didn't mention any man in her life and to be frank, I never asked."

She turned to glance at Chalmers to indicate they were leaving, then with a subtle nod to Susan, asked, "Perhaps you might see us out."

At the front door, her voice no more than a whisper, she told the young woman, "While the media will no doubt report that your mother was of no fixed abode or a homeless woman, you and your family and friends must anticipate that somehow they will discover your relationship and even your address, so if that should occur you must expect they'll be looking for a statement. My advice is not to tell them anything and if push comes to shove, let me know and I'll deal with it."

"How? I mean, how will you deal with it?"

"If it means putting a marked police car in your driveway to keep the nosy buggers away, then I'll organise that."

"Thank you," Susan softly replied with a nod.

In the car outside as Chalmers drove off, she said, "I'm sure you had your reason, boss, but knowing we can't rule anyone out, I thought you might have asked Mason where he was last night during the hours we suspect she was killed."

"Given that they were divorced, that would have been right and proper, Lucy," her brow knitted, "but you saw the state of the man. We can always ask for a formal statement at another time and put it to him then. Right," she arched her back and sighed, "back to the office and we'll see if anything else has turned up."

****

Right at that time, Constable Drew Taylor, his cap and raincoat on the bench beside him, was sitting in the smoke-filled police witness room in the District Court building in St Andrews Square. The red-bricked building, the former home of the City of Glasgow's Central Police Station, had seen better days since its construction in 1906 and to be kind, could best be described as shabby rather than derelict.

At that time, Taylor's thoughts were not as they should be on his witness statement for the trial to which he was cited, but on his neighbour, Roz Begley.

The hubbub of noise from his fellow police officers, smoking, laughing, reading their copy statements or sipping from the plastic beakers their machine issued insipid coffee or tea, didn't distract him. His thoughts turned to last night's argument with his girlfriend, Sharon, who arriving directly from an event at her city centre hotel, had come seeking a straight answer from him.

Yet, though he had initially been attracted to Sharon by her undoubted beauty and catwalk model figure, he had in the time they were together realised he was never completely…his brow furrowed when he sought the word - then settled on – never completely *comfortable* with her.

Odd, he mused, that whenever he and Sharon were together, whether in company or alone, he couldn't fully relax and sometimes found himself walking on eggshells lest she for some frivolous reason, found fault or took umbrage with what he said or did.

He smiled when he recalled a former, but now retired Ayrshire colleague's description of some women, describing them as 'all body and nae brains.'

It was then he unconsciously realised, more and more frequently he found himself comparing Sharon to Roz and continued to find his girlfriend wanting, for whereas he could work a shift with Roz and be completely at ease, in fact discuss any subject under the sun, it was not the same with Sharon who after a short time unfailingly set his nerves on edge.

"Penny for them."

He turned to see his trial neighbour, Ian Parker, staring at him, the football magazine he'd been reading now on his knees.

"Sorry," Taylor drew a breath, "I was miles away there."

"Aye, no doubt thinking about that absolute darling you're hooked up with," teased Parker with a grin.

It was out before he could help himself when he replied, "Well, if you fancy her so much, she's yours."

His eyes widening with surprise, Parker asked, "Oh, oh, trouble in paradise, pal? You breaking up with her?"

Taylor's face creased and he rubbed at his forehead when he replied, "I think so. Eh, honestly, I don't know."

"You don't know or you haven't decided?"

Parker, though five years junior to Taylor, had in the time they'd worked on the same shift become close friends and so it was to him that Taylor confided, "Sharon arrived at the flat last night and told me in no uncertain terms that if I didn't get off my arse and produce an engagement ring, she wasn't hanging about for me."

"Wow!"

Visibly shocked, Parker asked, "How did you react to that?"

He sighed when he replied, "I didn't. I just kind of shrugged and asked if she wanted a cup of tea."

"You're at the madam!" Parker stared wide-eyed at him. "You didn't say yes and grab the opportunity to net yourself a beauty like her, but you *asked* her if she wanted a cup of tea! Are you off your head or what?"

His face again creased when he agreed, "The thing is, Ian, aye, she's a delight to look at and I can see the envy in guy's faces when I'm with her. But sometimes, when we're out together…" he slowly shook his head, his cheeks puffed as he exhaled.

"Look," he bowed his head towards Parker to quietly say, "the best way to explain it is if we're out for dinner, say, and I want to talk about what's going on in the world, what's happening in the country or even in the city, a film or a book or even what I did that day, Sharon's on about some Hollywood star, what him or her wore in a magazine photo, who's divorcing who and why and well, crap like that. I *can't* have a conversation with her that's not all drivel. Oh, and if I try to talk about news headlines or politics or whatever, she shuts me down and tells me that she's not interested in *that* sort of stuff! Honestly, good looking though she is, I feel that the lights are on, but nobody's at home."

"But you get to spend the night with her, so it can't be all bad," Parker grinned.

"Trust you to come back to the sleaze," he scoffed, then conscious of the number of officers sitting around them, quietly continued, "Last night, apart from the ultimatum, I got the tears too."

"The tears? What, because you refused to agree to an engagement?"

"Ian," he frowned, "the tears switch on when she doesn't get her own way. Then, when the tears don't work, I get the door slammed because usually I'm sorry and she knows I'll race after her to apologise."

"But I'm guessing you didn't this time, did you?"

"Not this time, no," he shook his head.

"So, are you officially broken up or have you still to break the bad news? I need to know just in case I'm in with a shout," he grinned.

"Well, you're my pal, so I was thinking of asking you to go and tell her."

"What! Me! No way!" he vigorously crossed his hands.

"I'm joking," Taylor smiled at him, then grimly added, "I'll phone her this evening and arrange to meet her tomorrow morning for coffee before I start work."

"You remember we're reporting for the game tomorrow at Ibrox?"

"Remind me," sighed Taylor, a man curiously never really interested in Scotland's national sport. "Who is it again?"

"The Gers are playing Dundee in the quarter-finals of the cup," replied Parker, a fervent Celtic supporter. "It's a twelve-thirty report at the ground."

"Oh, right."

"And Sharon?"

"Sharon," Taylor moodily replied, then said, "She's on early shift at the hotel and there's a coffee shop in Bath Street that we've used before, so I'll meet her there during her break."

"Well, good luck with that and if you don't appear at Ibrox," he shrugged, "I'll just assume she's stabbed you to death."

"Thanks for your encouragement," Taylor drily replied, just as a portly woman dressed in the uniform of a court usher entered the room to call out, "Constables Taylor and Parker?"

"That's us," Parker replied.

"Case against Arthur Grieve. You're free to go. The accused pled guilty," she glanced down at her clipboard, then said, "Fined eighty pounds for breach of the peace with time to pay."

Eyes narrowing with suspicion, Taylor asked, "When did he plead, do you know?"

Peering down at her clipboard, she then replied, "Two-fifteen."

He exhaled when he irately replied, "An hour and a half ago, and we're left sitting here like a pair of muppets while he's likely in a pub?"

The room was suddenly silent before red-faced, the court usher snapped, "I've only got the list back. If you've a complaint to make, then take it up with the PF."

One hand on Taylor's arm, Parker raised the other hand, then sighed, "No problem, missus."

Turning to the angry Taylor, he added, "I got the bus into town, so it's me and you in your motor back to the office."

****

Chief Superintendent Jimmy Thompson's phone chirruped and when he answered it, his secretary said, "That's the Deputy Chief Constable's secretary on the line, sir, telling me you've to stand-by for a call from Miss Clarke."

He didn't fail to notice the warning in his secretary's voice and after the heads-up from his Chief Inspector, Lizzie Whitmore, knew that his decision about young Devlin's acting rank was about to descend upon his head.

When his secretary hung up, he heard the phone ring on the other side of the line, then the English accented voice of Paula Clarke, the Deputy, who formally greeted him with, "Mr Thompson, how are you today?"

"Very well, Ma'am, and yourself?"

"Oh," she sighed, "still smarting from the tongue lashing the Chief decided to flay me with after he learned that you have appointed Constable Devlin as an acting sergeant."

Paula Clarke, a forty-seven-years old Yorkshire woman who had been in the post of Deputy for just over a year, commenced her service with South Yorkshire Constabulary before being promoted to the Metropolitan Police, where she attained the rank of Assistant Commissioner.

Highly regarded by both the UK Government's Home Secretary and her peers as a dedicated police officer, the word was the unmarried Clarke was destined to be the first female Commissioner of the Met. What made the call more difficult was that albeit she was a woman and younger by several years, on the few occasions he had met her, the crusty and admittedly old-fashioned copper that he was,

Thompson had come to like and respect Clarke nor failed to notice that she was an extremely attractive blonde woman, too.

Fortunately, both forewarned and expecting the phone call, he carefully replied, "As you undoubtedly are aware, Ma'am, I am both understaffed and lacking experienced supervisory officers, so in my defence, as the *current*," he emphasised the word, "Divisional Commander, I *will* use what resources and experienced officers are available to me to run the Division to its best advantage."

The slight pause was ended when he heard Clarke sigh, before she replied, "And yes, I am aware you are doing a good job, Mr Thompson, but to fly in the face of a decision made by the Chief? Well, *that* really is not on, particularly when Constable Devlin's demotion was barely a day old!"

A few seconds pause finished when she hissed, "Jesus, Jimmy, but for the fact you're due to retire, had you any service left with the possibility of promotion, you know that your decision just killed it off!"

Realising that the formality of rank was over, he softly smiled when he asked, "Tell me, Paula, was the bugger raging?"

"Raging hardly describes it," she replied and his eyes narrowing, he suspected she was choking back a laugh.

Then she said, "I take it you stand by your decision?"

"My Division," he wheezed, "my decision. Unless the Chief wants to come down here to Craigie Street and relieve me of my position?"

"We both know he won't do that, Jimmy," she sighed. "The morale throughout the Force is bad enough, what with the pay situation and the lack of resources, so he'll huff and puff, but there's no way he's going to remove a Divisional Commander because of this for to do so would suggest to all the Divisional Commanders that they cannot exercise full control over their Division."

With a start he realised it was as Thompson and several of the senior management already suspected and confirmed by her imprudent comment.

Clarke had no real regard for the Chief Constable, himself an appointment based on political contacts, rather than experience or ability and privately considered by more than just Thompson, to be a buffoon.

A slight pause ended when she said, "And Devlin. You know why he was demoted, I presume. Nasty what happened to him, so how is the lad bearing up?"

"Good of you to ask, Paula," he replied and thought, that is what makes her a woman worthy of her rank.

"Well," he continued, "I only had that one dealing with him when I appointed him to the acting rank, but his Inspector, a good man, tells me he was very downcast when he arrived yesterday, but from what Lizzie Whitmore tells me…"

"Whitmore. I know that name. She's your Chief Inspector?"

"Yes, and good at her job. Lizzie tell me she did a background check on Devlin and up until his fall from grace, he was a rising star, extremely competent and good things were expected of him. In short, she persuaded me that he is worth me earning the Chief's rebuke," he admitted and surmised such admission would not go further.

"That's what I gathered from his assessment reports," Clarke replied. Again there was a slight pause as though she were considering her next words, then she said, "In confidence, Jimmy, I can tell you that the Complaints and Discipline have taken on the investigation into his wife's bigamy. Not usually their responsibility, as you know, but they are trained investigators and in this case it seemed to be the Chief's favoured choice they make the inquiry. I can disclose that they've discovered where she is residing and in due course will be knocking on her door to charge her with Section 24 of the 1977 Act. As you'll guess, Devlin will be the primary witness in the case against her, so likely the media will learn of it. You might want to ask Mrs Whitmore to keep an eye on him. For his sake, I mean."

"Thanks for that, Paula, and yes, I'll let Lizzie know."

"Now, as you are aware, Mr Thompson," he heard her exhale when once more she adopted a formal attitude, "as the Deputy Chief Constable, it is my remit to exercise discipline when any officer, regardless of their rank, has disrespected the Chief Constable or in any manner brought disrepute to the Force."

He unconsciously braced himself, then smiled when she added, "In that case I take on board your defence for your action in appointing Devlin as an acting sergeant, but you will consider yourself formally rebuked."

When the call had ended, Thompson stretched back into his chair and lighting a cigarette, slowly drew the smoke into his already beleaguered lungs, then smiled.

With senior management such as Clarke, he thought, perhaps in the future there was some hope for the police service as a whole.
****

It was just after eight-thirty in the day, the evening now mild, the rain gone, their raincoats left in the office and Mattie Devlin wearing his tunic with his new stripes when he and Smiler McGarry found themselves strolling down Pollokshaws Road and just as the busy social scene was beginning to take off in the pubs on the southside of the city.

Chewing the fat as they strolled along and with Smiler nodding at or greeting the passers-by, they heard what sounded like a commotion coming from a pub just a few yards further on.

Glancing curiously at Devlin, Smiler upped his speed towards the hostelry, only to be confronted with what every uniformed officer in the city dreaded.

Reaching the pub, the double doors swung open to discharge over a dozen women whose ages ranged from late teens to mid-fifties, all dressed in brightly coloured and on some, extremely revealing garments and all who were at best tipsy or worse, half way to be steaming drunk.

To both Smiler and Devlin's horror, they saw it to be a hen party. The younger women were as expected among the most scantily dressed, with some banging spoons on saucepans, while others rattled plastic buckets filled with coins and practised the age-old custom of soliciting 'donations' for the bride from the pub's patrons in the full knowledge that no man dare deny their requests; not if he wanted to keep his trousers on.

As for the bride, they saw her to be a young woman no older than eighteen or nineteen years and wearing a tightly fitting white knee-length dress and a straggly veil lopsidedly on her dyed blonde hair. Her make-up smudged, her glazed eyes and her slack jaw betraying her alcohol intake, it was clearly obvious she was drunk and being supported on either arm by a middle-aged woman, presumably her mother and a younger woman, likely a bridesmaid.

The large, home-made cardboard 'L' plate hanging by a string around her neck seemed to both Smiler and Devlin to contradict her swollen belly that suggested she was no novice to coitus.

Seeing both officers, the women whooped with joy and with cries of, "It's the polis!" or "Give us a shot of your cap, Sergeant!" or the blatant sexual innuendo, "Get your baton out, big man, and let me stroke it!"

Panic-stricken, Smiler grabbed Devlin by the arm and surrounded as they were, had little option but to drag his neighbour to stand with him with their backs to the pub's wall.

Dozens of hands reached for them as the two besieged men, one hand firmly pressing their cap to their heads and the other protecting their short, wooden batons located in the custom-made pocket on the right leg on their uniform trousers.

Vainly, they tried to dissuade the crowd of women from their gleeful assault upon them, but their words were lost in the uproar and they could feel the hands inappropriately grabbing at their groins and reaching for their batons, while some others attempted to plant kisses upon the trapped men.

Devlin suffered far worse than the taller Smiler, who continued to grin while vainly attempting to calm the resolute women.

Almost a minute passed before salvation came in the form of a tall, well dressed but very drunken, middle-aged man who staggered from the pub and with a bank note in his upraised hand, loudly called out, "A fiver for a kiss from the bride!"

A fiver!

Distracted, the women turned almost as one towards the drunk, permitting Smiler to snatch at Devlin's tunic collar, then hiss, "Run!"

Making a break for it and scattering women as they did so, both men sped away, ignoring not only the catcalls and pleas from behind, but the indignity of being seen by passers-by of the two of them running away from a crowd of amorous women.

Turning a corner into Alison Street, they breathlessly sneaked into a tenement close.

As one, they burst into laughter with Smiler admitting, "It's a long time since I was caught like that, Mattie."

"Aye, well I suggest we take a couple of minutes to catch our breath before we head back out there," he replied, then asked, "The guy waving the fiver that saved our arses. Is he one of the pub's regulars?"

"You know, Mattie," his face thoughtfully creased, "it wasn't a face I recognised."

"What, Smiler McGarry admitting there's actually somebody on his

beat he *doesn't* know?" Devlin teased with a wide grin.
It was then, with a hint of mischief in his eyes, Smiler decided not to mention the smeared lipstick on Devlin's cheeks, that he'd let the acting sergeant find out for himself when they returned to the office.

CHAPTER NINE: Saturday, 10 March, 8.15am.

DCI Laura Gemmill arrived in the incident room to discover her office manager, DS Danny Sullivan, already at his desk and leafing through a pile of reports.
"Morning, Danny," she laid her handbag down onto his desk. "Anything doing?"
He glanced up at her before he continued with the reports, then with a shake of his collar length, fair-haired head, said, "Nothing at the minute, boss, though I'm still waiting for the rest of the team to get in. If you can maybe find a minute to let me know how you want them divided up?"
"Is Sammy in yet?"
"In the DI's room, yes," he nodded.
"Right, I'll have a word with him and we'll let you know when we've decided."
"Boss," he acknowledged with a further nod.
Making her way along the corridor to the DI's room, she found Sammy Pollock poring over a list of personnel, then greeting him, asked, "Is that the teams you're making up?"
"It is," he confirmed, then handing her the sheet, added, "Five teams of two and leaving the rest on the book. I've also drawn in four extra DC's, from Castlemilk and the Gorbals offices if you're okay with that, though needless to say, both the DI's, Mark and Joe, aren't happy about us taking them away when they're already short-staffed."
"I agree about calling them in and I'll speak later with Mark and Joe," she scanned the list. Her eyes narrowed when she asked, "That big cop yesterday at the mortuary, eh..."
"Smiler? Constable McGarry. Why do you ask?"
Her eyes narrowed in thought when she explained, "I was wondering if there's any benefit to us by bringing him on board for the

investigation. From what both you and Lucy Chalmers tell me, he not only knew our victim well, but he also has a unique knowledge of the area, particularly the low-life's. What do you think?"

His face creased when he replied, "Right enough, boss, Smiler would be a definite asset, but as you already know, the uniform is under even more pressure than we are for boots on the ground so I think if you were to speak with Lizzie Whitmore, it's likely she'll resist losing another cop on the street. However," he exhaled, "perhaps we could request that Smiler be *our* cop on the street, that he can be directed by us while he's working his beat to make some discreet inquiries."

"That's a better idea," she acknowledged, then added, "I'll have a word with Lizzie today…"

"Oh shit, it's Saturday," she frowned. "Lizzie won't be back till Monday, so in the meantime, I'll speak with Smiler's Inspector, who is…?"

"That'll be Iain Cowan. He's a good man and I don't think you'll get any argument from him."

"Right," she nodded, "I think I've met Inspector Cowan before. In the meantime, you let the team know who's working with who while I grab a coffee and prepare my briefing."

****

The coffee shop located in Bath Street just off the junction with Renfield Street was popular during the working week with office workers as well as shoppers and Monday to Friday, and difficult to find a table during those days.

However, just after ten-thirty that Saturday morning, Drew Taylor, his anorak hung on the chair behind him and wearing a grey coloured sweater over his police shirt and tie, attended early at the café and secured a table at the rear of the premises, watching the door while nervously waiting for his girlfriend, Sharon, to arrive.

His mouth dry, his foot automatically tapped on the floor beneath the table as he again went over in his head how he'd break the news that he wanted to split from Sharon.

Glancing around the café at the half dozen or so early customers, most he guessed tourists from the hotels dotted about the Sauchiehall Street area, he wondered at his foolishness in choosing such a public place for he knew in his gut that when he broke the news, Sharon was not beyond kicking up a fuss.

So engrossed was he in his thoughts that he missed Sharon entering the café and startled when she appeared at the table.
Glancing up, he shot to his feet and stared wide-eyed at her.
He wasn't alone for more than a few customers turned to smile at the glamorous blonde, her hair tied back in a perfect French braided pony tail and who wore a white blouse and a fitted navy blue, knee-length skirted business suit; a poster-woman for her hotel chain.
"Hello, lover," she breathed at him, then when he stood, she turned her head to permit him to kiss her cheek, for Sharon's make-up with glossy lips was flawless and not even the man she professed she loved would dare smudge it.
Taylor held her chair and watched as in one practised movement, she slid onto the seat, aware that just at that moment, she was the centre of attraction.
Stooping to lay her handbag on the floor beside her, she sat upright just as the young waitress with an admiring glance, appeared at her elbow.
"Cappuccino," she snapped, "and ensure it's warm, but not too hot. I hate tepid coffee. And a china cup and saucer, not a mug," she dismissed the young woman with a haughty wave of her hand.
When the young girl let the table, Taylor took an inward breath, for those short words sharply reminded him of another thing that bothered him about Sharon.
Though an accomplished receptionist with a practised smile and courtesy, it irked him that whenever they were out dining or even like now, having a coffee, she herself was often rude to waiting staff working in the service industry.
It was then he saw her as she really was, that Sharon wore her beauty like a mask, but beneath the veneer she was a very shallow and dislikeable woman.
"Well," her expression changed and she smiled benignly at him, a practised smile, her eyes bright with anticipation. "Am I to guess why we're meeting so early this morning?"
Licking at his suddenly dry lips, Taylor nervously glanced at the other customers, then heard Sharon eagerly ask, "Is there something you want to ask me, Drew?"
Oh, God, he inwardly thought. She's thinking I asked her here to propose.

His stomach-turning somersaults, he leaned across the table and with a lowered voice, began, "It's not what you think, Sharon. I'm not here to propose we get engaged."

He could see the confusion on her face that suddenly paled, then as if realisation dawned, her lips tightened before she said, "Why exactly am I here then, *Andrew*!"

Andrew. She only ever called him Andrew when she was angry with him.

All the practised excuses abruptly were lost to him, his throat suddenly tight and as though he were someone else, heard himself say, "I'm sorry, Sharon, but it's over between us. I've given it a lot of thought and I don't think you and I are suitable for each other."

He watched her face that if possible, grew even paler and saw her nostrils flaring before she hissed, "Not *suitable* for each other? Who the hell do you think you are!" her voice increased in volume, attracting the attention of the other customers.

"You…" her face full of vehemence, she almost choked getting the words out, her face a mask of hatred. "You're lucky to have someone like *me* in your miserable fucking life!"

It was unfortunate that just then, the waitress arrived with Sharon's coffee.

Grabbing the cup from the younger woman's hands, Sharon stood and threw the contents over Taylor who gasped as the hot liquid hit him in the face.

Reaching down for her handbag, Sharon swiftly turned and raced from the café, knocking over the waitress who stumbled backwards then fell to the floor.

Dabbing at his face with a table napkin, his face burning, Taylor stood and helped the stunned waitress to her feet, aware that a silence had fallen in the room and all eyes were upon him.

His sweater and shirt stained with coffee, curiously his first thought was if he was quick, he'd just enough time to return home to his flat to change into a fresh shirt before reporting for duty to Ibrox stadium.

His hands shaking, he fetched his wallet from his anorak pocket then thrust a ten-pound note at the young waitress, telling her, "Sorry about that and please, keep the change."

Happy with what would be a sizeable tip, she grunted before she replied, "Thanks and can I just say, pal, you're better off without that stuck-up bampot, so you are."

His face now redder than a beetroot and not just from embarrassment, but the coffee too, Taylor could only nod in return then made his way outside, aware that more than a few sympathetic glances were cast his way.

But it was done, she was gone from his life, he sighed and hurried towards his car parked in a bay in Bath Street.

He was free of Sharon and felt an enormous sense of relief.

But to his later regret, he was to learn that Sharon was not yet done with him.

****

Standing at his front window, a mug of coffee in his hand, Smiler watched her drive off from the street, his hand raised in a wave as she cheerfully waved back through the front windscreen.

It had pleased him no end when he'd arrived home the previous evening to find her there, in the kitchen waiting for him and with a light meal prepared for them both, once more grateful that he had all those months before decided to entrust her with a key to the house.

Turning away from the window, Smiler continued to think of her and again, though he no longer raised the issue, it troubled him that though they'd known each other for over a year prior to them getting together as a couple a little over six months previously and though there was a notable difference in their ages, she seemed determined that he was the one.

His problem, he realised, was that he did not believe himself to be worthy of her.

But that was not what truly troubled him.

Though she had survived a bad marriage and was divorced these last three years, unlike him she came without…his brow furrowed, trying to recall again what the word was.

Yes, baggage, he'd heard it called.

Smiler had his two children, albeit both were now adults and he was a grandfather and though early in their relationship, he pointedly told her that she would likely be better off with a younger man, she crossly told him that *he* was her choice, so he'd better get used to the idea.

Yes, he happily sighed, definitely a woman with a mind of her own.

In the meantime, she had agreed that for now, they would keep their relationship strictly between them both, that anyway, she had firmly told him, it was nobody's business but theirs and she was quite happy to wait till such time he decided to disclose their liaison to his children.

Glancing at the wall clock, his gaze dropped to the sideboard, then to the framed photograph of him and Cheryl; the photograph taken onboard the cruise ship on their twentieth anniversary and the most expensive holiday they'd ever had.

He found himself smiling when recalled the first time when he'd brought her home and forgotten that the photo of him and his late wife was on the sideboard.

Trying to be discreet, he'd attempted to lay the photograph flat, but she'd seen him and smiled, "Don't be silly. That's the woman who made you happy and gave you two children. I hope you're not ashamed of her?"

He recalled his face turning red and stuttering, "Of course not, it's just…"

But she'd interrupted when stroking gently at his cheek, she said, "I couldn't be jealous of a woman who made you happy, Stuart, and if anything, it only serves to remind me how lucky I am to have found you."

Still smiling, he took a deep breath, then made his way upstairs to get ready for the twelve-thirty report to Edmiston Drive, outside the east gate at Ibrox football stadium.

****

As was his custom when attending the local football duties, Inspector Iain Cowan called in to Craigie Street police office to park his car and collect his gear, before travelling to Ibrox in the shaky old Divisional Transit bus along with those officers who like him, parked at the station or didn't own cars.

It being Saturday and with the bosses being off at the weekend and so not using their allocated bays in the rear yard, after parking his Morris Marina, Cowan made his way into the building to collect his cap, tunic and raincoat from the Inspector's room where he found a note on his desk, requesting he contact DCI Gemmill when he resumed duty.

Deciding to attend upstairs rather than phoning, he made his way to the incident room where he found Laura Gemmill in discussion with the incident room manager, DS Danny Sullivan.
"Looking for me, Ma'am?" he greeted her.
"Inspector Cowan," she smiled, "I was wondering if we could have a wee chat."
Without waiting for a response, she led him from the room into her own room along the corridor, then turning said, "Your Constable McGarry, Smiler. I'm told he has a rare knowledge of the office beat area and more importantly, was familiar with our victim, Jeannie Mason."
"When you say familiar, Ma'am…" Cowan defensively replied, only for Gemmill to hold up a hand and grimace when she interrupted, "Sorry, poor choice of words. I mean, he knew her and also of her background."
With a nod, Cowan said, "Smiler, Ma'am, is without a doubt, my best constable. In fact, he's the glue that holds the shift together. By that I mean they're a young shift and in the main, lacking experience, though they're eager and resilient too and for that I'm fortunate for right now I'm short of at least a half dozen constables. If I'm honest, it worries me that the pressure the job puts on them will burn them out or force them to pack it in and I pray that this pay rise Westminster keep promising does happen because if it doesn't, God alone knows how the Force will survive."
His rant over, he softly smiled when he said, "But that's not what you want me for, is it?"
She returned his smile when she replied, "Actually, what I'm hoping is that we can share Smiler for the duration of the murder investigation?"
His face expressed his confusion when he replied, "Share him?"
"The thing is, Iain…can I call you Iain?"
"Of course, Ma'am."
"The thing is, I'd prefer to have Smiler seconded to the investigation, but I know you can't afford to lose him off your shift. What I need from him is access to his unique knowledge of the area and its residents to assist with my investigation and I'd like to be able to use him to make some inquiries on my behalf, but during the course of his own duties when he's walking his beat and not involved in other issues. Now, it might be that it involves some

overtime, but rather than come from your own shift budget, I'll speak with Liz Whitmore and get that cleared."

"Let me get this right. You want Smiler, when he's not attending Divisional calls, to make inquiries on your behalf? In essence, he'll be wearing two hats?"

"Exactly," she nodded. "Anything we give him would be within his own beat area and be intelligence led. By that I mean he'd be following up information my team obtain from sources that come in, such as the door to door visits or any witnesses we might find. I'm also hearing he's quite a shrewd individual, so I'll be looking for him to assess any information that does come in, whether it's worth following up or whatever."

"But surely you have your own detectives to attend to those inquiries?"

"I do, yes," she patiently explained, "but I'm led to believe that Smiler is so well known and regarded in the area that there's a real likelihood the locals will respond to him, whereas they might not be so forthcoming with my team. Let's face it, Iain, even the most helpful people will lie to the police, though they won't consider it to be lying, but only telling us what *they* think we want to know."

She paused for a few seconds, then continued, "From what Sammy Pollock and Lucy Chalmers tell me about your man, Smiler. Well," she wryly grinned, "they not only describe him as an old-fashioned polis who's straight as a die, but also consider him to be a walking collator."

"I'll not argue with that description," he smiled, then thoughtfully nodding, he added, "We're back here for the rest of the late shift after the game at Ibrox. At the minute, I've Smiler introducing my acting sergeant to the beat area, so if you're still here, I'll send them both to see you when they return."

"Oh, I'll still be here, Iain," she sighed, "and I appreciate your cooperation."

****

In her officer and at her desk with Sammy Pollock seated opposite, DCI Laura Gemmill could not hide her disappointment when she said, "So, the initial door to door at the flats directly opposite the locus has disclosed nothing? Nothing at all?"

"The problem is, boss, that unless they're actually looking out of the windows into the Park and don't forget, not only have the few lights that illuminate the paths been vandalised, but it was raining last night, so it's unlikely anyone would be hanging around. If you want my tuppence worth, I'm thinking that our victim was accompanied into the Park by her killer and either she or him knew about that spot where we discovered the body is protected by the canopy of foliage overhead. From what the SOCO recovered, the number of empty bottles, tins and junkie's paraphernalia," he sighed, "the place is not exactly a state secret."

"You don't think she was followed there, Sammy, that she intended sleeping rough there?"

"No," he shook his head. "From what we've learned and from what big Smiler told us, she prefers tenement closes to sleep in, out of the bad weather and that seems to be corroborated by the number of reports we've had from residents who complained that if she's drunk, she causes a ruckus in the close."

He watched Gemmill slowly shake her head when she softly muttered, "I know that as the SIO I'm supposed to be objective and detached from the victim, that it's my job to find her killer, not sympathise with her, but I can't help myself. I can't even imagine how she found herself living like that."

She was rubbing wearily at her forehead when he asked, "How did you get on with Iain Cowan?"

"The Inspector? Oh, he's agreed to Smiler being loosely attached to our investigation on an *ad hoc* basis. On that point," she continued, "the Inspector will let him know we're looking for him, so when he arrives back after his football duties, can you have a word with him and explain what we need from him."

"No problem, boss. Anything else?"

"Can't think of anything right now," she shook her head, then added, "but though I was reluctant to tie up the troops with it, I can't see any other option at the minute, Sammy, than to extend the door to door to the flats around the whole bloody Park."

She held up her hand when she continued, "I know there will be the usual moans, but tell Danny Sullivan to get it sorted."

"Will do, boss," he rose from his chair and turned towards the door, but stopped when he said, "The pubs, boss, and particularly the ones our victim hung about. When do you want the troops canvassing them?"

"Let's complete the door to door in the flats around the Park first;

then on that point, bring it to the attention of your man, Smiler, and find out from him which ones he thinks she favoured."

Her eyes narrowed when she said, "I'm of the opinion he's more likely to get a result from the pub staff than we will."

CHAPTER TEN.

Arriving at Ibrox stadium, Inspector Iain Cowan directed the constable driver of the marked police Transit bus to turn from Edmiston Drive into the playground of the primary school opposite the stadium, where all the police vehicles were parked under the scrutiny of two constables manning the gate.

Getting out of the front passenger seat, Cowan directed the four constables from the bus to head towards the Copland Road entrance to the venue, telling the senior constable, "I'm away to the briefing in the control room in the main stand, so tell the rest when they arrive I'll get them at the entrance gate."

"Sir," the constable tipped two fingers to the peak of his cap.

Fifteen minutes later, just as a number of noisy Rangers and even noisier Dundee supporters were arriving at the stadium, Cowan joined acting Sergeant Mattie Devlin and his shift of six constables that included not only the four early shift constables who had accompanied Cowan in the Transit bus, but three additional volunteer constables; civilians who gave up their time to act as Special Constables and who received police training over a lengthy period, wore police uniform and when on duty, had the same powers as regular officer that included the authority to arrest offenders.

"All present and correct, sir," Devlin greeted him with a smile.

Nodding at the two ranks of constables, Cowan said, "Afternoon, ladies and gentlemen," then waving the sheet of paper in his hand, he continued, "Sergeant Devlin will pair you off and allocate your aisles and it's the same routine that we've come to know and love," he grinned at them. "On this occasion, we're on the aisles among the travelling support from the east coast who'll be shepherded towards the Govan West corner, so is there anyone here who speaks Tayside?" his question provoked a laugh.

"Right," he waved a hand to calm them, "while there's no intelligence to suggest that there will be trouble, if you do arrest anyone, then all arrests to be walked to the Force portacabin located outside the Govan gate. As soon as you can, complete the arrest proforma, then get yourselves back into the stadium because as you already know, we're short enough of boots on the ground as it is. Okay then, any questions?"

Predictably and to the quiet groans of his colleagues, the only question was asked by Constable Keith Telford who said, "What about a break during the game, Inspector?"

"Heaven's sake," Cowan irritably shook his head, "we're only here for a couple of hours and might I remind you, it's overtime. Grab a pee and Bovril before you take up your post. Any *other* questions?"

The shaking of heads finished, Cowan dismissed them to their duties, but calling Smiler and Devlin to him, then quietly said, "The murder investigation. DCI Gemmill has requested you to assist their investigation when you're out on the beat, Smiler," then turning to Devlin, added, "and as he's still showing you around the area, Mattie, I'd like you to attend as well to hear what she has to say."

"Sir," they both acknowledged, then turning to his neighbour for the afternoon, Smiler nodded that he and Harry Dawson head for the Govan entrance to the stadium.

****

To those he was known too, he'd always been Moxy, though very few of them knew or cared his real name was Albert Moston.

Aged thirty-eight, Moston, a tall, skinny man with thinning brown hair, a seriously misshapen nose and usually unshaven other than for the occasional family funeral or wedding, lived with his mother, Irene, a seventy-five-years old woman whose GP suspected she was in the early stage of dementia. Their first floor flat was located in a tenement in Govanhill Street and situated directly across from the corner of the Park where the body of Jeannie Mason was discovered. As such, it was one of the first to be visited by a pair of detectives on the door to door detail.

Now all four were seated in the two armchairs and couch in the front room where the bay window overlooked the park.

No, both Moston and his mother agreed, they hadn't heard a thing on Thursday night with Irene reminding the detectives it had been raining heavily and besides, she was an early bedder.

But then her sons surprise, she turned to him to say, "But you were at the pub that night, Albert. Did you see or hear anything?"

His face turned red and inwardly angry at his mother for grassing him into the polis, Moston shrugged, then stuttered, "Me? No, I had a skinful in me and just came home and aye," he quickly nodded, "it was pelting down, so it was. I had my head down and just hurried home to my bed."

As his mother turned her head away, Moston quickly made a circling motion with his forefinger at his own head, suggesting his mother wasn't quite right.

"And when was this?" the young detective, DC Barbara McMillan, politely asked, acutely aware that for the first time, the skinny bugger had shifted his beady eyes from her crossed legs.

"Eh, I don't know for certain," he shrugged, "but closing time had been shouted. It's what, about a ten-minute walk from the pub to here?"

"And what pub was that, Mr Moston?"

He found himself swallowing with difficulty, then replied, "Eh, *The Resting Soldier* on Alison Street. On the corner of Belleisle Street? You know it?"

"Ah," she nodded, memories of being a uniform cop and attending more than a few disturbances in the dark and dismal hostelry where the clientele made it known the police were never welcome.

"*The Resting Soldier*. You a regular there?"

"Eh, yeah, I suppose I am," he nodded, nervously faking a smile.

"The victim found in the park over there," she pointed with her pen through the closed window, "was a woman called Jeannie Mason? Did you know her, Mr Moston?"

His chest tightening and his hands clenched to stop them shaking, he nodded when he replied, "If it's her, then I suppose I knew her to see. Wee Jeannie? A down and out? Used to hang around outside the pubs, begging for money? Is that who you mean?"

The young detective didn't immediately respond, but then slowly nodded when she said, "That's seems to fit the description we have of her, yes. So, she *was* known to you?"

"Well, like I said," he grimaced, "only to see. I mean, I never knew her to speak to. Clatty wee woman, so she was."

With a quick glance at the mother, the detective turned to him to ask, "You never availed yourself of her services?"

"Availed myself what? You mean, used her like…" he paused, then red-faced, snapped, "Are you kidding?"

Though he worked hard at sounding genuinely outraged, even curling his lip in disgust, McMillan was not that easily fooled. Sneering, he said, "Did you not know her? She was, well, I don't like speaking ill of the dead, but she was filthy so she was. No," he rapidly shook his hands in front of him, "I wouldn't have touched her with a barge pole."

It was the mother, her face expressing her curiosity, who hesitantly asked, "What do you mean, hen, availed himself of her services? What does that mean? What services?"

But McMillan decided that was a question best left for the son to answer, then hurriedly said, "And on your walk from the pub on Thursday night, Mr Moston, last orders having been shouted, you said, so we can assume it was about eleven that night?"

Her eyes narrowed when she continued, "You didn't see Jeannie Mason on your walk home?"

Vigorously shaking his head, he said again, "Like I told you, it was teeming down and I was just wanting to get home, so I never saw her or anyone."

"Did you know of anyone who might have harboured ill-will against Jeannie? Anyone who would have wanted to harm her?"

"Only the guys who might have caught something from her," he sneered at his own joke, but staring at the dead-pan expression of the young woman, realised it was the wrong thing to say.

McMillan stared at him for several seconds, then with a tight smile, rose from the chair and nodded to her neighbour that she'd heard enough.

"Thank you for your time, Mrs Moston, and you too, Mr Moston. If there's anything you can recall, you know where to find us."

"I'll show you out," he insisted and led them to the flat's front door and it was then that McMillan noticed he limped slightly on his right leg.

They were gone just seconds when he strode over to the front window and from behind the curtain, saw the two detectives meet on the pavement with two other detectives, then watched them standing conversing for several minutes while they seemed to compare notes. To his shock the female turned to point up at the first-floor flat window, causing Moston to hurriedly step back behind the curtain.

"What's going on, Albert? What you looking at?" his mother queried from her chair.

"I'm just watching them, Ma, the polis," he explained, then turning, hissed at her, "Why did you have to go and tell them that I was out late on Thursday night?"

Her brow innocently furrowed when she said, "Because you *were* out late, Albert. You didn't get in till nearly midnight. Why?" her face adopted a worried crease when she asked, "Are you in trouble, son?"

"No, Ma, I'm not," he hastily replied.

His head reeling, he rubbed at it with the heel of his right hand. Albert 'Moxy' Moston could not with any certainty say who murdered Jeannie Mason, but he had a damned good idea who might be responsible and that information, while of obvious value to the police, was a great deal more valuable to him.

In fact, his eyes narrowed in thought, for that information might just put a sizeable lump of cash into his pocket.

His problem now was how to make good on that information; how to squeeze the money out of the man he saw that night with his arm around wee Jeannie's shoulders and who was leading her through the open gate into Govanhill Park.

****

Smiler and his neighbour for the match, Harriet 'Harry' Dawson, stood watching the dejected Dundee fans passing by on their way to the parked buses that surrounded Ibrox, having seen their team trounced six goals to three by an invigorated Rangers, apparently taking their revenge for being beaten one-nil earlier in the week by Cologne in the European Cup quarter-finals.

In the distance on the other side of the stadium, they could hear the joyous chants and songs of the Rangers fans.

"Are you interested in football at all, Smiler," the red-haired Dawson turned to stare up at him.

He took a deep breath, then sighed before he replied, "I was brought up supporting a team called Third Lanark, but that was before your time, Harry. They went to the wall in nineteen-sixty-seven, so I kind of lost interest after that. And you, you like the football, do you?"

"I grew up supporting the Celtic because my family all do, but then," she mischievously grinned, "I discovered boys."

"So, got anyone in particular at the minute?"

"There's a guy over in Baird Street I was at the police college with and who I've kept in touch with, but nothing definite. Well," she smiled, "not yet that is. I'm kind of leading him along at the minute," she grinned up at Smiler, her tongue pushing against the inside of her cheek, then added, "I'm waiting on the right time to invite him to my flat and if he's lucky, I'll hint he can bring an overnight bag."

Smiler didn't dislike Dawson, but thought her to be a selfish young woman and nosy too; definitely not someone he'd share his inner thoughts with. However, as far as he was concerned, her private life was her own and as long as she did her job when they were neighboured, it was none of his concern when off duty, what she got up to.

With the last of the Dundee supporters trickling past, some half-carried by their more sober mates, he glanced at his watch, then nodding at their dejected backs, told her, "We'll walk them along to the roundabout where the buses are parked, then head down Broomloan Road and back to the Govan station to collect our cars."

"Are you picking up a supper before you get back to Craigie Street?"

"No, I've a pasta salad in the motor," he shook his head, then with a soft smile, added, "You get to my age, a moment on the lips is a pound on the hips."

"Fortunately," she airily replied, "I don't have that problem."

He resisted the urge to glance at her wide hips and with an inner smile, thought, aye, keep telling yourself that, hen.

****

The pretty, young female Special Constable, a clerical assistant at the nearby Southern General Hospital, had always harboured an ambition to join the police and spent over a year as a Special trying to make her decision whether to continue in her admin job or joining the Force.

But today had not been a good day.

Neighboured with Keith Telford, who was not previously known to her, she had listened for almost two hours to his boastful tales, all of which featured him as the hero in the arrests of bad guys with outrageous stories of Telford disarming men with broken bottles, knives and on one occasion, so he said, talking down a man with a sawn-off shotgun.

Young though she was, the Special recognised Telford was attempting to impress her as a prelude to asking her out and almost immediately decided there was not a snowballs chance in hell she'd accept any invitation from him.

The pretend awe and fixed smile as she listened to the stories had made her jaw ache and now when they were making their way to collect their cars, here he was, grabbing a lone, drunken young Rangers supporter in his late teens who looked no older than a schoolboy and whom she didn't think warranted being arrested.

It had to be, she could only guess, that the young, stick-thin supporter was Telford's final opportunity to impress her.

Spinning the supporter around, then slamming him against the brick wall of the stadium, she listened as Telford told him he was being arrested for a breach of the peace.

In vain, she protested with, "He was only singing because his team won, Keith."

"Aye, well the game's over and he's causing a breach," he scowled at her, grabbing with a free hand at his handcuffs in the small pouch on the back of his trousers belt.

The young man, totally compliant, tried to turn to protest his arrest, but was again slammed against the wall by Telford.

The Special, through gritted teeth, had had enough and said, "No handcuffs, Constable Telford. I'm not speaking to a breach of the peace when he's not done anything wrong other than singing as he was making his way *lawfully* along the road!"

His face chalk-white, Telford realised he was losing control of the situation and turned to snap back, "You're only a Special! You'll do as you're told! Now, help me cuff him!"

Hearing the argument between them, the supporter, his tears blinding him, cried out, "I'm sorry, I'm drunk. I don't usually drink. Honest. I was only singing. I need to go home now."

Folding her arms, the Special stared at Telford, then hissed, "Look at him, he's just a wean. You'd better be letting him go or I'm informing the Inspector you've made a false arrest!"

Shaking with anger, Telford turned the supporter to face him, then snarled, "Right! I'm letting you go with a warning! Now, bugger off!"

Red-faced, the supporter stared at Telford, then his cheeks bulged when unable to hold back the vomit, it erupted and sprayed across

Telford's police issue raincoat.

"Shit!" Telford danced back, but too late to avoid more vomit hitting his police trousers and shoes.

Stepping back and well asway from the vomit, the Special fought the grin that threatened to explode across her face, then told the supporter, "On your way, son, and no more drink tonight, eh?"

"Yes, Miss," the young man dully replied and having expelled his stomachs contents, staggered off.

"This is your fault!" Telford screamed at her, but the Special, having suffered him long enough, merely turned and wordlessly made her way to the school yard to collect her car.

****

DC Barbara McMillan, blonde haired, a shapely twenty-seven-years-old with piercing blue eyes and who was more often in many of her colleagues' thoughts than she realised, sat quietly in the front passenger seat; quiet enough to provoke her older neighbour, DC Morris Kerr, to ask, "Okay, spill it. What's worrying you?"

McMillan grimaced before she replied, "That guy living with his mother at number ten, first floor flat. Albert Moston. I think he's lied to us."

Kerr had neighboured McMillan for almost a year and though she was younger by ten years and less experienced, he had come to respect her intuition, explaining to his wife, "I think it's a female thing. Barbara seems to be able to sense when she's being told a load of porky's Uncanny, so it is."

His eyes on the road, he asked, "What makes you think he's lying?"

She turned to stare at Kerr before she said, "Tell me this, first. You've been out on the randan, you've got more than a few pints in you and you're making your way home in a public street. A *Glasgow* street, mind. Do you walk with your head down or this being Glasgow, you know that if you've a drink in you and particularly it being a Friday night, you're always liable to run into some idiot who thinks he's harder than you. In short, you know you've drunk too much and you're so more vulnerable to being assaulted than usual."

"And you're point being?"

"Moston said he kept his head down, didn't see anyone. I'm thinking that if he lives here and *particularly* it being a Friday night, he'll be aware there's always trouble lurking around here; cars getting screwed, teenage gangs hanging around, the pubs emptying and fights going on."

"Wait," he risked a glance at her, "based on him saying he kept his head down and didn't see anyone, you're thinking he's lying? On that one issue alone?"

"A ten-minute's walk he told us, Morris, and he saw nobody. Nobody at all," she continued to stare at him. "Doesn't that strike you as odd? Ten minutes here, in a busy tenemented area in the southside?"

Kerr frowned, then with a sigh, said, "When we get back to the station, take a turn into the collator's office and check his files. See if Moston's known to us."

****

Arriving back at Craigie Street police station, almost twenty minutes passed before Inspector Iain Cowan discovered that Keith Telford had not returned from Ibrox stadium.

Striding into the Sergeants room, he sighed, recalling that Mattie Devlin was likely upstairs with Smiler, speaking to the DCI and was about to turn away when the bar officer, barely keeping the grin from his face, met him in the corridor.

"Keith Telford was on the phone, Inspector. Says that he's had to go home to change his trousers, that a drunken supporter vomited on him."

Nodding his thanks for the heads-up, Cowan's eyes narrowed, trying to recall who had neighboured Telford at the stadium, before recalling it was the young female Special Constable who like the other Special's, was now off duty.

Nobody then to corroborate if Telford was being truthful, for in the time Cowan had been his Inspector, he'd quickly learned that not only was his constable a shirker and unreliable, but it didn't take a genius to realise that Telford was neither liked nor trusted by the rest of the shift.

While Cowan didn't like to label any officer as a coward, he knew there was a strong feeling amongst the shift that Telford was not a man to have anyone's back, that regardless of his boastful stories, he would run a mile rather than face an angry man.

That and his all too infrequent arrest cases usually comprised of drunk and incapable men or women or petty offences where a seasoned constable might have been inclined to issue a warning, rather than charge the individual.

Never an accused for a fighting breach of the peace nor anyone who argued with Telford, but usually individuals too drunk or too meekly docile to resist Telford's arrest.

A bully in uniform, but only to those unable to speak or argue back and Cowan had met more than a few of those in his time.

In short, he inwardly sighed, had there been sufficient resources to properly staff the shift, Cowan would long ago have petitioned the Chief Inspector, Liz Whitmore, to get rid of Telford who was no more than a uniform carrier and in reality, a waste of space.

Unfortunately, getting rid of an officer once the obligatory two-year probationary period had been served, was extremely difficult and Cowan inwardly cursed his predecessor for not invoking the section twelve clause for Telford; the clause that would mean dismissal for any number of reasons and included being unsuitable for the role of constable, but instead permitted him to see out his probation.

Now in his own office and seated at his desk, Cowan was all too aware that Lucy Chalmers and the previous shift sergeants had all attempted to motivate Telford, but to no avail.

With a humourless smile, he wondered if Mattie Devlin might have more success, but unconsciously shaking his head, doubted it.

He turned when the door was knocked, then opened to admit Devlin, closely followed by Smiler.

"Got a minute, Inspector?" the sergeant asked.

"Of course," Cowan straightened up in his chair. "How did it go with the DCI?"

"It's as you said, sir," Devlin nodded with a grin. "She's keen for Smiler to use his local knowledge where she suspects her DC's will get the bums rush."

Turning his head to address Smiler, Cowan nodded to both empty chairs then asked, "How do you feel about that?"

Removing their caps, both Devlin and the big man sat down, then Smiler frowned when he replied, "Only too happy to help try and find who murdered wee Jeannie, Inspector."

"Any thoughts on the killer at the minute?"

For several seconds, Smiler, his eyes narrowing, chewed at his lower lip before he replied, "We both know that Jeanne had sunk as low as a woman can go and I'm thinking that her killer didn't see her as a woman or even as a sex object, but just as a…" he paused, then taking a deep breath, said, "some sort of hindrance perhaps? But a hindrance to what, I have no idea," he shook his head, the continued. "The DCI told us that the post-mortem didn't find any suggestion that any sexual activity occurred before she died, but that doesn't mean the killer didn't *attempt* to have sex with her, but I'm also thinking that in her state she wouldn't have been able to resist being molested. So, that begs the question. If her killer didn't want her for sex, why was he there with her in that hideaway in the Park? According to the DCI, her clothing, I mean her undergarments, were not interfered with. I'm thinking," he unaccountably blushed, "that whoever killed her might have been attempting to obtain oral sex with her, but somehow even that doesn't sit well with me, for even if that's true, why kill her?"

Devlin interrupted when he said, "You might be interested to know, Inspector, Smiler shared his theory with the DCI and she hadn't considered it."

Cowan's brow furrowed when he thoughtfully asked, "Then, Smiler, if what you're suggesting did occur, the killer's likely to be a man?"

"Yes, sir, there is no doubt it was a man."

"How can you be so sure?" Cowan probed.

"Oh, I'm not that intuitive," he softly smiled, "but the DCI intimated that the SOCO obtained what appears to be size nine boot or shoe prints on Jeannie's clothing and skin, suggesting that indeed it was a man."

"Which also suggests a man of ordinary height, so what, five feet seven to five feet ten perhaps?"

"That's the theory, yes," Smiler nodded, then continued, "There's also little doubt that the killer must have been bloodstained too, but at that time of night, it's unlikely anyone passing the killer would notice bloodstaining on his clothes, particularly as it was raining heavily."

"And still no witnesses found yet?"

"The DCI says no," Smiler shook his head.

Nodding, Cowan then asked, "So, what's her instruction to you for this evening or have you an idea how to commence your inquiries?"

"Well," Smiler drawled, "I'm thinking of introducing Sergeant Devlin here to some of the less reputable pubs in the area, the ones where Jeannie primarily hung about offering her services. Maybe speak with some of the staff, see if anyone can recall seeing her on

Thursday night at closing time."

"Right then, I'll let you get on with it," Cowan nodded their dismissal, but then said, "Mattie, a word before you go?"

"I'll grab us radios and get you at the uniform bar," Smiler nodded to Devlin and stepped out into the corridor.

When he'd left the room, Cowan said, "Keith Telford. He's going to be late, claiming he'd to go home to change because some drunk vomited on him."

"You don't believe him?"

"If Telford told me today was Saturday," Cowan sighed "I'd still check the calendar."

"You want me to keep my eye on him," Devlin astutely guessed.

"Aye, and on top of everything else I'm asking of you, try and motivate him because sure as hell everyone else who has attempted it, myself included, has failed miserably."

Devlin grinned when he replied, "I'll do what I can, sir."

"Good man," Cowan nodded.

****

DC Barbara McMillan's visit to the collator's office and a check of his files discovered that Albert Moston, AKA Moxy, was indeed known to the Division and had accrued a number of convictions for minor thefts and breach of the peace.

Reading the file, McMillan's eyes widened, then she slowly smiled when she read that one of the convictions for breach was awarded some eight years before after a local woman had complained that in the dark of a late evening, Moston had followed her through the Govanhill Park, then pulled at her arm and tried to solicit the woman for sex.

It was his misfortune that the woman was married to a rugby playing physical training teacher who later that night, knocked on Moston's door and that, McMillan grinned, must have accounted for Moston's crooked nose.

The teacher was also charged with seriously assaulting Moston, but it seemed at the trial, the streetwise Sheriff took account of the circumstances that led to the assault and wagging a finger at the husband that he never again take the law into his own hands, admonished him.

Not so the unemployed Moston who was fined eighty pounds, but with time to pay.

Drumming her fingers on the filing cabinet, McMillan decided then that Moston's attempted solicitation meant the DCI must agree he was certainly worthy of a further visit by her and Morris Kerr.
****

Constable Drew Taylor joined his neighbour in the van, then asked, "Have you had something to eat or do you want me to stop off at a chippy?"

"Eh, sorry?"

His eyes narrowed when he stared at her, then said, "You seem a wee bit distracted, Roz. Everything okay?"

She took a deep breath, then slowly exhaled before turning to him to reply, "Just a bit of personal news. Nothing for you to worry about," she forced a smile.

Eager as he was he neither knew how to raise the subject nor break the news of his break-up with Sharon.

"Okay," he slowly drawled, "so chippy or not?"

"Ah, no, I'm fine," she reached for her seatbelt and clicked it on.

He started the van's engine, then deep in thought, manoeuvred the vehicle through the arch and out into Craigie Street.

CHAPTER ELEVEN.

After a quick refreshment break, Smiler and Mattie Devlin were back on the street, their first port of call that evening was one of the pubs the older cop knew to be regularly visited by Jeannie Mason, *The Resting Soldier*, that was located on Alison Street near to the corner of Belleisle Street.

Upon their arrival, Devlin glanced up at the rusting sign above the door that depicted a Napoleonic British soldier, wearily resting on his Baker flintlock rifle.

Smiler shook his head and remarked, "It's usually quiet at this time of the evening, Mattie, but a den of iniquity any time after nine o'clock. That and there's unattributed information that a local worthy called Jo-Jo Donnelly, a right nasty bugger and who fancies himself as a hard man, has taken to dealing that new drug in the pub, the one that's being bandied about as lethal, the eh…"

He was lost trying to remember the name of the drug, but was prompted by Devlin who said, "You talking about crack-cocaine? The drug that's said to be coming up from England?"

"Aye," Smiler sighed, "that's it, Mattie."

"What about the licensee, any issues with him?"

"Her," Smiler corrected Devlin with a frown, stopping just outside the main door of the premises. "Cathy McHugh. Local blonde bombshell who about six years ago now, won something like eighty-odd grand on the football pools and bought herself this place. Runs it like a private club."

"How so?"

"If your face fits, you're okay to stay, but if it doesn't or for any reason Cathy takes a dislike to you, one or both of her bouncers throw you out the door."

"So, doesn't that prevent trouble?"

"Not really," Smiler sighed and stepped aside as a punter exited the pub and who suspiciously frowned when he saw the two officers loitering outside the door.

"It's common knowledge the locals know that Cathy turns a blind eye to wheeling and dealing in the place, whether that be selling knocked off property or drugs and that, as I said, encourages the local worthies to use the place like a private club. Anyone who seems suspect, isn't a known face or thought to be a polis tout is identified and expelled, usually with a slap to the jaw. Sadly, no complaint is ever made and no matter how many times the Divisional drug squad or the licensing sergeant has attempted to enforce the Licensing Act, Cathy always seems to survive."

"So, what kind of reception are we expecting here," Devlin nodded towards the pub's door.

"You've seen the John Wayne movies when he walks into a cowboy bar, haven't you?" Smiler grimly smiled, then added, "Just don't expect anyone to catch your eye. If this were a film, we're the bad guys."

Pushing open the door and followed by Devlin, Smiler strode into the pub and it was as he'd said, conversation among the thirty or so customers hushed and heads turned away.

At the bar, Smiler addressed the multi-tattooed, balding, man in his late thirties, whose face blank, was slicing lemons on a wooden cutting board and who said, "Nobody called you people, officer."

In turn, the big man politely asked, "Is the licensee on the premises?"

Wordlessly, though Devlin didn't miss the sullen glance at Smiler, the shaven-headed bartender turned away to pull back, then call through a curtained doorway, "Cathy, the polis are here looking for you."

"Right," a voice called, "I'll be out in a minute, Cokey."

Seconds passed, then the curtain was pulled back to disclose a woman with shoulder length, auburn-coloured hair and who dourly crooked a finger at the officers to indicate they follow her through the curtained door.

Following Smiler behind the bar then through the doorway, Devlin found them in a large room that seemed to double as both an office and a storeroom then behind him, heard the hubbub of craic in the bar, resume.

His first impression of Cathy McHugh, though he guessed her to be in her mid to late-forties, was her good looks belied her age and with a figure many younger women would envy.

Wearing just the minimum of make-up, McHugh wore what seemed to be diamond studs in her ears, at least three gold chains around her neck, several heavy gold bracelets on each wrist and a number gold and diamond rings on each hand, but saw no ring on the third finger of her left hand.

He choked back a laugh when it occurred to him Tutankhamen's wife was probably less jewelled.

Dressed in a silk red blouse, black knee length leather pencil skirt and red high heeled shoes, there was little doubt McHugh was an extremely attractive and sexy woman.

"So," she at last smiled, "what can I do for you, Smiler?"

Turning to Devlin, he nodded, "This is my boss, Mattie Devlin," then continued, "You'll be aware, Cathy, that wee Jeannie was murdered?"

"A bad business," she solemnly agreed with a nod.

"I'm seeking any information or anything you might have heard or know about regarding her movements on Thursday night, particularly around closing time."

"You know I have no interest in speaking with the police, Smiler," she sniffed, "so why are you asking me this?"

He sensed rather than heard Smiler take a deep breath before the big man slowly responded with, "I'm not asking you to like me or the polis, Cathy, and of course I'm well aware of your intransigence towards us, but this is different. We're talking about wee Jeannie here and I know that while you never suffered her to come into your pub and you'd never encourage her drinking, you weren't beyond bringing her in here to this back room to feed her a couple of pies from your bar or to give her an old warm jacket you were finished with."

Devlin saw the surprise on McHugh's face, who first shrugged, then stuttered in reply, "Well, you know the old saying, Smiler, there but for the grace of God and all that."

The big man slowly smiled when he softly said, "I know you like to think you're a hard business woman, Cathy McHugh, but I'm hoping beneath that tough exterior there's still a heart beating that wants us to find out who killed a helpless wee woman like Jeannie."

Devlin saw her face redden before she replied, "Nobody but you, Smiler, would get away with that comment."

Nodding, Smiler replied, "Well, we'll be away now, Cathy, but if you were to hear anything about what happened to her, you know where to find me," only for her to surprise him when she quickly retorted, "And you know where to find me too."

Returning through the curtained door, on this occasion the customers ignored the two officers and continued with their conversations.

On the pavement outside, they began to walk to the next pub on Smiler's list, but he turned when Devlin teased him with, "She fancies you, you know."

"Who, Cathy? Nah," Smiler slowly shook his head in dismissal.

"And I thought it was me who was a poor judge of women," Devlin airily said, then fighting the grin, added, "After you told me about her, I didn't know what to expect, but she's a bit of a looker is Cathy McHugh. And," he continued to tease him, "just about your age, though of course she looks a lot younger."

"What's the penalty for punching a sergeant?"

"Oh, touched a raw nerve, have I?" Devlin widely grinned. "Don't tell me you can't see she's a cracker, is Cathy?"

"Aye, I'll give you that," Smiler sighed, "but to my knowledge, there's been nobody in her life since her husband, Micky, took off with her best pal."

"What's the story there then?" Devlin asked, idly seeing that a group of noisy young teenagers across the road who heads down, quietened when they spotted the polis.
"I mentioned that she'd won a tidy sum on the pools?" Smiler continued.
"Eighty grand, you mentioned."
"A little over that, if memory serves me correctly. Anyway, seemingly it had been Micky's dream to be a pub landlord and soon after they won, they bought *The Resting Soldier* from the previous owner who had run it into the ground. I'd called in a few times to introduce myself and at that time, the pub was running fairly smoothly with no issues. But Mickey, he was a bit of a player with the women," he shook his head and his face creased in thought when he said, "and I think it was about three, maybe four months after purchasing the pub, Mickey took off with Cathy's best pal and what remained of their winnings, something close to forty grand I heard at the time. Can't blame Cathy for being embittered about men after he left her."
"Ouch, that must've been a sore one for her, losing not only her husband but the rest of the money too."
"Word is Micky's down south somewhere with the pal, but in fairness to Cathy," he cocked his head, "whether or not we like the way the pub's being run, she's made it a success and I'm hearing there's a lot of money goes across the bar every month."
"More importantly, do you think she'll come back to you if she does hear something about the murder?"
Stopping and turning to Devlin, Smiler stared thoughtfully at him before he replied, "You know, Mattie, I believe she will."
****
Constable Willie Strathmore and his neighbour, Harry Dawson, tasked to attend a disturbance in Stanmore Road, turned when the Divisional vehicle, Foxtrot Mike Two drew alongside and stopped. Winding down his window, Drew Taylor greeted them from the passenger seat and said, "We were passing by and thought we'd hang around in case your disturbance kicks off."
"Grateful for that," Strathmore nodded, acutely aware that his neighbour, for all her enthusiasm, had a habit of running off at the mouth and even the most innocent situations could develop into a brawl for like it had been said of her many times, Harry could cause

a fight in an empty house. In fact, Strathmore privately believed that Dawson enjoyed the confrontation, that she got some kind of kick out of arresting punters.

"Keith Telford arrived at work, yet?" Dawson addressed Taylor.

He turned to glance at Roz Begley and seeing her shake her head, replied, "Not to our knowledge. We were out sharpish in the van to cover while the Inspector was reading the DBR to you guys. Why, is there a problem?"

Strathmore inwardly sighed, knowing that not only was Dawson a nosy bugger, but any opportunity to spread salacious gossip where undoubtedly, she'd put her own spin on it too, would be like petrol to a fire.

"No," Dawson pouted, "but I heard he'd had a wee accident with his trousers. I'm thinking someone must've said boo to him and he's shit himself."

"Harry!" Strathmore raised his voice in rebuke. "You haven't heard that at all, you're making it up and that's a nasty thing to say about anyone, okay?"

Her face reddening, Dawson glared at him before she snapped back, "Well, we all know what he's like, don't we," then turned to Taylor and Begley as though seeking their support.

But it was Roz who leaned across Taylor, then sighed, "I was there in the bar, Harry, collecting our radios when Keith phoned in to say he'd be late. Apparently some drunk puked on him, so he went home to change."

"Oh," Dawson, blushing fiercely, said, "that's not what I heard."

Or more than likely made up, Strathmore thought, but instead said, "Right, we'd better get to this call and yes, thanks for coming by, guys. We'll give you a shout if it kicks off."

Glancing at the 1960's-built council three storey tenement building and watching Strathmore and Dawson turn into the close, Taylor told Begley, "Might as well switch off the engine, Roz. We'll hear better if there is a rammy in the close."

****

Arriving at Craigie Street the subject of Harry Dawson's mischief making, Keith Telford, was still apoplectic with anger.

Sitting in the driver's seat, his knuckles white from gripping the steering wheel, he was still seething at the drunken teenager for puking all over him, but more than that, livid at the Special who not only failed to back him up, but accused him of making a false arrest. Bitch!

What did she know with her weekly, two-hourly sessions on how to be a cop.

She had no idea what it was like out on the streets, dealing with society's riff-raff, then having smarmy lawyers defend them in court. No idea, at all.

Well, he unconsciously shook his head, she had ruined any chance of him asking her out and his eyes narrowed as he gave thought to how he might revenge himself on her.

One idea played over and over in his head.

He'd ask her out and when she arrived at the restaurant, he'd dizzy her, smiling as he imagined her waiting there for him and he not turning up.

That would teach the bitch, so it would.

Or maybe taking her back to his house then at the door, telling her to fuck off, that he didn't want anything to do with her.

Or even…

His breathing became rapid as he thought about her, wearing her NHS clerical uniform, suddenly finding himself becoming aroused…

The sudden beep of a car horn startled him and to his surprise, he hadn't realised the supervisory panda had stopped alongside him with the Inspector glaring at him from the driver's seat.

Hurriedly winding down his window, he gulped and nervously smiled, only for the Inspector to bark through the panda's open window, "Constable Telford, you're late enough as it is for your shift without you sitting in your motor there, playing with yourself. Get into the station, grab your radio and head out to meet your neighbour. Understood?"

"Sir," red-faced, he nodded and breathed a sigh of relief as the panda car drove off.

Slumping into his seat to catch his breath, he was still angry at the drunk, the Special and now the Inspector who had thought him…well, he wasn't, was he?

His teeth gritted, he vowed that sometime this evening, he'd find someone to take out his anger on, someone who would get the jail and feel his wrath.

****

Smiler's plan to visit the three other pubs on the beat that he knew Jeannie Mason hung around didn't quite go to plan.

Outside the second pub on his list, he and Devlin encountered three men, two against one and worse the wear for drink, arguing, pushing, shoving then finally swinging at each other and in general, creating a nuisance.

As they made their way towards the men who by now were attracting a crowd of jeering and booing patrons that had exited the pub to watch the fight, Smiler, apparently irked by the inconvenience, told his neighbour, "There's an old and standard tradition we in the Glasgow police use, Mattie. Breaches of the peace get one warning, then if they ignore that warning, it's the jail for them. It's worked since time immemorial and the Glasgow punters know it too. So, time to practise it, eh?" he sighed at Devlin.

As they arrived at the commotion, the crowd of a dozen hecklers suddenly parted and muttering, began to drift back into the pub, cardboard hardmen pretending that the arrival of Smiler and Devlin didn't really intimidate them, but acutely aware that the arrival of the polis meant someone was about to get the pokey and they weren't getting caught up in it.

Devlin grabbed one of the protagonists by the collar of his jacket and physically heaved him to one side, while Smiler, similarly holding the other two, loudly boomed, "Now, now, gentlemen, what seems to be the trouble, here?"

Devlin's man and one of Smiler's immediately desisted, their arms falling to their sides, but the second individual held by the scruff of his neck, turned to stare at the big man towering over him and drunkenly snarled, "Fuck off, it's nothing to do with you!"

Ignoring him, Smiler turned to the other two and politely said, "I take it you pair are off home then?"

"Aye, Smiler, sorry, big man," Devlin's man responded for them both whereupon both he and his former pugilist pal were released and together, stumbled off along Allison Street.

However, Smiler's second man continued to struggle and was slammed face first against the pub wall, then calmly informed, "You had your chance, Fergie, so you know the rules. It's the jail for breach, now stop struggling or you'll make me angry."

Devlin thought that Fergie must be known to Smiler after all for the man, who he guessed to be in his mid-forties, stopped struggling and was immediately contrite, begging not to be jailed, reminding Smiler that it was Saturday and with his convictions, he'd be detained till the District Court on Monday afternoon.

It was fortuitous that at that very moment, Inspector Cowan, driving the supervisory car, stopped on the road way beside them then leaning out of the driver's window, cheerfully called out, "One for Craigie Street, lads?"

"Aye, Inspector, it's our Fergie again," Smiler confirmed knowing his prisoner, who he shoved into the rear of the panda and who was joined by Devlin while the larger Smiler occupied the front seat.

They were just a few minutes into the journey when the drunken Fergie piped up, "Is that right about wee Jeannie, Smiler, that she got herself murdered?"

Beside him, Devlin tensed, wondering how Smiler would respond to the suggestion Jeannie Mason was the architect of her own death.

However, Smiler, without turning, simply replied, "Aye, it is, Fergie. Sad news, eh?"

"Aye, wee Jeannie never hurt anyone," Fergie slurred. "Me? I liked her when she was sober, but a bad wee bitch with a right wicked tongue on her when she was drunk, you know?"

"No reason to hurt her though, eh Fergie?"

"No, big man, you're bang on. I mean, the size of her, she couldn't punch her way out of a wet paper bag, eh? I hope you get the bastard that killed her, so I do."

It was then that Devlin realised, like the Inspector, he was unconsciously holding his breath, for nothing loosened the tongue quite like alcohol.

"Any ideas yourself, Fergie, who might have done it?" Smiler casually posed the question.

"Me," Fergie smirked. "No harm to her now she's dead, but you must know what she was like, Smiler," he breezily replied. "A shag or a blowjob for a half bottle of the cheap stuff."

Sitting behind the Inspector, Devlin saw Smiler's shoulders tense and inwardly prayed that the big man wouldn't react to the callous comment, but heard Smiler ask, "Can you pull over here, sir?"

Without questioning why and to his surprise, Cowan slowed then stopped the vehicle at the side of the road in Calder Street, then switching off the engine, simply stared ahead through the windscreen into the dimly lit road ahead.

Turning in his seat to stare back at Fergie, Smiler softly said, "As I recall, your convictions might mean sixty days or more and am I right in thinking, you just started work a week or two ago, labouring at that tile factory over in the Dixon Blazes industrial estate?"

Beside him, he sensed Fergie tense and replied, "Aye, I did. How did you know about that?"

"And is it fair to say," Smiler didn't bother explaining, "if you get the jail on Monday, the job's out the window? And if that happens," he voice dropped almost to a whisper, "and if I'm correct in recalling, your missus says you're out on your ear?"

Devin turned to glance at Fergie, seeing his throat tighten and his face pale as though the reality of his situation was now hitting home. Before Willie could respond, Smiler softly continued, "Think back, Fergie. Thursday night. Do you remember seeing Jeannie at all? Oh, and before you reply, we're not at Craigie Street yet and you've not been formally charged at the uniform bar, so the truth *might* be helpful to your predicament, if you get my meaning."

By now, Devlin saw Fergie's legs were shaking and his throat dancing like a hula girl on speed.

"Think about it," Smiler softly and slowly continued so that what he said could not be misconstrued by the inebriated Fergie.

"I'm not interested if you ever used Jeannie's services, though I suspect your wife might be, but just so you know. Anything said in the car here, stays in the car. Do you understand, Fergie?"

Licking nervously at his dry lips, the anxious man took just seconds to consider the threat, then quickly asked, "There's a guy, a local guy. I don't know his real name, but everybody calls him Moxy. Drinks in our pub sometimes, but usually hangs about the Soldier. Now," he shook both hands in front of him in denial, "I'm not saying he did anything to Jeannie, but the word is that this guy Moxy, he was using her every now and again. People are starting to talk, you know? Some are thinking it was Moxy that done her in."

"Moxy," Smiler slowly repeated, though Devlin sensed the big man knew exactly to whom Fergie was referring.

"Just to be clear. Skinny big guy, nose like a battered fish. Drinks in *The Restful Soldier*, you say?"

"Aye, that's him," Fergie swiftly agreed.

Turning to Cowan, Smiler told him, "I think in this case, Inspector, a street caution re our Fergie's future conduct is appropriate, rather than have him locked up and separated from his nearest and dearest, eh?"

Taking his cue, Cowan loudly sighed before he replied, "As you say, Constable McGarry, perhaps Mr Ferguson will take a warning," then turning to the fearful man, told him, "That's a huge favour you owe Smiler here, pal, so I'd bear that in mind when he speaks again to you."

Nodding eagerly, a relieved Fergie almost leapt from the car when Smiler opened the door, then him sent on his way.

Returned to the front passenger seat, Smiler said, "Thanks, Inspector. Moxy is an Albert Moston who coincidentally, lives with his mother in a flat overlooking the Govanhill Park."

"And what do you think, Smiler? Is this guy capable of murder?"

"Isn't everyone," Smiler replied, more sourly then he intended, then added, "I do know he's accrued several minor convictions and if memory serves correctly, one was for soliciting a woman in the Park."

"Well done, guys. That'll give the CID a starter for ten," Cowan grinned, then starting the engine, drove towards Craigie Street.

****

As it happened, just twenty minutes later, the subject of the conversation in the panda car, Albert 'Moxy' Moston, was lingering in a darkened close in Annette Street, waiting for the man he'd seen and recognised that dark, Thursday night when he was returning home from the pub; the man with his arm around Jeannie Mason and who was leading her through the open gate into Govanhill Park.

The man that Moston knew so very well.

Standing just inside the in the coldness of the close, he shivered and his leg ached as it always did when he was in the cold.

The leg that broke when he fell.

He was early for the meeting, but it gave him time to practise again, to go over in his head what he would say and decided to add another couple of hundred onto the sum he would demand for his silence.

His eyes narrowed when he saw a police panda car passing by and stepped back into the close, though he was certain they couldn't have seen him.

The polis.

He hated them.

And of them all, he unconsciously bent to massage his aching leg, he hated that big bastard McGarry even more.

Always smiling, always pretending like he was a good guy.

If people knew the truth, his teeth gritted as he snarled.

If it hadn't been for that boss man detective, if he hadn't agreed to tout to the CID, McGarry would have seen him get the jail; *bastard* that he is!

Deciding it might be wiser to move, he stepped even further towards the rear of the close, but then just seconds later, he took a deep breath when he saw the figure enter the close, then slowly walk toward him.

"So, Moxy," the man began, "what exactly is it that you want?"

His mouth suddenly dry, Moxy's eyes flickered when he realised that maybe this wasn't such a good idea, telling him first what he'd seen then meeting him here and alone.

"Eh," he took a deep breath, then his throat tightening, he stuttered, "I saw you with wee Jeannie."

"And what did you see, Moxy?" the man calmly replied, taking a step forward, his face now no more than inches from Moxy's squinty nose, his breath smelling of the drink he'd consumed.

It was then Moxy felt real fear, knowing that if this got out of hand, he'd no chance against this brute of a man, that even if he cried out, there was no one to help him.

It didn't help that he needed to pee and could feel his stomach constricting, inwardly praying that he wasn't about to shit himself.

"Nothing," his voice almost a squeak, he vigorously shook his head, unconsciously now backed against the cold, stone wall of the close. "I didn't see nothing at all."

"Unlike me, Moxy. What were you telling her when I saw you the other night? Were you telling her about us, about all those years ago?"

"Eh? What?" Moston was confused, then hurriedly added, "No. Of course not."

"I don't believe you, Moxy."

"But I didn't tell her anything about you or me, about what happened back then," he was cringing now, unable to prevent his bladder from discharging the hot urine down his leg.

"Then why are you telling me that you saw me with her? Why did you want to meet me here? Oh," the man humourlessly smiled as if in realisation. "Was it to screw money out of me, Moxy? Is that why I'm here?"

"No, honest," he was almost pleading now and hating himself for it. "It's just that…" he stammered, but Moxy got no further, for with his gloved right hand, the man shoved and pinned Moxy by the shoulder against the wall, then from behind his back he produced the large bladed kitchen knife that he shoved deeply into Moxy's stomach.

Moxy's eyes widened and though he tried to stutter a plea, with a quiet, but audible sucking noise, his killer withdrew the knife from Moxy's stomach then once more forcefully plunged it again into Moxy's abdomen.

His legs suddenly giving way, his eyes stared into his killer's emotionless face while his killer, unable to hold Moxy's dead weight with one hand, let him slide sideways down the wall.

The killer's final act before leaving the close was to pull the knife from the dying Moxy's stomach, then wipe the blade clean on his victim's anorak.

CHAPTER TWELVE: 07.48am, Sunday, 11 March 1979.

Peter McCaskill yawned, then his stomach protesting and threatening to loosen his bowels, gritted his teeth against the blinding headache and once again regretted both last night's steaming hot curry and the several pints accompanying it.

Burping loudly and once more tasting the bold and spicy vindaloo, he mentally crossed his fingers and knew he knew he'd be lucky to make it back to the van before he had an accident.

Head down against the drizzling rain, he shifted the torn and threadbare postbag on his shoulder before he turned into the close and once more wondered why he'd agreed to take the job this early on a Sunday morning.

But then the lure of cash in hand to supplement his unemployment benefits when jobs in general were hard to come by, had persuaded him.

The leaflets in his hand, already prepared for dispatching through the tenement's letterboxes, was already damp from the rain, then peeling off and discarding the elastic band holding the pile together, yawned again as he approached the ground flat doors.

So intent on separating the mail, McCaskill didn't immediately notice the drunken man lying slumped on the close or as he later told the detectives, that's what he thought the body was.

It was only when he stepped closer and saw the pool of blood and the terror on the corpses face; the eyes wide open and the gaping mouth.

Horrified, he couldn't quite believe what he was looking at, but then heard himself loudly scream as he dropped the leaflets right into the middle of the pooled blood.

****

It was the first thing that greeted DCI Laura Gemmill when she arrived at her Departments general office, the unwelcome news that a body had been discovered in a tenement close in Annette Street.

Just what I needed, she thought. A second murder investigation.

"What do we know about the victim," she turned to her DI, Sammy Pollock.

"Other than it's a male, nothing yet, boss, but I've sent two of the team straight down there, the first two who were in the office before me, DS Chalmers and young Barbara McMillan. That and I've the uniform early shift cops protecting the locus. I've also contacted the duty SOCO team, so they should be on their way once they get their gear together."

He glanced at his wristwatch, then continued, "The Duty Officer downstairs is calling out the casualty surgeon to meet us at the locus and I've also contacted the duty PF who will also attend."

"No question that it *is* a murder?" she sighed.

"None," he ruefully shook his head, for like Gemmill, he didn't relish the idea of running two murder investigations at the same time, for all it did was divide the already under resourced staff and Craigie Street, being an old office, would also mean difficulties running two incident rooms.

They both turned when DC Morris Kerr entered the office and nodding a greeting, then hurried towards a ringing telephone.

"On the ongoing murder investigation," Gemmill asked, "anything in through the night?"

"Yes, an information note from Constable McGarry; Smiler," he added but before he could continue, from across the room, Kerr called out, "Boss. That's Barbara McMillan on the phone with an update."

Striding across the room, Gemmill took the phone from Kerr's outstretched hand and said, "Barbara, speak to me."

"You'll recall, boss, that Morris and I spoke to a man called Albert Moston that we suggested might be worthy of a second interview?"

Rubbing at her forehead, Gemmill thought hard, then nodded, "Yes, I do. Why?"

"Well," she could hear the strain in the younger woman's voice, "I can positively identify our victim here in the close as Moston. Lucy says to tell you it looks like two stab wounds to the abdomen and that the blood loss has coagulated, so she's of the opinion that the murder took place at the very least several hours ago. That and Moston is stone cold."

Her head reeling at this development, Gemmill quickly asked, "Anything else you can tell me? Like, who discovered or reported finding the body?"

"It was a guy delivering leaflets for an estate agency. I asked why he's doing it so early on Sunday, but he's worried someone he knows would recognise him working and he's worried they'd tell the DHSS he's working for cash in hand, so needless to say he's been very cooperative. He's currently in the back court with Lucy, puking his guts up. He used a tenant's phone to call in the finding of the body. I'm calling from the same flat and with the householder right now." McMillan lowered her voice when she added, "The lady has been very helpful and we've use of her phone, boss. That and she's got the kettle on for when you get here."

Gemmill smiled, then said, "Right, Barbara, keep the postie there and the DI and I will be with you in ten minutes."

Gemmill thought McMillan to be a shrewd and eager young detective and aware the younger woman was relatively new to the Department, almost as an afterthought she lowered her voice to ask, "And you, are you okay?"

In the same low voice, McMillan admitted, "To be honest, boss, this is my first murder scene so I'd be telling lies if I didn't admit to feeling a bit squeamish right now."

Gemmill couldn't help but smile when she replied, "Get yourself a big glass of water and stay where you are. We'll be there soon," she reiterated.

When she returned the phone to its cradle, she turned to both Pollock and Kerr, then said, "We have an ID for our victim; Albert Moston, the man you and Barbara spoke with, Morris, during the door to door. Right," she took a breath, "Sammy, you're with me. Morris, keep everyone here till we return from the locus."

****

Wakening late that morning in his bedroom in his parent's home, Keith Telford was still angry and frustrated at how the Special Constable had treated him the afternoon before.

His parents, both retired teachers and at home when he'd returned the previous afternoon with his vomit stained trousers and boots, had discreetly retired to their conservatory at the rear of the house rather than engage him in yet another lie, for neither his father nor his mother believed half of what Keith told them.

The elder of their two sons, Keith had in their opinion wasted his life with his lies and half-truths, unlike his younger sibling, now living in his own home and happily married with a young child and employed as a senior administrator with a prestigious insurance company.

No matter that Keith had been offered every advantage, the sad truth that his parents had to accept was that educationally, their son just did not apply himself and expected that his life would proceed with every advantage being provided by his parents.

The driving lessons, the paid holidays, the handouts when he was often unemployed; all amounted to far more attention than was ever given to his sibling who, with the minimum of support from his parents, had gone on to excel not only in his education, but his professional and social life too.

What made it more difficult for Mr and Mrs Telford was that though he still had several months before his sixty-fifth birthday, their dream to retire to Spain had for the time being been put on hold, for it seemed their only son had no interest in either moving out or indeed, finding himself a partner or a wife.

In fact, had it not been for the magazines that Mrs Telford regularly discovered hidden under Keith's mattress, he obviously forgetting that it was she who both changed his sheets and daily, made his bed, the lurid pictures in such magazines seemed to allay both her own and her husband's fears that their son was homosexual.

Why then, they wondered, for all his bluster and boastfulness of his female companions, had they never been introduced to any of these women or even the friends in his shift he constantly referred to? The friends, who according to Keith, were in awe of his rising career.

And so, lying in his bed his hand moving rhythmically beneath the quilt cover, Telford's thoughts again turned to the Special Constable who by now deserved every sexual perversion that his mind dreamed up. That he'd get his revenge, he was absolutely certain and as his vivid imagination moved on, once again saw himself as the hero of the shift, admired by all.

His eyes tightly closed, he again turned his thoughts on the Special Constable, now wearing her police uniform. Such was his excitement his breathing became erratic and with is free hand, threw back the quilt, his hand thrusting fast and furiously…until the door knocked and his mother barged in, a mug of tea in her hand.

Red-faced, he screamed, "Get out!" startling his mother who face flushed, quite obviously could see what he was doing and who in her haste to exit the room, spilled half the mug of tea onto the carpeted floor.

The door closed behind her and now, tears of shame biting at his eyes, Telford bit savagely at his lower lip.

For several minutes, he lay there, sobbing at how his life had gone, then with reluctance, rose from the bed and pulling on a robe, headed for the bathroom in the hallway.

****

Seated in the front passenger seat of the CID vehicle, Gemmill turned to Pollock to say, "You mentioned when I arrived this morning that our uniformed cop, Smiler, had left some information?"

Pollock sighed when he said, "Curiously and assuming it's the same man, it was about our murder victim, Moston. Smiler had learned that Moston might have been a client of Jessie Mason and apparently there has been local rumours he might have been involved in her murder. Smiler had suggested Moston could be worthy of interview, but the info's a bit redundant now, I suppose," he wryly added.

Gemmill huffed, exhaled then eyes narrowing, speculated that it was too coincidental that Moston, mentioned regarding Mason's murder, should also find himself murdered and as every detective knew, there was no such thing as coincidence.

Minutes later, Pollock slowed, then stopped the CID car at the rear of the marked police Transit van.

Exiting the vehicle, her anorak pulled up against the fall of rain, Gemmill nodded to the uniformed cop at the close entrance who noted both their names and time of arrival in his issue notebook. The cop went on to inform them that the detectives were in the ground flat to the left, that the SOCO had still to arrive, though just minutes earlier, his controller informed him the casualty surgeon was en route.

Nodding her thanks, Gemmill led Pollock into the cold tenement close where they saw the body lying just a few feet past the stairs and about ten feet short of the rear door that lay ajar and led out into the rear courtyard.

Standing several feet from the body to negate any further contamination that might have occurred already, Gemmill sighed and shook her head.

Like Pollock, she had attended numerous murder locations, but it was never anything that a police officer would get used to and if indeed any officer did become use to the sight of a murder victim, the psychological implications must in her opinion, affect their professional judgement, a view shared by many of her colleagues.

Turning to Pollock, she sighed, "Let's hear what young Barbara has to say about our victim and while we're in there, Sammy, I'd like you to make a phone call."

"Boss?"

****

She called out that he was wanted.

Vigorously rubbing the towel at his hair and wearing his knee length robe, Smiler hurried down the stairs and took the phone from her hand as she whispered, "Says his name is Sammy Pollock."

He watched her turn away, slowly unwrapping the bath towel that covered her, then deliberately teasing him with a sexy wiggle as she turned through the kitchen door and out of sight, leaving him wondering and for the umpteenth time how he had come to be so lucky.

"Sammy," he greeted him.

"Smiler, the note you left about the guy, Moxy Moston."

"Yeah?"

"I'm calling from a ground floor flat in a tenement close in Annette Street. Moston's lying in the close inside near to the back door. He was discovered just about an hour ago, stabbed to death. The casualty surgeon has just arrived and estimates death occurred between eight and ten hours ago, so presumably late last night."

He paused before he continued, "I'm aware you're supposed to be on shift, but the boss," he lowered his voice, "she's in the kitchen here, having a cuppa while we're waiting on the SOCO arriving. She asks if you can come in and speak to us about what you know of Moston."

He heard Smiler take a breath, then choking back his laughter, quickly added, "Assuming that it's not interfering with anything too, eh, pressing that's going on there, right now?"

"Aye, very droll, Sammy," he replied, aware that Pollock knew him to be a widower and though Smiler liked and respected him, was in no doubt the DI would be curious about the woman who had answered the phone.

"Uniform or civvies?" he asked.

"Suit yourself, but I expect the boss might want you for most of the day."

He listened as Smiler sighed, then said, "Right, I'll take ten minutes to organise myself, then I'll be there in another twenty."

"Nothing you can do here, Smiler, so better you head towards the station. That's where you'll find the DCI. I'm remaining for the time being at the locus, but I'll see you there later."

After he'd hung up the phone, Pollock smiled for as Smiler had correctly thought, he wondered who the female might be.

****

Pollock had no sooner ended his call with Smiler when the SOCO team arrived and immediately began their examination of the body and the locus.

Returning to the cold close entrance, Gemmill and Pollock watched as the photographer commenced the procedure, then turning to her DI, she said. "I'll get back to the station, Sammy, if you can maintain a presence here. Perhaps when SOCO has…"

She stopped and wryly smiled, then with a shake of her head, said, "Granny and eggs?"

He grinned when he replied, "I'll have young Barbara and her neighbour started on knocking doors, boss, and hopefully being a Sunday morning, we'll get someone at home in each of the flats."
"Right, then, you know where to find me," she took the CID car keys from his outstretched hand. "I'll have Danny Sullivan organise a team to come down and knock on doors both sides of the street, but if the Doc's correct, it's highly unlikely we'll have much success."
"Ma'am?"
She turned to see one of the SOCO's team beckoning to her.
Stepping gingerly past the body, she and Pollock followed the young woman to the open door then heard her say, "With the rain last night, it's left a patch of mud on the left as you exit the rear door into the back courtyard," the SOCO pointed to the mud. "Now, as you can see, the metal fencing that used to divide the rear courtyards that serve the tenement's closes has long gone for scrap or been broken down."
"And your point is?" Gemmill asked, but knew there was something more to be said.
The SOCO bent down, her knee still barely inches within the concrete floor of the tenement then with a high-powered torch, shone it onto the muddy patch.
"Do you see the two footprints there?"
"Yes," Gemmill nodded, that old tickling feeling she invariably got in her stomach when she was about to learn something important.
"Left and right, I'm thinking?"
"Yes, Ma'am, left and right," the SOCO agreed with a nod, then continued, "It's the right one I'm concentrating on because as you know, it was my team who attended your murder locus in the park on Friday last. Well," she exhaled, "actually, it was me who lifted a right footed print from beside the victim's body and unless I'm wrong, I do believe I'm now looking at the tread marks from the same shoe or boot. Of course," she grimaced as she shrugged, "I'll need to take a plaster cast and make a comparison check, but stand on me because I'm convinced that pound to a penny it's the same footprint."
Gemmill smiled at the younger woman's enthusiasm, but also felt her stomach righting itself and with a frown that was tempered by a sense of relief that they had no need to divvy up the team, she

quietly said, "It's as we feared, Sammy. Our murders are connected after all."

CHAPTER THIRTEEN.

Inspector Iain Cowan took the phone from his wife, then said, "It must be important if you're calling me at home, Smiler."
"I've just had a phone call from Sammy Pollock, Iain, so I thought you should get a heads-up too."
Cowan had known Smiler, both formerly City of Glasgow cops, for almost twenty-two years and when it was just the two of them, the formality of rank was ignored, for though they'd never disclosed their close friendship, he, Smiler and their wives had been firm friends.
The death of Cheryl McGarry had been a dreadful blow to Cowan's wife, Elizabeth, who considered Cheryl her best friend, but it was to her credit that grieving though she had been, she was there to help Smiler and his children through their sorrow, a fact that the big man was eternally grateful for.
So respectful of Elizabeth's opinion, before he commenced his new relationship it was to her that Smiler confided. Meeting in a café in Newton Mearns shopping centre, he admitted he was considering seeing another woman, a much younger woman.
Almost shamefaced, he had sought her approval and to his relief, Elizabeth had immediately agreed that he move on with his life, reminding him that Cheryl would never have wanted him to mope through the remainder of his life alone.
And so, aside from his children who he yet had to inform of his new relationship, he received the blessing of the one person that both he and Cheryl unreservedly trusted.
Now, learning of the news of Albert Moston's murder, Cowan breathed into the phone, aware why his old friend had phoned.
His thoughts trying to deal with yet another hiccup in his shift pattern, he said, "I'm assuming you'll be away helping the CID, then?"
"Likely, aye."

Cowan unconsciously rubbed at his forehead when he said, "I'll get onto the early shift and try to persuade them to keep someone on to stand in for you till seven this evening, then when I'm in the office, I'll call the night shift Inspector and see if I can get one, maybe even two of his lads out on overtime."

With the poor salaries that currently existed, Cowan knew the problem wasn't persuading cops to do the overtime, it was trying to stretch the individual shifts budgets to accommodate the extra payments. While Chief Inspector Lizzie Whitmore, responsible for the management of such budgets was a sympathetic listener, her byword was usually, "Elastic only stretches so far."

He slowly exhaled, then rubbed at his forehead when he added, "I'm grateful for the heads-up rather than arriving at the office and trying to work miracles with what numbers I've got left."

"I'm guessing asking for stand-ins to cover will knock your budget to buggery."

"Needs must, Smiler, and if it helps you catch the bas…" he paused, then saw the reproving face of Elizabeth peeking out from the kitchen door.

"I mean, catch the man who murdered wee Jeannie, then so be it. Besides," he suddenly grinned, imagining her face when he spoke with her tomorrow, "Lizzie Whitmore owes me a favour or two, so I'll knock her door tomorrow and take my begging plate with me."

"Right, well Iain, I'd better get my backside in gear. Give that lovely woman of yours a hug from me."

"I'll do that. See you at the station."

****

Roz Begley sat at the kitchen table, the breakfast that her mother, Nan, insisted was a Sunday morning ritual finished and knowing that the heavy cooked meal would last her right through to her break where she planned on having a pasta.

Her father, Ronnie, turned to his youngest daughter to remark, "You haven't mentioned Derek in the last week. Everything okay between you two?"

Her face betrayed her to her father while at the sink, her mother, picking up on Roz's hesitation, stopped washing the dishes to ask, "There a problem, hen?"

Roz sighed before she said, "He's asked that we take a break for a while."

She didn't miss the sharp glance between her father and her mother, so brow suspiciously furrowing, asked, "What?"

Clearly nervous, it was her mother who replied, "Last week, I was over in Dumbarton Road and just stepped out from the fruit and veg shop when I saw Derek in a motor that was stopped at a red light. I was about to give him a wave when I saw that the driver was woman, a blonde-haired lassie, and they were laughing."

Her stomach tightening, Roz shrugged when she replied, "So?"

"Nothing," her mother's face flushed.

"They just looked, eh, kind of," her mother fought for the right word, then said, "*comfortable* together."

"Comfortable, mum? Really?" her nostrils flared. "What does *comfortable* mean?"

"He was, eh, stroking the back of her hair."

She glanced at her husband and added, "Then just before the lights turned green, he leaned across to kiss her on the cheek."

Seconds passed before Roz quietly asked, "You think he's cheating on me, don't you?"

Her father reached across the table to tightly grasp at her hand when he said, "Your mother's just, well, actually the two of us, hen," he glanced again at his wife. "We've never really taken to Derek. Never really trusted him," he grimaced.

She stared from one to the other, then downcast, slowly shook her head.

Roz had always been a realist.

Even as a small girl, the youngest of their three children, she'd quickly impressed her parents and teachers by her pragmatism and common sense. While her peers developed as children do, Roz was always considered to be one step ahead of them in both social issues and education, even believing herself too to be a good judge of character; but then she met Derek.

Though he hadn't been her first boyfriend and wise though she was, she'd soon accepted that the handsome and popular Derek was a flirtatious man, but forced herself to believe that at least he was faithful.

Caught up with her growing attraction for him, the first seven months of their relationship had been a whirlwind of progressively intimate dates, but then some three or four weeks ago, a lingering doubt of his commitment to her had occurred when within his flat she had answered the phone to a woman who asked for him, then abruptly hung up when Roz identified herself as Derek's girlfriend. The telephone call had bothered her, though at the time he had laughed it off as someone probably just fooling around.

But that seed of doubt had then been sown and so other small things began to niggle at her.

Derek's insistence that Saturday's were for playing or attending at football games with his mates, though on at least two occasions she heard his pals criticise him for not turning up and on one occasion, her brow furrowed, in fact just a week previously, his close friend at the estate agency where Derek worked, phoned her at home on her day off asking if she knew why Derek wasn't at work.

When she'd confronted him…no, when she'd *asked* him, he excused himself by telling her he'd had a heavy cold, yet there had been no evidence of that a day later when they'd met for dinner at his flat. And now this, her mother seeing him in a car with a blonde-haired woman.

Conscious that her concerned parents were staring at her, Roz sighed, "Don't worry, I'll get it sorted between us."

Excusing herself, she left the kitchen and made her way to her bedroom at the rear of the flat where closing the door behind her, she finally gave way to her tears.

But they were not tears of sadness or loss, they were bitter tears, for Roz was now accepting that Derek, the man she had thought cared deeply for her, was in fact deceiving her.

****

Across the city and out in the town of Coatbridge, Constable Willie Strathmore had that morning ditched the notion of studying for his police exam in favour of taking his eleven-years-old twin daughters out for a walk to Drumpellier Country Park, the large open-air space located in the suburb of the town.

Watching the twins gallop ahead towards the entrance gate, Strathmore assured his wife, Julie, "Look, I've put in a lot of hours and with the examination this Wednesday, I'm as ready as I'll ever be."

Broodily, she reminded him, "You're thirty-nine in December, Willie, and time's marching on if you want promoted. Even if you do pass Wednesday's exam…"

"What, you think I might not pass?" he teased her with a smile.

But she wasn't to be put off and continued, "Even if you do pass on Wednesday, that's just the first exam. You'll then have to pass the Inspector's examination next year and from what you tell me, that's a lot harder."

"I know, I know," he nodded, inwardly uncomfortable that though he'd tried to sound confident, he was anxious that of the three test subjects, Crime, General Duties and Traffic, it was the Traffic paper that worried him most.

"I'm worried about you, you know," she stopped, her hand on his arm to halt him, but with one eye on her daughters thirty yards further on and seeing them just about to pass through the park gates. He smiled when taking her hand in his, he replied, "Look, if I pass, I pass and if I fail; well, I'm still in a job, okay?"

"Yes, but you've worked so hard studying. I'm worried that if you don't pass, you'll *feel* a failure when you're not."

Continuing to smile, he shrugged when he said, "I've got you, the girls and we're all in good health, Julie, and the financial jump from constable to sergeant isn't huge, so let's just say I'm doing this for my own pride, eh?"

"Okay," she sighed and leaning into him, then urged on by their daughters, they continued walking towards the gate.

"Anyway," she smiled at him, "If you did get promoted, you'd miss the shift, the guys I mean, wouldn't you?"

"Most of them, yes," he nodded, "but not all of them."

"That guy, what's his name? the one you talk about. Trafford, is it? That who you mean?"

"Telford, Keith Telford," he corrected her with a nod. "Should never have been a polis in the first place. Going to get someone hurt one day, he is."

"Well," she squeezed his hand, then gimlet eyed, stared at him when she added, "just bloody make sure it isn't you, Willie Strathmore." The six feet tall Strathmore smiled down at his diminutive wife, then said, "Right, if the ice-cream van's there, it's cones all round, then half an hour on the swings before we head back up the road, missus. I've a late shift to attend."

****

To say that Harriet 'Harry' Dawson was disappointed was an understatement.

Contrary to her previous days' boastful confidence to Smiler McGarry at Ibrox Stadium, that a serving officer working out of Baird Street station had a romantic interest in her, had she been truly honest with herself she would have admitted that the pursuit of such a relationship was to date, one-sided.

To be fair, there was indeed such a young man, but she did not know for certain if he was aware of her infatuation for him nor if he even fancied her at all, for to date he had not responded to several telephone messages left for him at the Baird Street uniform bar. Dawson, imagining herself to be one hell of a catch for any man, chose to believe that her messages were not being relayed to him and was now seriously considering door-stepping the station to catch him coming off duty.

It did not occur to her that her actions might be considered to be those of a predatory woman, a stalker as the term was becoming widely known, and had she sought the advice of any of her female colleagues, it is likely there would be little doubt she would have been warned off such an action.

Unfortunately, Dawson trusted no one in her shift to confide in and with so few individuals she could loosely describe as friends and no close female relatives, it was left to her imagination that persuaded her the source of her infatuation was simply not receiving her messages.

Now, brooding in her upper cottage flat in Western Road in the Cambuslang area, a warm pink cotton blanket wrapped around her with her knees drawn up, she lay huddled on the old worn couch. Frustrated and a little angry, Dawson once more considered leaving a message for the Baird Street constable, but then quite randomly, her thoughts turned to the late shift that afternoon and her colleagues.

She knew that she was very popular, that all the men on the shift wanted to bed her.

Nor was she oblivious to the sly glances at her chest when they thought she wasn't looking and yes, she confidently thought, they all definitely fancied her. Well, all the eligible men, for she wouldn't include old Smiler in that group nor that ratbag Telford. Smiler was all right, if a little standoffish with her at times, but that was probably because he was old. Her brow creased when she wondered, maybe he'd been a bit of a looker in his heyday, but now he was definitely past it, she smiled.

As for Keith Telford, she involuntarily shuddered for like the rest of the shift she recalled the day he had ignored a general lookout when Roz Begley was chasing a ned.

Thinking of Begley caused her to consider her neighbour, Drew Taylor. Not a bad looking guy, she pursed her lips, but just as quickly dismissed him for she remembered one night at a shift function, he had brought along his girlfriend, Sharon something, and even Dawson realised with that good-looking the blonde on his arm, it was unlikely he'd play away.

Bugger it, she thought she reached for the phone.

She'd leave one more message and if he failed to respond *this* time, he was dumped.

****

Smiler had opted for a sky-blue coloured shirt, maroon coloured tie, beige chinos and his new straight-out-of-the-carrier-bag navy blue dress jacket.

Arriving at the CID general office, he was met by Sammy Pollock who whistled then quietly said, "You scrub up well for an old guy."

It was then that it occurred to Pollock that while Smiler always turned out smartly in uniform, his civilian dress sense seemed to have the touch of a woman about it.

"Less of the old guy, Sammy, or me and you will fall out," he pretended to growl.

"Right then, where's Ma'am?"

"I'll take you along to her office," Pollock continued to grin, but then asked, "Have you had breakfast? Do you need a coffee or something?"

Not realising he was walking into a trap, he replied, "No, I'm fine."

"Oh, right," Pollock's face was the picture of innocence when wide-eyed, he added, "I take it the maid brought you breakfast in bed, then?"

Smiler stopped, his face flushed, then in a low voice responded with, "You've known me too long to be sarcastic, Sammy. If you've a question, come out with it."

"Sorry, Smiler," Pollock raised both hands in apology and contritely exhaled. "I was teasing and you know it. Whatever's going on in your life, good luck with it. Now, I'll take you to the DCI and by

way of apology, I'll fetch you a coffee. Yeah?"
"Just milk, no sugar," he smiled in return.
Knocking on Gemmell's door, Pollock pushed it open then said, "Smiler's here, boss."
"Oh, come in," she beckoned them forward, then pointing that Smiler sit down opposite, unconsciously impressed she noted that for an older man and his broken nose aside, he was a right handsome big bugger.
Then she asked her DI, "Who have you left in charge at the locus?"
"Young Barbara McMillan with the instruction when the team gets out there, she'll let us know. Right now, Danny Sullivan is dishing out the door to door duties and the guys will be on their way within the next five minutes."
"Good," she nodded, "I'm just off the phone letting the Div Commander know we've another murder on our hands."
"Oh, that'll please him no end on a Sunday morning," his voice dripped with sarcasm when he shook his head, then asked, "I take it you told him you suspect the two murders to be related?"
"I did, yes," she nodded, then eyes narrowing, said, "You wouldn't be fetching yourself a coffee?"
"On my way to make three cups, so I'll be back in a couple of minutes," he nodded with a grin and left the room, closing the door behind him.
Gemmill arched her back and turned her neck to ease the ache before she said, "Thanks for coming out early, Smiler. Did the DI update you about the murder?"
"No, Ma'am, but I'm aware simply that in response to some information I left, the subject of the note, Albert Moston, has been discovered stabbed to death in a close in Annette Street."
"That's correct," she nodded. "A guy out leafletting found the body early this morning and…"
"Leafletting so early on a Sunday morning?" he interrupted.
"Aye," she allowed herself a smile, "He was earning a few bob on the side and trying to avoid anyone recognising him and telling the DHSS. Unless anything else comes in about him, at the minute I'm happy to treat him as a witness."
"Anyway," she continued, "I'd sent young Barbara McMillan and a neighbour down to the locus first thing and she positively identified Moston from the door to door inquiries. In fact, she had asked Danny

Sullivan if she could return to re-interview Moston because she had a feeling he was lying to her."

"Aye, sounds like Moxy," he sighed, then added, "Moxy. That was his nickname. A weaselly individual who wouldn't know the truth if it smacked him in the face with a shovel."

"Okay," she slowly drawled, then said, "The reason I asked you to come in early, Smiler, is to provide me with as much background information as you can about him. Now, let's start with your note."

He shrugged when he said, "Last night and in furtherance of your instruction, I persuaded a local man who drinks in a pub I know Jeannie Mason hung about, to tell me what the word is about her murder. Now," he held up the flat of his hand to her, "I don't suspect this individual of being involved, but like most of his cronies, he's there when the rumour mill is pumping out the gossip. What he told me is the rumour circulating is that Moston was using Jeannie Mason for sex and there's a suspicion he might have killed her."

"And you believe this individual?"

"Aye, Ma'am, I do or rather, I believe *he* believes what he told me," he nodded.

She glanced down at her desk, then replied, "I've Moston's previous convictions here and I see that one is for harassing a woman in Govanhill Park. What do you think, Smiler? Could he be our killer?"

"I don't need to tell you, Ma'am, that everyone is capable of murder. However, if Moston *did* kill Jeannie, then it begs the question; who killed him and why? Revenge?" he shrugged, then shaking his head, added, "I really don't think so, because the only people who'd want revenge for her murder would be her family and if you, the CID didn't identify Moston as a suspect for her murder, how would they possibly know about him?"

He paused for a few seconds, then continued, "It could be explained that Moston's murder is coincidental, but I know as you do, there's no such thing as coincidence. I think and mind," he stared at her to make his point, "it's only my humble opinion, I believe that you are correct. The murders are linked. Moston was well known in the area and of course, knew a lot of the locals too and what was going on."

The door was opened by Sammy Pollock, who carefully balancing three china mugs on a plastic tray, laid them down before Gemmill and Smiler, then wordlessly took the empty chair beside the big man.

Nodding her thanks for the coffee, Gemmill lifted her mug, then said, "Go on, Smiler, I asked for you to come in because I value your knowledge and experience with the locals here, so what's your humble opinion telling you about Moston's murder?"

He knew she was gently teasing him, then drawing a short breath, he replied, "Moston was a real lowlife, Ma'am, and as a younger man, probably even until his murder, was not beyond using violence when his victim was weaker than him.

He paused, then then as though remembering, thoughtfully said, "In his early twenties, him and another waste of space would target the elderly collecting their pensions from the post office in Cathcart Road and they weren't beyond hurting the old folk if they resisted. In short, he had no compunction about hurting people, regardless of their age or gender. But that said," he shook his head when he added, "I don't figure him for Jeannie's murder. If I were to present you with a supposition, I'm thinking he might have known something about her murder and *that's* why he was killed; to silence him."

Her brow creased when she again glanced down at the previous conviction file, then said, "There's nothing about him committing robberies in this file. Wasn't he identified for the robberies?"

Pokerfaced, Smiler replied, "He was, Ma'am, though he steadfastly refused to identify his associate and that because I believe he was more frightened of his pal than he was of us or the courts. Unfortunately, when he was discharged from hospital one of your predecessors," his voice grated when he continued, "a man who I will admit I was never overly impressed by, decided that Moston was more of value as a source to what was going on locally than a prisoner, so he was never charged with the crimes."

Her face expressed her incredulity when she hissed, "You're saying the DCI at that time ignored the charges that could be laid against Moston?"

Smile shrugged when he replied, "As I say, one of your predecessors was an ambitious man, Ma'am, and signing him on as a tout didn't do his career any harm, regardless of who Moston had hurt or robbed."

She could tell from his expression and the change in his voice that the decision still rankled with Smiler, guessing it was a bad decision that denied Moston's victim's the justice they deserved, then guiltily thought if they're still alive, maybe his death will bring the victim's some closure. Nor did she ask but inwardly guessed the identity of her predecessor who because of family's political connections, continued to serve, but now as an Assistant Chief Constable (Crime) in a neighbouring Force; a man who, she suspected, like Smiler, she and many of her CID colleagues had absolutely no regard for.

"Sorry," her face revealed her confusion. "You say discharged from hospital? What happened to him?"

"Ah, well, you see when he was identified as one of the pair robbing the elderly, the arresting officer chased him into his first floor flat where he resided with his mother. Moston tried to escape by jumping from the bay window into Govanhill Street and broke his right leg so badly it let him with a slight limp."

Gemmill didn't miss Pollock's red face as he choked back a laugh.

"What?" she stared hard at her DI.

"Not the story I heard," he sniggered.

"Sammy!" Smiler's face reddened when he turned to flash a warning glance at him.

Glancing between them, Gemmill's eyes narrowed when she softly said, "*What* story?"

"It was a long time ago, now Ma'am, but the story *I* heard," Pollock nodded at Smiler, "is that the big man here simply administered some summary justice."

It was Smiler who wearily sighed when he explained, "Moston alleged I threw him out of the window, Ma'am."

"And *did* you throw him out of the window?"

He stared at her with narrowed eyes before he replied, "Like the DI said, Ma'am, it was a long time ago."

To his surprise, Gemmill grinned when she said, "Assaulting and robbing the elderly? Sounds to me like some summary justice was required, Smiler. Now, bad guy or not, I'll have to break the news of his death to his mother. DC McMillan has already explained she's in the early stages of dementia. You know her, I presume?"

"Yes, Ma'am, there was never any harm in old Irene. A nice woman with a nasty son who like any mother would, defended him to the hilt."

"Okay, then, if you're a familiar face to her, I'd like you to accompany me, Smiler."

"Of course, Ma'am," he politely nodded, then rising from his chair, told her, "I'll collect a set of car keys and a personal radio and be

ready when you are."
****

Just as she was being discussed, Irene Moston rose from her bed, her toilet needs overtaking her patient wait for her son, Albert, to bring her morning cuppa to her.

She glanced at her bedside table just to check if he had indeed brought the tea, but there was no cup and saucer there, so assumed he had not.

Rising from her bed, she donned her old, tattered cotton robe and opened her bedroom door, then called out his name, but there was no reply.

Pushing open her son's bedroom door, she stared into the untidy room, the unmade bed, the scattering of the magazines he liked and then sniffed at the smell of unwashed clothes and the other smell; the smell of the sweet and funny looking roll-up cigarettes that he liked, then shaking her head, turned towards the bathroom.

After making her toilet, Irene sighed and decided just to get her own tea, so stepping into the kitchen, she lifted the white plastic electric kettle from its base plate, then took the kettle to the sink and half-filled it with water.

With a sigh, she placed the kettle onto the cooker, then pressed the electric ignition button to light the gas ring beneath it.

CHAPTER FOURTEEN.

Drew Taylor, changed from his coffee stained uniform shirt and trousers, was still upset after his encounter with his girlfriend Sharon.

He wryly smiled when he thought, his *former* girlfriend, Sharon.

If he were honest, he felt a little unhappy at the break-up, but more how he'd handled it rather than saying goodbye to her. Of course, he knew that the benefit of hindsight would always present his handling of it in a different light, that he could have said this or done that or perhaps even chosen a better venue to break the news to Sharon. However, he also knew that no matter how or where he told her, today simply proved she would not and did not take it well.

Well, he told himself, what's done is done and there was no going back because though had had known but hated to admit it even to himself, Sharon was a vindictive woman, recalling with sudden clarity an incident that had occurred some two months after they'd got together.

She had taken him to an afternoon party in the hotel in one of the meeting rooms, being held for one of her fellow and very popular senior receptionists going on maternity leave.

Sharon told him the party was what the Americans called a baby shower and so most if not everyone brought a gift, though Sharon had apparently been unaware of this custom.

As he recalled, besides the woman's family, there had been a dozen off duty staff present, representing every department from management to housekeeping and while drink was available, it was more an intimate than boisterous event.

For whatever reason, what he had not known was the pregnant woman, whose name he couldn't recall and Sharon disliked each other. According to Sharon at the time and he had no reason to doubt her, her colleague was forever complaining and knit picking about Sharon's competence in the job.

He recalled and though Sharon later thought it to be a huge joke, less than twenty minutes into the party, she had disappeared to the ladies toilet and while she was gone, the fire alarm activated.

Of course, not just the meeting room, but the entire hotel had to be evacuated into what was a cold, blustery and wet afternoon.

As a result, the partygoers, dressed in their finery and huddled together in the rain with the hotel guests, almost as one offered their apologies to the pregnant woman and her husband then left, thus prematurely ending the party.

While at the time he was curious at Sharon's indifference…no, not her indifference, her delight at seeing her colleagues obvious dismay, he did wonder if she had been responsible for activating the alarm.

Now, knowing her as he did, that seed of doubt grew and even without anything to indicate her guilt, he was certain it was she who had set off the alarm.

Of course, she could never admit to such an act, not even to him, for to do so and given the cost to the hotel as well as the fee charged by the Fire Brigade for the arrival of three tenders arriving at the locus to find out it was a deliberately activated fire alarm, she would have been instantly dismissed without reference.

Funny, he thought with a shake of his head, how all those little doubts now manifested into one eye-opening realisation, causing him to believe he had been conned by Sharon during the time they had been together. That the woman who he first thought was his ideal partner should turn out to be such a mean, conniving and scheming…

He couldn't even say the word, his dignity forbidding him to sink to her level while inwardly admitting it was he who had been the fool, that before now he should have recognised the signs.

Call yourself a policeman, Drew Taylor, he mocked himself in front of the hallway mirror. There she was, right in front of you and you couldn't see what she really is, he sighed.

Grabbing at his car keys, he headed for the front door.

****

Getting out of the driver's seat of the CID vehicle, Smiler McGarry glanced up at the first-floor bay window, then said, "This early on a Sunday morning, Ma'am, and with her having the dementia, I don't think there's any doubt that Irene will be at home."

Closing the passenger door, a thought occurred to Gemmill when she asked, "Mrs Moston. Do you happen to know with her having dementia, are the social work involved?"

"No idea," he shook his head and followed her into the close. "I'd imagine that if her son was looking after her, he'd likely be registered as her carer, though how good that care would be," he sighed, "again, I can only imagine."

At the half landing, she sensed rather than saw him hesitate and turning, asked, "What?"

His nose twitching, he replied, "Either somebody's burning the toast or…"

He hurried past her and stopping at Moston's door, snapped, "Smoke. I can smell smoke."

Startled, she watched him hammering with his fist on the door, then placing the back of his hand against the door knob, he turned to tell her, "The handle's warm. I think the flat's on fire!"

Handing her the personal radio, he quickly snapped at her, "We need the Brigade here now. Stand back. No," taking off his jacket, he literally bundled her back down the flight of stairs and added, "in fact don't come in unless I call you!"

Before she could protest, he had taken a short run at the door, then with his right foot raised, kicked the door at the lock. It was to his good fortune that the lock was no match for his size thirteen foot and with the weight of a six-foot three inch determined man behind it, the door crashed open.

Smiler, his jacket thrown across his head to create a makeshift hood, was immediately engulfed in thick, acrid smoke and as Gemmill used the radio to summon assistance, she saw him dart into the hallway and was immediately hidden by the pall of smoke.

"Smiler!" she cried out, but whether he heard or not, he was already gone.

As quickly as she could, Gemmill relayed her call for help then decided if the fire took hold, it would be wise to evacuate the building.

But that would mean leaving Smiler, who might at any second need her.

Angry at her indecision, she literally hopped from foot to foot, screaming his name into the doorway that by now was issuing black smoke.

In the hallway, Smiler realised the seat of the fire seemed to be located in the kitchen where the polystyrene tiles on the ceiling were ablaze.

"Irene!" he shouted over and over, then coughing and spluttering, heard what sounded like a soft wailing coming from the behind the closed toilet door.

On the smoke ridden landing outside, Gemmill, her eyes and throat stinging from the acrid smoke, banged on the door opposite Moston's flat that was opened by a young woman wearing a dressing gown and holding a toddler in her arms.

"Fire! Get out!" Gemmill pulled at the woman and shouted, "Is there anyone else in there?"

The shocked woman, no more than mid-twenties, gasped as she took a lungful of smoke and shaking her head as she coughed, covered the now crying toddlers face with her free hand.

"Go, go, go!" Gemmill half ushering, half pushing her downstairs, but then turning, wisely pulled close the woman's flat door behind her.

Wiping at her eyes with a handkerchief, Gemmill screamed again into the flat, "Smiler!"

That scream unwittingly caused her to inhale some thick, black smoke and gagging, bent over in a coughing fit.

Seconds later, coughing and choking, the big man, his face and shirt blackened by smoke, emerged from the interior carrying the slightly built Irene Moston in his arms.

"She's alive," he managed to gasp, then thrusting her towards Gemmill, spluttered, "Get her outside. I'll warn the rest of the building."

She didn't argue, but still coughing and trying desperately not to inhale more smoke, took the elderly woman, relieved she was no weight at all, then awkwardly turned and made her way downstairs, but not before seeing Smiler pulling the door closed behind him and trusting that he had enough strength left to warn the rest of the tenants in the upper flats.

Staggering outside into the cool morning air, wheezing like a sixty a day woman, her lungs feeling as though they were on fire, Gemmell staggered across the road, then dropping to her knees, laid her burden gently down onto the pavement.

She hadn't noticed the young woman, but suddenly there she was with her toddler son, thumping Gemmell's back in the mistaken belief it would help her breathe easier.

"Enough," she snapped, but raised a grateful hand to the overly-helpful woman for her effort, then turned her attention to Irene Moston who lay with her toothless mouth open and who had apparently stopped breathing.

Now old Irene was the focus of Gemmill's attention and her body shaking, was hardly fit to do so, but in those few seconds she tried hard to recall her training from all those years before and the instructions for resuscitating a patient who'd stopped breathing while trying to ignore that she was about to lock lips with a set of toothless gums.

"The neighbours, they're coming out," the young woman patted her shoulder and pointed across the road.

Instinctively she turned to see a six or seven men and women who were assisting some confused children, hurrying from the close entrance onto the street while in the distance she could hear the sound of police and Brigade sirens.

Turning back to stare down at Irene Moston, to her surprise the old woman gave a loud gasp and her eyes opened wide.

Her grey hair smudged and her dressing gown reeking of smoke, she stared up at Gemmill before she quietly explained, "Albert didn't bring my tea this morning."

****

Over a half hour had now passed and the fire that fortunately and mainly due to Smiler's forethought in closing over the front door, had been confined to the Moston's flat and was now extinguished, though the Brigade's narrow jet hoses that snaked into the close and up the stairs were still being sprayed in the flat's kitchen and particularly on the smouldering ceiling.

A cordon of early shift, uniform cops held the public back and particularly the young kids who were keen to sneak among the three tenders and the accompanying police vehicles.

In an ambulance parked outside the adjacent close, Smiler, a blanket around his shoulders and wearing a mask attached to an oxygen bottle by his side, sat on the stretcher bench opposite the DCI, whose throat still hurt and whose voice was hoarse. On the seat beside Smiler was his new jacket, reeking of smoke and peppered with small burn holes.

"Mrs Moston," she began with a nod and a sigh. "The Brigade's station officer tells me that the seat of the fire was a melted plastic electric kettle they found on the cooker's gas ring. That in turn set fire to what he thinks was a tea towel and he says the resulting flames in turn set off the polystyrene tiles in the ceiling. Says the polystyrene tiles are a bloody menace and give off a choking smoke that is responsible for most of the fire related deaths they encounter. They're so flammable that half the tenement fires in Glasgow involve them. According to him too, we're lucky the cooker didn't go up and blow the whole building away."

He grunted through the mask, his throat sore and had the sudden desire to pick at his crusty nose, thinking it was likely clogged by soot, but to do would not only mean removing the mask, but he was too embarrassed remove the snot in front of the DCI.

She stared at him before she softly said, "You took a hell of a chance, Smiler, going into that smoke filled flat. I was worried you might not come back out."

Already warned by the ambulanceman not to speak, that there was the possibility of damage to his larynx, he shrugged and tried to look sheepish.

Gemmill wasn't fooled and attempted a grin herself, though it pained her throat to do so when she added, "They want to take you to the hospital, so that's where you're going and no protest, big man."

He accepted he had to be examined anyway, so merely nodded.

"Is there anyone I can phone for you? Family, I mean?"

"Oh," she suddenly recalled he wasn't supposed to speak and fished in her handbag for her notebook and pen.

"I can deal with that, Ma'am," she turned to see Inspector Iain Cowan at the open rear door of the ambulance, who then added, "I arrived early for the late shift and thought I'd take a turn up to see how my man Smiler and yourself are doing. I'm hearing both of you have been through the wars."

He suddenly grinned when he added, "The two of you are the talk of the steamie back in Craigie Street, how you saved that old woman and all the tenants."

"Well," she nodded towards Smiler, "the truth is if it hadn't been for your man here, Inspector, we'd have been looking at a calamity, but I can hand on heart say, everything I've heard about him seems to be true after all."

"And you, Ma'am," Cowan's eyes narrowed, "you don't seem to have escaped unscathed. You sound a bit like that actress who married Humphrey Bogart, her with the forty-fags-a-day voice."

Even Gemmill had to smile at that before she replied, "Lauren Bacall, you mean. If I looked like her I'd *be* in Hollywood," she wryly smiled, "not sitting in the back of an ambulance in the southside of Glasgow smelling like a barbeque."

Privately, Cowan considered that Gemmill wasn't at all a bad looking woman and idly wondered if the rumours about her man cheating on her were true and if they were, more fool him, he thought.

"Boss," she turned and saw Sammy Pollock arrive, then stand behind Cowan.

"I've brought Barbara McMillan with your car. Now the medics have cleared you, she'll run you up the road in your motor then her neighbour will bring her back. As of now, I'm signing you off for the day."

"What," she pretended to be annoyed, "you taking over my Department, Detective Inspector?"

"No, nothing like that," he sniffed as in disdain, "but I'm not wanting you in the office looking like you've stuck your head in a bonfire and you're also reeking of smoke. It just so happens that F Division CID has a certain dress standard for its detectives."

She didn't have to force a smile when she quietly replied, "Thanks, Sammy. I'll take the day to recover then if I'm fit for work tomorrow morning, I'll be in. In the meantime, you'll know what needs to be done."

"Boss," he nodded in agreement.

Rising to her feet, she stooped to place her hand on Smiler's shoulder, then bending towards him, said in a low voice, "You did well today and I'll not forget it."

Making her way to the back door of the ambulance, she felt her legs a bit shaky and involuntarily reached for Pollock's hand, telling him, "Maybe see me to my car, Sammy, and Inspector," she turned to Cowan, "I think it's time that ambulance was away and taking Smiler to the Viccy."

****

Returning the phone to its cradle, a dazed Adam McGarry turned to his wife, then said, "Dad's been in an incident. That was his pal, Iain Cowan on the phone. He says not to worry, that dad's okay, but he's suffering from smoke inhalation and is in an ambulance being taken to the Victoria Infirmary over in Langside and suggests I might want to go there."

His wife Grace, a no-nonsense primary school teacher, briskly replied, "Right. Get yourself dressed and I'll phone Jean and let her know. Now," she urged then pushed her dazed husband towards the stairs.

Tall like his father, though just an inch shorter, the twenty-eight-years-old Adam stared down at his raven haired, five-foot two-inch wife, then nodding, raced away.

Shaking her head as she watched him sprint upstairs, Grace, two years older than her husband, knew that professionally, Adam was a smart and decisive man, yet since his mother died, he constantly worried about his dad.

Though her husband and his sister, Jean, met with or visited him regularly and Stuart had a close-knit group of friends, Adam thought maybe his father should now consider 'putting himself out there,' as he confided it to Grace, yet didn't know how to approach the subject. As for their two children, wee Stuart and his sister, Bella, they absolutely adored their Papa and young as they were, constantly nagged her for time with him.

Reaching for the phone she dialled Jean's number and when it rang, mentally composed how she would break the news that Stuart was being taken by ambulance to hospital.

****

Returning to the Inspector's office, Iain Cowan negotiated with the early shift Inspector for a constable replacement for Smiler and to his relief, was offered two officers when his colleague intimated, "After what the big man did today, it'll be kudos for the Division, Iain, so I can't imagine Lizzie Whitmore arguing against paying the overtime bill."

With the shift sorted, Cowan decided to phone his wife to let her know that Smiler was off to the Viccy, but that he was fine, though maybe he'd be admitted for a couple of days."

"And he's definitely okay?" he could hear the relief in Elizabeth's tearful voice.

"He's fine, love. You know Smiler, he'll be arguing with the staff to let him out, so I might have to go there and order him back to bed," he joked.

"What about the kids, do they know?"

"Phoned them before I phoned you."

"If he's been in a fire, he'll need a change of clothes."

Trust Elizabeth to be way ahead of me about that, he thought, then replied, "When I put the shift out, I'm going to see him for a visit, so I'll fetch his keys and get one of the shift to grab something from his house."

His eyes narrowed when she didn't immediately respond, then heard her softly say, "No, don't bother. I have an idea about that."

"Eh, what? What idea?"

She softly exhaled in his ear before she replied, "There's something you should know, something Smiler shared with me some months ago. Something he didn't want to share with anyone till he'd told his family."

****

It was Drew Taylor's turn to drive that late shift and turning into Caird Drive, saw Roz already waiting for him at her close entrance. Getting into the car, she said, "You been listening to Radio Clyde's news this morning?"

"No, why?"

"Craigie Street's been on the news. Seems like there's been another murder, though they didn't know anything other than a body has been discovered. That and there was a fire in a flat in Govanhill Street and a resident and a cop, one of the early shift I'm guessing, has been taken to the Viccy, though it didn't say who he or she was and what their condition is."

He glanced at the dashboard clock and saw it to be a few minutes to one, so his own news would have to wait for now and turned on the radio.

At one o'clock, the news bulletin offered no further information than Roz had related and with just a twenty-minute drive to Craigie Street, it seemed pointless trying to guess what colleague had been injured.

"In other news," he sighed, "I had a meeting this morning with Sharon. Met her in a coffee shop we've used before, up in Bath Street before she started her shift at the hotel."

Smiling, she turned to face him when she coyly asked, "Am I to presume that this meeting had something to do with a ring?"

He'd practised how he was going to break the news to Roz, but just as he'd practised his break-up statement to Sharon, once more his preparation failed him and so he shrugged, "Not exactly. I ended it with her. Broke up with her, I mean."

Stunned, Roz's jaw dropped, then she stuttered, "But I thought, I mean," she paused with a shake of her head. "I thought you guys were so tight it was just a question of time before you…"

She turned to stare through the windscreen, her thoughts a riot, then quietly said, "I'm so sorry, Drew. I didn't realise you guys were having problems. Is there no chance of a reconciliation?"

"No," he sighed and slowly shook his head. "I'd been having my doubts for a while now, some months in fact and well, I don't want to make her out to be the bad guy, but I should have challenged her on a number of things before now, only I didn't have the balls to do that."

"Wait, you had doubts months ago? Why didn't you tell her then?"

He sensed a change in Roz's initial sympathy and wondered, is she annoyed with me?

"I…" his throat was suddenly tight. "I don't know. I suppose I was worried that I might lose her and…"

"But you didn't lose her, Drew, you dumped her! And in a *coffee* shop, you said? With people around you who were probably listening and watching? Is that what you're telling me?"

He knew he'd made a huge mistake sharing his meeting with Sharon, then snatched a glance at her when he foolishly asked, "What are you getting at?"

He could not know that Roz herself was being dumped, that worse, her boyfriend, Derek, was seeing another woman and she was already an unlit fuse; that is, unlit till Drew had shared his information.

Now, he was about to be on the receiving end when she vented her fury.

"What I'm *getting* at and God knows though I really did *not* like Sharon, to lead her on for those months you talk about when you had your doubts!" she snarled. "What the hell were you thinking! That was just so *bloody* cruel of you! That and you dumped her in *public*!"

Angrily, she shook her head then crossing her arms, stared moodily out of the passenger window and he knew that any further conversation was now extremely unlikely.

CHAPTER FIFTEEN.

During his long service at Craigie Street, through the years Smiler McGarry had escorted many victims of assault and the occasional prisoner for treatment to the casualty ward of the Victoria Hospital and so become known to the permanent medical and nursing staff. He'd also on occasion attended there to assist the staff when they'd been threatened by drunks or confrontational families, demanding immediate treatment for their partners, siblings, sons or daughters who in the main, were usually drunk or suffering the effects of some or other illicit drug.

It was no surprise then that when a number of the long-serving and seasoned staff heard the popular and well-liked police officer was being admitted by ambulance, he was met by the on-duty nurses and doctors, all keen to guarantee that their favourite polis would receive the best treatment.

After several minutes of fretting over him and sympathetic greetings, it was the Ward Sister who finally took charge and waved the rest to their duties, herself ensuring that Smiler was quickly ushered into a receiving cubicle and the most senior consultant on duty summoned. Still spluttering through the plastic oxygen mask from his smoke inhalation, Smiler, taken aback and more than a little overwhelmed at the concern being shown him, waved his thanks before the curtains were pulled closed, then was startled to find himself being undressed by two of the young nurses who continued to fuss over him as though he were a favourite uncle.

The curtain was pulled aside by the duty consultant, a woman Smiler's age who grinning, said, "Nice to see you again, Smiler, if a little surprised at the circumstances."

Lifting her stethoscope from around her neck, she continued, "I'm hearing you're a bit of a hero, pulling an elderly lady from her burning flat," then seeing the apprehension in Smiler's eyes, quickly held up her hand when she added, "Don't worry, she's in another cubicle and I've already examined her and I expect her to be fine," her eyes narrowed, "though she is a little disorientated at the minute."

Pulling down at his mask, Smiler whispered in a gravelly voice, "Dementia."

"Ah, then that explains it," the consultant nodded, then turning towards the Sister, told her, "Might be an idea to have someone pop down from the Geriatric Department."

The Sister nodded then in turn, nodded at one of the nurses who left the cubicle.

The initial examination of his torso completed, the consultant gently removed the oxygen mask, then suggested Smiler take a short breath before examining the big man's mouth and throat.

"Hmm," she stared down at his patient, "other than some sooty phlegm and likely a sore throat to follow, you were wise not to inhale to deeply, Smiler, but we'll keep you on the oxygen for

another couple of hours, just to be safe. Sister?"
She turned again to her.
"Please remind me in say," she glanced at her wristwatch, "two hours and I'll pop back down to see our man here."
With a wave, the consultant was gone just as the remaining young nurse handed Smiler a glass beaker and straw to sip at the water it contained.
Seconds later the oxygen mask was replaced and Smiler was instructed by the nurse, "Now, lie back and relax."
****
Acting Sergeant Mattie Devlin slapped his palm down onto the old lectern then stared around at the shift that now included two early shift officers earning some overtime, one of who, a young policewoman was yawning widely.
Now having their attention, he began, "Likely the rumour mill has already informed you that our very own Smiler is in the Victoria Hospital's casualty department where the Inspector has gone to visit him. For those of you who haven't heard the real story, Smiler and the DCI were intending visiting the mother of the latest murder victim, Albert Moston, but instead discovered Mrs Moston's flat on fire."
He paused, then continued, "Though of course I only know what I'm told, so don't be asking anything I can't answer, but it seems that Smiler put the flat's door in, then rescued the mother who is also now detained at the casualty. As far as I'm *aware*," he stressed, "Smiler is suffering from smoke inhalation, but should be okay and hopefully will be discharged in a day or two."
He didn't fail to notice the smiles and grins, though thought it a little odd that while the cops and their two early shift colleagues were at least pleased with the good news, Keith Telford seated in the second row, remained pokerfaced, perhaps even a little distracted.
Devlin could not know that in those brief moments, Telford had in his mind replaced Smiler McGarry as the hero of the hour and was imagining himself being the one receiving the plaudits for his bravery.
"Right," Devlin broke into Telford's thoughts, "in the absence of the Inspector, I'm putting the shift out, so here's the latest in the daily briefing register."
At that time, Drew Taylor was driving the response Transit van,

Foxtrot Mike two with Roz Begley huffily sitting in the passenger seat.

Since their arrival at Craigie Street and the handover from the early shift crew, there had been a stony silence between them, broken only with the brief work-related dialogue.

Now turning into Butterbiggins Road, Taylor took a slow breath, then quietly said, "Okay, I messed up, but I can't believe that you're prepared to go through a whole shift in a bad mood with me."

Roz slowly turned to stare at him before she replied, "Oh, I'm *more* than capable of going through a shift and not speaking to you. And yes, you really messed up, Drew. I always considered you to be one of the more sensitive guys in the shift, that you…"

"Sensitive?" he snapped an angry glance at her. "You mean like that I wasn't the type to argue back, that I was supposed to let someone like Sharon run my life for me?"

"I didn't say that," she defensively replied. "What I mean is…"

"Look," he raised a hand from the wheel. "Yes, I could have handled the break-up better, I admit that, but Jesus, Roz, you've met her and you've even admitted you did *not* like her! I've always credited you with being astute and able to suss people, so don't tell me that you couldn't guess how controlling or manipulative she is. There, I've said it!" he hissed at her. "I'm far better off without her and even though I did mess up, I don't for one-minute regret ending it!"

She bit back her retort because she knew exactly what he was talking about, recalling in those few seconds the first time she had met Sharon.

It had been a weekday, a Wednesday before they resumed the early shift on Friday. With some of Lucy Chalmers family members and cop friends, Roz and four or five of the shift had been out in a pub in the city centre's Hope Street, celebrating the sergeant's thirty-fifth birthday or as Chalmers had said at the time, any excuse for a party. Two women wearing business suits had wandered through to the back lounge to investigate the music and the hilarity and it was the glamorous Sharon who had almost immediately caught the eye of most of the men there.

But it quickly became obvious it was Drew Taylor who Sharon fixated upon, encouraging him to buy drinks for her and her friend, both of whom had just finished their shift at the hotel reception desk.

There was no doubt he was completely mesmerised by the good-looking Sharon, but when Roz who admittedly had consumed more gins than was good for her, had tried to introduce herself, she was rebuffed and cold-shouldered.
However, tipsy though she had been at the time, she did not fail to notice the proprietorial Sharon's obvious play for Drew; the hand resting gently on his chest, the leaning into him to permit him to smell her very expensive perfume and even noticed the slight nod to her friend, who picked up on the hint to turn away, that Sharon had scored.
Roz's eyes narrowed when she recalled thinking then with a smile that Drew, in the Glasgow vernacular, had so easily been nipped and he didn't even realise it.
But now, she sneaked a glance at his angry face, it caused her to wonder though he did handle the breakup badly, maybe he did the right thing after all.
Her thoughts were interrupted when the All Stations radio activated with their call sign and the instruction to attend a report of a pair of violent shoplifters within the Cooperative Hypermarket in Morrison Street.
"But that's G Division, isn't it?" she turned to him.
"Aye," he nodded, his concentration fully on the road ahead, "but we must be the nearest call-sign," then lightly pressing down on the van's accelerator, activated the blue's and two's to warn any traffic in his way that Foxtrot Mike Two was coming through.
****
Smiler McGarry's son, Adam, and his daughter, Jean, sat together, the palpable relief on their faces when they realised that their father was not badly hurt, that the likelihood was he'd soon be discharged, possibly even later that day.
"I can't wait for your thirty years to be up," sniffed Jean, reaching across the bed to grab at her dad's hand.
"What time do you have left anyway, dad?" Adam asked.
Smiler's face creased in thought then pulling down the oxygen mask, exhaled before he slowly drawled in a slightly less hoarse voice,
"Well, I finished my trade training in March, '49, but though I'd been accepted and a couple of weeks before I was signed up by the City of Glasgow Police, my National Service papers came in the post and I was away in the army for two years."

"That was when you were sent to Korea, wasn't it?" Jean stared at her father, who though his voice was still a little hoarse, nodded, then continued, "Fortunately, after I was discharged from the mob, the polis finally accepted me and in a deal struck a while after I joined, later awarded me almost a year for my military service towards my pension. So, Adam, to answer your question, I believe with my accrued annual leave, I could probably retire in about eight months or so."

"And not before time," his daughter huffed, but it was obvious her scowl was of concern for her father's health.

The three of them turned when the curtain was pulled back by a woman, Jean guessed to be in her thirties, with cropped blonde hair and a worried look on her face.

Wearing a green knee length coat, she carried a brown leather holdall in her left hand that curiously, Adam recognised as a recent Christmas gift to his father from him and his wife.

"Stuart," the woman, her free hand on the curtain and her eyes bright with unshed tears, stared at him, then apparently noticing Adam and Jean sitting there, stuttered, "I'm sorry. The nurse didn't say you had visitors."

She was about to turn away when Smiler beckoned at her as he tore off the mask and called out, "Sally! Don't go! Please! Come back."

"Here," Adam, his curiosity written all over his face, leapt from his chair and gestured that she sit down.

With obvious hesitation, Sally stepped into the cubicle and with a red-faced nod to Adam then Jean, sat and laid the holdall down onto the floor.

Both his son and daughter stared at their father, waiting for him to explain, but it was Sally who introduced herself and said, "I recognise you both from your photographs."

Jean's eyebrows knitted when she repeated, "Our photographs?"

With a tight smile, it was Adam who told her, "Don't be slow, sis, this is dad's friend. Sally. The woman he told us about."

Her face creased when she snapped back, "I don't recall dad telling…" then paused as the penny dropped and said, "Oh. Yes, of course."

It was blatantly clear that both were struggling to understand, but were saved from further embarrassment when Sally, making a visible effort to compose herself, smiled then interrupted with a sigh,

"He's been meaning to break the news to you both for some time. About me, his dark secret, but you know your dad. He didn't want you to think that; well, I can only guess how much you must miss your mum and the very thought of your dad seeing someone else…"
She tailed off and turned to stare at Smiler, then continued, "Sally Rodgers and yes, I'm thirty-six, almost thirty-seven and so I'm younger than your dad and that worries him, though for the life of me I can't imagine why."
She took a deep breath and unconsciously shaking her head, her lips trembling, added, "When Elizabeth phoned me to say you'd been taken to the hospital, Stuart, I didn't know what to think."
"Auntie Elizabeth? You know her?" Jean gasped.
"We've met, yes," Sally nodded, then unable to help herself, the tears finally spilled over onto her cheeks.
To her surprise, she felt Jean's hand in hers and squeezing gently, then heard the younger woman say, "Well, he's fine. Bloody obstinate and secretive, but he's fine, okay?"
Sally took a deep breath, the pent-up emotion released in a long sigh, then nodding, was rising from her chair when she began, "I'll let you…"
But she got no further, for Adam placed a gentle hand on her shoulder and told her, "No, sit where you are and visit with dad. Jean and I are just going to find ourselves a coffee. Right, sis?" he glared wide-eyed at her, but there was no need for a warning for Jean, smiling widely, replied, "Good idea, big bro."

****

Sitting in the Inspectors office, dealing with that day's shift correspondence, Mattie Devlin lifted the phone to be told by the Duty Inspector, Marion Bruce, that Foxtrot Mike Two was leaving the Division to attend a call in G Division, that if any of the beat cops needed vehicle support, could he make himself available in the supervisory panda.
"No problem, Inspector," he replied, pleased to be doing something other than paperwork.
Grabbing his cap, raincoat and car keys, he headed for the door only to be met by the Divisional Commander, Chief Superintendent Jimmy Thompson, who noticeably unshaved, was wearing a plaid shirt fraying at the collar, brown corduroy trousers with unfashionable turn-ups and a sports jacket that seemed to be almost

as old as was he and who greeted him with, "Morning, young Devlin. Where's Iain Cowan?"

Taken aback, he replied, "The Inspector was gone before I arrived for the late shift, sir, but I'm told he's away in his motor to the Victoria Hospital, sir, to check on Constable McGarry. I'm guessing that's why you're here?"

"Aye, correct," Thompson sighed. "I had a phone call from the DCI about another murder, then shortly after that her DI phoned to say she and Smiler were involved in the rescue of a woman from a tenement flat on fire. Any word how the big man is?"

"As far as I'm aware, sir, Smiler's suffering from smoke inhalation, but other than that, he's okay. As for the DCI, the DI told Inspector Bruce at the uniform bar she's away home for the day."

Thompson seemed to ponder this, then nodding, said, "Right, then. You okay handling the shift on your own?"

"Yes, sir, I don't foresee any issues."

"Good man," Thompson nodded, then added, "I'm off to the Viccy, but if I miss Inspector Cowan in the passing, let him know I was here."

"Will do, sir, and can I ask that you tell Smiler we're all asking after him?"

"Of course I will," Thompson grimly smiled, then took his leave of Devlin.

****

An approximate minute from the Cooperative Hypermarket in Morrison, Street, Drew Taylor switched off the blue's and two's, then upon their arrival at the front entrance, they saw a tall and heavy-set man apparently in his mid-fifties, wearing a security shirt and trousers standing with a radio in his hand.

Waving to them, Taylor drew up alongside him then when Roz wound down the window, the security guard gasped, "Two of them. Him and her. Well known to you guys at Orkney Street and according to my neighbour," he waved the radio at them, "they're in the drinks aisle and they've lifted a bottle of whisky each that they're hiding under their jackets. He says…."

Just at that, the radio cackled in his hand and a tinny voice was heard saying, "That's them on their way to the exit, Bobby."

There seemed little point in explaining that they were not G Division officers and so, with a deadpan expression, Taylor, his voice politely

sarcastic, asked, "If you've witnessed them taking the whisky and you know them to be shoplifters, why haven't you escorted them to a till or challenged them to ask if they intend paying for the whisky?"
His face aghast at the very suggestion, the security man blurted out, "They're a right pair of violent buggers, the two of them. It's not my job to get assaulted, that's your job."
"Aye, very good," Taylor drolly replied, then nodding at Roz, they exit the van and with the security guard, strolled over to the entrance to await the arrival of the two shoplifters, hearing on the guard's radio the same voice, but now whispered, "Twenty seconds from the entrance, Bobby. Are the cops there yet?"
"I'm with the officers now," the guard confirmed, then turned to stare at them with the very obvious expression that he'd done his job and it was now down to Strathclyde Police to do theirs.
Within seconds, Taylor and Roz saw the two suspects, each with a hand under their jacket and presumably holding their stolen bottle of whisky, pushing their way through the first set of glass doors, then hurriedly pushing through the outer doors, only to come to a dead stop when they saw the guard flanked by two uniformed police officers.
The male, a man in his mid to late-forties with shoulder length greasy dark hair, wore a pair of soiled tracksuit bottoms and a faded, green coloured parka jacket while the woman, younger by at least fifteen to twenty years with short, dyed jet-black hair and a haggard face and who also wore a black coloured parka jacket and a short denim skirt with stained, once-white trainers.
The pair, obviously dumbstruck stared at the three of them, but it was Taylor who loudly said, "We can do this the easy way or the hard way. Hand the bottles over and come quietly or," he reached down and pulled his wooden baton from his leg pocket, then meaningfully held it low against his leg, "you can go to the jail via the casualty department at the Southern General Hospital."
Roz fought her grin, knowing that her neighbour was bluffing, that Taylor would not use his baton unless it was to defend himself or her, that his threat was simply a bluff.
A tense few seconds passed, but then the male suspect slowly took out the whisky, then bent to lay the bottle down onto the ground before raising his hands, just at the second security guard, a grey-haired man in his fifties, burst through the outer doors.

However, to everyone's surprise, it was the young woman who withdrawing the bottle of whisky from beneath her own jacket, held it by the neck and raising it above her head, with a loud scream suddenly attacked Roz Begley in the apparent belief she was the smaller of the three, so less likely to stop her fleeing.

In the few heartbeats it took for the suspect to race across the ten or so feet to where Roz was standing, whether by instinct or perhaps after watching some of the martial art films so popular at that time, the young officer leaned forward onto her left foot, then bent over. As she did so, the suspect collided with Roz's back just as almost immediately, Roz stood upright.

The suspect's momentum carried her over the young officer, tossing her head over heels, the whisky bottle flying from her hand to shatter on the ground where she painfully landed spread-eagled on her back as the air burst from her lungs.

Turning to the whimpering suspect, Roz fetched her handcuffs from her pouch and turning the now compliant suspect onto her front, secured both wrists before smiling at Taylor, who stunned, grabbed the male suspect and similarly, handcuffed him.

"I hope you know that the police will be responsible for paying for that broken bottle of whisky," the guard called Bobby sniffed at him.

"You ungrateful git," Taylor snapped back at him. "If you pair had done your job and detained these two like you're paid to do…"

But he didn't finish, just took a deep breath, then continuing to stare at the red-faced guard, said, "Roz, secure these two in the back of the van while I take this pairs statements and get labels signed for the whisky."

"What," wide-eyed, Bobby protested, "you're taking the other bottle with you? My boss won't be pleased at that," he vigorously shook his head. "The other cops usually just get a label signed in lieu."

"Well," Taylor angrily stared at him, "if your boss wants to complain, I'll be more than happy to explain that you pair did nothing to detain these two, that you left us to stand in harm's way when you copped out of the job *you're* paid to do."

It was Roz who slamming the rear door of the van on the suspects, calmed the situation when she intervened with, "Drew, maybe let AS know the result of the call and I'll get the details, eh?"

Wordlessly, he nodded and returned to the van while Roz, with a disarming smile at the security guards, fetched her notebook and pen from her handbag and calmly said, "Now then, who's who and what was is the value of the whisky they stole?"

****

Plastic beakers of coffee in their hands, Adam and Jean McGarry were seated on the unforgiving tubular and plastic chairs in the casualty department's waiting room when they saw Inspector Iain Cowan enter the foyer area.

"Uncle Iain," Jean called out and rising from her chair, her beaker in her hand, awkwardly embraced him.

"How's your dad?" Cowan stared from one to the other.

"Better than he should be," Jean moodily replied, while Adam, with a reproving glance at her, said, "He'll be fine, uncle Iain. From what the Staff Nurse told us just five minutes ago, as there's no apparent damage to his larynx and his lungs sound okay, he'll be detained overnight for observation then discharged tomorrow after the consultant has seen him again. That said, he's going to have a sore throat for a couple of days but thankfully, that's all."

"Well," Cowan breathed a sigh of relief, "that's good news. You know he saved an elderly lady and all the tenants from a burning flat, him and the DCI?"

"So we heard," Adam nodded. "Our dad, the hero," he smiled.

"Is he okay for a quick hello?" Cowan stared from one to the other.

It was Jean who replied, "He is, but there's someone with him at the minute. His girlfriend."

"Ah," Cowan grimaced as Jean seized upon his hesitant reply and accusingly asked, "You knew?"

"Not till half an hour ago," he shook his head. "I was going to arrange for someone to pick up a change of clothes and his toothbrush from his house, but then your auntie Elizabeth informed me that she was making that arrangement with a woman called Sally who *apparently* has a house key."

"Yes," Adam nodded, "we've only just met her."

He smiled when he added, "Dad's dark secret."

"And you guys are okay with him having a girlfriend?"

"We are," Adam stared meaningfully at Jean who exhaled, then slowly nodded before she added, "He's been long enough on his own without mum, so maybe it's time someone else worried about the old bugger."

Then she asked, "Why did auntie Elizabeth know and you didn't." Cowan shrugged when he shook his head to reply, "The ways of women. Apparently your dad was waiting on the right time to break the news to you guys first, that he's a little embarrassed that this woman Sally is younger than him. I've only just learned that he'd met some time ago with your auntie Elizabeth to ask her advice and of course, remembering she was your mum's best pal, he felt he needed her blessing before he broke the news. Quite correctly, Adam, she wouldn't tell me before he told you both."

"That's dad," Adam wearily smiled, "always thinking of everyone else before himself."

"She seems okay," Jean's brow furrowed. "Very pretty too and she was genuinely upset about dad being hospitalised."

"Would this be her now?" Cowan nodded behind them.

They both turned to see Sally walking towards them, Smiler's burned jacket carried over her arm and softly smiling at the three of them, though a little uncertain what her reception would be.

It was Adam who greeted her with, "Sally, this is Iain Cowan, dad's best friend. Uncle Ian, Sally…" his face creased, "I'm sorry, I don't know your surname."

"Sally Rodgers," she extended her hand to Cowan, then explained, "I've been sent out because the nurses are changing him into a hospital gown. The Sister said it's likely he'll remain overnight then be discharged in the morning."

"That's what we were told," Adam agreed.

A short silence fell among them, broken when Sally hesitantly said, "Look, it's Sunday and there's not a lot open. The Sister said that after Stuart," she smiled, "your dad, I mean. After they've changed him into a gown, they'll be sending him to a general ward for the night and want him to get some rest and they've suggested that further visiting should now be this evening. So," she glanced at Jean, then Adam, "I live a ten-minute walk away in Arundel Drive. If you'd like to come back for a coffee…?"

They could not know what the offer meant to Sally, that she dreaded the response if it was no.

"Well," it was Cowan who replied for the three of them, "thank you, but I'm due back at the office for late shift. However, I see no reason why you pair can't take up Sally's offer."

"Coffee it is then," smiled Jean, inwardly eager to learn more about this woman who had come into her father's life and who seemed to know much more about both she and her brother while they knew nothing of her.

****

Their prisoners handcuffed and locked in the rear of their van, it was when they were travelling to the G Division headquarters at Orkney Street, that Roz said in a quiet voice, "Look, Drew, about what I said earlier. You and Sharon, I mean. It's really nothing to do with me and I apologise if I came across as huffy. You're a grown man and you must do what is best for you and if it makes you feel any better, you're correct. I really didn't like Sharon. I'm certain you'll find someone who is right for you."

She took a deep breath, then continued, "But if you dump another girlfriend like that, it makes you no better than the likes of Sharon."

He didn't respond other than to nod, but she could not know how much better that simple statement made him feel.

CHAPTER SIXTEEN.

DI Sammy Pollock sat at the office manager's desk in the incident room, reading the daily synopsis of Jeannie Mason's murder, disappointed that there was nothing to add to indicate who killed her. The newly created file for the murder of Albert Moston lay closed and contained just a few pages that included photostat copies of the statements of Peter McCaskill, who discovered the body and negative results from the tenements door to door knocking.

"Here you go, Sammy," he turned to see the office manager, DS Danny Sullivan handing him a much-needed brew before sitting down in the chair opposite.

"So," Sullivan began, "you and the boss are in no doubt the murders are connected?"

"It would certainly seem so," Pollock nodded, "though what the connection is between wee Jeannie and this guy Moston, apart from him using her for sex, is still unknown."

Sullivan's face twisted when he said, "I didn't know Mason, but from what I'm hearing and though I'm speaking ill of the dead, she wasn't the prettiest whore in the parish."

"Don't let Smiler McGarry hear you calling her a whore," Pollock warned. "According to the big man, wee Jeannie was a woman who fell on bad times because of her alcoholism and lost everything, even her dignity. In fact," he sipped at his mug, "I think Smiler had a soft spot for her and looked out for her when he was on the beat."

"Speaking of Smiler, I'm hearing he deserves a medal for pulling Moston's mother out of the burning flat. What do you think?"

Pollock smiled when he replied, "I think it takes a special kind of courage to run into a burning flat, Danny, when the rest of us would be running away from it; so aye, the big man deserves some kind of recognition. Now, back to the murders. I know it's Sunday, but have you managed to make an arrangement for Moston's post-mortem?"

"Tomorrow at midday," Sullivan confirmed. "Oh, and the SOCO expect to deliver the book of photos from the locus sometime this afternoon."

"What about the footprint the young SOCO lassie thought might be the same at both loci?"

"No word about that yet," he shook his head, "but I'm hearing there was a murder last night over in the Milngavie area, so likely the SOCO will be stretched dealing with that too."

Pollock's brow furrowed, wondering how he might be able to progress the investigations that day, then slowly said, "Moston. He was murdered in a close that wasn't too far away from the busy thoroughfare in Calder Street. Now, Saturday night?"

His face twisted. "I'm guessing there was more than a few punters winding their way home along Calder Street from the pubs on Pollokshaws Road. We'll continue with the door to door on Annette Street and let's see if we can persuade the Media Department at Pitt Street to put out a request for information on Radio Clyde and the 'Glasgow News,' something along the lines of where you in the vicinity between the hours of…"

His brow furrowed, then he continued, "Say sometime between ten pm last night and one o'clock this morning."

Hesitating, Sullivan asked, "You don't want to run a public appeal past the boss before you put it out, Sammy?"

He smiled at Sullivan before he replied, "Laura Gemmill has left me in charge today, Danny, so right now, I *am* the boss."

"Fair enough," Sullivan rose to his feet. "Leave me to draft

something that I'll run by you before I get onto Pitt Street."
****

Their prisoners locked up at G Division's headquarters in Govan and the statements turned over to the CID, the crew of Foxtrot Mike Two returned to their vehicle and intimated to the Pitt Street control room they were back on call.

Driving out through the arch onto the cobblestones of Orkney Street, Drew Taylor remarked, "That was a smart piece of thinking, sending that woman over your shoulder, Roz."

"Well, it was either that or being dunted on the coupon with a bottle of whisky," she grinned.

He smiled when he replied, "I think we'll take a turn past Craigie Street and ask how Smiler's doing, if that's okay with you?"

"Oh aye, fine by me," she smiled, inwardly pleased that they seemed to have got over their spat and were now back on level terms.

They were five minutes into their return journey when she took a short breath, then admitted, "You're not the only one breaking up. I'm finishing with Derek. It seems he's not as keen on me as I thought he was."

Seconds passed before Taylor replied, "Oh."

"Oh? Is that it?" she turned towards him.

"Well," he slowly drawled, "whatever I say about you breaking up, I'm guessing I'll get it wrong and you'll fall out with me again, won't you?"

She found this funny and grinning, said, "No, not this time."

"If I'm not being too personal, can I ask what happened between you two?"

"No big drama, but it seems that I wasn't the only love of his love," she sighed.

"He's cheating on you?" his head snapped around to glance at her.

"Apparently so," she shrugged. "My mum saw him in a motor with another woman and from the way he was paying the woman attention, she wasn't a relative or just a casual friend."

"Bloody idiot," Taylor fumed.

"Why, because he was caught, you mean?"

"No," he felt his face burn, "because he cheated on you and now he's lost you."

He turned swiftly to ask, "He has lost you, hasn't he?"

What a curious question, Roz thought, but nodded, then pursed her lower lip when she replied, "Oh, aye, betrayal is something I won't abide."

What she could not guess was that her admittance her boyfriend Derek was to be dumped was the best news that Drew Taylor had heard for some time.

****

DC Barbara McMillan, with nothing for her or her neighbour to show after tramping up and down three tenement closes, trudged up yet another set of tenement stairs, then stopped at the first landing to catch her breath before knocking on the door of the flat.

Presumably her neighbour, DC Morris Kerr, was still within the ground floor flat opposite to where she'd come from, noting details and enjoying a cuppa from the elderly tenant who seemed delighted to have a handsome man call at her door on a dreich Sunday morning.

Her clipboard folder in her left hand, she knocked firmly on the door that half a minute later, was opened by nervous old man, in his seventies she thought, who stared suspiciously at her, then croaked, "I don't do religion, hen. Now, if you don't mind…"

He began to close the door as McMillan raised her free hand and quickly said, "I'm a police officer. CID. I'm only looking for a wee word, sir."

"You're a polis?" his head bobbed up and down as he continued to stare suspiciously at her. "My, but you're awfully glamourous to be a polis, hen."

"Here, look at this," she held out her laminated warrant card, attached around her neck by a plastic ball neck chain.

The old man leaned forward to peer myopically at it, then sighed, "How can I help you, hen; eh, I mean, Detective?"

McMillan graced him with a warm smile, then replied, "Maybe I could come in and I'll tell you why I'm here?"

Pulling the door fully open to admit McMillan, he led her through a darkened hallway to a musty smelling front room where a two-bar electric fire blazed in the hearth.

As if in explanation, he said, "I'm at that age where I feel every chill. Please," he motioned with his hand, "sit down."

The worn, but comfy couch sank beneath McMillan who tiring as the day had drawn on, almost immediately felt a little drowsy from the oppressive heat in the room and so asked, "By any chance, Mr, ah…"

"Davy Collins. That's me, hen."

"Mr Collins. Could I possibly have a drink of water, please?"

Collins returned two minutes later with a glass of water in which two ice cubes floated.

"There you are," he toothlessly smiled at her, then handing her the glass settled himself in the armchair opposite.

Gasping at the chilled water, McMillan felt a little more refreshed, then placing the glass down onto a small wooden side table asked, "You live here alone, Mr Collins?"

"I do, hen," he nodded. "The wife passed two years ago and no sad loss either. Bloody nag she was towards the end," he shook his head.

"Oh," she didn't know how to respond to that.

"Now," she began, "the close two along in Annette Street. Are you aware that a body was discovered there this morning?"

His eyes arrowed when he asked, "Is that why there was polis cars parked there and a white van? I saw them there when I went out to fetch the Sunday paper."

"That'll be correct," she nodded. "A man was discovered murdered in the close at the bottom of the stairs."

"Ah, right," he solemnly nodded as though confirming his thoughts.

"We're checking the flats on the street to try and find any witnesses who might have seen or heard something that could assist us. We believe the murder was committed between the late hours last night or very early in the morning. Where you at home during that time?"

"I'm always at home, hen," he grimaced. "My days of going to the pub are long gone. Three flights up and at my age with my arthritis, I'm more content to get a couple of cans in and watch the Saturday night sports on the tele."

"So, no discoing or dancing then," she smiled at him.

He laughed when he replied, "Not these days, though my missus and I, we were fond of the jazz and the Bepop back in the forties, so we were."

"And being in last night, did you see or hear anything, a fight, shouting, screaming, anything at all?"

His brow furrowed when his lips compressed and he shook his head before he said, "No, hen, sorry, nothing at all, but that said, by half past ten, I'm usually in my bed and the room faces onto the back court, so I don't even hear the bampots travelling along Anette Street after they leave the pubs."

McMillan reached for the water and taken another sip, sighed and rose to her feet when she said, "Well, I'll not bother you anymore, Mr Collins, but thanks for your time and the water."

It was when she saw him narrowing his eyes and his face creasing, some inner sense, some curious feeling caused her to ask, "What?"

"Her below me on the ground flat. Not directly below me, the flat on the other side of the landing."

"Yes?"

"I don't really speak to her, though her and the wife had been pals for a while. Anyway," he shrugged, "it might not be anything, but I know that she's always leaving her bedroom light on at night and right through to the early hours. I think she might be scared of the dark."

"And what is it that you think might be nothing?"

He softly exhaled as he stared at McMillan, then by way of explanation, said, "The wife, she got be a right nag towards the end, picking me up for this and that and used to chin me about smoking in the bedroom. When I had my last fag of the night, she made me open a window and stand there to blow the smoke out of it. Okay," he held up his hand, "I know she's gone, but I kind of got into the habit of smoking at the window now and, well, I'm not even sure of what I might have seen."

McMillan could feel herself tense when she slowly said, "Tell me anyway."

She watched him lick at his lips before he replied, "I thought I heard a noise down below under my window and when I peeked out, it was a figure; a man I'm sure it was, down below and passing her lit window. Bent over too, he was like he'd not wanted to be seen. Look, hen, with my poor eyesight and that, like I said…"

"It's okay, Mr Collins," she suppressed the excitement in her stomach, "please, just tell me what you *think* you saw."

"Well, like I said, a man and he was wearing one of them posh coats."

McMillan's blinked in surprise when she repeated, "A posh coat?"

"Aye, posh. Well, I mean, I couldn't afford one on my wages. It was one of them fancy green ones you see the farmers and the country toffs wearing. Like it's waterproof and with a brown corduroy collar."

"Wait, you mean like a wax jacket or rather, a wax coat?"

"Aye," he was pleased she recognised his description, "That's the one. A long wax coat with a brown collar. Oh, and he was either very fair-haired or bald. I'm sure of that. In fact, I'd probably go with bald."

"How sure are you of that, Mr Collins?"

"Well, pretty sure, because the light was shiny on his head."

****

Moved to a Nightingale general ward, Smiler was still wearing the oxygen mask when he saw a young nurse accompanying his Divisional Commander, Chief Superintendent Jimmy Thompson, enter the ward.

"Here's your man then," the nurse smiled, then turned to point, "Mr McGarry."

Lowering himself down into the chair by the bed, Thompson grimaced when he greeted a confused Smiler with, "Bloody job I had getting in here to see you. That Sister in the casualty, she was like one of Caesars Praetorian Guard and it was only when I told her I was your older brother she said I could have ten minutes. Anyway, Smiler, how you doing?"

Pulling down the mask, he grinned when he replied, "My older brother? You've some nerve, Jimmy. Well, apart from a sore throat, I'm okay and the word is I can be discharged tomorrow."

To anyone watching and who would be unaware of the difference in their ranks, it would seem evident that both men were on friendly terms and now, out of earshot of passers-by, the formality of rank was dropped because Smiler was comfortable to be familiar with the older man he considered to be a friend.

Slowly shaking his head, Thompson said, "That was some risk you took, big man. You could have found yourself trapped in that bloody flat."

"It had to be done, Jimmy, and if I recall back about what, twenty years? When you were a rookie Inspector at Partick. Didn't you launch yourself into the River Clyde after a woman who had drunkenly fell in?"

"All right, all right," Thompson grinned when he raised a hand. "You're admitting you are as daft and I was, so let's call it even.

Anyway, I'll be putting your name and Laura Gemmill's forward for a citation from the Chief, though if it's coming from me, he might just ignore it."

Astutely, his eyes narrowing, Smiler quietly asked, "Is that because of Mattie Devin?"

"Aye, I'm in the bad books as likely you'll know, but with my time left…"

He suddenly had a coughing fit, a hacking cough that bode ill for his health.

When he'd recovered and was again composed, it was Smiler who quietly said, "Tell me you're getting that seen to, that you're not ignoring it, Jimmy."

"Too far gone," Thompson shook his head, then added, "But mark my words, Smiler, I'll see my time out, don't be worrying about that. I wouldn't give that shiny-arse at Pitt Street the pleasure of seeing me go on an ill-health."

They sat in comfortable silence for almost a minute, two old coppers, regardless of rank and each lost in his thoughts before Thompson said, "Your man Devlin, was he worth me giving him back his stripes, albeit temporarily?"

Smiler's face creased when he replied, "You and me, Jimmy, we're old school and we think we've seen and done it and yes, sometimes we privately mock the naivety of the modern cops. But some of these young guys and lassie's in the job now. If they stick it, if the powers that be recognise they need a decent, living wage, there are some really good hardworking people in the job. So, to answer your question, yes; my gut tells me in the short time I've known him, Mattie Devlin will make a right decent boss someday."

"Just like yourself," he added with a wide grin.

"Aye, very good, but pattering me up won't get you any extra overtime, Constable McGarry. Now," he rose from the chair, "I know they're killing me, but I'm heading out now because I'm gasping for a fag."

Leaning forward, he extended his hand and grasped Smiler's hand tightly in both of his.

He continued to hold Smiler's hand when he said, "It's been a long road for me and you, Smiler, and we've not far left to travel. But I'd like to think that if I decide to have a wee farewell doo, you'd come along?"

"Just tell me what telephone kiosk you're having it in, Jimmy, and I'll be there," Smiler laughed.

"Always the joker," Thompson shook his head with a wide grin, then when he turned away, he gave a backward wave of his hand.

****

Leaving her neighbour, DC Morris Kerr, at the rear of the close in Annette Street, Barbara McMillan made her way back to the incident room in Craigie Street to report her discovery of a possible witness to a suspect fleeing the locus of Albert Moston's murder.

Now seated opposite Sammy Pollock with Danny Sullivan listening too, she recounted her conversation with Davy Collins.

"And you say this man Collins, he's seventy-nine years old?" asked Pollock. "What's his eyesight like?"

"He admits it's not great, boss," she grimaced, "but he was looking down into a bright light. So, when he says it was a man he saw wearing a wax coat and more likely bald than fair hair, but that's my assessment," she stressed, "then I believe him."

"Okay, we'll go with that for now."

"Aye, boss, but that's not the best bit," she excitedly exclaimed. "While Morris asked the woman in the ground flat about keeping her light on and she confirmed she does through the night because she's worried about housebreakers thinking her flat might be empty, I went into the rear court to have a look outside her window."

"And?"

"You recall the SOCO woman discovered footprints at the rear of the close at the locus?"

"I do," he nodded, already guessing where this was going.

"Well, there's at least five good footprints in the muddy ground outside the window. I used metal bin lids to cover them as best as I could and I called in for a SOCO examination before I left Annette Street."

With a wide grin, Pollock said, "Nice one, Barbara. I take it someone's standing by the bin lids?"

"Morris volunteered to stand by and liaise with the SOCO when they arrive, boss."

"Excellent. Well," he glanced from Sullivan to McMillan, "if the footprints match those at both murders as I bloody hope they do, we've cut down the suspects to a gender; a man, perhaps bald and who was *probably* wearing a wax coat with a brown coloured collar."

Almost as an afterthought, he asked, "What direction in the back court was the suspect heading to, Barbara, and where might he have exited. Can you shed any light on that?"

"Assuming he was passing Mr Collins view from left to right, he was heading through the rear courts in the general direction towards Calder Street. I had a quick check on the doors to the back of the closes in Annette Street, all of which were unlocked, but there was no indication that the suspect had used any of them to exit onto Annette Street and to be honest," she sighed, "the couple of closes that led into the rear closes in Calder Street; well, he could have used any of them to get out of the back courts. That and there's easy access because most of the boundary fences are gone or broken down."

Nodding, Pollock replied, "Okay, Barbara, grab yourself a coffee, then get back and join Morris. It's Sunday and as Danny pointed out, SOCO might be tied up with a murder over in the north of the city, so it could be any time before they arrive to examine your locus. On that point, the weather's closing in again so do what you have to do to protect the locus and ensure those footprints are there when SOCO arrive."

"Boss," she nodded and stood to leave, only for Pollock to tell her, "You did well, Barbara. I'm phoning the DCI later to update her and to be honest, yours is the only good bit of news I have to pass on." McMillan smiled and left the room.

"What you thinking, Danny?" he asked him.

"Aye, our Barbara's a good-looking woman."

Pollock grinned, then said, "Now, don't be naughty. Her information?"

Sullivan's forehead creased before he replied, "I'm thinking our suspect is local, that he likely knows the area and wherever he exited back onto the street, it was far enough from the locus of Moston's murder so as not to draw any suspicion upon himself."

"Agreed," Pollock nodded.

****

Acting Sergeant Mattie Devlin was out on his own in the supervisory panda when the radio cackled into life, requesting he return to Craigie Street to uplift Inspector Cowan.

"Five minutes," he quickly responded, then upon his arrival, saw Cowan standing waiting for him in the entrance arch to the building, his raincoat draped across his arm.

"How you getting on?" Cowan asked when he settled himself into the passenger seat.

"Fine, sir, and thanks for arranging those two early shift cops. Made it a while lot easier putting the shift out and they're now all neighboured."

"Anything doing?"

"Foxtrot Mike Two attended a call to the Govan side, the Cooperative Hypermarket, where they arrested two shoplifters. The last I heard is that they've handed over the suspects and the paperwork, so they should be back in the Division now."

"How's the big man?" he glanced at Cowan.

"I didn't get to see him, but his kids were there. I say kids," Cowan smiled, "Adam's twenty-eight now and married and his sister, Jean, I think she's now twenty-two or twenty-three."

Cowan didn't mention Smiler's girlfriend, believing that was a story for his old friend to tell.

Cowan continued, "According the what they told me, Smiler didn't suffer any real damage to his throat and will probably be discharged tomorrow sometime."

"Good," Devlin sighed. "I've not known him for too long, but he comes across as a right decent man."

His eyes narrowed when he asked, "Did you see the Div Commander when you were at the hospital?"

"Mr Thompson?" Cowan's face expressed his surprise. "No, I didn't."

"He popped by when you had gone, asking for you and said he was going to the Viccy to see Smiler."

Cowan shook his head, then said, "We've obviously missed one another. Now, who's neighbouring who on what beat?"

While Devlin explained who was where, Cowan's thought were elsewhere and he wondered, why was Jimmy Thompson taking the time to visit Smiler, but then inwardly decided that was the old guy's style, that Thompson was a boss who looked after his people.

"Right," he began when Devlin had finished his report, "let's get the shift's locations and start signing a few notebooks.

****

Smiler's son, Adam, and his daughter, Jean, bid their farewells at the door of Sally Rodgers flat and as she closed it behind them, she leaned her back against it, then sighed deeply. That had gone better than she had thought or even hoped for.

All those months of worrying what they might think of her, a divorced woman who was fifteen years their father's junior, dreading they might consider her to be some sort of floozy, a gold-digger only out to fleece Stuart of his pension and commutation, just like that woman he had told her about, the wife who had did the same thing to his new neighbour.

She smiled almost with relief when both had agreed that she alone visit Stuart that evening, that they would call upon him tomorrow when he had returned home, also agreeing that if she was up for it, she could be the one to pick him up when he was discharged.

And on that point, her eyes narrowed when she mentally made a note, I'd better phone and let my assistant manager know I'll not be coming in tomorrow.

Making her way through to the front room, she lifted the empty coffee mugs and with a satisfied smile, returned them to the kitchen and placed them in the basin in the sink.

But then, stood staring out of the window into the rear court below, her thoughts turned to her own dark secret; the secret that she knew must eventually be disclosed if she continued their relationship and her brow creased with apprehension.

A cold chill swept through her, causing her to tightly wrap both arms around herself when she wondered; how then, when Adam and Jean found out, would they react to their father's girlfriend having a criminal record?

CHAPTER SEVENTEEN: 09.05am, Monday 12 March 1979.

Chief Inspector Lizzie Whitmore was her usual early self and at her desk when just after nine o'clock that Monday morning, her door was knocked then pushed open by a slim man with receding fair hair, who wore a white shirt, red tie and blue two-piece business suit. The man, she saw, was accompanied by a dark-haired woman a little shorter than his five feet eight, who wore an open-neck grey blouse over a charcoal two-piece skirted suit and who wore a frown on her plain, unattractive and make-up free face.

"Lizzie Whitmore," the man greeted her with a smile.

"Well, well, Marty McKenna. Long-time no see," she stood up from her desk and with a wide grin, extended her hand, then her brow creasing, asked, "What are the rubber heels doing calling on me, then?"

It didn't escape Whitmore's notice that the woman seemed to scowl at Whitmore's joking reference to the Complaints and Discipline Department's derogatory nickname, commonly used amongst the officers of the Force.

Grabbing one of the two chairs in front of Whitmore's desk, McKenna sat down then with a hand towards her, introduced the woman.

"This is my neighbour, Sergeant Shona Mulvey."

Tight-lipped, Mulvey barely nodded at Whitmore before she too sat down in the second chair.

"Right, no doubt this isn't a social visit," Whitmore sighed, "so before you give me the bad news, can I offer you guys a tea or a coffee?"

McKenna pursed his lips when he replied, "Yeah, that sounds fine to me. Coffee for us both, milk only."

When Whitmore again rose from her chair to leave her office and collect the drinks, McKenna also rose from his chair, telling her, "While you're doing that, Lizzie, I'll nip to the gents. Too many early morning cuppas'," he grimaced.

Leaving Mulvey alone in the office, it was in the corridor outside that McKenna, lowering his voice, stopped Whitmore with a raised hand to confide, "Listen, Lizzie, I didn't want her hearing. I've been saddled with Mulvey for over a month now and she's a right tight-arse when it comes to dealing with complaints. No discretion whatsoever. Everything is black and white to her. Good guy, bad guy, know what I mean? That and I suspect she's a boss's tout too."

Whitmore had known McKenna, who like her was now a Chief Inspector, since both had been uniform sergeants serving in Easterhouse and believed him to be one of the Force's good guys.

"Thanks for the heads-up," she sighed, "now I'll fetch the coffee and when I get back, you can tell me why you're about to ruin my day."

****

Returned to her desk, Lizzie Whitmore first phoned the uniform bar to intimate that she was not to be disturbed, that she was currently in a meeting, then turning to McKenna, formally asked, "So, Chief Inspector McKenna, what seems to be the issue?"

"First and foremost," he began, "Sergeant Mulvey and I are in the very early stage of what seems to be a serious complaint against one of the constables stationed here at Craigie Street. A Constable Andrew Taylor."

Surprised, Whitmore's eyes narrowed when she repeated, "Taylor? Yes, one of our harder working officers and currently crewing Foxtrot Mike Two. He's on late shift at the minute. Can you disclose the nature of the complaint?"

"As I said," McKenna exhaled, "the complaint only come in this morning. A telephone call from a former girlfriend alleging he was violent towards her. We've yet to formally interview this young woman, but likely as you know, we usually obtain the veracity of the complaint before informing the officer's Division, but we go a long way back, Lizzie," he smiled at her, "so take this as a courtesy visit, giving you a heads-up."

Whitmore glanced at Mulvey's face and guessed that McKenna's decision did not sit well with the sergeant.

"So," McKenna continued, "if you have any insight that you can share of Taylor's private life or relationship with the ex-girlfriend, a woman called Sharon Crosbie, it would be useful in assisting with our investigation."

Whitmore took a deep breath before she shook her head and replied, "I've no knowledge of Taylor's private life, but knowing him as I do, he's one of the last people I'd imagine would be violent to a girlfriend or for that matter, any woman."

"But then again," Mulvey spoke for the first time in what Whitmore later described as a cold and emotionless voice, "you admitted yourself, *Ma'am*, you don't know anything about his private life."

It didn't escape Whitmore's attention that Mulvey almost spat out the word, 'Ma'am.'

But then she replied, "And it's a telephone call. How can you conduct a discreet investigation based on a single telephone call?"

It was McKenna who replied in a voice oozing sarcasm, "You know the polis, Lizzie. Everyone is guilty till we prove them innocent."

That earned him a sharp, reproving glance from Mulvey, who snapped, "I don't think that's entirely fair, sir!"

"Lighten up, Sergeant," he smiled humourlessly at her, then turning to Whitmore, added, "Well, we'll interview this young woman and see what she's got to say for herself and I'll keep you posted. However, as you'll be aware, no doubt…"

"I don't inform Taylor of the complaint," she sighed.

"Indeed," he took a last sip of coffee then rose to his feet.

Turning to Mulvey, he told her, "I'll get you downstairs in the car, Sergeant."

It was clear from her expression she didn't like being so summarily dismissed, that she suspected the conversation about the complaint would continue without her.

Turning, she left the office.

Whitmore nodded at the closed door when she said, "You've got your work cut out with that one."

"Aye," he shook his head, then with a grim smile, said, "When we get back to Pitt Street, I've no doubt that after she's had a word with him, the Superintendent will be wanting to see me later today about my attitude to the job."

He turned to leave, then stopped to say, "I'm hearing at headquarters that your boss, Jimmy Thompson, has incurred the wrath of the Chief? Something about promoting a cop who the Chief had *demoted*?"

"Yes," she nodded. "A young guy, Mathew Devlin. Jimmy's made him an acting sergeant for the time being, seeing as how we're so short of supervisors and Devlin has experience in a supervisory role."

"Devlin," he nodded, his eyes narrowing. "Yes, I recognise the name. Two of our lot are looking for his former wife. Something to do with her being a bigamist, is that it?"

"That's it. Took the poor sod for his savings and almost wrecked his career."

"I'm not completely *au fait* with the case, but I understand they had an address for the ex-wife, but it turned out to be a bummer, so they're still looking for her."

He too shook his head when he replied, "You never know the next in this bloody job, do you? Anyway," he stared meaningfully at her, "a word to the wise to your boss. The Chief has made it *very* clear to anyone who'll listen that he's gunning for Thompson and between you and me, I'm hearing he's planning a surprise visit, hoping to catch him smelling of drink. Does that mean anything to you, Lizzie?"

She took an inward breath before she replied, "I'm grateful for that, Marty. That's definitely one I owe you."

"No, Lizzie," he shook his head and stared for several seconds at her before he softly added, "You covered my arse more than a few times at Easterhouse, so you owe me nothing."

More sprightly now, he said, "Right then, I'll be off, but I'll stay in touch regarding this young cop, Taylor. Oh, and if I *should* hear anything about a surprise visit…"

He left the rest unsaid.

When he'd gone, Whitmore phoned down to Thompson's secretary, Doris, then said, "Tell him I'm coming down and can you organise two cups of strong coffee, please."

****

Returned to work that morning, DCI Laura Gemmill sat at Danny Sullivan's desk and perused the timeline file of Albert Moston's murder, her eyes lighting up when she read of DC Barbara McMillan's discovery of a potential witness and the footprints in the rear court.

"This paragraph here, Danny. Am I to assume that SOCO did recover footprints?"

"They did, boss. That young SOCO lassie travelled over from the murder locus in Milngavie to personally take plaster casts and she reckons she'll have a result by midday, today. Seems she stayed on well past her finishing time *and* it seems that the SOCO's overtime budget too is exhausted, so fair play to her. Oh, and you're aware the PM is set for midday as well."

"Good."

Her brow furrowed when she glanced around, then asked, "Is it me or is the DI late getting in?"

"Ah, car trouble again, boss," his eyebrows raised. "That old car of his broke down on the way to work."

She slowly shook her head when she remarked, "That's two or three times this month. When the hell is Sammy going to get himself something reliable?"

Sullivan grinned when he replied, "He keeps insisting the old

Humber is a classic, but it's more a wreck that's held together by its last paint job and string."

As if on cue, his face red from rushing upstairs, Sammy Pollock staggered into the room, his face purple and gasping for breath.

"Sorry…I'm…late…boss," he deeply inhaled.

"Bloody…car…broke…down…again."

Gemmill fought back her laugh, then with a shake of her head, said, "No problem. Danny, can you muster a cuppa for the DI?"

"On my way, boss," Sullivan nodded with a grin.

Giving him a minute to compose himself, Gemmill was about to speak, but stopped when Pollock raised a hand to ask, "How are you this morning? Any ill-effect from your smoke inhalation?"

"No, I'm fine, thanks Sammy. I'm hearing too that Smiler should be discharged sometime today, so that's good news and the old woman, Mrs Moston?"

"She recovered quicker than did Smiler," he shook his head, "and she's now in the care of the social work. I visited her and tried to explain about her son's death, but to be honest, boss, it went right over her head. I'm no expert, but I think she's too far gone for any lucidity. When I tried to explain about her son, Albert, she hardly even recognised the name. It seems to me the fire and the stress of it all has sent her over the edge."

He grimaced when he added, "You know, boss, it might be a blessing in disguise for her, because she won't have to suffer the loss and pain of knowing he's been murdered."

"About that," she held up the timeline file. "Good work by young McMillan."

"She's a smart one right enough" he nodded.

"Now, the PM. I'm thinking of taking Lucy Chalmers with me while you man the fort here, so who else do you suggest?"

"Why not McMillan and her neighbour, Morris Kerr? I'd already considered them to handle the productions for Moston's murder."

He continued with, "I'm just being cautious, boss. I didn't want to combine both murder productions in the *unlikely* event they are separate investigations, albeit we do believe them to be connected. Besides, Morris is an old hand at dealing with productions and it's an ideal opportunity for him to tutor Barbara on the system."

"Okay, I agree. Keep both murder productions separate in the meantime until we have conclusive proof the murders *are* related. I

suspect when the young SOCO lassie returns with the results of the footprint plaster casts, it will confirm the same suspects footprints for both murders, then we can link both productions as one investigation. Let Kerr and McMillan know to attend the PM."
"Right," she reached for the second timeline file.
"Jeannie Mason's murder. Nothing new come in over the last twenty-four hours, then."
"No, boss," his face creased.
She glanced at her wristwatch, then said, "I'm nipping downstairs to brief the Div Commander on the little we have so far. In the meantime," she sighed, "and I know it's a bloody pain, but carry on with the door to door."
****
Mattie Devlin was at home when the phone rung and answering it, his heart sank when the caller identified himself as a Chief Inspector McLean of the Force's Complaints and Discipline Department.
"Not wanting to pour petrol on an open wound, Constable Devlin…" McLean hesitated, then with an apologetic sigh, said, "Sorry, I understand it's acting Sergeant Devlin."
"That's correct, sir. A temporary appointment to supplement the shortfall of junior supervisors in the Division."
"Okay, then let's make this easier. Can I call you Mathew?"
"Of course, sir."
"Well, Mathew, you'll be aware that responsibility for tracking down the woman who bigamously married you was handed to my Department, though God alone knows why, but there we are. The Chief commands and we obey."
Devlin's eyes narrowed as he wondered, was there a trace of bitterness in McLean's voice? "As it happens," McLean continued, "we thought we got lucky with an address for her, but it turned out to be a no go. However, on Monday last week, it seems that Janice Goodwin used her passport in her own name, that's if it *is* her real name," Devlin heard the Chief Inspector sigh, "as photographic identification to hire a car from a city centre garage in Mitchell Street. The young woman who dealt with the hire was a bit suspicious of her, though I'm not sure why because I haven't yet spoken with the assistant. What I do know is the assistant at the car company reported the hire as suspicious to a bar officer at Stewart Street police station, but it sounds like nothing was done at the time.

It also begs the question if the assistant was *that* suspicious," Devlin could hear the anger in McLean's voice, "why the hell she went ahead with the bloody hire at all."

After a few seconds pause during which it sounded like McLean was composing himself, he continued, "That said, it took five days before the car company reported the forty-eight-hour hire was overdue. On the basis of that information, on Saturday afternoon a retrospective PNC lookout for the vehicle's registration was issued by Stewart Street CID and almost immediately, they got a hit. It seems that on that very morning, the vehicle boarded a Belfast bound ferry in Cairnryan. Regretfully," Devlin could once more hear the irritation in McLean's voice, "and again I have no explanation why, the vehicles registration was checked, but of course wasn't at that time on the PNC as logged stolen, so there was no cause to question the driver. Anyway, a further check later that afternoon with the Ports Control Unit at Cairnryan recorded the driver of the car identified herself to the PCU cops as Janice Goodwin and produced a passport in that name and the assumption is, it *was* our suspect."

"So, she's travelled to Northern Ireland, sir?"

"And therein lies the problem," McLean sighed. "I'm not sure if you're aware, Mathew, but no extradition treaty currently exists between the UK and Southern Ireland, so if you want my opinion?"

"Yes sir, of course."

"I'm thinking that our suspect has scarpered south over the border, then likely boarded a plane abroad, so she could be anywhere at the minute."

"And we've no way of knowing where she could be?"

"Well, not officially no," he heard McLean wheeze. "However, I do have a *quid pro quo* agreement with a contact in the An Garda Siochana and earlier this morning, I requested a check be made for the stolen hire car at Dublin airport and other airports that serve flights to Europe. If we can trace the hire car then we might be able to backtrack what flight destination our suspect took. Needless to say, as the primary witness and complainer in the case against Goodwin, I'll contact you if I get a positive result."

Devlin rubbed thoughtfully at his brow, then asked, "The short answer then, sir, is that at this time, Janice is on the run and the case against her will be shelved unless she returns to the UK?"

There was a pause before McLean slowly replied, "I can only guess that you would have wanted this to be resolved as quickly as possible, Mathew, but yes; you're absolutely correct. Even if I do trace her destination abroad and if that country has an extradition treaty with the UK, whether or not a Scottish court will issue an international warrant for a charge of bigamy…oh, and theft of the hire vehicle," he added almost as an afterthought, "I'm not certain. However, as you know, bigamy is a common law criminal offence in Scotland and more unusual than you might think. However, I will be submitting a case to the Procurator Fiscal. Our suspect, who we know as Janice Goodwin, will remain on the PNC as wanted here in Scotland, so if she should return to the UK under that name, she will be arrested."

After the call had concluded, Devlin stood for several minutes at the small table in the hallway, the phone still clutched in is hand, his anger knowing no bounds that Janice was getting away with it, that her deceit and theft, not only of his hard-earned money, but his dignity and his rank too…

The beeping of the phone in his hand brought him back to his senses and with a resigned sigh, he replaced the phone into the cradle and made his way into the kitchen.

****

Unaware of the allegation made against him, Drew Taylor cheerfully whistled his way out of the shower and wearing his bathrobe, made his way into the kitchen to prepare his breakfast.

Roz Begley's admission the previous day, that she was dumping her unfaithful boyfriend, had cheered him no end and for the first time since they had met, he believed there might be an opportunity to court her.

But how to go about it without seeming to be taking advantage of her break-up?

Thoughtfully, he prepared his breakfast, his mind considering several says he might display his interest in Roz, dismissing each one and knowing that smart as she is, she'd see through them.

Flipping the eggs and sausages in the frying pan, he finally decided that frustrating as it would be, the only solution to his problem was to continue to remain as her friend, to be there for her and let the future take its course.

****

That morning, waking later than she had for some time, Sally

Rodgers, felt the effect of her fitful night and wearily arose from her bed.

Not usually a woman with issues sleeping, meeting Stuart's children yesterday had unnerved and concerned her, not least because her first thought being she was deceiving them, that she was not the woman they might think her to be.

After making her toilet, her first phone call was to her assistant manager to inquire if the early morning routine within the City Bakeries shop in Allison Street was running as usual, that there was nothing requiring Sally's attendance.

"No, you're fine, hen, you just see to your friend getting out of the hospital," her assistant told her, though not admitting it was killing the older woman not knowing who the friend might be and who suspected it was likely a man.

Sally could not know that she was a popular boss to the eight full and part-time staff and though younger than most of them, could be relied upon to have their back and when they genuinely needed a few hours or even a day off, would mark them as working and ensure their pay was not docked by the head office management.

And so if Sally, who rarely if ever took time off, needed a day to herself for whatever reason, the staff to a woman covered for their boss.

But that didn't prevent their mutual curiosity and so it was decided among them when she returned on Tuesday, she would be teased mercilessly to find out if indeed at long last, there was a man in Sally's life.

Her second phone call was to the general ward at the Victoria Hospital to inquire how Stuart McGarry was that morning and if there was any information about his discharge.

"The consultant will be doing his rounds sometime after ten this morning," the nurse told her. "Perhaps give us a call back about half past or nearer eleven?"

Thanking the nurse Sally slowly exhaled, then decided on a bath. Twenty minutes later, luxuriating in the hot and scented water, her thoughts turned once more to Stuart's son and daughter and her chest tightening, she involuntarily shivered when she wondered; how could he break the news about her past and what would be their reaction?

Of course, they had discussed it at length, what he would tell them, and while Stuart had assured her that Adam and Jean would understand, Sally was not to certain, even reminding him that she knew if it became public knowledge he was dating someone with a criminal past, it might possibly affect his job with the police.

She smiled when she recalled his reaction to that, reminding *her* that she was more important to him than any job and also that with the time he had left in the Force, what did it matter?

If only she had someone she could discuss the issue with, then her brow furrowed when a further thought came to her.

Though they had not met other than converse of the phone, she was aware that Stuart absolutely trusted his deceased wife's friend, Elizabeth, and idly wondered; if he did, why then, shouldn't she?

****

As expected, the pathologist informed DCI Laura Gemmill and her team that the post-mortem examination concluded with the result Albert 'Moxy' Moston was indeed fatally stabbed and therefore, murdered.

"However," the pathologist, a small paper production bag in his hand, had in a dramatic voice more suited to the amateur productions that he so enjoyed, "there is something of significance that you should be aware of."

Returning to Craigie Street, Gemmill's disappointment that there was no further information that might have identified Moston's killer was alleviated somewhat when following her into her office, Pollock said, "The SOCO lassie arrived shortly after you left for the PM, boss. She confirms the plaster casts from the locus of Jeannie Mason's murder and that of Moston are identical."

"Well," Gemmill breathed a sigh of relief, "that confirms what we suspected, Sammy."

"And further," he smiled, "she said the shoes are a size nine, so if we can trace the shoes she'll match them to the casts."

Though he was stating the obvious, she didn't comment on it, but merely nodded before asking, "Any word on our man, Smiler?"

"Word is he's to be discharged today, boss, but I'll keep my ears open for any further news."

"Right then," she took a breath, "coffee then we'll review what little we have."

****

When he pushed open the door to the Sergeants Room, Inspector

Iain Cowan sensed that there was something amiss with his acting sergeant, Mattie Devlin, and so asked, "You okay?"

Devlin, how forehead knitting, quietly replied, "Before you put the shift out on patrol, sir, you got a minute?"

Cowan drew up a chair and sitting opposite, rested his clenched hands on his lap when he said, "What's up, Mattie."

He took a deep breath before recounting the phone call from the Complaints and Discipline's Chief Inspector McLean.

"And she's in the wind, then?"

"Sounds like it," Devlin sighed.

"I have to ask. Is that a good thing or a bad thing?"

"How do you mean?" Devlin was puzzled.

"Well, if she's on her toes and likely to be gone for good, say, then no trial and no reporting in the media."

"And no red face for me or pointed fingers from the rest of the Force?"

"Well," Cowan grimaced, "that's surely a good thing, yes?"

"And the bad thing being if she *is* arrested, then I'll forever be known as the idiot who was completely taken for a mug by a woman pretending to be my wife."

Cowan shrugged in reply.

"So," Devlin wryly smiled, "I'm to hope she gets a clean getaway?"

"Hmm, think of it as more, out of sight, out of mind."

The desk phone rang and when Cowan heard Devlin respond with his name, saw the sergeant raise a finger, then glance towards the Inspector when he told the caller, "Yes, sir. I'm just about to commence late shift."

Almost a full minute followed with Cowan watching Devin, who listening intently, then said, "Thank you, sir, and yes," he nodded, "I'll send a statement to your office."

When he returned the phone to the cradle, he told Cowan, "That was Chief Inspector McLean from the rubber heels. His contact over in the Irish police reported the hire car was discovered in the long stay car park at Dublin Airport. It seems from the ticket on the windscreen the car was parked there on Saturday and further inquiry revealed that a woman calling herself Janice Goodwin caught a late flight that evening to Barcelona."

"So," Cowan gently smiled, "she's definitely in the wind then?"

"Seems so, sir," Devlin softly exhaled.

"Money you can always save up again, Mattie, but pride and dignity are a little harder to recover, so let's tell ourselves that's a good thing, eh?"
Before Devlin could reply the phone again ran, but this time when he answered it, he glanced over when he handed it to Cowan and said, "It's Chief Inspector Whitmore."
"Ma'am," Cowan replied, then Devlin heard him say, "Two minutes."
Handing the phone back, Cowan, who seemed visibly puzzled, said, "Seems like you're putting the shift out, Mattie. I'm wanted upstairs, though why," he shook his head, "I have not a clue."

CHAPTER EIGHTEEN.

Chief Superintendent Jimmy Thompson was no fool and though he doubted the Chief Constable would surprise him with a visit in an attempt to catch him smelling of booze, realised that Liz Whitmore believed it and so that was good enough for him.
Three strong coffee's and a half packet of spearmint mints swallowed that his secretary, Doris, had fetched from the local grocers, Thompson critically examined himself in the full-length mirror attached to the back of the door in his tiny, private toilet, then dabbed with a damp handkerchief at the unidentifiable stain on the right-hand breast pocket of his tunic.
"Bugger it," he muttered to his reflection, "If the sod does arrive, I'll have to do as I am."
Returning to his desk, he fetched a bottle of Brut aftershave from the top drawer and liberally splashed some on his face, then called through to Doris to come in to see him.
When she pushed open his door, he asked her to prepare a tray of cups and saucers and have the kettle boiled.
"Not a good idea, sir," she shook her head.
"Why ever not?"
"This is supposed to be a surprise visit," she explained. "I don't suppose the Chief's that stupid, so if you have things prepared he'll guess you were tipped off."

"Ah, right, and that's why you get paid the big bucks to manage me," he grinned at her.

"Aye, if only," she frowned at him, then waved her hand in front of her face before she added, "You using that aftershave again?"

Before he could respond, she glanced at the room carpet, then said, "Give me a couple of minutes to grab the hoover from the cleaners cupboard in the corridor and while I'm doing that, can I suggest you tidy up your desk? It looks like you've had a couple of toddlers playing football on top of it."

Doris had just closed the door when she opened it again, her eyes wide in warning when she stammered. "The Chief Constable to see you, Mr Thompson."

She'd hardly had time for the announcement when behind her, the portly figure of Chief Constable Arthur Donaldson rudely pushed passed her, closely followed by a young and smartly turned out uniformed Superintendent, who Thompson recognised as the flunky brought from Donaldson's previous Force when he arrived at Strathclyde.

Respectful of the rank whether or not he liked the man, Thompson rose to his feet and with a forced smile, greeted Donaldson with, "Good afternoon, Chief Constable. This is an unexpected..." he hesitated, for it was no pleasure, then added, "visit."

Donaldson did not respond, other than to turn to Doris and snap, "Tea, white, two sugar and a white coffee for the Superintendent." With a wave of his hand, Doris was dismissed, but it didn't escape Thompson's attention that her eyes were murderous.

Striding towards Thompson's desk, Donaldson leaned across it then taking a long sniff, said, "Seems to me, Mr Thompson, you appear to be wearing perfume. Place smells like a bloody brothel in here."

With a soft smile, he nodded, "I bow to your own experience, Chief Constable, for I myself have never actually *been* inside a brothel."

Donaldson's mouth gaped open and his usual ruddy complexion reddened even more, but a retort escaped him.

Nor did it escape Thompson's notice the Superintendent, who stood in the corner of the room, fought his own grin.

Donaldson's mouth tightly set, he slumped down into the chair in front of the desk, permitting Thompson to resume his seat while the pokerfaced Superintendent moved the second chair to a position some feet behind Donaldson. Then to Thompson's surprise, the

Superintendent removed a police notebook from his tunic pocket. Opening it, he sat with it on his lap and pen in hand.

"So, sir," Thompson addressed Donaldson, "what might I ask is the purpose of your visit today?"

The Chief glared at Thompson with what he believed to be an intimidating stare, something he had practised many times in front of mirrors, before he replied in his trademark bullish voice, "I understand that following my demotion of a sergeant to the rank of constable last Thursday, upon his arrival at F Division, you almost immediately appointed him to the rank of acting sergeant and in direct contravention of my instruction."

Thompson adopted a blank expression when he replied, "I'm sorry, sir, but you've lost me. What instruction?"

"Eh, well, after I demoted him," Donaldson blustered.

"I don't recall any specific instruction coming from your office that I could not appoint Constable Devlin to the acting rank, for as likely you know, I am seriously short of junior supervisors. It seemed to me that not to utilise Devlin's previous experience was a great waste."

In those few seconds that followed Donaldson's outraged silence, Thompson reminded himself of the Chief Constable's career.

A recruit to Grampian Police, Donaldson was appointed as a constable to a small village outside Aberdeen; Cults, Thompson thought it called, where he'd spent four years doing nothing. Those four years of idleness had permitted Donaldson time to study and back to back, achieve both his standard and elementary police examinations. The rumour was then that having gained both certificates, a supportive family member of influence had a word in the right ear that saw Donaldson promoted to sergeant at police headquarters in Aberdeen, where he was to spend the next five years, finally achieving the rank of Inspector. It was at this rank the Force's Personnel Department decided the newly promoted Inspector should accrue some street experience and posted him to the rural setting in Fairley that neither involved shift work nor anything other than administering the local officers. Nor, it was widely suggested, did it involve detecting or arresting miscreants.

On this occasion, with plenty of spare time on his hands, Donaldson took an interest in Accountancy and in 1971, was one of the first students to commence studies at the new Open University, finally gaining a second-class degree.

With a degree in hand, his rise was thereafter meteoric, transferring to an administration post as Chief Superintendent in the Lothian and Borders Police, then an appointment as an Assistant Chief Constable with the Cumbria Constabulary. Hardly in place six months, Donaldson was readily available to assume the post of the incumbent Deputy Chief Constable of that Force when the Deputy suffered a serious health issue that resulted in his early retiral.

And so when in 1978, the post of Chief Constable of Strathclyde Police became vacant, Donaldson was the successful applicant, though neither Thompson nor many others ever understood the Police and Fire Committee's logic of hiring a man with so limited practical police experience.

However, it soon became apparent that Donaldson was hired as a hatchet man, having assured the committee that he was keen to cut the Police budget and commenced with what he described as the deadwood; officers who had suffered injuries that prevented them from operational duties, but had been kept on in administrative roles to enable them to finally claim their pensions. As a result, within his first year Donaldson had disposed of several dozen such officers and further damaged the bruised morale of a Force already suffering financial hardships.

And so, having inflicted such cuts, he was *not* a popular Chief Constable.

The door was knocked, then pushed open by Doris with one hand while in the other, she balanced a tray with three cups and saucers and a plate of plain digestive biscuits.

Thompson choked back a snigger, knowing that his secretary kept a packet of Jammie Dodgers in her desk drawer, but obviously didn't consider the Chief Constable worthy of them.

To his credit, the young Superintendent jumped up from his seat to help her and with a smile to Doris, took the tray, then dished out the cups and saucers.

Noisily clearing his throat at the distraction, Donaldson stared again at Thompson, then directly snapped at him, "Have you been drinking, Mr Thompson? The scent you are using. Is that to cover the smell of booze? Drinking alcohol, I mean, *not* tea," he added, thinking himself clever to pre-empt a smartarse response from

Thompson.

The atmosphere in the room became immediately tense and caused Doris, just about to leave, to stop and turn to stare in turn at the Chief, then with alarm, at Thompson.

But then to Doris's dread, Donaldson added, "I believe a breath test should be conducted."

Even the Superintendent's eyes widened in disbelief at the suggestion.

As calmly as he dared, Thompson returned Donaldson's stare before he lifted the phone on his desk, then dialling an internal number, calmly said, "Chief Inspector Whitmore. I have the Chief Constable with me. Please attend at the uniform bar and collect an unused breathalyser kit, then come to my office. Thank you."

"Mrs Whitmore will be just a few minutes, Chief Constable," his voice remained calm, though his stomach was turning summersaults. Staring over Donaldson's shoulder, he said, "You may return to your desk, Doris, and thank you for the tea and coffee."

The next six minutes passed in absolute silence, broken when the door was knocked and then pushed open by Liz Whitmore, who greeted Donaldson with a nod and "Sir."

"You took you time," Donaldson harshly responded.

"Chief Inspector Whitmore," Thompson stared at her, his eyes indicating that no blame was to be attached to her, "in response to an allegation made by Chief Constable Donaldson that I have alcohol in my system while on duty, you will apply a breath test to me."

"Sir?" brow knitting, she turned to glance at Donaldson, who ignored her.

"Chief Constable," Thompson turned to humourlessly smile at him, "are you happy for the Chief Inspector to conduct the breath test?"

Donaldson, satisfied from what he had learned of Thompson, was confident that there was no way the older man could possibly pass the test, so nodded with a satisfied smirk.

"Chief Inspector," Thompson nodded at her to begin.

They watched a now pale faced Whitmore break the seal on the previously unopened green coloured, rigid plastic box, then removing one of the small, clear glass phials from within, proceeded by breaking both ends of the phial that contained the minute, yellow-coated crystals the breath must pass through. That done, she inserted the balloon on one side of the phial and the new mouthpiece in the other end, thereby completing the process.

With a glance at the Chief Constable, she said, "As you're aware, sir, when I apply the test, Mr Thompson will blow into the mouthpiece and if the chemicals react to alcohol in his breath, they will turn green."

"Yes, yes," Donaldson irritably replied. "I know all that, just get on with it."

"Sir," her gritted teeth indicated her unexpressed anger.

When she held the mouthpiece towards Thompson, Donaldson eagerly sat forward to ensure there was nothing amiss, that the older man fully inflated the bag.

As the few seconds it took to inflate the small bag passed, Thompson returned the item to Whitmore to inspect.

Removing the bag and the mouthpiece, she stared at the glass phial in her hand, then bluntly said, "Negative. The crystals have *not* turned to green."

"What!" Donaldson screamed then held out his hand for the phial as Whitmore, handing it over, added, "The crystals are *completely* yellow, sir, so no trace of alcohol whatsoever. It's a negative test."

Staring unbelievingly at the phial, he angrily threw it down, then watched it skitter across the desktop to fall into a far corner of the room.

"Again!" Donaldson hissed at her, but Whitmore shook her head, then replied, "No, sir, as the officer conducting the test and regardless of your rank. I will *not* conduct a second test on my Chief Superintendent because you simply refuse to accept the result of the first test!"

"You…you…" pointed a finger at Whitmore. "You did something to the test!"

Her eyes widening and face expressing her shock at his allegation, she said, "Are you accusing me of faking the test, sir? Is that what you're implying?"

"Chief Constable, sir!"

They all turned to see the uniformed Superintendent now on his feet, his pronounced English accent clearly directing a warning to Donaldson.

"I really think it's time to go, sir," he stared hard at him.

"But before you do go, Chief Constable," Thompson calmly addressed him, though his stomach was again twisting in his guts, "I must remind you that you made a completely malicious allegation against me, my character and my good name in front of not only my Chief Inspector, but a civilian employee too. That and you accused my Chief Inspector of falsifying a breath test. Please be under no illusion that I intend making an *official* complaint against you."

With a final, hateful glance at both Thompson and Whitmore, Donaldson wordlessly left the room, followed by his Superintendent who gently closed the door behind him, but not without a meaningful glance at Whitmore; a glance that somehow unsettled and confused her.

His legs shaking, Thompson slumped down into his chair as Whitmore moved around the desk to slump down in the chair vacated by Donaldson.

"Well, I never," he gasped. "Never in a million years would I believe I'd pass a breath test, Lizzie."

He watched her smile, then his brow creasing, asked, "What?"

She reached across the desk with her closed left hand, then opening it, dropped a glass phial onto the desk where within, the crystals could clearly be seen to be bright green.

Stunned, he raised his head to stare at her when she explained with a wry grin, "When I was at the uniform bar, I grabbed a second breath kit, then blew into a bag before I got here. The phial I gave the Chief was my negative test."

****

Returned to his desk in the Inspector's room, Iain Cowan was stunned.

Lizzie Whitmore's revelation, made in the strictest confidence, that Drew Taylor was under investigation for assaulting his former girlfriend had come as more than a shock.

The name, Sharon Crosbie, meant nothing, but he recalled the young woman who was Taylor's current girlfriend, a stunning blonde who would turn any man's head; or, he wondered, is *she* the former girlfriend making the complaint and have they had some sort of falling out?

That must be it, his brow furrowed.

His problem was he couldn't ask any of the shift about Taylor or his girlfriend, for Lizzie Whitmore had sworn him to secrecy and informed him simply to question his own knowledge of Taylor; primarily, she had asked, was the young cop ever suspected or even thought to be capable of assaulting women?

Had Cowan been asked the question before being told of the allegation, he would categorically have said, no, but the fact the rubber heels were investigating Taylor had sown the seed of doubt, though his instinct continued to tell him the woman was lying.

But why?

Slumped in the chair, he slowly exhaled. He had always believed he knew his shift, the good workers like Taylor and the young probationer, Roz Begley, as well as young Ian Parker who always without fuss, turned in a good day's work. Then there were the utterly dependable old sweats like Smiler and Willie Strathmore and of course, the ones to watch like the impetuous Harry Dawson, who couldn't be trusted to work herself and the skiving feartie, Keith Telford. Even his new acting sergeant, Mattie Devlin, had impressed him, but now?

He slowly shook his head.

Just how much do I know them all, he wondered.

The knock on his door startled him and turning, he saw a smiling Lucy Chalmers poking her head in.

"Just passing," she began, "so thought I'd stop to ask after Smiler."

His eyes narrowed and though Lizzie Whitmore had sworn him to secrecy, he replied, "Well, now that you're here, can I have a word?"

****

Patrolling along Durward Avenue in Foxtrot Mike Two, Drew Taylor listened as Roz Begley acknowledged an All Stations call to attend an anonymous report of suspicious persons loitering at the rear of the shops located in Sinclair Drive.

That done, Roz immediately used the Divisional radio to inform the controller that they were attending the call and then heard the civilian controller, Mary Wiseman, relay Roz's information to the beat man, Ian Parker.

"Blue's and two's, please Roz," Taylor said with a grin, then stamped down onto the accelerator.

Weaving through the afternoon traffic, it took Taylor just under four minutes to drive the mile to Sinclair Avenue and, as Roz witched off the blue's and two's, they saw Ian Parker, cap in his hand, running on the pavement along Battlefield Road towards the junction.

Though Parker had but three hundred yards to the locus, Taylor screeched to a halt to permit the breathless constable to climb into the rear of the van.

Gasping, Parker called through the small cut-out opening in the wooden partition that separated the cab from the rear of the van, "This is the third time in a month there's been a report of neds hanging around the rear of the shops, but I've always been too late to catch them. If I'm right, I think they're waiting for the staff of the pharmacy on the corner to open the back door for a smoke, then maybe run in and grab what drugs they can from the dispensary."

"Where should I stop, Ian?" Taylor called out.

"Drop me at the pharmacy on the corner and I'll go through the adjoining close in Sinclair Drive to the back court. You guys go on to Battlefield Gardens, the next junction on the right, so if they run I'm guessing they should emerge from the close there at number four."

Within seconds, Taylor had again screeched to a halt whereupon Parker jumped from the rear door, then slamming the door closed, raced into Sinclair Drive.

Seconds later, Taylor had driven on the hundred yards or so to the junction, then turned right into Battlefield Gardens and stopped outside the red sandstone, tenement building at the first close.

Hurriedly exiting the van, Taylor and Begley could hear distant shouts coming from what seemed to be the rear court.

Just at that moment, the door of the close at number four was pulled open and two young men, both wearing blue parka jackets and jeans, but more significantly, black balaclavas covering their faces, dashed literally into the arms of the two officers.

A short struggle ensued during which Taylor, his arms wrapped around the taller of the two suspects, fell through the four feet high hedgerow bordering the six-foot path to the close entrance while Roz, one arm wrapped around the second suspect's neck and her cap falling from her head, fell to the pavement with her on top of him as screaming obscenities, he thrashed around trying to free himself from her tight grip.

Seconds later, the entrance door was again pulled open, but this time by Parker, who seeing his colleagues struggling with the verbally abusive suspects, decided to first assist Roz.

Having been violent, the suspect was handcuffed to the rear and with Roz maintaining a grip on her groaning suspect, Parker leapt onto the second suspects back to pull him off Taylor and together, both officers handcuffed the squirming and violent suspect, again to the rear.

"Any more of them?" Taylor wheezed as he dragged his suspect to the back of the van.

"Just saw the two of them," panting, Parker shook his head, but then added, "Hang on, I'll be back."

Returning back through the close, he was gone just a few minutes before he returned carrying what seemed to be two home-made wooden batons and clutching two black bin bags.

"They dropped these at the back door of the pharmacy when I came through the close on Sinclair Drive and as I thought, they must have been waiting on the staff opening the back door. I usually pop by there now and again and I knew because they're not permitted to smoke in their small refreshment room," he explained, "they take their smoke breaks out the back door. I'm guessing that this pair," he nodded to the suspects, "must've been waiting on the door opening, then they intended barging in and robbing the place of the drugs."

With a satisfied grin, Taylor placed both the sullen suspects, now minus their balaclavas and revealing them to be in their late teens, into the rear of the van.

"Good job, guys," he nodded to Roz and Parker in turn.

****

Just as the suspects were being bundled into the van, Mattie Devlin, with Keith Telford in the passenger seat, arrived at the locus.

A grinning Ian Parker recounted the circumstances to Devlin, who turning to them in turn, asked, "You guys okay? Nobody injured in the arrest?"

"I've injured my knee, Sergeant," Roz innocently stared at him.

His eyes suspiciously narrowed when he asked, "When you hit the ground?"

"No," she pouted, "when I kneed him in the balls."

"Well," Devlin fought his smile, "I'm certain by the time that you arrive at Craigie Street, Roz, you'll be feeling much better."

"If it's okay, Sarge," Parker interrupted, "can Drew and Roz take this pair to Craigie Street. I'll need to get some statements from the staff and knock on a few doors in the close above the pharmacy to

try and trace the anonymous caller."
"You think it was a resident in the tenement?"
Parker nodded when he replied, "There's no window in the pharmacy facing the rear courtyard, so I'm guessing it was someone looking out of their back window in the block. Even if I can't identify them, the CID can't claim I didn't try," he grinned.
"Okay," Devlin nodded, then turning to Telford, said, "You travel in the rear with the suspects, Keith. I'm staying here and I'll give Ian a hand with the statements."
"Yes, Sergeant," Telford formally nodded.
When Telford climbed in the back of the van, he sat on the wooden bench seat facing both suspects and waited till Taylor and Roz had climbed in the front.
When the vehicle was moving, Telford leaned forward then with a glance at the cab in the front to ensure he wasn't being watched through the cut-out opening, put on what he believed was a fierce scowl, a look intended to intimidate the suspects.
Turning to glance at each, both the suspects began to laugh with the elder of the two remarking, "What's wrong with you, pal? Touch of the runs, eh?"
His face red with both anger and embarrassment and both suspects now laughing as well as being conveniently handcuffed to the rear, Telford reached forward and slapped him on the face, only for the youth to grin and sneer, "You slap like a lassie, ya wanker."
His face a mask of vehemence, he raised his hand again, but Telford was unprepared for the suspects together to press their back against the side of the van, then with their feet raised they begin to kick at him.
Suddenly fearful, he began to scream, "Help! Help! They're attacking me!"
His feet raised and his hands protectively around his head, he slid to the floor as both suspects continued their merciless kicking, then began stamping on him.
Suddenly aware that something in the back was amiss, Taylor slammed on the van's brakes, the resulting sudden stop caused both prisoners, unable to use their hands to save themselves, to literally fly through the air and tumble together against the wooden partition separating the rear from the cabin.

Exiting the cabin at a rush, Roz and Taylor run to the rear of the van and pulling open the back doors, saw Telford lying curled up in the foetus position on the floor, his cap crushed by a foot and his eyes brimming with unshed tears, moaning and groaning, though Taylor suspected he was playacting, that he was not really hurt.
The suspects, also lying in tangled heap, were groaning after their impact with the wooden partition, the younger of the two bleeding from a fresh cut to his forehead where he had obviously struck the edge of the wooden bench seat.
With a weary and disgusted glance at Telford, Taylor turned to Roz, then sighed, "That's all we need. Now we'll have to explain how a suspect got injured while handcuffed and in custody."

CHAPTER NINETEEN.

Shaved, showered and dressed, Smiler McGarry was waiting patiently in the chair by the hospital bed when the staff nurse led Sally into the Nightingale Ward, then with a smile, said, "You can have him. He's been nothing, but a nuisance since he got here, demanding this and that."
"Oh, nurse," Smiler began to protest, but then realised he was being teased.
"Here, for your staff room," Sally handed a plastic bag containing cakes, biscuits, a box of teabags and a jar of coffee to the staff nurse that was gratefully received.
"Right," she grinned at him, "ready for the off then?"
Grabbing at his brown leather holdall, he stood up and bent to kiss her cheek, though a little self-consciously with the nurse watching.
With, Sally clutching his arm, they walked through the many corridors to the small car park located outside the casualty department, when at last he said, "I'm sorry you had to meet Adam and Jean like that. I was hoping I could have explained to them…"
"Look," she stopped, pulling for him to do so too, "it had to happen sometime, Stuart. Now that's it's done and over with, maybe we could bring them and your daughter in law and your grandchildren to yours one day? This Sunday perhaps? I could cook lunch."
"Aye," his face lit up with pleasure. "That sounds like a good idea,

love. As long as you're okay with it?"
They resumed walking and she inwardly sighed, for that seemed to be another hurdle over with.
Now, she thought as her stomach lurched, all I have to worry about is how do I tell them about my past?
In the car, she was surprised when Smiler turned to her to ask, "Before you take me home, Sally, would you mind running me past Craigie Steer police station? I had al last night to think about something and I'd like to share it with the CID."
****
DCI Laura Gemmill, in conference with DI Sammy Pollock and the incident room manager, DS Danny Sullivan, posed the question, "How do we progress the investigation with no witnesses, no obvious motives and the only Forensic evidence being that the killer of both Jeannie Mason and Albert Moston wore size nine footwear?"
She continued with the pathologist's conclusion that the two, one-inch wounds on Moston's torso indicated the weapon used to murder him was sharp-edged with a quarter-inch heel, more commonly referred to as the widest part of the knife and the bruise left on the skin by the bolster, the thick piece of steel where the blade meets the handle, suggested a kitchen implement, possibly similar to that used in a butchers shop.
Though not commonly known by the public, a common practise by Senior Investigating officers in murder investigations was to hold back a vital piece of evidence, what might be regarded as a safeguard.
Such evidence was not disclosed because too often many individuals, for whatever reason, often provided false or misleading information to the police, whether claiming to be the killer or knowing something of vital evidential value. Most, if not all, who provided such erroneous evidence were soon disapproved by the police, while the safeguard information not publicly disclosed, must only be known to the real killer.
At Albert Moston's post mortem examination, the information held back by Gemmill and other than Pollock and the two production officers, DC's Morris Kerr and Barbara McMillan, but *not* disclosed to the team, was that during his examination, the pathologist had discovered the broken sliver of blade, the quarter inch tip of the murder weapon that had, presumably because of the force used to

drive it into Moston's body, somehow snapped off against the victim's rib cage and recovered from his liver.

Unaware of this fact, the office manager, DS Danny Sullivan, chewed on the stem of his unlit pipe, then said, "The fact that the knife was driven into Moston's body with such force, boss, does that not indicate the strength of the killer and maybe also killing Moston might have been personal?"

"How do you mean, Danny," she stared curiously at him.

"Well, that time of night? It was unusual for Moston to have been hanging around the close in Allison Street when he's living in Govanhill Street, eh? There's nothing to indicate he was forcefully dragged there so, a meeting perhaps? A meeting that's gone wrong?"

"And if it *wa*s a meeting," Pollock sat forward when he interjected, "then the killer has gone there tooled up, so are we to surmise that the intention was to murder Moston and if it was, that then begs the question. Why?"

He shrugged when he continued, "There's nothing indicate that Moston was the victim of a robbery. I mean, his clothing was intact and he was carrying a wallet, albeit there was only a couple of pound notes in it as well as some loose change in his trouser pocket."

"So," Gemmill's brow furrowed when she arched her fingers in front of her nose, "possibly a meeting with his killer, *not* a mugging gone wrong, but the killer, who we can safely presume had *already* murdered Jeannie Mason, came prepared to kill Moston. That suggests a connection between both victims that goes beyond any sexual liaison, does it not?"

It was Sullivan who slowly suggested, "What's your thoughts, boss, that perhaps the connection between Moston and Mason is that the killer knew or presumed they had something on him, that he killed them to stop them talking about it?"

Silence settled on the room as all three gave it some thought, then Gemmill, renowned as a boss who heeded the advice of her staff, made her decision.

"With no other evidence to lead us in the direction of a suspect, I think that we should consider Danny's idea. Okay," she took a short breath then exhaled through pursed lips, "that's our new line of inquiry, guys. We need to establish some sort of connection between our victims that goes beyond Moston having intercourse with Mason. Something that connects them to the killer."

"Sammy," she turned to him, "we need a full and thorough background of Jeannie Mason and the same with Moston. Anything at all that indicates where both have crossed paths and I don't mean just the locus of her murder, yes?"

"Understood, boss," he began to rise from his chair.

"Danny," she turned to him, "Good work. Now, start thinking about who best to assign those lines of inquiry too."

"Boss," he acknowledged with a nod.

While Gemmill and her detectives were inwardly excited at this possible new line of inquiry, they could not know that the connection they sought between Jeannie Mason and Albert Moston was in reality, all in the paranoid mind of their killer.

****

Her early morning telephone complaint made to the police at their headquarters in Pitt Street still in her mind, Drew Taylor's former girlfriend, Sharon Crosbie, walked into the hotel that morning full of confidence that the police would deal with him; that at worse he'd be disciplined and at best, lose his job.

With a self-satisfied and very smug smile, she greeted her colleague manning the reception desk, then strode through to the rear staff room to leave her jacket and handbag there before commencing her shift.

The middle-aged man already there, Jonas McWilliams, her partner for the late shift, turned to greet her with, "There was telephone call for you just as I came into the foyer. A policeman who said he'd pop by this afternoon to take a statement or something."

"Oh, right," she felt her face flush, but whether with nervousness or excitement, even she couldn't tell.

"You in trouble with the law or something," he teased her.

"Eh, no. Nothing like that," she gushed, then a curious feeling overtook her, a sensation that made her feel empowered, that what she told the policeman would ultimately decide Drew's fate, perhaps even end his career.

If nothing else, her nostrils flared when she shrugged of her coat and hung it in her locker, it would teach the bastard that he couldn't just dump Sharon Crosbie and get away with it.

"So, what *have* you done, sweetie?" Jonas persisted.

She turned to face him, then with a sly grin, changed the subject when she replied, "You know I've finished with Drew?"

"Eh, no," Jonas seemed surprised, "I hadn't heard."

"Yes," she sighed as though it were such a trial, "he was getting too pushy, wanting to get engaged, pressing me for an answer. So really," she shrugged her shoulders, "I had no choice but to end it."

Jonas stared suspiciously at her, recalling when working the reception desk together the many conversations that they'd had, how she loved her boyfriend's flat, her plans for changing this and that when she moved in with him, that she was confident he'd pop the question any day now.

To Jonas, it just didn't seem to tally with her ending their relationship because he was…too pushy?

"How did he take it, dear?" he turned to her. "You ending it with him?"

"Oh, tears and snotters," she flippantly replied, checking her makeup in the mirror attached to the inside of the locker.

"Yesterday morning, in fact," she continued. "I'd arranged to meet him for coffee and well, he was so upset that I felt *really* bad about dumping him."

"Now," she turned back to Jonas with a brilliant smile, "did this policeman say exactly when he was coming to see me?"

She still hadn't explained why the police officer was keen to meet with her and that caused Jonas to be even more suspicious, so shaking his head, he simply replied, "No, it was the desk that took the call, just asked me to let you know."

"See you at the desk," she strutted out of the locker room.

Watching her leave, he continued to be confused.

A gay man in his mid-forties and overtly effeminate, Jonas had no love for the police who in previous years had hounded and harassed both him and many of his close circle of friends; however, he'd met Drew Taylor at several functions to which the young police officer had accompanied Sharon and found him to be nothing but polite and courteous, very sociable and completely ignored Jonas's obvious gender preference.

That and Jonas was not blind to Sharon's predatory nature as evidenced by her preference in dealing with any male guests who displayed affluence. In fact, it had surprised not just Jonas, but several colleagues that she had attached herself to a young police officer who likely was not at all so well-heeled.

Why then, if as she said she'd dumped young Drew he wondered, was a police officer coming to interview her?

****

Standing at the uniform charge bar, Inspector Iain Cowan nodded to the Duty Officer, Inspector Marion Bruce, that she go ahead and request the attendance of the casualty surgeon to examine both suspects and Constable Telford, who continued to whine about his so-called injured pelvis, alleging it to be the result of the vicious assault upon him.

Turning to her bar officer, she instructed him to make the call from her desk, then both Inspectors watched the constable leave.

The suspects, now both prisoners and in cells awaiting the arrival of the doctor, as well as their interviews by the CID about their plan to rob the pharmacy, had both very volubly complained that they had reacted to the assault on them by Telford, that they had acted in self-defence, the elder youth alleging the constable had slapped him first. With the crew of Foxtrot Mike Two now in the Inspector's room awaiting him interviewing them about the incident, there was just the two Inspector's at the charge bar.

"What do you think, Iain?" Bruce quietly asked. "I mean, Telford's your cop. Do you believe that he was attacked by that pair, given that both were handcuffed behind their backs?"

"Not for a second," he shook his head with a weary sigh. "I'm thinking Telford's provoked them and as the young guy said, Telford's slapped him across the chops, maybe because the young guy said something to him."

"Is that Telford's style? I mean, is he a bully?"

"Worse, Marion. He's a cowardly bully. I'm guessing mind, but I think Telford's tried to act the hard man and the pair of them have lashed out at him after he's belted the young guy across the jaw. Can I prove it? Not a chance," he pursed his lips when he shook his head again.

"Telford knows that he's uncorroborated, so he'll stick to his story. My problem now is, with the younger guy being injured, do I hand the issue over to the rubber heels or try to deal with it myself?"

Her arms crossed, she stared suspiciously at him when she asked, "And how would you propose to do that?"

He lowered his voice when he replied, "Persuade them that in addition to the charge of conspiring to rob the pharmacy and for which the CID have the evidence of not just Parker, Taylor and Begley's statements, but balaclavas that will no doubt have their hair follicles attached as well as the home made batons, there will be a further charge of attempting to escape lawful custody by attacking Constable Telford."

Her face expressed her dubiety when she said, "That's really pushing it, Iain."

"Aye, but will they know that," he shrugged, then shaking his head, said again in a low voice, "But if I report the issue to the rubber heels, it also presents the opportunity to get rid of a bad and cowardly cop that Telford is. To be honest, Marion, he's a bloody liability so he is and my real fear is that one day because he *is* a feartie, he'll end up getting one of my people injured or worse. That and he's incompetent too."

They both turned when the door to the rear yard was pulled open to admit Smiler McGarry, who stepping into the charge bar area, stared at them both when he said, "This a union meeting or are you pair conspiring for some dastardly deed?"

A popular man with all ranks, they both grinned and it was Bruce who greeted him with, "Nice to see you back, Smiler, but shouldn't you be off on the pat and mick?"

"Ach, I'm fine, Inspector. Just popped by to have a word with the DCI upstairs, so if you will excuse me," he smiled at them both then headed towards the stairs.

When he'd gone, Bruce turned towards Cowan to tell him, "Well, I'll leave you to decide what you plan to do, Iain, and I'll keep Telford in the turnkey's room till the doc's seen him and the prisoners, then I'll let you know once he's examined the three of them."

Making his way through to the Inspector's room, both Taylor and Roz Begley, who he guessed had been talking in low voices before he entered, jumped to their feet when he entered, but waved them back down into their seats.

"Right," he sat down at his desk then glanced at them in turn, but addressed his question to Taylor, "What's your version of wat happened?"

With a glance at Roz, Taylor recounted the cry for help from the rear of the van causing him to stamp on the brake and that, he grimaced likely accounted for the younger suspect colliding with the bench seat and causing his wound.

"Sorry, Inspector, but I reacted to Keith calling out and maybe I shouldn't have stopped the van so quickly. That and maybe I should have had Roz in the back of the van, neighbouring Keith."

"What, with two *handcuffed* prisoners? And you're saying you think you caused the injury by stopping the van?"

Taylor's face creased when he nodded.

Cowan stared at him and realised that Taylor was trying to downplay Telford's stupidity and guessed that the younger man also believed the prisoners story, that it was Telford who had provoked them into assaulting him.

With a sigh, he softly said, "Then let me assure you, you are *not* responsible, Drew. Any one of us would have reacted as you did."

"Roz," he turned to her, "what exactly did Telford say when you opened the back doors?"

"Eh," her face creased as she tried to recall, then shrugging, she replied, "he didn't really say anything, sir. Just lay there moaning and groaning."

"But prior to the van stopping, you both heard what?" he turned again to Taylor.

He didn't miss the glance that the younger man gave his neighbour, before Taylor said, "Keith shouting for help, that he was being attacked."

"But nothing before that?"

"No, sir," they replied in unison.

Iain Cowan was basically an honest man and had his own thoughts on both the law and what was right and wrong. During his lengthy career there had been many occasions when he saw or didn't see things and made decisions that was between him and his conscience. However, above all, he would never see an innocent man unjustly charged with a crime or an offence.

In his heart he knew that Telford was lying, that he *did* slap the handcuffed prisoner and likely did so to make himself feel like a big man; an act that had backfired and left Telford, uncorroborated, now facing two statements from handcuffed prisoners that it was he who was the aggressor.

Staring at Roz Begley, he was suddenly reminded of the time Telford had ignored an All Stations call when the young woman had bravely pursued a thug into the back courts and tackled him; an act that could have gone so wrong had she not been as tenacious as she is.

On that occasion Telford, by ignoring the call, had put her safety at risk and the likelihood is, he angrily thought, he could do so again with someone else if he isn't stopped.

Bugger it, Cowan inwardly decided, I'm handing this to the rubber heels to deal with.

****

Knocking on the DCI's door, she glanced up to see Smiler standing there and widely grinning, greeted him with, "Come in, come in. I hadn't been told you'd been discharged, Smiler. Tea or coffee?" she begin to rise to her feet.

"I'll not hang about, Ma'am," he raised his palm towards her, "I've someone waiting in the car downstairs."

He smiled at her when he continued, "But I thought on the way home I'd pop by because there's something that's been bothering me."

"Wait," her brow furrowed, "shouldn't you still be in hospital?"

"Ah, well, much as I appreciated the Viccy's all-inclusive hospitality, Ma'am, they decided that I ate too much and I was a liability with my snoring, keeping the other patients awake, so they threw me out."

"Aye, I'll bet they did," she grinned at his humour and motioned that he sit down opposite before asking, "So, what can I do for you, Smiler?"

His face creased when he began, "I hope I'm not speaking out of turn, you being the CID and all, but lying in that hospital bed, I've been thinking. The murder of Wee Jeannie and Moxy. There has to be a connection between them, something that the killer knows about them both or something that they knew about him that made him feel threatened by them. Oh, and I don't think it's anything to do with Moxy and Jeannie, you know," he cleared his throat in embarrassment, "having sex in the Govanhill Park."

Her eyes widened, recalling just twenty minutes earlier her conversation with Sammy Pollock and Danny Sullivan, then she hesitantly asked, "Have you any thought on what that connection might be, Smiler?"

"Well, actually, Ma'am," he stared narrow-eyed at her, "I do have an idea."

****

Handing him a mug of tea, Sally asked, "Don't you think you should maybe lie down for a couple of hours?"

Smiler grinned at her when he replied, "If that's an offer, then how can I refuse?"

"Dirty minded bugger," she leaned over to kiss the top of his head, then said, "Look, I know I have the day off, but I've a meeting to attend, so will you be alright for a couple of hours without me?"

He laid the mug down onto the nearby table, then without warning, grabbed her arm and pulled her towards him, rolling her over to lie beside him on the three-seater couch, then replied, "I don't know if I can let you go. I have this irresistible urge to carry you up to bed and do naughty thing to you."

Squealing with delight, she pushed him off, then falling giggling onto the floor, breathlessly said, "Can it wait for a couple of hours?"

"Oh, I don't know if I can, because something's just come up," he pretended to leer, then sighed, "Okay, but only if you promise to come right back when you're finished your meeting. I mean," he petted his lips, "I'm not a well man."

"Aye, right," she stifled her laugh, then added, "I promise."

She sat up and reached to grab his face in both hands before planting a slobbery kiss on him.

Rising to her feet, Sally patted herself down, then bending, kissed him again and said, "I won't be too long. Promise."

Five minutes later, pulling away from the kerb outside the house in her Vauxhall Viva, Sally gave thought to the meeting and realised she was extremely nervous, which was not at all like her, for she considered herself not just to be a strong-willed individual, but having endured what she'd gone through, believed herself to be both resilient and did not need anyone.

Well, that was until she'd met Stuart and she involuntarily sighed. At first, she'd thought the big lump was nothing more than just another bolshie, misogynistic policeman, but as she come to know him, saw beneath his exterior to the gentle man he really was; a complete contradiction to the man and the police officers she had known before.

Their first date, a Greek restaurant located in a basement on Sauchiehall Street near to Charing Cross, had been a complete disaster.

Neither of them recognised the foods described in the menu and when finally, after some advice from the staff, ordered and commenced eating their meal.

They had just started eating when the four-waiting staff, obviously that evening's entertainment, had danced holding hands into the small, compact room in what was some sort of poor imitation of Zorba's Dance, then after the dance concluded, began throwing unglazed crockery to the floor that startling all the customers shattered like shrapnel.

"Oh, come on," Stuart had irately shaken his head, then said, "I think we've had enough of this."

Settling the bill with notes left on the table, they had exited the restaurant, watched by the bemused staff and the other customers who evidently were themselves too embarrassed to leave.

In the street outside, the rain falling heavily, both had succumbed to fits of the giggles and finally, suggesting they grab some fish suppers from the chippy in Elmbank Street, shared a bottle of Irn-Bru and ate their carry-out in Stuart's car, parked in Holland Street.

She involuntarily smiled when she recalled him driving her home, apologising for such a disastrous evening until she leaned across then said, "It's been a while since I've had such fun. Thank you."

Dropping her outside her close in Arundel Drive, he'd walked her to the close and while she'd prepared herself to fend off any attempt by him to coerce her to invite him upstairs, he'd simply said, "If you might consider another date, Sally, I promise that I'll keep away from foreign restaurants. Maybe the cinema, if that's okay? If you say no, I'll completely understand."

She recalled seeing his face, how hopeful he was she would say yes and she did, then stood on her tiptoes to lightly kiss his cheek farewell.

Making her way upstairs she couldn't believe that he'd been such a gentleman and remembered with a blush that she'd hoped he found her as attractive as she did him.

Since then, they'd gone from strength to strength and though he'd been worried about the age difference, it mattered not a jot to Sally who wanted nothing more than to have Stuart in her life; permanently.
She startled, not realising she was driving on automatic pilot for she was almost at the café on Paisley Road West where her meeting was to take place.
Not familiar with the area, she gently braked in the inside lane, preparing to stop at the turning on her left prior to the row of shops and where she'd been told she could park at the rear of the building.
She knew she was near for there was the school on her right, Lourdes Academy, she recalled being told, so the turning was only a little further on.
There, she inwardly breathed a sigh of relief.
Braking, she turned into the service road that led to the block of flats above the row of shops below.
Parking the Viva in one of the empty covered bays, Sally checked her make-up in the rear-view mirror, then getting out of the car, glanced at her wristwatch and hurried around to the row of shops.
The small café was the third premises in the row and taking a deep breath, pushed open the door and stepped inside.
Nervously glancing around the brightly lit interior, she saw a fair-haired, well-dressed woman rise from a chair on her left and beckon her forward.
Extending her hand, the woman smiled when she greeted her with, "Sally. You're just as you described yourself. I'm so pleased to finally meet you. Please, call me Elizabeth."

CHAPTER TWENTY.

Now that her team had all returned from their inquiries, DCI Laura Gemmill, with Sammy Pollock standing beside her, held the briefing in the incident.
Pollock was at that time the only person she had shared Smiler's suggestion with and to her relief, he had agreed it was definitely worth pursuing.

She began with, "After a discussion with the DI, I have decided that we will focus our investigation into any possible link between out victims for the purpose of finding out who in common they knew or associated with."

Holding up her hand, she added, "While I realise that both were well known locally, it is my belief that the killer, for some reason as yet unknown, has silenced both victims because of something that they knew about him, some information that he fears if it became widely known or reached our ears, might incriminate him. Again," she took a soft breath, "what that information is we have no idea. However," she glanced around the room, "it has been suggested that a possible link is as follows."

She paused to gather her thoughts, then continued, "It has come to my attention that about sixteen or seventeen years ago, our victim, Albert Moston, was with another male involved in street robberies, predominantly assaulting and robbing pensioners in the sub-Divisional area."

Deciding not to mention Smiler as her source, she saw several heads turning and curious glances directed at her, guessing her detectives would wonder why this had not been previously disclosed, but raising her hand, then explained, "While Moston was positively identified and for reasons that are not at this time clear, it seems he was never charged with any of these crimes nor was his accomplice identified."

It literally stuck in her throat that she could not further explain that the then ambitious DCI, simply to further his career, had used his rank to pervert the justice the elderly victims deserved. However, she also realised that slinging mud so many years later would serve nobody any good, though guessed more than a few of the more senior detectives would recall the muggings and realise who she was talking about.

And so she said, "Our aim now is to identify the male accomplice who conspired with our victim in these crimes and who might, though it's not definite, be the link we're looking at between both victims."

She stared at the faces who stared back and guessed more than a few considered this line of inquiry to be no more than a shot in the dark.

"To that end," she continued, "Danny Sullivan will appoint some of you to research the City of Glasgow Police files for reports of these crimes and I realise, while many of the complainers, elderly at that time and so might have since died, we're looking for any information that might offer a description of Moston's accomplice. Anything that can identify him."

Again she paused before she said, "I know it's a long time ago and that the files might be in one hell of a state, but if you can't find what you're looking for at Craigie Street, my understanding is that all the criminal files of the Forces who now make-up Strathclyde Police are stored in the cellars at police headquarters in Pitts Street. DI Pollock will arrange for the janitorial staff at Pitt Street to offer you every assistance in locating these files. Questions?"

A subdued murmuring ensued, then a hand was raised; Barbara McMillan, she saw and knew she was about to be asked the question she did not want asked.

"Ma'am, I'm sorry if I've missed something, but if he was identified for these street robberies, why exactly wasn't Moston charged..."

McMillan startled when her neighbour, Morris Kerr, sharply dug her in the ribs with his elbow.

She turned in surprise to stare at him and saw his eyes narrow when he subtly shook his head.

With a soft smile, Gemmill held up her hand and all eyes turned to her when she said, "It's okay, Morris, Barbara's asked a perfectly legitimate question."

Licking at her lips, she glanced around the room before she began, "You're all experienced police officers so I'll ask you to respect what I'm about to disclose for if this gets out, it will come back and land at my desk. Right," she slowly shook her head, "no names and no pack drill, guys, but suffice to say that someone in the chain of command at that *time*," she stressed, "decided Moston was of more value as a source of local intelligence, than pursuing a conviction for the street robberies."

"Aye," called a voice at the back, one of the more senior DC's in the Department, who then loudly added, "and that same wanker's now an ACC over in Lothian in Borders Polis."

The room erupted in a hubbub of comments, for there was now no doubt who the culprit was.

Gemmill fought her grin when she called for silence, then said, "Okay, the damage was done a number of years ago, guys, but we have the opportunity now to at least fix some of it. Moston's dead, so he's paid his price for his crimes, but let's try and find his accomplice. Any further questions? No? Right, I'll leave you to collect your inquiries from Danny Sullivan."

Leaving the room with Sammy Pollock, he waited till they were out of earshot of the incident room, then told her, "That went better than I thought, boss."

"Perhaps," she sighed, "but I just hope we're not putting all our eggs into the one basket, Sammy."

In the corridor, he stopped, causing her to turn and stare curiously at him when he solemnly said, "Call it a gut feeling or intuition or whatever, boss, and don't ask me to explain it," he shook his head, "but something's telling me that our man Smiler just might be on the right track."

But that said, Pollock could not ignore the niggling doubt that the DCI was indeed, as she said, putting all the eggs into the one basket.

****

Chief Inspector Marty McKenna and his DS, Sergeant Shona Mulvey, were led by Sharon Crosbie into a small anteroom off the main foyer of the hotel where they declined tea or coffee.

Seated together on the spacious couch, Sharon sat in the single chair opposite, her skirt riding up to her thigh and as he later admitted to his wife, McKenna would not have been a normal heterosexual man if he hadn't taken those few seconds to admire the stunning blonde and her long, tanned legs.

When they commenced the interview, it was McKenna who led Sharon through her statement while the pokerfaced Mulvey took notes.

She began her statement by mirroring her earlier disclosure to her colleague, Jonas McWilliams, that she had dumped Constable Drew Taylor, but with the lengthy and tearful addition that she had little choice because her former boyfriend, who throughout their relationship had been both verbally and physically abusive.

Twenty minutes later, lightly dabbing at her eyes with a tissue, she asked, "What happens now that I've told you? Will he be sacked?"

McKenna, however, was no fool and recognised the eagerness behind her question, realising his sympathetic questioning had heartened Sharon who though he didn't know it, seemingly believed that she was about to gain her revenge.

Calmly, he replied, "Oh, no, not right away, Miss Crosbie. First, we'll interview him and of course likely he'll be suspended from duty. Then, when you provide some friends who witnessed these assaults and abuse, we'll obtain their statements and Constable Taylor will be charged. Thereafter will follow a court case and when presumably he's found guilty…"

"Wait, what?" her face suddenly pale, her eyes narrowing, she stared at McKenna when she raised a hand, "You want me to give you the names of my friends? For what purpose?"

"Well," he smiled, then politely repeated, "we must have corroboration of your allegation that…"

"Corrob, coborr…what's that?" her face creased with a lack of understanding.

Patiently he explained, "You said you were together about nine months? Surely there must have been friends or family who saw your injured face or the bruising on your body after he's slapped and punched you. Or perhaps you attended at a casualty ward," his eyes widened as though being helpful, "or maybe a friend has helped you after you were assaulted? These are the people who we need to speak with and who…"

Her nostrils flared and her teeth gritted when she leaned forward and hissed, "You're all the same, you lot! You're trying to confuse me with your fancy legal patter! You don't believe me, do you! Isn't *my* word good enough?" she snapped at him, suddenly on her feet, her tears now genuine that she was not to be taken seriously.

"I'll go to the papers," she hissed at them in turn, "Tell them what your man did to me!"

Staring up at her, McKenna coolly replied, "Of course, that's your prerogative, Miss Crosbie, but as I said, if you wish to pursue the complaint against Constable Taylor, then all we ask is that in your nine-month relationship with him, you must have at some point told someone of your fears and distress, not to say the bruises you allege to have received. An independent witness to his violence towards you. Again I ask, is there such an individual?"

"Allege? You mean you think I'm making this up, don't you!" her fists balled and her lip curled.

McKenna did indeed believe she was lying, but it wasn't his place to say and getting to his feet as did Mulvey, he raised the palms of both hands towards her when he replied, "As I said, Miss Crosbie, we seek witnesses to provide evidence to pursue a complaint against him; evidence that will stand up in a court case should you wish to continue with your complaint against Constable Taylor. All we ask is you bring forward someone to support your allegation."

Staring vehemently at him Sharon turned on her heel and rushed from the room, slamming the door behind her.

Seconds passed in silence, broken when Mulvey, replacing her notebook into her handbag, shrugged, "She's a lying cow."

"On that, Sergeant," he nodded, "we both agree."

There was no sign of Sharon at the reception desk when McKenna and Mulvey crossed the busy foyer towards the mahogany and glass doors.

Stepping out into the busy city centre street, they had walked just twenty or so yards to collect their parked, unmarked car when they heard a voice from behind call out, "Excuse me! Officers! Wait!"

They both turned to see a middle-aged, rotund man with dyed blonde collar length hair and wearing a three-piece suit with the hotel's logo on the breast pocket, hurrying towards them.

Breathlessly, his face red with his burst of exertion, he stopped with one hand on his chest, then with a nervous glance behind him, said, "I work with Sharon. Please," he implored them in a sotto voice, "the young man she is supposed to have dumped, Drew. I think it's all a lie what she's telling you. For whatever the reason, she wants to get young Drew into trouble and believe me, she's *more* than capable of being spiteful."

"Would you be willing to provide a statement as to her character, Mr, eh...?"

"Oh, no, I can't do that," his face expressed panic. "I have to work with her and believe me, officer, she can be *more* than vindictive and I have my job to think of," he again glanced behind him.

"One more thing," he licked nervously at his dry lips, "she told me that she dumped Drew. I think it's more than likely he's realised what *she's* like and *he's* dumped her."

"Sorry," he began to back away, his hands waved in apology, "I have to return to work. I hope that helps."

They watched the man quickly make his way back to the hotel entrance, then Mulvey, her brow knitting, turned to McKenna and in a flat voice, shook her head when she said, "I knew it as soon as she opened her mouth. She's definitely a lying cow."

****

Sitting opposite Lizzie Whitmore in her office, Inspector Iain Cowan reminded her she was getting the story third-hand, but he'd no reason to suspect that his constables, Drew Taylor and Roz Begley, had told anything but the truth, then added, "Of course, Telford denies slapping the prisoner and continues to allege that he was unexpectedly assaulted."

"And the casualty surgeon said that apart from some bruising to his groin…"

"He took a boot in the balls, Liz. Greeting and whining like a wee schoolgirl for an hour because of it," Cowan mirthlessly grinned.

"What about the prisoners?"

"Well," he drawled, "the doc applied a couple of steristrips to the young guys napper, but other than that, they're both okay."

"And they both adhere to their statements that Telford instigated the rammy, that he slapped the older youth?"

"Yes," Cowan nodded.

"You're satisfied that they're not making the allegation in the belief we will cut a deal and drop or reduce the charges?"

"My opinion is that they know they're caught bang to rights for the conspiracy to rob the pharmacy, but yes," he shrugged, "I suppose that *is* possible."

"But you don't believe that, Iain, do you?"

"No, on this occasion, I think this pair are telling the truth."

He paused then said, "You know me, Liz, I'm not beyond admitting that on occasion when I've had to deal with a violent arrest, I've used my fists and yes, sometimes even my feet to subdue a prisoner, but never, *ever*, have I resorted to assaulting a prisoner with his hands handcuffed behind him. That's the worst type of bullying."

Whitmore rubbed wearily at her forehead then with a resigned sigh, said, "It's not as if I've nothing else to deal with that the minute."

Cowan smiled when he suggested, "Look, Liz, I came to you because it's protocol, but I'm quite happy to contact the rubber heels myself and report the incident."

Her eyes narrowed when she replied, "If those two wee scroats continue with their allegation, Iain, Telford could look at being charged and maybe even losing his job."

"Honestly, Liz," he shook his head, "I've had enough of him anyway."

He paused and slowly shook his head when he said, "Like you have, I've met some dodgy characters in the job, guys and a couple of women too that I hated working with and for a number of different reasons, but I never thought I'd ever say hear myself say this. Telford should never have passed the vetting process and as far as I'm concerned, he's not just a liability on my shift, he's a menace to the health and the safety of the rest of my guys."
"That's how you honestly feel?"
"It is," he sighed.
"Okay then, but leave it with me. I'll deal with Telford and on that point, where is he now?"
Cowan took a breath before he said, "He persuaded the casualty surgeon that he wasn't fit to continue and has been signed off on the sick. Based on that, I'll have to complete an injured on duty report that I'll send you when I'm finished with it."
"So, he's away home?"
"He is and of course, the next two days are rest days, so he's not due back on shift till Friday."
"That's if he doesn't see his own GP and get an extension to his sick line," she snorted, then added, "Like I said, leave it with me and I'll deal with him whenever he resumes duty."
"What about that pair downstairs in the cells? You know as soon as they arrive for the custody hearing tomorrow at the Sheriff Court and get themselves appointed a lawyer, that's the first thing they'll complain about."
"We'll just need to deal with that when it occurs and *if* they decide to press a complaint."
However, staring at him, Whitmore knew she hadn't reassured herself, let alone Iain Cowan.

****

Returned to duty in Foxtrot Mike Two, Drew Taylor and Roz Begley were patrolling in the Battlefield area and discussing the issue with Keith Telford.
"He's a lying git," Roz shook her head "I don't believe for one minute those two suspects attacked him, not with their hands handcuffed behind them. I mean, I'm not condoning what they did, but it's Keith Telford and we all know what he's like. He talks being a hard man, but he's just a bully boy."
"I agree," Taylor nodded, "but it's two statements against one and

the fact that they were about to commit a robbery using batons, then struggling with us when they were arrested, that'll count against them when the rubber heels get involved."

"You think it'll come to that," she turned to stare at him, "an official complaint?"

"Bound to," he nodded, unwittingly agreeing with his Inspector when he added, "once they speak to a defence lawyer when they got to court tomorrow, I'm thinking that'll be used as a bargaining chip with the Fiscal."

"Changing the subject," he glanced at her, "what's planned for your days off?"

"Washing, ironing and maybe a meal then a movie with my pal, Beth. You?"

"Same as you, catching up with the washing and shopping and what needs done in the flat," he smiled, then literally holding his breath as he stared through the windscreen, he added, "Don't suppose you fancy meeting up for a coffee tomorrow or Thursday in Byres Road?"

Roz didn't get the opportunity to respond, for the All Stations radio burst into life, instructing their call-sign to attend a road traffic accident, an RTA, at the busy junction of Cathcart Road and Dixon Road, the controller adding that an ambulance was en-route.

"Here we go," he said, "blue's and two's please, Roz."

Stamping down onto the accelerator, he wondered if his suggestion would be remembered once they'd finished attending the call.

****

They'd finished their coffee and cake and the small talk over, Elizabeth stared at her when she asked, "So, Sally, what's the real reason you asked to meet me today?"

She sensed the younger woman was nervous, so added, "Look, I know from what Stuart's told me in the past that you are a little worried about the age gap, but like I told him, that should not be an issue. If you two are happy together, then that's what counts."

"It's a little more than that, Elizabeth. What worries me is, well, I've met Adam and Jean and they're very nice, but there's something that Stuart hasn't told them about me, something that might cause them to choose between them and me, to finish with me."

Elizabeth's eyes narrowed when she stared at Sally, then in a lowered voice, softly said, "Surely whatever it is, dear, it can't be that bad."

Sally's throat suddenly felt very tight and beneath the table, her hands twisted and her stomach knotted before she stuttered, "I've been in prison. Eighteen months."

She drew a deep breath, then added, "For stabbing my husband."

CHAPTER TWENTY-ONE.

Laura Gemmill glanced up when her door was knocked, then pushed open by her DI, Sammy Pollock, his face unusually sombre.

"Two things, boss," he began, "that's Danny issued the team with their jobs and there's a couple on their on their way to Pitt Street while two of them will check the basement here at Craigie Street for any of the old CID files containing statements or crime reports."

"Good. And the second thing?"

He nodded at one of the two chairs in front of her desk and she motioned he sit down.

"Just had Jeannie Mason's daughter on the phone. She was very upset when I told her we couldn't release her mother's body at this time, that the investigation was still proceeding."

Gemmill sighed, knowing while the murder was still an open case, the victim's body must remain in the custody of the Procurator Fiscal for if or rather when, she fervently hoped, an accused was arrested, the defence team representing the accused were entitled to conduct their own post mortem examination and thus the body remained until such time there was an arrest or the investigation stood down.

"Would you like me to phone the lassie?"

"No point right now," he shook his head. "She went off on one, but even though I did try to explain, she wasn't listening. Maybe when she's calmed a little, I'll give her a phone call later today."

They sat in silence for several seconds before Gemmill said, "It's hard on the family, even harder when the loss is due to a murder."

He slowly nodded in agreement, then asked, "Smiler. Do you still want him back on the team?"

"More than ever," narrow-eyed, she nodded, then explained, "I'm thinking that sometimes we in the CID tend to become fixated when we're investigating murders. By that I mean and quite rightly, we usually stick rigidly to the old MAGICOP way of viewing a murder."

"Motive, ability, guilty intent, identification, conduct after the crime, opportunity and preparation," Pollock slowly recounted the meaning of the acronym, then asked, "And how does Smiler coming on board differ to how we look at a murder?"

"Well, for starters, he's already thinking out of the box, bringing us the supposition that for whatever the killer's reason, he might have murdered our victims because of what occurred all those years ago."

"You mean, he's suddenly got the heebie-jeebies that after all this time, Moston and wee Jeannie are a threat to him?"

"Yes, Sammy, that's exactly what I *am* thinking and besides, what harm will it do if Smiler does join us? Let's face it," she sighed, "we're getting nowhere at the minute anyway."

"It's my job as your deputy to question your decisions if I have my own doubts, boss, but to be honest, I agree with you. It'll do no harm if Smiler comes back on the team and anyway, he's given us the only real possibility of a lead anyway."

"Good," she smiled at him, inwardly pleased he wasn't going to argue, then added, "can I leave you to phone Smiler and ask if and when he's ready, regardless of what shift he is supposed to be working, he can come back to us?"

"Consider it done, boss," he nodded.

****

She couldn't ignore the quick glance the older woman cast around the café's other customers before she began, "I can't say that I'm not shocked, Sally," Elizabeth Cowan began in a low voice.

"However," to her surprise, Elizabeth reached a hand across the table to lay it upon Sally's, then continued, "I'm certain that Stuart must know about you…ah, being in prison, and if he does and still has such strong feelings for you, there must be a story as to why you went there."

Her chin dropped and she took a soft breath before she replied, "I was married at twenty-one to Thomas, a man who had slapped me several times during our relationship, but was then very sorry and always regretful. I naively thought when we were married that he'd change, that his temper would…well," her face creased, "I was young and foolish and wouldn't listen to my parents or my friends," she shrugged.

She paused then nervously licked at her lips before she continued, "The first few months of our marriage went okay. He'd stopped drinking heavily and gambling and I thought this was going to work. Then about a year after we'd married, he was caught by the police drunk driving, lost his licence and his job as a drayman with the brewery. So, with the job slump back then, he had time on his hands and just mooched about the flat. With him not working, that left me as the breadwinner, even though I found myself pregnant and it was a bad time for me, with the vomiting and the occasional bleed."

Sally fought the tears as the memories flooded back, then heard Elizabeth say, "Take your time, dear. There's no rush."

"Can I get you anything else, ladies?" they both startled as like a wraith, the young waitress appeared at their table.

"Yes, please, a fresh pot of tea," Elizbeth forced a smile.

When she'd gone, Sally, dabbing at her eyes with a napkin, continued, "Like I said, with time on his hands, he started hanging around the bookies with his old mates, then increasingly arrive home later and later and once again, the slapping started, but this time he grew more violent."

Elizabeth could feel her face pale and beneath the table, her hands balled tightly into fists.

"The first time Thomas punched me," Sally said, her throat tightening as she fought to get the words out, "he knocked me against a wall and split the back of my head. I tried to fight back, but by then I was over three months pregnant and I was no match for him."

She sighed when she said, "I remember the nurse at the casualty in Stobhill Hospital telling me that she'd phone the police, but believe it or not, I was so ashamed that my husband had hit me, I told her no," she grimly smiled, "I didn't want to tell the police."

She stopped when the waitress arrived with the pot of tea and fresh milk and cups, then continued, "It was a week later, in the kitchen I caught him rifling my purse to take money out for the horses and drink and when I tried to explain he was stealing the rent money…"

She stopped again, unshed tears glistening, took a deep breath, then determinedly said, "He punched me in the face, then in my stomach. I fell back against the worktop and I really, *really* thought he was going to kill me this time. God, I remember the pain in my stomach like it was yesterday," she unconsciously rubbed gently at her abdomen.

"I knew I was bleeding, you know, down there," her eyes dropped to her lap.

"The next thing he had his hands around my throat and was squeezing the life out of me and telling me he was going to effing kill me. I was bent back against the sink and I reached into the plastic bowl and grabbed a knife. A steak knife it was because Thomas," she slowly shook her head when she humourlessly smiled, "even though we were living on my shop assistant wages, he always wanted the best food, so it was steak for him while I was left eating pasta or cheap fish fingers."

She watched Elizabeth pour tea into both cups, then milk them both before she continued again, "I stabbed him out of sheer terror, right here," she pointed to her own left shoulder.

She paused and again dabbed at her eyes.

"He fell back screaming that I was trying to kill him. Me, kill him? After what he'd done to me?" she fiercely scowled.

"I was still holding the knife and my legs were shaking and then because I was bleeding, my legs just gave way and I just crumpled onto the floor while he run out of the kitchen. Turns out he'd run across the landing to the old woman who lived there to use her phone," she stopped then said, "Sorry, I should have explained. We lived in a council flat over in Lenzie Street in Springburn at the time."

"Anyway, I don't know how long it was that passed before two policemen and an ambulance man came into the kitchen and the next thing I know is I'm being taken to the casualty at Stobhill and," her lips quivering, the tears trickled down her cheeks, "they told me I'd aborted. I lost my baby, Elizabeth."

Her eyes dulled when she whispered, "He'd killed my baby when he'd punched me."

Stunned, Elizabeth felt her own eyes tear up when she asked, "And he was arrested?"

"No," Sally shook her head.

"The detectives that arrived, they believed Thomas when he said I had attacked him and they weren't really interested in my side of what happened, so as I was the one found holding the knife, I was arrested and charged with attempting to murder Thomas."

Elizabeth tightly closed her eyes, recalling that even in the so-called enlightened society that was supposed to recognise women's right, those troubled days continued to exist, as well as the almost indifferent attitude that many police officers had when dealing with violent domestic situations; an attitude of 'you made your bed, now lie in it,' that did not serve women well.

In those few seconds she also recalled too her husband Iain's frustrations through the years, telling her of many of his colleagues unsympathetic and misogynistic outlook. Officers, male and curiously, some female too, who preferred not to be involved in such situations.

And so she asked, "But your lawyer, if you were convicted, am I to assume he did not fight your case?"

Sally's brow creased when she replied, "My lawyer was a she, a young woman appointed by the legal aid system who at the trial was completely out of her depth. It didn't help either that the Sheriff, a man called Arthur Wyatt…"

"Wait," Elizabeth frowned, "do you mean, Arthur Wyatt who was in the news, when was it again?"

Her brow furrowed as she fought to recall, "I think it was about four years ago? The retired Sheriff who publicly stated that it was not in the public interest to convict a husband who, if on occasion, slapped his wife to keep her in her place? *That* Arthur Wyatt?"

"That's him," Sally sighed. "He was still sitting as a judge in those days and sentenced me to four years in Cornton Vale women's prison, but when that article about him being a misogynist came out, my lawyer, she visited me and started an appeal against my sentencing."

She softly smiled when she added, "I think the poor lassie completely believed my side of the story and never got over me being sentenced."

"Anyway," she shrugged, "cutting a long story short, my lawyer contacted a group called the Nuffield Foundation who not only supported, but paid for my appeal too and after serving just under the eighteen months, the Parole Board released me prior to the formal review of my sentencing. A little after two months later, I was informed that my sentence must stand, but was reduced to time served."

Shocked, Elisabeth loudly exclaimed, "What!"

Then with a guilty glance about her, she leaned forward to hiss, "You weren't fully exonerated?"

Sadly smiling, Sally replied, "My lawyer, who was as upset as you are, explained it was all to do with politics. The Crown Office said that to exonerate me would have opened the floodgates for every prisoner sentenced by Sheriff Wyatt and *particularly* women," she pointedly stressed, "to appeal and so I was required to agree that I would accept the deal. In my defence, Elizabeth," she sighed, "after eighteen months in prison, I would have signed anything and agreed to any deal to get out of there."

Too dumbstruck to respond, Elizabeth, with tears in her eyes, again reached a hand across the table to tightly clasp at Sally's, then managed to stammer, "My dear, dear girl. I can't imagine how you survived not only a violent marriage, but the whole judicial system treating you as the criminal. And as for that…" teeth clenched, she hissed, "that *bastard* who treated you so badly. What become of him, do you know?"

"Oh, Thomas," she shrugged.

"Well, the Nuffield Foundation paid my lawyer to raise a divorce action that he didn't contest and they also helped me find a job, so now I'm the manageress of the City Bakeries in Alison Street. As for my ex-husband, I'm fully divorced and I have neither any idea where he is now nor do I care. He's out of my life and that's all that matters."

"The shop is in Allison Street, you say? Where presumably you met Stuart?"

"Yes," she slowly drawled, then smiled when she added, "Given my previous experience of the polis, it wasn't exactly love at first sight, but after he'd visited the shop for a few weeks, I kind of warmed to him."

"And your story, how did he react to that when you told him?"

"You've known him for far longer than I have so as you'd expect; he listened just like you did, Elizabeth, then reacted with the same anger and outrage."

"And you're worried that Adam and Jean might not react as we did?"

"Yes," she quietly replied. "I know from what Stuart has said in the past, they're very protective of their father."

Several seconds passed before Elizabeth softly said, "If you can find it in yourself to trust me, Sally, then can I ask that you leave Adam and Jean to me?"

****

The injured driver now being conveyed to the Victoria Infirmary and the preliminary details of the RTA and witness statements recorded in their notebooks, Drew Taylor and Roz Begley handed the incident to the attending officers from the Road Traffic Department, then returning to their vehicle, informed AS that they were again available for calls.

With nothing pending, Taylor suggested they head towards the Dixon Blazes industrial estate and visit the fast food van located there for a cuppa.

A little over ten minutes later, with Roz as the junior officer coerced into paying for two teas and the obligatory chocolate biscuits, Taylor said, "Ah, you never said yay or nay about meeting for a coffee in Byres Road, tomorrow or Thursday, whichever day suits."

Hurriedly sipping at his scalding plastic beaker of tea to hide his flushed face, he saw Roz's face contort as she gave it some thought before she replied, "I've a few things to catch up on Thursday, so how's about tomorrow morning?"

"Yeah, great," he responded, a little bit more enthusiastically than he intended, then cleared his throat when he added, "How about eleven at the University Café?"

"Yeah," she drawled, "that'll be fine, then maybe you can show me your flat? You do know I've never actually been inside, even though I've picked you up from there about a thousand times."

"Eh, what? You've never been *in* my flat?"

"Nope," she grinned at him. "I've always imagined it to be a dark and dismal bachelor pad with soiled clothes everywhere and the kitchen sink full of dirty dishes and the bin overflowing with old takeaway cartons."

Pretending anger, he said "I'll let you know, Constable Begley, I happen to run a tight ship and I'm fully domesticated, so less of the disparaging female assumption that us men are incapable of looking after ourselves."

'Well" she stared slyly at him, "we'll see."

It was then through the open passenger door, they heard the radio call, "AS to Foxtrot Mike Two, over."
****

Lizzie Whitmore glanced up as her door was knocked then pushed open to admit Chief Inspector Marty McKenna and his neighbour, the sullen faced Sergeant Mulvey.

"Got a minute?" he raised his eyebrows.

"Of course. Coffee or tea?"

"No, we won't bother, thanks anyway. We'll not be here that long, Lizzie," he replied as he dragged out one of the two chairs opposite her.

"Actually, Marty," she exhaled when she replied, "you might be, because I have another situation that will probably involve your department."

Glancing at Mulvey, he nodded when he said, "Tea for us both. Milk only."

Phoning down to the uniform bar, Whitmore requested that a tray of tea for three be delivered to her room.

Fifteen minutes later and with a mug in his hand, he detailed the interview with Sharon Crosbie and also recounted the information provided by her work colleague.

McKenna concluded when he said, "So, subject to confirmation from my boss and without any corroborating evidence at this time, unless something turns up in the future which I sincerely believe will not happen, I'll be writing off Miss Crosbie's complaint as malicious."

"You believe because young Taylor finished with her, it's her way of revenging herself on him?"

To both their surprise, it was Mulvey who sourly replied, "Crosbie's a right gorgeous looking young woman, Ms Whitmore, and she knows it too and undoubtedly with an ego to match her looks. There's no doubt in my mind and likely Mr McKenna's too, that she is vindictive and I'd guess, devious as well, as intimated to us by her workmate. She isn't the sort of woman who gets dumped; she's the sort that *does* the dumping and for Taylor to end it? Well," she snorted, "what better opportunity than to use us, the police, to get her revenge. The only thing that *really* bugs me," she leaned forward in her chair, tiny flecks of spittle at the edges of her mouth, "is that because the Force don't want to inhibit the public from making genuine complaints against the police, Mr McKenna and I can't go and charge the bitch with making a false allegation."

Suddenly getting to her feet, she excused herself, saying, "I need to go to the ladies."

When she'd left the room, McKenna stared wide-eyed at her before he gasped, "In the time I've worked with Mulvey, that's the longest speech I've ever heard her make."

"So," she returned to the subject of Drew Taylor. "If my constable is being maligned, do we tell him or let it go?"

"My suggestion," he slowly began, "is to bring him in and have a private word with him. There's a likelihood this woman Crosbie won't let the issue rest, albeit I'm satisfied that Taylor is completely innocent of the allegation she made against him."

"Do you want to be present when I speak with him?"

No," he shook his head, "I think it's better you keep this in-house, but let him know to keep a weather eye and his ears open for her to try and make trouble for him."

"He's on late shift right now, so I'll have him come and see me before I finish up today."

The door opened to admit Mulvey who resumed her seat just as McKenna said, "Now, Lizzie, what's this other situation you're talking about?"

****

Sitting in his front room, reading that days delivered 'Glasgow News,' Smiler unconsciously shook his head at the Editorial page that lambasted the Craigie Street CID who according to the article, were nowhere near discovering the identity of the man who murdered Jeannie Mason and Albert Moston.

If anything, apart from the usual diatribe against the police, the article told Smiler two things.

Someone and likely with knowledge of the investigation, which in turn meant a police officer or member of the civilian staff, had touted to the newspaper that both murders were linked; the second thing that the killer was a man.

Smiler was no stranger to seeing confidential information published in the media, but it still rankled that a trusted and vetted employee of Strathclyde Police, whether for a backhander or perhaps simply boasting that they were 'in the know,' would divulge such information that might or not be crucial in identifying the killer.

He himself, one evening many years previously while guarding a murder locus, had been approached by a crime reporter from the 'Glasgow News' who had attempted to solicit information by producing a crisp, ten-pound note; a princely sum at that time.
It was fortunate that because of his attempted solicitation, the reporter was not in a position to make a complaint, for he had found himself taken by the throat and shoved hard against a tenement wall, being choked.
Though it had occurred so long ago and on any occasion he had cause to visit Craigie Street, the reporter had since that time given Smiler a wide berth.
The phone ringing in the hallway broke into his thoughts and caused him to hurry through whereupon answering it, discovered it to be the DI, Sammy Pollock.
After confirming that the big man was fit and healthy, Pollock made the DCI's request.
"I'm supposed to be days off Wednesday and Thursday, Sammy, but if you can guarantee I'll get them back as time in lieu, I'm your man," Smiler assured him.
"I'll see your shift Inspector, Iain Cowan, is informed, Smiler, and thanks," Pollock ended the call.
Replacing the handset, Smiler turned as the door opened to admit Sally, who with a wide smile, opened her arms and was crushed in his.
"Miss me?"
"A wee bit. What's for dinner?" he teased her.
Slapping lightly at his arm, she replied, "Wait and see."
"How did your meeting go?"
"It went well, in fact better than I thought," she sighed, for she'd sworn Elizabeth to secrecy, having decided she would tell Stuart of her fears when the time was right.
"I'm thinking of taking tomorrow off," she smiled at him. "Maybe spend the day together."
"Ah, yes, well," he grimaced, "there's a wee problem with that."
"And that is?" her eyes narrowed.
"The boss at the CID has asked me to go in to assist with their murder investigation."
"Oh, right. Well," she reached up to gently stroke at his cheek, "if you must then, you must, but please be careful. The doctor told us

that you had a lungful of smoke and you really should be taking it easy, out walking and getting some fresh air."

He stared peculiarly down at her, then to her surprise, he softly said, "I like it when you worry about me. Makes me feel, I don't know," he shrugged, "loved and wanted."

****

DC Barbara McMillan's face registered her disgust at working in the dusty, dank and creepy basement of Craigie Street police station. Feeling dirty after handling dozens of the grimy box files, she was already planning that when she returned home to her flat that evening, it was to be an immediate hot bath, her business suit destined for the dry-cleaners and her blouse and undergarments thoroughly machine washed.

It didn't help when her neighbour, Morris Kerr, laughed at her discomfort, then said, "Be careful when you disturb the paper files there, Babs. There might be spiders nesting among them."

"Aye, very good," she grunted, but inwardly shivered for eight legged arachnids were definitely not her favourite creatures, regardless of their size.

It was curious that though McMillan wold square up to a violent man with a broken bottle, as she had done in the third year of her service outside a pub on Battlefield Road, the very thought of facing a spider the size of her fingernail, filled her with dread.

Holding her breath, her face contorted as she delicately picked her way through the old box files, half expecting each one to disclose a big black hairy spider, then suddenly realised the dry, musty air in the basement caused her to feel parched.

Turning to Kerr, she brightly suggested, "Why don't I nip back upstairs and grab two mugs of coffee?"

Kerr grinned, knowing the real reason McMillan was that his neighbour wanted a five-minute break, counter-suggested with, "Look, I'm needing a pee anyway. You continue down here and I'll grab the coffees."

Before she could object and with his back to her so she could not see him grinning, he was away and heading to the door that led to the tight, circular stairs up to the ground floor of the station.

"Bugger," she hissed after him, then gingerly pulled yet another file from the seemingly hundreds that filled the free-standing metal cabinets standing against the walls of the basement.

With a heavy sigh, then almost choking from the dust that rose as she wrestled the next file from the shelf, she stood back and opened the lid of what was the latest of several dozen files she had so far examined.

The crime reports and statements contained within the unmarked box file were, similar to those files she had already sifted through, lying loose and with no apparent index to indicate their origin and once again, McMillan mentally cursed the lazy detectives or admin staff who had so thoughtlessly filled the file.

Sitting herself down onto an old, rickety wooden chair of undetermined age, one of three spider-webbed that she and Kerr had discovered in the basement, she balanced the file on her knee, then groaned when she saw that the skirt of her suit was now stained with some undetermined greasy or oily substance adhering to the bottom of the file.

"Shit!" she loudly cursed, then irately began to examine the contents of the box file.

Removing the first of a number of crime reports, the paper dry and rustling and some of which had multiple statements attached with now rusting paperclips, she laid those files she'd examined in a pile by her feet.

Halfway through the contents, she read a file and was about to lay it with those at her feet when she stopped, then reread the top crime report page.

Her eyes narrowed as she read that a man called Robert Reagan, a seventy-three-years old retired shipyard welder, reportedly one evening on 18 October, 1963, exited a pub on Allison Street, then ten minutes later, been bundled into his close in Ascog Street by two men who proceeded to punch and kick him, before robbing him of his wallet.

All thoughts of spiders, her stained skirt and where she was sitting disappeared and an excited McMillan read the attached statement of Reagan, that he had been taken to the Victoria Infirmary where he was treated for a broken right arm and multiple bruising.

What was more exciting to the young detective was that when interviewed by the detective and though Reagan had been drinking, the old man was sufficiently *compos mentis* to provide rough descriptions of his assailants, one of whom had a funny shaped nose.

Unable to contain her excitement, McMillan unconsciously took a deep breath, then when the dust mites and heaven alone knew what else was floating in the basement air, struck the back of her throat, she involuntarily coughed and brought up dirty phlegm onto a handkerchief.
But disgusted or not, that didn't bother her for the rough description of the assailant with the 'funny shaped nose' must, she breathlessly thought, had to fit their victim, Albert Moston.

CHAPTER TWENTY-TWO.

Foxtrot Mike Two's last call of that afternoon, a report of a man acting suspiciously while hanging around the houses in Kingsacre Road in the Kings Park area, had proved to be a false alarm with good intent when the man was discovered to be the new boyfriend of a young woman who had invited him to meet her mother.
However, the highly embarrassed boyfriend had lost his girlfriend's address and a stranger to the southside of the city, become confused by the number of roads, drives, crescents and avenues in the area whose addresses were preceded by the word, 'King'.
Driving the boyfriend to a nearby telephone kiosk, an amused Taylor and Roz waited while he telephoned his girlfriend, then sheepishly confirmed the address to be located in Kingsbridge Crescent, again an address not known to him.
"What do you think, Roz?" Taylor winked at her.
"Who are we to stand in the path of romance," she lightly replied, then invited the boyfriend to again jump into the rear of the van before minutes later, depositing him at the address.
The young man's thanks were gratefully received, then as they drew away, Taylor's personal radio activated with the instruction that if the crew were not involved in a call, they were to attend Craigie Street where Taylor was to report to Chief Inspector Whitmore.
"Now," he wondered as he turned to stare quizzingly at Roz "what's that all about?"
****
Dressed in his pyjamas and sitting at the desk in his bedroom, a cup

of tea cooling on his bedside table, Keith Telford broodily gave thought to what had occurred earlier that day.

He thought of how everyone had let him down. Him, the best cop of the shift and none of the *bastards* supported him when he really needed it.

Drawing deeply on the Kensitas cigarette, the smoke adding to the already foetid air in the disorderly room that his mother had long ago gave up trying to tidy, he vowed that one day he'd get even with them all and in particular, that bitch Roz Begley and her backstabbing neighbour, Drew Taylor.

They were supposed to have his back like he always had theirs, conveniently forgetting that neither of the two nor any of the shift would ever trust Telford to have their back.

Shifting uncomfortably on the chair, his balls still aching from where one of those murderous thugs had stamped on him, his memory of the event in the back of the van now suited the story he had spun to his parents.

Arriving home and theatrically groaning, he had staggered through the front door to tell them of his heroism, recounting how he had been injured and almost killed when acting alone, he had arrested two of the most wanted men in Scotland who were robbing a pharmacy, then prevented their escape when two of the clueless idiots in his shift had forgotten to handcuff them.

"Dear God," his wide-eyed mother had slapped her hands across her mouth at such a dangerous story, while his father, a little more circumspect, inwardly thought it to be yet another of his sons Walter Mitty stories, but said nothing.

Dragging himself upstairs, he had called back down to his parents that he was not to be disturbed, that the doctor had examined him and recommended bedrest.

In the privacy of their front room, his parents whispered conversation queried why if he was so injured, he had arrived home alone, why had none of his colleagues accompanied him and most curiously, why did Keith tell them that the arrest was to be considered a secret, that the TV news and media was banned by the police from reporting this supposedly very serious incident?

"Because it *didn't* happen, dear," his father stared sadly at his wife, ashamed that his son had grown to be a man who could not be trusted to tell the truth.

"You mean, he's lying again?"

"Of course he is," the father replied with a resigned sigh. "Which begs the question, his late shift is due to finish at eleven at night, so why has he really been sent home in the afternoon?"

Had he known of this conversation, their son might have included his parents in that long list of individuals with whom he promised to get even and which now included Inspector Cowan, who also refused to believe his side of the story.

His anger knowing no bounds, Telford vividly imagined himself once more emerging as the hero, with his shift begging forgiveness for their betrayal of him.

But then those pleasant thoughts turned darker when he considered ways that he could revenge himself on them and perhaps, he grimly smiled, commencing with Roz Begley.

****

On foot and doing the round of his constables out on the street, acting Sergeant Mattie Devlin called for the position of Constable Willie Strathmore, then minutes later, met with Strathmore at the corner of Albert Avenue and Victoria Road.

"Anything doing, Willie?" Devlin asked as he signed and timed Strathmore's notebook, adding the locus where they had met; an unofficial stamp, as it where, that the constable was noted to be present and on his beat at that time and place, thereby safeguarding him against any allegation of shirking or dereliction of his duties.

"Nothing at the minute, Sarge," Strathmore shook his head. "A couple of calls regarding some of the old jakies loitering in the back courts bevying and I had a word with them regarding wee Jeannie Mason's murder, but it was the usual three monkeys; see, hear and speak no evil. That said," he sighed, "Jeannie never hurt a soul and she was well liked in the bevy community, so like the polis or not, I'm thinking if they *did* know anything, they would say."

"Looking forward to your days off?"

"Well," Strathmore glumly replied, "I've the elementary exam to sit on Wednesday, then likely on Thursday, my missus will take me for a consolatory dinner."

"Well, for one," a surprised Delvin stared at him, "I hadn't realised you were going for the exam and two, what makes you think you'll fail? I mean, if you're putting the work in, you should get by."

"Ah, well, yes, I have been studying hard as my Mrs Happy will tell you, because I'm missing a lot of time with the weans, but you'll know yourself how many get through the exam. I've been told that the pass rate for Scotland is something like fifteen percent, while for the advanced exam, it's less than ten percent."

"One exam at a time, Willie. Wednesday," Devlin thoughtfully said. "Are you off tomorrow to cram?"

"No," he shook his head, "I didn't think it was worth it. I mean, if I haven't done enough by now, one more day won't make that much difference."

"I disagree," Devlin's lip curled as his face creased. "There's nothing wrong with putting in another nine hours of study rather than doing a late shift pounding the streets around here."

He took a breath then again stared thoughtfully at Strathmore before he asked, "You got any time in lieu lying available?"

"Aye, I have. Nearly fifteen hours, I think. Why?"

"How do you feel about using nine of those hours and taking tomorrow off? I can square it with the Inspector, if you like."

"Eh, yeah, that'd be great. I could hit the library for the day and get some more time under my belt, but me being off, Sarge. That's going to leave you right short on the shift."

"Leave me and the Inspector to worry about that, Willie. Hmm," his face creased, "as I recall, Harry Dawson is on her variable rest day tomorrow. I'm sure I can persuade her to work for time in lieu if she knows she's doing you a favour. Might cost you a box of chocolates," he smiled.

Strathmore, his hopes gradually mounting that on Wednesday morning, he'd not be attending the exam centre tired after a late shift, eagerly nodded, then said, "I'm grateful, Sarge, if you can fix it for me."

"Leave it with me," Devlin smiled, then added, "How's about you and I neighbour up for a half-hour, eh?"

****

DCI Gemmill's door was knocked, then pushed open by Sammy Pollock, closely followed by DC Barbara McMillan.

One glance at McMillan's eager face was enough to raise Gemmill's hopes when she asked, "You found something, Barbara?"

"Yes, boss, this," she laid the file down onto the DCI's desk.

"Before I read it, what does it contain?"

Her throat dry from the dust she'd swallowed, McMillan swallowed her phlegm before she began, "Back in 1963, one of the DC's from the Department dealt with a complainer called Patrick Reagan, who was seventy-three at the time. He was mugged in his close in Ascog Street and…"

"Ascog Street? Where's that?" Gemmill interrupted when she turned towards Pollok, but it was McMillan who replied, "Not far from Calder Street, boss. In fact," her forehead creased, "it's just a couple of streets away from Govanhill Park."

"And Govanhill Street, I suppose, where Moston lived," Gemmill nodded, then said, "Go on."

"At the time, boss," McMillan continued, "Reagan gave a brief description of his two assailants, admittedly not brilliant descriptions, but describing one as having a funny shaped nose."

"Moston!" Gemmill slapped a hand down onto the desk, then said, "Good work, Barbara."

Glancing down at the green coloured paper crime report, it was the half-page size supplementary report, attached to the front with a rusting staple that immediately drew Gemmill's attention; green like the crime report, a supplementary report whose white copy would have been dispatched to the City of Glasgow Police headquarters, then located in the city centre's Stewart Street.

Her eyes narrowed when she read the small summary, writing off the crime as unsolvable, but it was the signature and rank that really attracted her attention.

And her inward fury.

'J M Crawford,' she read, then under her breath, muttered, "John Michael Crawford, DCI."

Watching her, both Pollock and McMillan sensed her anger, but neither commented.

Forcing herself to be calm, Gemmill glanced up to address McMillan when she said, "Now, Barbara, if your complainer was seventy-three when he was assaulted and robbed in 1963, that would make him, eh, ninety-eight or -nine," she groaned, "and likely deceased. However, if he's ever related that story of him being robbed to a younger person …"

She licked at her lips, then addressed McMillan with, "It's a bit late now, but tomorrow first thing, Barbara, you and your neighbour interview the residents of the locus in Ascog Street to try and find anyone recalls Reagan living there and if any of them remember him being robbed, but more particularly, if he ever described to them who robbed him."

"Boss," McMillan tried to contain her excitement.

Returning to the incident room, McMillan saw her neighbour, Morris Kerr, with two mugs of coffee and who stared at her, then asked, "What?"

****

Chief Inspector Lizzie Whitmore glanced at her wristwatch and wondered why she hadn't just had young Taylor come to see her tomorrow, then she'd not be late getting away home.

When the door was knocked, she called out, "Come in," and was relieved to see it was Drew Taylor, his cap held under his arm.

"You're looking for me, Ma'am," he asked with a smile.

"Yes, I am. Please," she gestured to the chair in front of her desk, "sit down."

When he was seated, she said, "I'll come straight to the point, Drew. There was a complaint made against you, one that could have meant the termination of your career had it not been nipped in the bud, so to speak."

His jaw dropped and his face paled when stunned, he muttered, "Ma'am?"

"I understand you were recently in a relationship with a woman called Sharon Crosbie?"

"Sharon? Eh, yes Ma'am. But we broke up. No," he shook his head, then after a few seconds pause, said, "Actually, I broke up with Sharon, to be more precise."

"And I take it the …*ending* of the relationship was acrimonious?"

"She didn't take it well, Ma'am, if that's what you mean," he softly replied, then added, "To be honest, I didn't handle it well either. I told her in a public place, a café in the city centre. Just on Sunday morning, there."

"Eh," his face expressing his curiosity, he leaned forward to say, "can I ask what she's said about me, what the complaint is?"

"That during the relationship, you both verbally and physically abused her."

"What!" he cried out. "She's saying I *hit* her!"

Whitmore saw his body was shaking with outrage or was it anger, she wasn't quite certain, but raised her hand to calm him, before she replied, "Needless to say, the complaint has been investigated by the

Complaints and Discipline Department at Pitt Street, but they found the complaint to be completely unfounded."

Such was his distress, Whitmore saw him to be close to tears, then more gently, added, "I'm telling you this, Drew, to warn you to stay away from this woman. The Chief Inspector and his sergeant who interviewed Miss Crosbie are in agreement and of the considered opinion she is likely to be vindictive and might try to press her unfounded complaint in some other way, such as speaking to a reporter."

"But Ma'am," he stared at her, "my information is that if a complaint is lodged against an officer, whether unfounded or not, it remains on that officers personnel file for the remainder of his career. I've passed both my elementary and advanced exams, so what if was to be considered for promotion? Will this complaint hinder my chances?"

"Yes," she nodded, "you're correct, Drew. Complaints *do* remain on personnel files, but trust me. The Chief Inspector who interviewed your former girlfriend has assured me that in this case, he will speak with his boss and when the official report is attached to your personnel file, it will clearly state there is no hint of any wrongdoing on your part. In fact, his sergeant is just so peeved that she can't go after Miss Crosbie and charge her with a malicious accusation. As for your opportunities of being promoted, if you can trust *me*, then I assure you this complaint will not preclude any opportunity for promotion."

Taylor took a deep breath to compose himself, then asked, "Am I to understand from what you say, Ma'am, that she might continue this, this…I don't know what I'd call it," he was angrily distressed, then settled for, "This *vendetta* against me?"

"We both know I can't answer that question, Drew, but what I will suggest is that if you do hear from her again or suspect that she's trying to contact you, take a note of the time, date and circumstance and immediately report it to me. You do *not* deal with it yourself. Is that agreeable with you?"

There was a several seconds pause and she could only guess what was going through his mind, but at last he replied, "Yes, Ma'am, and thank you."

"Right then, I know you're on the response vehicle, so you'd better get back to it."

"Ma'am," he nodded, then rising to his feet, left the room.

When the door closed behind him, Whitmore sighed, then glancing at her wristwatch, wondered if she might beat the evening rush after all.

****

Sally Rodgers decided that after she'd made dinner for them both, she'd return home to her flat.

"Is this because I'm working tomorrow?" a disappointed Smiler asked.

"Absolutely not," she'd smiled as helping her clear the table, he followed her through to the kitchen. "You're just out of hospital and you need a good night's rest and besides, if you're working tomorrow, then I'm returning to the shop, too. There's no point in me taking another annual leave day if I can't spend it with you," then seeing his eyes narrow, quickly added, "and that is not me giving you an ultimatum, Stuart. You know I'm not like that, but I do know that finding this man who murdered the woman on your beat; that's important to you, okay? Besides," she grinned at him, "how would the CID possibly find the killer without my favourite sleuth on the trail?"

He stared down at her before he softly whispered, "I do love you, you know."

"And I love you too," she curled into his outstretched arms.

****

Stooped over the cutting board, the bald man expertly sliced his way through the bags of lemons, then used the blade to sweep the cut lemons into the large, glass jar.

Tunelessly whistling to himself, his eyes narrowed and he stopped, the knife hovering over the half lemon as he stared down at it.

Curious that he hadn't noticed it before, that the tip of the knife was missing.

Lifting it to eye level, the wide, shiny blade smelling of the lemon juice, he closely examined the knife and saw the ragged metal where the tip was broken off.

His thoughts turned to that night in the close, driving the knife into the body of that grass, Moxy, then wondered; but no, the knife was

Sheffield steel and it was unlikely the bastard's soft body wouldn't have been what caused the tip to break off.

Some bastard has been using my knives, he savagely snatched a glance around him, and whoever used it probably dropped it onto the concrete floor.

His anger lasted for several seconds before his body relaxed, satisfied that his explanation must the correct one, then staring at the knife, remembered that night in the close.

Anyway, it was done and he was safe.

That wee drunken cow Jeannie and her pal, Moxy, were both gone, the only two who could finger him for what him and Moxy did all those years ago.

Slowly releasing his pent-up breath, he continued whistling while he finished cutting up the lemons.

CHAPTER TWENTY-THREE: 08.15am, Tuesday 13 March 1979.

Opening the door to the incident room, DC Barbara McMillan smiled when she saw Smiler McGarry, wearing a white shirt, tightly knotted navy-blue coloured tie and a dark grey suit.

"Smiler," she happily greeted him, "how are you after your fireman rescue?"

"Oh, it wasn't just me," the big man blushed with a wide grin, "your DCI was with me too."

Behind McMillan, the door opened again to admit DI Pollock, who seeing them both said, "Barbara, your neighbour's missus has gone down with a stomach bug and he's scrambling to find someone to childmind the kids, so in the meantime, you carry on with the inquiry in Ascog Street and, eh," his eyes narrowed in a quick decision, "in the meantime take Smiler with you. You can tell him the story on the way there."

"Boss," she nodded, then when Pollock moved away, asked Smiler, "Don't happen to fancy a cuppa somewhere before we start?"

"I know the very place," he smiled at her.

****

Drew Taylor awoke just after eight that morning with a thumping headache, having tossed and turned most of the sleepless night, then finally fell asleep when his digital clock read six-fifteen.

Swinging his legs from his bed, he slowly exhaled, unable to decide whether to lie on or get up and shower.

Finally, he stood up from the bed and made his way through to the kitchen, deciding first to have a strong coffee, then shower.

Though the Chief Inspector had been adamant that Sharon's complaint against him would not hinder his promotion chances, Taylor was not convinced and lying awake in the darkest depths of the night, even considered resigning from the police and looking for opportunities elsewhere.

However, tired though he was, he decided that he would not let Sharon win and ruin his career because of her lies.

Yes, he'd always known she was a manipulative and deceitful woman and yet he had foolishly if not *stupidly*, overlooked those nasty traits. Why, was the question he now had to ask himself and if he were honest, he'd allowed himself to ignore them.

Fool me once, he shook his head, shame on you, Sharon; fool me twice, he took a deep breath, shame on me and I deserve what's happening to me.

Filling the electric kettle, he spooned a large dollop of coffee into a mug, then milked it.

Minutes later, pouring the boiling water into the mug, his thoughts turned to Roz Begley and her curiosity when he'd returned from the Chief Inspector's office.

His first thought had been to share the news of Sharon's complaint, but found he couldn't bring himself to admit his part in it for like it or not, he was as much to blame for ignoring Sharon's vile character as she was using the police to get payback on him.

Of course, almost immediately Roz had sensed something was wrong and after being politely, but firmly rebuffed by him, they finished the shift in almost total silence.

His brow furrowed when he thought, just as the manner in which he'd finished with Sharon, once more he'd handled it badly.

Now seated at the kitchen table in the galley kitchen, he sipped at his coffee and made his decision.

Today, when he resumed the final late shift, he'd speak with Inspector Cowan and share his concern about the complaint affecting his chances of promotion, then seek his advice.

****

Chief Superintendent Jimmy Thompson glanced up when his door was pushed open by his breathless secretary, Doris, who flushed-faced and who wide-eyed, hissed at him, "That's the Deputy Chief Constable to see you, sir. Shall I tell her to come in?"

Inwardly grateful that he had not had an early morning tipple, Thompson nodded as he stood, then unconsciously pulled at the hem of his tunic.

Seconds later, the Deputy, Paula Clarke, smiled as she walked through the door and greeted Thompson with, "My apologies for not announcing my visit, Mr Thompson, but between us, I'm not really here."

Surprised, he indicated the chair in front of his desk and when she sat down, told his secretary, "Tea for two, please, Doris."

His curiosity aroused, he resumed his seat, then repeated, "Not really here?"

"Cards on the table, Jimmy?"

"Always, Paula," he stared narrow-eyed at her.

She drew a short breath before she said, "I'm aware what occurred here in your office, yesterday, and frankly I'm appalled that the Chief ordered you to take a breath-test."

His mind racing, he asked, "Can I assume it wasn't the Chief who told you?"

"No, but I'm certain you'll work it out," she replied with a droll smile.

The only other witness to the visit was Lizzie Whitmore and Thompson knew she wouldn't have mentioned it to anyone, so that left just the one other person who had been present.

With his own smile, he said, "I take it the Chief's aide, the Superintendent, is one of yours then, Paula?"

"We have a history in the South Yorkshire Constabulary, yes," she nodded, "but that aside, he's a good man and is neither pleased by the way the Chief conducts himself nor what is asked of him."

"And why are you telling me this?"

She paused for several seconds as though weighing whether or not to disclose the full story, then said, "I had a call at home several nights ago from the Deputy Chair of the Police and Fire Committee. In confidence, she told me that due to a number of complaints from both officers as well as members of the Force Support Officers union," then held up a hand to before she continued, "though I'm not party to those complaints, the Committee are reviewing the Chief's contract with a view of requesting his resignation, rather than proceeding with his dismissal."

His brow creased when he sighed, "And after yesterday's visit you believe that my complaint against the Chief might be the, what shall we call it, the icing on the cake?"

"Exactly."

"And where does that leave you, Paula?"

"We're both grown-ups, Jimmy," she stared meaningfully at hm. "Initially, I'll be asked to step up as the acting Chief while the job is advertised, though we both know very well that leaves me in the pole position for assuming the Chief's job."

He wryly smiled when he asked, "Is this really the way you want to get the top job, Paula? I mean, you've proved yourself to be an able and very capable Deputy. Like it or not, you're conspiring to oust him and that doesn't strike me as being your style."

She frowned when she shook her head and said, "You're right, of course, it's not how I wanted things to go. But Jimmy, the truth is Arthur Donaldson is a bloody incompetent and a liability who, as they say, has never seen an angry man in his life. He's absolutely no experience in any department other than administrative ones and we both know he's led a charmed life throughout his career. As far as I'm concerned, I might not have been here at the unification of the Forces and the commencement of Strathclyde Police, but in the short time I have been here, I've come to love working in this Force and I'm damned if I'll see that fool run it into the ground! My God, Jimmy," she fumed, "have you any idea at all how bad our officer's morale is?"

Thompson knew exactly how poor morale was, but decided to let her rant on.

"I regularly visit stations throughout the Force area and it's always the same complaint; undermanned shifts, poor or old equipment and vehicles and all the while Donaldson is ranting at his senior commanders, blaming them for *his* shortcomings."

She took a breath just as Doris meekly knocked on the door and entered with a tray on which she balanced a pot of tea, cups and saucers, milk and sugar bowl along with a plate of Tunnocks caramel wafers.

Glancing at her, seeing her downcast eyes, Thompson had little doubt Doris had heard every word.

When the door had closed behind her, Clarke continued, "Are you aware that he's instructed the Scenes of Crime photographers to produce a set of eight large *framed* prints of himself posing at various locations throughout the Force area; that he used the Force helicopter to travel to scout out these locations and that the cost of the whole project, the use of the chopper, the SOCO's time and their resources, is the composite price of several brand new Ford Granada cars for the Traffic Department?"

"I did hear a rumour," he quietly admitted.

She slowly shook her head when she added, "He's also demanded his office be completely refurbished and brought his bloody wife in to supervise the decorating, so God alone knows what *that* will cost."

"That I *didn't* hear," he softly smiled.

"The thing is, Jimmy, he's using money from our Force budget, money we can't afford to be squandering. Look around you at this station," she waved a hand. "Can you imagine what you might have done with that money to improve your officer's accommodation and facilities?"

He raised his eyebrows in silent agreement, then drew a breath before he asked, "Am I to assure that no matter if I complain or not, he's being sacked anyway?"

"Yes," she nodded, "he's going, Jimmy, though he doesn't yet know it."

He surprised her when he said, "Will *you* be a good Chief Constable, Paula?"

She drew a short breath when she grimly replied, "Time will tell, but I know one thing for sure. I'll be a *better* Chief Constable, Jimmy, and there's a wealth of experience at Pitt Street among the Assistant Chief's that I can draw upon, so yes, I should be okay."

He reached for the teapot and filled both cups as he formally said, "Well, in that case, Deputy Chief Constable, I must inform you that I wish to submit an official complaint against Chief Constable Donaldson."

****

Leading Barbara McMillan through the rear door into the back shop of the City Bakeries, Smiler introduced her to the manageress, Sally

Rodgers, then said, "Barbara and I have a wee inquiry to conduct locally, but wondering if we might have a cuppa?"

"I'll see to it," Sally smiled at Barbara, then left to return to the front of the shop.

"This your regular howf, then," McMillan glanced around the room.

"One of them," he smiled at her as the curtain parted to admit Sally, who carried a tray with three mugs of tea and a plate with two rolls and bacon.

"Oh, thank God," McMillan snatched a roll and bit into it, dropping crumbs onto her jacket that she swept away with her hand as she muttered, "I left the house this morning without any breakfast."

"Still living with David?" Smiler asked as Sally drew up a third chair and reached for a mug.

McMillan nodded, then taking a second bite, mumbled, "Can't get rid of the sod, so I suppose he's there for keeps."

"And you, Smiler," Sally turned to him, "I'm hearing you were quite the hero the other day."

"Ah, no, not really. Just in the right place at the wrong time."

"Oh, right," she stared at him; a stare that wasn't missed by McMillan.

"Here," he passed the second roll to McMillan, who acknowledging his courtesy with a nod, bit into it as Sally asked, "And this job you have with the CID, Smiler, is that to be full time, working shifts like you do uniform?"

What an odd question, McMillan thought, then saw Smiler's face redden before he replied, "Oh, probably dayshift I think."

Slurping his tea, he glanced at his wristwatch, then hurriedly said, "Maybe time to get away, Barbara."

"Eh? Aye, okay, Smiler," she rose to her feet, then thanking Sally, followed him through the rear door to the courtyard at the back of the shop.

Walking towards the close that would return them to Allison Street, she teased him with, "She definitely fancies you, big man."

"Not at all," he quickly responded; too quickly thought McMillan, who decided then not to say any more.

Arriving some minutes later in Ascog Street, McMillan stared up at the red sandstone, council properties said, "If I recall from walking the beat here, these flats are two-bedroomed. Is that right?"

"Aye, spot on, Barbara. Two ground flats, two upper storeys, so six flats in all. This shouldn't take us too long, assuming that the tenants are at home and not out working."

They found the first flat on the ground left was clearly unoccupied, judging by the lack of furniture in the rooms and this was confirmed by the young woman who answered the opposite door, a toddler on her hip and clinging to her neck.

"Aye," she wearily said, "the old busybody that lived there died months ago, but the council haven't reallocated it yet."

Two minutes later, assuring Smiler and McMillan she'd never heard of a family called Reagan who lived in the close, she admitted she'd only been there for four years.

The two doors on the next flight up were both at home, a middle-aged man who was recently tenanted there by the council after declaring himself homeless and an elderly woman with hearing difficulties, but who didn't know of a Reagan family.

On the top landing, there was no response to the first door they knocked while the second door was an elderly man, who seemed confused and who believing them to be Jehovah's Witnesses, slammed the door in their face.

"Well," a disappointed McMillan said as they trudged back downstairs to the CID car, "that was a wash-out."

"Hmm, maybe not," Smiler slowly replied.

She stopped in the close entrance, then turning to stare at him, asked, "What do you mean?"

"That old guy, believing we were Jehovah's. That got me thinking. Patrick Reagan. What foot do you think he kicked with?"

"Eh?"

"Patrick Reagan," he repeated. "What do you think his religion might be with a name like that?"

"I don't know," she shrugged. "It sounds Irish, so maybe Catholic?"

"Aye, Catholic," he smiled, then his brow knitted when he thoughtfully said, "I think the nearest Catholic church is over in Albert Drive."

"That's over the boundary in G Division, isn't it?"

"Aye, but I don't suppose God's got boundaries for his worshipers, wee pal. As I recall, curiously enough, the church is called St Albert's," he smiled, then added, "Right, let's me and you go and visit the priest in St Albert's and see if he's any knowledge of the family Reagan."

****

Still depressed after learning of his former girlfriends' malicious complaint against him, Drew Taylor swithered whether or not to cancel his coffee date with Roz Begley, particularly after the previous evening when he had all but ignored her for the remainder of their shift.

Besides, he told himself, even though Sharon's complaint was false, there would always be those who learning of it might believe that if mud's flung, something will stick and the last thing he wanted was for anyone, let alone Roz, think that he was an abuser of women. Showered and now towelled dry, he sat on the edge of his bed then made his decision.

Roz was no fool. If he was upfront with her and told her of the allegation, there was no doubt she'd believe him.

Or so he hoped.

No, he unconsciously shook his head, she *would* believe him, for the simple reason that after he'd admitted badly handling the break-up with Sharon, Roz had scolded him, even though he strongly suspected she didn't like Sharon, she had admitted, albeit in a roundabout way, he'd done the correct thing.

Curiously, that made him feel a whole lot better, the glancing at his bedside clock, realised he'd time to head out grocery shopping before he had to get dressed for work.

****

Sitting in front of her boss, Chief Inspector Lizzie Whitmore listened as he recounted the visit from the Deputy Chief Constable.

"You'll want a corroborating statement from me too, then," she slowly nodded.

"It would help, but if it goes apeshit, you could be ending your career and settling for a job in some God forsaken station in the middle of nowhere."

"Jimmy," she sighed, "since the management learned of my gender preference and by *management* I mean that bigot Donaldson and his type, my career's already blighted, so what more can they do to me?"

He grimly smiled when he replied, "Yes, Lizzie, a statement from you would be most helpful. Now, I'm assuming you have some other business with me?"

"I need a favour."

"And that is?" his eyes widened.

Recounting the allegation against Constable Drew Taylor and the result of the Complaints and Discipline investigation, she concluded with, "He's a good, hard working young cop, is Taylor, and I'd like you to assure him that though the complaint will remain on his personnel file, it will not affect his promotion opportunities."

"You do believe the complaint is malicious?"

"According to Marty McKenna, a man I trust, then yes. I do believe it's malicious."

"Okay, ask that Inspector Cowan instructs Taylor to come and see me when he arrives for his late shift. No point in keeping it hanging over the young man. Now anything else I should know?"

"It was then the door was knocked and pushed open by his secretary, who said, "DCI Gemmill to see you, sir."

"Send her in, Doris," then when Whitmore rose to leave, he said, "No, stay, Lizzie. You should hear what Laura has to say."

Greetings exchanged, Gemmill took a chair by Whitmore and began with, "Firstly, sir, no good news on the murder investigations; however, I'm concentrating the team on a number of historical crimes that were committed in the Division about sixteen years ago."

"Go on," his eyes narrowed.

Over the next few minutes, Gemmill related the circumstances of the assaults and robberies committed by Albert Moston and an accomplice, not yet identified.

"And Moston," Thompson asked, "was identified, but never charged because the then DCI decided to use him as a tout on local crime?"

"It would appear so, yes," she nodded with a frown.

"Jesus," he wearily rubbed a hand across his brow. "If that gets leaked to the media, even after all these years, it will cause a bloody stink because though the victims might have since passed on, their children and grandchildren could kick up one hell of a fuss."

"On the other hand," Whitmore quietly suggested, "if the media were to identify who the DCI was at that time…"

She left the rest of her statement hanging in the air, but watched it draw a smile from both Thompson and Gemmill, who said, "Serve the bugger right, using his career advancement on the back of a number of pensioners being beaten and robbed by Moston and his pal."

"And quite correctly," Thompson added, "would scupper any thoughts he might have of continuing his career in the police or even worse, returning here to Strathclyde as a Deputy or, the good Lord forbid, as Chief Constable."

It was Whitmore who asked, "While I'm not privy to everything going on in your investigation, Laura, it does rather seem that you're placing all your eggs in one basket, going after this alleged accomplice."

"The truth is, Lizzie, we've no witnesses and very little Forensic evidence, other than the shoeprints and a Production I'm not at liberty to discuss."

Both Whitmore and Thompson understood the necessity of an SIO keeping something back and didn't question what that Production might be.

"Is there any good news in your investigation, Laura?" Thomson stared at her.

"Well," she drawled, "one of my DC's, Barbara McMillan, has identified a complainer from back then and is currently trying to track down any family members of that individual who might recall the complainer describing Moston's accomplice. She's currently out now with one of the cops, Smiler McGarry, but I've not heard anything back yet."

"Smiler," Thompson grinned. "If there's someone to be found, then he's your man."

"Right," he slapped a hand down onto his desk.

"I'll let you get on, ladies, and Lizzie," he reminded her, "I'll see your Constable Taylor when he's back on shift."

When both Whitmore and Gemmill had gone, Thompson lifted his desk phone and dialled the direct number for the Deputy Chief Constable's office, then asked to be put through to her.

"Paula," he began. "Following on from our conversation this morning, my Chief Inspector Lizzie Whitmore has agreed to forward a statement of the Chief's visit yesterday to my office. And another thing," he licked at his dry lips, "in the strictest of confidence, should the Police and Fire Committee decide to approach a certain Assistant Chief Constable (Crime), who is known to us both and currently serving in our neighbouring Force, you *might* wish to apprise the Chairwoman of the following information."

CHAPTER TWENTY-FOUR.

Knocking on the chapel house door, it was opened by a stocky built woman in her mid-fifties," McMillan guessed, her greying hair knotted in a tight bun on her head and wearing a lengthy wrap-around apron and who stared suspiciously at Smiler and Barbara McMillan.
"Hi, we're from the police," McMillan smiled when she flashed her warrant card, then added, "Is the parish priest at home?"
In a soft Irish accent, the woman replied, "Father is in the vestry. I'm Mrs Rosie Donovan, his housekeeper. Can I ask what it's about?"
"We'd like to speak to him about a parishioner, if the priest might have known him."
"On that issue," Smiler interrupted, "can you tell us how long Father might have been serving here at St Albert's?"
"Oh, let me see…" she stared thoughtfully at Smiler, then her face lit up in a huge smile when she said, "It's you, Smiler, isn't it? You're the polis that works around Allison Street, aren't you now? I didn't recognise you with your clothes on."
His face reddening, he saw McMillan turn to him with a huge grin when he replied, "You mean, out of my uniform and wearing my suit, of course?"
"Aye," she seemed confused, "what did you think I mean?"
"So," Smiler hastily continued, "how do we get to the vestry?"
"Come away in and I'll take you through," she stepped to one side to permit them to pass her by.
After closing, then locking the front door behind them, Rosie led the two officers through the house to a solid wooden door that in turn admitted them to the interior of the church, then followed her along the line of pews to the altar.
To one side of the altar was another solid wooden door that led to the priests dressing room and yet another door, that she knocked.
"Come in," barked a gruff voice.
Pushing open the door, Smiler and McMillan saw a dark-haired man of about forty years of age, dressed in a black shirt with a priest collar, black trousers and his black dress jacket hung over the chair on which he sat in front of a desk.

Smoke from a lit cigarette curled up from an ashtray on the desk that was laden with a number of black coloured hardback ledgers.
Staring curiously at the officers, he said, "What's this then, Rosie?"
"Ah, sorry to disturb you when you're at the books, Father, but it's two polis looking for a word."
It was Smiler who extended a hand, then nodding at his neighbour, said, "Detective Constable McMillan and I'm Constable McGarry, Father, eh…?"
"John McNamara," rising from his chair, the priest instinctively took Smiler's hand, then asked, "What can I do for you?"
Smiler turned towards McMillan, who gave him the subtlest nod to go ahead, then he said, "Can I first ask how long you've been the parish priest here, Father?"
McNamara glanced at Rosie before he replied, "Oh, that'll be coming up for three years now. Would that be right, Rosie?"
"Aye, Father. April nineteen-seventy-six, as I recall," she nodded, then making the sign of the cross, she added, "Just about a month after we lost poor Father Johnstone, may God bless him, though admittedly he was a trial at times," but thought it better not to mention the old priests' fondness for his native Irish whiskey.
Feeling a little deflated, Smiler shrugged when he said, "Sorry, Father, but it seems we might be wasting your time. We were hoping that you might have been the parish priest here a number of years ago, roughly sixteen years, to be frank."
McNamara smiled when he shook his head then explained, "Sorry, but no, though had you been here three years ago, I understand Father Johnstone had arrived in the parish in the Ark. Sixteen years ago," he grimaced, "I wasn't even ordained then. I take it what you're wanting to know must be important?"
"We think so, yes. We were hoping to learn something about a man called Patrick Reagan, who lived in Ascog Street. Maybe even if he had family and where they might be now."
They saw the priest's eyes narrow and did not miss the glance he gave Rosie, whose face paled.
"Am I missing something?" Smiler asked, turning from one to the other.
"Patrick Reagan, you say," Rosie stammered. "From Ascog Street? Why would you want to speak with him?"
Staring curiously at her, Smiler said, "We're following up a report

from sixteen years ago, the eighteenth of October, nineteen-sixty-five, to be exact, when Mr Reagan was assaulted and robbed in his close entrance and had his arm broken during the attack."
To Smiler and McMillan's surprise, her voice almost a whisper, the housekeeper replied, "His right arm."
"How could you know that, Mrs Donovan?" McMillan asked, her stomach tensing as though she had already guessed the answer.
They watched Rosie reach for the back of the priests chair as though to steady herself when she softly replied, "Reagan's my maiden name. Patrick Reagan was my father."

****

Roz Begley, ironing her uniform blouse while the radio played in the background, could not help but worry that something was amiss with her neighbour, Drew Taylor.

Her curiosity about his visit to the Chief Inspector's office and his reluctance, upon his return to disclose why he'd been beckoned was, frankly, killing her.

Her attempt to elicit the reason for his summons had fallen on deaf ears and the remainder of their shift that fortunately had been without incident, but any attempt at social conversation had also fallen on deaf ears.

Even the drive home before he'd dropped her at her tenement was in total silence.

She stopped and standing still, the iron firmly gripped in her hand, knew that it wasn't like Drew, that something awful must have happened.

But what?

She trusted Drew, a little surprised to discover that she actually trusted him more than anyone else she knew, apart maybe from her parents.

There was an honesty about him that she instinctively knew was genuine; a man who the shift liked and who liked the shift. Well, apart from that muppet, Keith Telford, her brow furrowed.

She found herself smiling when she thought about Drew, knowing that for all his experience as a police officer, there was still a naivety about him and particularly regarding women.

Women?

Not women, her eyes narrowed, but *a* woman.

That must be it, she decided with a start.

Drew was too good a police officer; smart, conscientious and ambitious to have done anything that would impact negatively on his career.

Whatever the Chief Inspector had said to him must be to do with his private life and, Roz found her teeth gritting, undoubtedly had something to do with Sharon Crosbie.

Convinced now she had discovered the reason for his mood, she now wondered; how do I get him to open up about it?

****

Keith Telford prepared his speech before he dialled the telephone number for the uniform bar at Craigie Street police station.

When the call was answered by the early shift bar officer, Telford groaned and said, "It's Keith Telford, here, from the late shift. Can you let Sergeant Devlin know that I'm still in a lot of pain after being assaulted and the doctor has prescribed me medicine that he says will make me drowsy, so I've not to drive."

The bar officer, a man with twenty years' service under his belt and who that morning had heard the story of Telford's fiasco in the rear of Foxtrot Mike Two, sniggered when he replied, "I'll pass that on, pal, but a boot in the balls doesn't make you a hero, so don't forget to send in your sick line."

Sick line!

Telford hadn't considered that he'd need one and stuttered, "Yeah, right, I'll do that," then hastily ended the call, inwardly cursing the bar officer, then adding him to the list of *bastards* he'd see sorted out!

Sitting in the front room with the door to the hallway slightly ajar, his mother and father had listened intently to his call, then heard him bad-temperedly stamping back upstairs.

They stared at one another before the father quietly sighed, "I'm thinking, dear, that our Keith won't be much longer in his job as a police officer. Maybe we should reconsider that offer for the house and like we planned, the two of us make our retirement move to Spain."

****

Now seated in the kitchen of the church house, Smiler and McMillan watched Rosie Donovan busy herself at the sink, filling the kettle. When at last she'd brewed and served the tea, she took a deep breath, then with a glance at each of them in turn, began her story.

"My father, Patrick wasn't a bad man, you understand, but weak with the drink and the gambling. My mother, she was from Donegal and when I was eight years of age, she returned there to Moville with me and my two brothers because she'd had enough of my dad and his errant ways."

"And that's why you have an Irish accent," McMillan smiled.

"Yes, even though I returned here to Glasgow some twenty odd years ago, after my mother died, I'm still taken for an Irish lass," she smiled in return.

"Anyway," she continued, "my two brothers, good men that they turned out to be, made their lives in Donegal and both made good marriages, one to a farmer's daughter where he now runs the farm and the other running a wee hotel in Moville. I was thirty-seven when I returned to Glasgow, unmarried and thinking myself to be an old maid. I moved in with my dad in Ascog Street, then a year later, after working in a shop in Battlefield, old Father Johnstone offered me the position of housekeeper. I think it was because of my accent; he missed the auld country and liked to hear the Irish spoken about him, you know? Anyway, when he passed, Father McNamara kept me on."

"And you're now Mrs Donovan?"

"Yes," she smiled. "Aiden and I met at the church social two years after I returned, him a widower with two children, so I found myself with a ready-made family," she smiled. "Course, that meant leaving my father's house, but I saw him every day; well, mostly every day."

Sipping at his tea, Smiler laid down his mug, then said, "Not wishing to sound abrupt, Rosie, but the night your father as mugged. Can you remember it?"

"Remember it, Smiler? I was in the house waiting for him to return and very angry I was too," she frowned. "The old bugger, God rest him," she once more made the sign of the cross, "was supposed to be at mine for his dinner and when he didn't show up…oh, I should say after I married Aiden, I'd moved in to his flat in Queen Mary Avenue. Anyway, to continue, it was about ten that night I'd been back and forth to the window, watching for the old scoundrel for as you'll have guessed he was still bevying, when I saw him lurching along the street. He was really staggering so I decided to go downstairs and…"

"I apologise for interrupting, Rosie, but where in the building was his flat?" McMillan asked.

"Eh, one up, on the left," she replied.

"Go on, please."

"Like I said, I'd just opened the door to the flat when I heard him shouting downstairs in the close. I thought he'd fallen over, him being so drunk and I raced down, just in time to see two bad buggers, pardon my French, stooped over him and him squealing as they thumped at him. I screamed and they saw me, then the cowardly sods, there's me using bad language again," she sighed as she shook her head, "well, they run away."

Stunned, McMillan stared at Smiler who said, "I know what you're thinking. Why wasn't this in the crime report?"

Turning to Rosie, he said, "Two questions. Firstly, did the close entrance have lights on?"

"Oh, aye," she nodded. "Back then in sixty-five, the closes still had gas lighting and the lamplighters, the leeries, we used to call them, were very regular lighting them in the evening and putting them out in the morning."

"So, you got a good look at these two thugs?"

"I did indeed, Smiler," she sniffed.

"Second question," Smiler mentally crossed his fingers. "After all these years, would you be able to describe them?"

"Yes, I can," she confidentially replied. "They were both wearing dark coloured parkas, them jackets with the fur lined hood that were popular back then. The one, the tall skinny one, his hood was up, but I got a good look at his face and I saw that he had a really funny shaped nose as though it had been twisted and bent at the same time. The other guy, the one I saw stamping on my father's arm, his hood was down and he was mean looking, I mean *really* mean looking with very fine, almost blonde hair down to here," she placed her right hand on her left shoulder. "That one, he was a little shorter than the one with the funny nose, maybe about my Aiden's height."

"And what height is Aiden?"

"Well," she smiled, "he's lost an inch through the years, but I think about your height, hen," she nodded towards McMillan. "About five feet six or seven, maybe?"

"And their ages?"

"Oh, I'm not good with ages, but I'd say both were around twenty, maybe twenty-two or twenty-three?"

"Right," Smiler drawled, then hesitantly asked, "What's the chances of you recognising that pair again, Rosie?"

She didn't immediately respond, but then stared him in the eye when she said, "Smiler, trust me. If they passed me on the street today, I'd know them. When I screamed they both stared at me before the cowards run away, so I got a right good look at the pair of them."

Seconds passed while Smiler and McMillan took this in, then she asked, "On that night, was it you who contacted the police?"

"It was," she nodded. "We didn't have a phone in the house, but there was a telephone kiosk on the corner of Victoria Road and Kingarth Street, so I'd to leave me poor old dad lying there in the close and run there to phone for an ambulance and the polis. When I got back to the close, the ambulance came first, so I went with him to the Victoria Infirmary and that's where the police turned up. Detectives, two of them."

"And you gave them a statement?"

"I did, yes."

"What about your father? Our information is that he gave the detectives a description of his assailants, particularly the one with the misshapen nose."

Rosie's brow furrowed when she shook her head, then slowly replied, "No, that can't be right. He was drunk and rambling. It was definitely me who gave the statement."

She didn't miss the glance between McMillan and Smiler, then asked, "Is there a problem?"

"It seems that somehow your statement for the crime report has become…detached, from the crime report, but that's not an issue, now that we've spoken to you."

"So," Rosie glanced at them in turn, "what happens now?"

Again, the faintest nod from McMillan caused Smiler to explain, "We believe that one of the men who assaulted your father, Rosie, might be responsible for two recent murders in…"

"Wait!" Rosie held up her hand. "Are you talking about wee Jeannie Mason and that man, eh, what's his name?"

"Did you know Jeannie?"

Rosie sighed when she said, "Jeannie sometimes came to a soup kitchen we'd open in the church hall on Tuesday's and Thursday's. A right poor soul she is…I mean was," she corrected herself and yet again, made the sign of the cross.

"Well, yes, we're talking about Jeannie and unless we're a million miles off, the man who was murdered, Albert Moston. We believe him to be one of the pair that assaulted your father. The one with the misshapen nose."

"Jesus, Mary and Joseph," a shocked Rosie once again crossed herself.

Smiler, struggling to avoid grinning, continued, "As for the other man, he is a viable suspect for those murders. Now, if we were to ask you to come to Craigie Street police station, Rosie, do you think you could have a look at some photographs of local men who are known to us?"

He face paled, but drawing back her shoulders, her chin jutted out when she replied, "I heard that man with the fine blondish hair snap my poor old fathers arm, Smiler, and for what; a handful of change in his pocket. You just name the time and day and I'll be there."

****

Wearing a knee length fawn coloured raincoat belted at the waist over her uniform blouse, her handbag slung across her shoulder and a Tupperware box containing her salad meal carried in her hand, Roz Begley stood in the entrance to the tenement close, once more considered perhaps it was time to make the move from her parents flat and find her own place.

Glancing at her wristwatch, she waited patiently for her lift, knowing that Drew Taylor was always either early or at worse, bang on time. Her thoughts turned to him and once more she wondered, what had caused him to be so droll after his meeting with the Chief Inspector, the previous afternoon? Was it as she thought, something to do with Sharon Crosbie?

The sound of an engine caused her to turn and see Taylor's car turning into Caird Drive, then stepping out onto the pavement, she smiled when he stopped beside her.

Getting into the front passenger seat, she cheerfully greeted him with, "Afternoon, neighbour, are we still on for coffee tomorrow morning?"

"Yes," he muttered when he pulled away from the kerb, "if you like."

They had barely gone fifty yards when she hissed, "Stop the car!"

"Eh?"

"Stop the car, Drew!" she repeated.

He halted the car in an empty bay behind a delivery Transit van, then turned to stare curiously at her.

"What's wrong?"

"What's wrong?" she shook her head and turned toward him. "You're what's wrong! Your face was tripping you after you went to see the Chief Inspector yesterday, for the full remainder of the shift with barely a word from you! I'm not going through that again, Drew Taylor, so what the *hell's* up with you?"

She watched his shoulders slump and his knuckles turn white as he fiercely gripped the steering wheel, then with a resigned sigh, he said, "Sharon. She made an official complaint about me, that I was physically and verbally abusive towards her."

Shocked, it was all that Roz could do to contain her anger, but hissed, "That lying, horrible, two-faced, Barbie cow!"

He found himself grinning when he said, "Don't hold back, tell me what you really feel about her."

Seconds passed before she stuttered, "I don't know what to say."

"Oh, don't worry about that," he sighed, "I think Sharon said plenty."

"What's happening? I mean, will you be suspended?"

"No," he shook his head, "Lizzie Whitmore told me that the rubber heels Chief Inspector who interviewed Sharon about her complaint is satisfied she was lying and apparently I'm in the clear."

Her eyes narrowed, not quite understanding when she asked, "But if you're in the clear, why the doldrums?"

He shrugged again when he explained, "Innocent or not, Roz, the complaint will remain on my personnel file and you know I've ambitions of being promoted."

"But if you're innocent, surely that can't be held against your chances of promotion?"

"Well, for one," he smiled, "not *if* I'm innocent, I *am* innocent, but I'm not convinced that the complaint will be so easily dismissed."

"And what else did Whitmore tell you?"

"In short, not to worry."

"Do you think she was telling the truth?"

"I believe *she* believes what she told me, but I have this nagging doubt, you know?"

Several seconds passed before Roz calmly said, "I don't believe you're the first cop to have a complaint made against him, Drew, and

I'm sure there must be more than a few supervisors and senior officers have been complained about for different reasons, yet went on to be promoted. Obviously, I can't say for certain, but look at Mattie Devlin, for example. He was bust from sergeant to constable, yet now he's back doing the acting rank. Maybe you should have a little faith in what the Chief Inspector told you, eh?"
He smiled at her, then said, "Roz Begley, ever the optimist."
Starting the engine, he pulled smoothly away from the kerb.

CHAPTER TWENTY-FIVE.

Barbara McMillan could hardly contain her excitement when she and Smiler McGarry returned to Craigie Street CID suite.
Halfway through her explanation to DI Sammy Pollock, he raised a hand then said, "Whoa! Stop right there. You and Smiler, follow me."
He led them through to the DCI's room where knocking on the door, he entered and said, "Sorry to bother you, boss, but we might have a result of sorts."
Sitting back in her swivel chair, Gemmill indicated they sit in the two chairs while Pollock went to fetch a third chair.
After he returned, she said, "What's going on, Barbara?"
With a glance at Smiler, McMillan recounted their visit to Ascog Street, then Smiler's suggestion they visit St Albert's church, drawing a wry smile from Pollock when she repeated Smiler's idea Patrick Reagan likely kicked with the left foot.
A little over five minutes later, with Gemmill and Pollock now hanging on her every word, she concluded that their new witness, Rosie Donovan, was willing to attend and view mugshots of local males arrested for crimes and in fact, volunteered to attend at Craigie Street around midday, just after she'd seen to the parish priest's lunch.
"Well, I never," Gemmill was clearly stunned. "You managed to track down a witness after all those years. Well done, the pair of you."

Glancing from one to the other, her eyes narrowed when she saw that the big man was clearly unhappy and so asked, "Something bothering you, Smiler?"

She was not prepared for him to turn to McMillan, then say, "Barbara, would you be offended if I asked to have a private word with the DCI and the DI?"

Taken aback, the young detective stared at him before she replied, "No, of course not, Smiler, Is it about me?"

He smiled widely when he said, "Other than to reinforce my pride in your ability, hen, then no. It's not about you."

Blushing furiously, she pushed up from her chair then wordlessly left the room, closing the door behind her.

"So, Smiler, what's up?" Gemmill asked.

"It bothers me, Ma'am, that Mrs Donovan was interviewed by detectives on the night her father was assaulted, yet that statement was neither discovered with the crime report nor was there any mention of her being at the locus."

"I agree, Smiler," she nodded, "and it seems to reinforce the suggestion that there was a cover-up by the DCI in charge of this Department at that time. Tell me," she fought back her smile, "when you, eh, shall we call it, *interviewed* Albert Moston who, ah, allegedly tried to escape from his front window, did he at all allude to being signed on by the DCI as an informant?"

"No, Ma'am, and that's another thing that bothers me," his brow creased.

"How so?"

"Truth be told," he glanced at Pollock, "after what Moston and his pal did to those pensioners, I terrorised the bugger and he could easily have claimed some kind of immunity, that he was working for the DCI who I'm surmising would likely have told me to back off, but he didn't."

It was Pollock who asked, "And that bothers you why?"

Smiler frowned when he replied, "I'm beginning to think now, maybe it *wasn't* Moston who the DCI was protecting. Maybe it was the other guy and that the DCI had signed on as a tout and Moston couldn't be charged without also disclosing the identity of his pal, so he walked free too."

Gemmill asked, "What was your opinion of Moston, Smiler? Did he have good intel about local crime here in F Division?"

He shook his head when he slowly replied, "I always thought of him as being a complete dullard, Ma'am. Sly and sneaky, yes, and an opportunist thief when the fancy took him. But bright? No," he again shook his head. "Not worth a DCI risking his career by interfering in criminal investigations just to sign him on."

"And I take it he didn't complain about you…I mean, him falling from the window because he knew that he *was* responsible for mugging those pensioners?"

"That's fair to say," he nodded. "Yes, Ma'am."

Gemmill stared at Pollock before she sighed, "This investigation is now getting out of hand, Sammy. It's not just two murders we've to solve, but is seems we're now being saddled with a number of crimes of perverting the course of justice."

"One more thing, Ma'am," Smiler leaned forward in his chair. "I've had a thought…"

"Please, Smiler," she wryly grinned, "you've already caused us more work. But go ahead anyway."

"Can I have your permission to collect the padlock keys to Mrs Moston's flat in Govanhill Street? I believe the Inquiry Department downstairs were given them by the joiner who boarded up the house when the Fire Brigade were finished with it. I'd like to have a look in the flat prior to the keys being returned to the Council Housing Department."

"Whatever for?"

"Just an idea," he grimaced, then added, "Oh, and young Barbara, she's going a good job. If I might, can I borrow her too?"

Gemmill glanced at Pollock, who said, "After what you've brought to the table, Smiler, no problem."

****

When Smiler had gone, Gemmill requested Sammy Pollock bring acting DS Lucy Chalmers into her office and when the younger woman was seated, Gemmill glanced at Pollock before she said, "Lucy, I have a job for you, but you have to know I must rely on your discretion and if you accept what I'm about to ask of you, it does not leave this office."

Her curiosity aroused, Chalmers nodded when she replied, "Of course, Ma'am."

"One final thing, Lucy. I'm seconding three of the team to work with you. You will have complete autonomy to use them as you see fit and make inquiry again as you see it. Once and *if* you get a result, that'll be the time to report back to me or the DI."

"Now," Gemmill stared at the younger woman, "here's what I need from you."

****

Acting Sergeant Mattie Devlin, unconsciously expecting at best an argument and at worse, a verbal reprimand, strode into the Inspectors office, then greeting Iain Cowan, said, "If you're okay with it, sir, I've given Willie Strathmore time off today in lieu of hours he has accrued. I've also arranged that Harry Dawson work her rest day, today and she's agreed to take the time in lieu."

Cowan slapped himself on the forehead, then replied, "Of course, Mattie. I'd forgotten that Willie's got his exam tomorrow and decent of Dawson to help us out. I'll add my thanks to her and good decision on your part."

A relieved Devin continued, "That still leaves us a man down though, with Telford phoning in sick. Want me to have a word with the early shift sergeant and see if he's got anyone keen to work on for, say, four hours?"

"No, leave it for now. We'll muddle through like we usually do," Cowan shook his head, then added, "Besides, if it comes to it, we can add ourselves to the numbers with the supervisory patrol car."

Devlin slumped down into a chair, then asked, "Any feedback from the murder investigation?"

"No," Cowan shook his head, "other than I saw Smiler in his suit, so he's likely been called in off the pat and mick to assist with his local knowledge."

His eyes narrowing, Devlin said, "I thought Drew Taylor was looking a bit down in the mouth when we signed off, last night. Everything okay with him?"

Cowan rose from his chair, then closing his office door, took several minutes to disclose in confidence the complaint that had now been proved to be false.

"Poor bugger," he grimaced. "At least the rubber heels got it right this time."

"And what about you? Nothing more from Pitt Street about your, ah…"

"Runaway wife?" Devlin smiled, then shaking his head, added, "The sad truth is the bugger's probably gotten away with what she did, so time for me to get on with my life."

"Good man," Cowan again rose to his feet, then said, "Right then, I'm going to try to catch young Taylor before he goes out in the van. Seems the Chief Super wants a word with him."

****

The assistant serving behind the City Bakeries counter stared at the nervous young woman who seemed too well dressed, albeit it wasn't *her* style, to be a snatch and grab thief, for God alone knew how many cakes and buns they lost in a week to those bloody nuisances. "Can I help you?" she politely asked.

"Ah, yes," the young woman forced a smile, "is Sally in today?"

"Sally? Aye, she is. She's in the back, hen, doing the books. Wait a minute and I'll fetch her," she nodded to her colleague to mind the counter.

A minute later, Sally followed the assistant through to the front of the shop where to her surprise, she saw Smiler's daughter standing there.

"Eh, Jean, come through," she beckoned her forward to follow Sally through to the rear storeroom.

Turning, she was surprised when Jean lunged forward and wrapped her arms around Sally's neck, then her head on Sally's shoulder, tearfully said, "Auntie Elizabeth told us the whole story. Oh, God, I'm so sorry that happened to you."

She felt herself welling up and unconsciously wrapped her own arms around the younger woman's waist, then held her tightly and whispered, "It's all in the past now, Jean. It's just a bad memory that through time will grow less painful and now that I have your dad in my life, I really am moving forward."

Lifting her head from Sally's shoulder, tears streaming down her cheeks, Jean's lips quivered when she replied, "Not just dad, but me and Adam and his wife, Grace, and their kids too. You're part of the family now."

Her throat was too tight to respond and choked, she could only nod. Then at last, finding her voice, she smiled, "Well, now that you're here, how about a cup of tea and a sticky bun, then?"

****

Returned to the CID car, McMillan asked, "What are you hoping to find in Moston's flat, Smiler?"

Settling himself into the passenger seat, he replied, "I'm not sure, but hopefully something that might connect Moston to his pal from all those years ago."

"And what might that be?"

He turned to smile at her when he asked, "How old are you now, Barbara?"

"Twenty-nine, going on the big three-o. Why?"

"Well, I'm thinking, what is the one thing you do when you go on nights out with your pals or on holidays or days away?"

"Apart from having a good bevy?" she grinned, then eyes narrowing, asked, "Is this some sort of quiz?"

"Right, let me make it a bit easier. How do you record your memories?"

"Well, I normally take…" her eyes widened. "You're talking about photographs!"

"I know it's a long shot," he smiled, "but what if Moxy has a photograph of his pal, the one person he trusted enough to go out and commit street robberies with."

Nodding, she replied, "Maybe it's not *that* much of a long shot."

Less than ten minutes later, they were at the padlocked door, the original lock rendered useless when Smiler had kicked the door open.

Even though days had passed, the overwhelming smell of smoke, combined with the dampness that had followed after the flat had been sprayed by the Fire Brigade, caused both to fetch their handkerchiefs and tie them around their noses as masks.

Entering first, Smiler led the way through to the bedroom that had been occupied by Albert Moston, pleased to see that when the fire had ignited in the flat, the door had been closed so apart from some water seepage to the carpets, the room was clear of fire damage, though the acrid stench of smoke was powerful enough to make him gag.

"I can't decide whether that awful smell," McMillan began, "is because of the fire or how that bugger Moston lived. Even seeing it as it is, the place must've been like a pigsty," she waved a hand in front of her face.

An old-fashioned wooden wardrobe with two doors and a full-length mirror in the middle stood against a wall, while against the opposite wall, was a wooden chest of six drawers.

"I'll take the wardrobe," Smiler nodded towards it.

Their search commenced, both breathing through their mouths that were covered by their handkerchiefs and McMillan thinking that if time permitted, she was nipping home to her flat to change, for the smell of smoke was bound to adhere to her.

Finding nothing of interest in the wardrobe and with McMillan, still working her way down the chest of drawers, her face beneath the hankie rippling in disgust at the creased and sometimes stained clothes she was rummaging through, Smiler turned his attention to the bedside cabinet, a rickety piece of furniture that wasn't even worth scrapping.

In the one drawer, he discovered a pile of well-thumbed men's magazines, mostly pornographic and to his disgust, discovered many of the pages stuck together with what he suspected, but didn't like to think about.

In the small cabinet area, his eyes narrowed at the sight on an old, blue coloured photograph album, the spine broken and the font cover lying loose.

Easing it out from under a pile of Rangers football programmes, Smiler gently laid in down onto the unmade bed, then decided not to sit on the grimy sheets, so bent over to turn the pages, one by one, seeing that most of the black and white photographs had come loose from the small, cardboard photo corners.

"What you got there?" McMillan's muffled voice asked.

"Well, it seems to be a family scrapbook and I'm guessing the child in the photos is Moston with his mother and father."

McMillan stepped towards him as he turned the pages, righting the photos that had spilled on top of others, seeing the progression of Moston from a toddle, to a primary schoolboy, then in one photograph, had turned from a previously smiling youth to a sullen teenager with shoulder length hair and a crooked nose.

"As I recall, I think it happened when he was in his late teens," Smiler observed, pointing to Moston's nose.

Turning two more pages towards what was the end of the album, Smiler stopped and stared down at a black and white photograph, like the others on that page, it was firmly glued to the second but last page.

The picture, seemingly taken on a bright, sunny day, of Moston and a similarly aged youth, who not as tall, wore a floral shirt with a wide, round collar a brightly patterned, sleeveless tank-top pullover and light coloured, flared hipster trousers.

Both youths, Smiler guessed about twenty years old or so, had shoulder length hair; Moston dark and the other youth very fair or blonde and both squinting towards the photographer.

Neither youth was smiling, indeed, both appeared to be scowling at the camera as though trying to project their indifference and leaning on their elbows against a metal railing with a ship, a ferry thought Smiler, passing in their background.

"Trying to be cool, the pair of them," grinned McMillan through her mask, "though wearing those clothes, I don't see them pulling any lassies."

"Aye," he too smiled beneath his hankie, "but that was the style back in the sixties."

"Do you think that fair haired guy might be the accomplice for the muggings?"

"I don't know, Barbara, but he's shorter than Moston and has fair, perhaps blonde hair. I'd like to show this to Mrs Donovan, see if she can identify him as the man who broke her father's arm. That and back in the day, people used to write on the back of photos to remind them when and where it was taken. That information might be useful."

Carefully he began to pull at the lower corner of the photograph and gingerly eased the photo a few inches from the page, but then stopped and muttered, "I'm worried about tearing it."

"Why not just take the album? We can nip up to the SOCO lab and see if they can peel the photo off for us."

"Good idea, but let's visit St Albert's first. If as we suspect this *is* Moston's accomplice, that'll make the trip to Pitt Street doubly important."

****

Seated behind his desk, Chief Superintendent Jimmy Thompson was dealing with the daily correspondence when his phone rang.

"Okay, Doris, send him in."

Seconds later, the door opened to admit Constable Drew Taylor, his cap on his head and who came to attention a yard from Thompson's desk, then said, "Good afternoon, sir. I'm told you want to see me?"

"Ah, Constable Taylor," Thompson replied, seeing the younger man was clearly nervous, then indicated he sit down.

Removing his cap and placing it on his lap, Taylor, his heart thumping, could feel his stomach tensing, until Thompson said, "First of all, Drew," he smiled to put him at his ease, "you're not in any bother. Chief Inspector Whitmore has apprised me of this scurrilous accusation against you and I want you to know you have my full support."

Swallowing with difficulty, the dozen or so reasons that he imagined the Divisional Commander wanted to see him faded as quickly as they had arrived.

In a faint voice, he replied, "Thank you, sir."

Thomson, recognising the strain Taylor must have been under, took a few seconds to reach for his cigarettes and lighter, then withdrawing a fag, lit it knowing that those few seconds was giving Taylor time to compose himself.

Drawing deeply on the cigarette, he said, "You don't smoke, do you, Drew?"

"Ah, no sir, I don't."

"Then don't start. These bloody things will kill you and yes, I'm speaking from experience," he wryly smiled.

"I understand from Lizzie Whitmore that you're worried that because the complaint will remain on your personnel file, it might affect your chance of promotion?"

"Yes, sir," he vigorously nodded. "I hate the thought that even though I didn't do what I was accused of, anyone considering me for promotion might be swayed by the thought I'm possibly an abuser."

"But you're not, are you?"

Taylor's eyes widened when he snapped back, "No, sir, I'm bloody *not*! I mean," his face flushed, but Thompson held up his hand and continued smiling when he replied, "It's okay, I believe you."

"I'm sorry, sir," he gulped, "it's just that…well, punching a man who deserves it is one thing. Hitting a woman? That's a no-no in my book."

Thompson didn't ask him to elaborate on what type of man deserved to be punched by his constable, so tapping some ash into his ashtray, instead said, "I'll not keep you, but I reiterate, this complaint will not in any way hinder your career. I've spoken this morning with the Superintendent in charge of the Complaints and Discipline Department and stressed my support for you and that *will* be recorded in your personnel file."

Taylor's jaw dropped and he sighed deeply, then with obvious relief, gasped "Thank you, sir. Thank you."

"Now," Thompson pretended to be gruff, "bugger off and go and arrest some bad guys."

****

After Jean McGarry had left the shop, Sally Rodgers's day just got better and better.

Knowing now that both Jean and Adam were aware of her past had been a huge relief to her; that and them both approving of her relationship with their father had dispelled any lingering doubts she had about being with Stuart.

Joining her assistants behind the unusually customer-free counter, they noticed the change in their boss, causing the older of the three to ask, "So, what's the good news then, and who was that young lassie?"

"My boyfriend's daughter,'" she sighed, unable to hid her grin.

"Oh," her assistant glanced knowingly at her colleagues before she said, "We didn't know Smiler had a daughter, did we girls?"

Almost immediately and to the three women's loud laughter, Sally's expression gave her away and she stuttered, "How did you know? Who told you?"

"You did, ya numpty. Do you think we'd not noticed that every time the big man visited the back shop, you were on a high? You must think we're daft," she giggled at Sally's discomfort.

Exhaling, Sally slumped down onto the stool behind the counter, then said, "Okay, I didn't realise I was so transparent, but yes. Stuart and I…"

"Oooh, Stuart and I," the three women repeated in falsetto voices and fluttered their eyes.

"Okay, enough with the leg-pulling," Sally grinned with them.

She took a deep breath, knowing they were expecting more, so said, "Stuart and *me*, we've been together over six months now and it's the best thing that's happened to me."

The older of the three strode forward, then throwing her meaty arm around Sally's shoulder, said, "Well, for what it's worth, we all approve," then to more laughter, added, "It's about time your face straightened anyway."

****

After Rosie Donovan confirmed without hesitation, the youth in the photograph was indeed he who had with Albert Moston, assaulted her father, Barbara McMillan used the chapel house phone to phone DS Danny Sullivan in the incident room to convey their intention to travel to the SOCO at Pitt Street.

"Good one, Barbara," he acknowledged. "I'll let the DCI know."

Now arriving at Pitt Street, Smiler suggested with a wide grin that McMillan use her undoubted good looks and charm to inveigle the commissionaire manning the underground car park to allocate her a bay.

Unfortunately, upon their arrival at the West Regent Street entrance, the commissionaire on duty was a female, who at last persuaded by Smiler's pleasant demeanour and patter, finally permitted them entry to a bay on the ground floor.

"What is it women see in you, you old charmer?" McMillan shook her head in disbelief, yet inwardly realised for a man his age, Smiler was really attractive man.

Winding their way through the building, they arrived on the first floor of the former Scottish College of Commerce and now since the amalgamation in nineteen-seventy-five, the Force's headquarters. Stepping down both entry steps to the SOCO department, almost immediately both heard a raised male voice, clearly berating someone and causing them to glance at each other.

"Somebody's not happy," muttered Smiler.

Continuing along the narrow corridor into the extremely large, general office, they were surprised to see the dozen or so staff present arrayed around benches and desks in the room and all silently watching the uniformed Chief Constable Arthur Donaldson, who bareheaded was shouting at a man that Smiler recognised as the civilian manager and head of the Department.

Standing pokerfaced and slightly behind the Chief was a uniformed Superintendent who unlike his boss, carried his cap tucked beneath his arm.

"I have no interest in what *priorities* you have," his hands bunched into fists, the Chief's face was barely inches from that of the manager, "but I do have an interest in *my* priority and if you wish to continue working for this Force, I want it completed as a *priority*!" the Chief hissed at the manager, who pale-faced, stared wordlessly back at him.

McMillan's first thought was that she and Smiler should back out of the room before they were noticed, but then to her horror, she heard the big man loudly call out, "Hello there, anyone available to handle an extremely urgent inquiry from F Division?"

Turning slowly to stare up at him, her mouth agape, she saw him to be inanely grinning, his eyes wandering the room as though seeking some assistance.

As she later explained, "You could have cut the bloody atmosphere with a blunt knife."

The tense few seconds of silence that followed, ended when the Chief, visible spots of saliva on his chin, approached Smiler to scowl, "Who the hell are *you* to interrupt *me*!"

Smiler, standing at six feet three-inches, bent his head forward to loom over the five feet eight-inch Donaldson, then smiled when he calmly said, "I'm Constable Stuart McGarry from F Division and you'll be the Chief Constable, sir? Pleased to meet you."

To McMillan's further horror and wishing she could somehow slide unnoticed away from her neighbour, Smiler extended his hand to be shaken.

Donaldson bent his head to stare down at Smiler's hand, then ignoring the gesture, raised his head to stare up at the big man. Finally finding his voice, he squeaked, "Are you being funny?"

"Sorry, sir," Smiler's brow furrowed when he stared questioningly down into the Chief's eyes, then asked, "do you mean funny hah-hah or funny, sarcastic?"

In the pregnant silence that followed, everyone in the room saw Donaldson's face turn a deep purple, then he croaked, "Why are you here?"

The big man smiled, then replied, "Well, my neighbour and I are seeking some help from the SOCO in the ongoing murder investigation being run out of Craigie Street, sir, but I'm guessing from what I heard," Smiler adopted a grave expression, "that you too have some serious inquiry going on. Well," Smiler nodded at him, "it's good to hear that the Chief Constable, you being such a busy man running the Force I mean, still finds the time to be involved in helping to investigate crime."

McMillan, cringing that Smiler included her in his explanation and already seeing the ruination of her career, tightly closed her eyes and prayed to God that if she stood *really* still, Donaldson might not notice her.

Clearly taken aback, Donaldson blustered, "I am *here*, Constable, on a *private* matter, not that it is any concern of *yours*!"

"Oh," Smiler thoughtfully stared down at him for several seconds. "Then," he shook his head as though misunderstanding, "what you're telling me, Chief Constable, is that your *private* matter can't possibly be as great a priority as is solving the murder of two individuals in the F Divisional area, namely Mrs Jeannie Mason and Mr Albert Moston, as well as a number of historical crimes of assault and robbery?"

Donaldson's eyes widened and for one awful moment, McMillan thought he was going to have a stroke.

Taking a deep breath that visibly expanded his chest, Donaldson made to push past Smiler, but forgot that his slighter frame could not make any impression on Smiler's muscular girth and deliberately colliding with the big man, almost fell to one side.

However, Smiler reached out a hand to grab at Donaldson's arm and steady him, then politely said, "Mind how you go now, sir."

Outraged, the veins in his neck protruding like purple string, Donaldson stomped towards the corridor that led to the exit door, but barked back over his shoulder, "Superintendent! Take that man's name!"

Smiler turned as the Superintendent strode towards him, but before he could speak, the Chief's aide raised a hand, then quietly said, "Don't worry, I already caught your name," then to Smiler's surprise, conspiratorially winked at him.

With them both gone from the Department, the manager strolled over to Smiler and with a grim smile, said, "Well, that's your career well and truly knackered, big man."

"What career?" Smiler responded with a wide grin.

CHAPTER TWENTY-SIX.

"You're in a happier mood," Roz Begley stared curiously at her neighbour.

Drew Taylor, slowly driving the Transit through the arch into Craigie Street, shrugged when he replied, "I've just had a talking too by the Div Comm and he set me straight about that complaint. Says I'm not to worry about it, that he's sent a note to the rubber heels supporting me and that's to be included in my personnel file."

"Well," her face creased in surprise, "you must be a favourite with the management if they're looking out for you and there you were, thinking you were being picked on."

"I never said that!" he risked an irate glance at her.

"No, but you were *thinking* it," she teased him with a smile, then added, "At least now I'll not have to put up with your huffy face all night."

"I'm not going to win this discussion, am I?" he sighed.

"Nope," she grinned and turned away to stare though the windscreen just as the All Stations radio used their callsign and instructed they attend a disturbance at a second floor flat in Annette Street.

Responding to the call, Roz sighed, "Here we go again."

****

DCI Gemmill poked her head into the incident room, then catching Danny Sullivan's eye, asked, "Anything yet from Barbara McMillan?"

"Not since she phoned in they were on their way to the SOCO at Pitt Street, boss," he shook his head.

"Okay," she slowly drawled, then said, "I'm popping in to see Lizzie Whitmore if you're looking for me."

"Boss," he acknowledged with a nod.

Minutes later, sitting facing Whitmore, Gemmill said, "Couple of things I'd like to informally discuss Lizzie, starting with Lucy Chalmers. She's doing a good job on the investigation and while I know it's supposed to be a secondment, I'm considering requesting her transfer to the Department. I know she's former CID, so undoubtedly she's been through the Detective Course down at Ayr, which is a plus for me. So, I'm here to ask, will you have any objections, given that it leaves you short a uniform sergeant for the Division."

Whitmore sighed when she said, "Aye, it *would* leave me short of another supervisor though as perhaps you're aware, I've Mattie Devlin from her shift performing the acting rank at the minute. That said," her face creased, "I can't in good faith stand in the way of

what Lucy will perceive to be a promotional transfer and she's made no secret during her annual appraisals of her desire to return to the CID. So the short answer is no, I won't offer any objection if she submits an application for her transfer."
Her eyes narrowed when she asked, "I take it you haven't yet mentioned this to Lucy?"
"No," Gemmill shook her head, "I wanted to sound you out first before I mentioned it."
"And the other thing?"
"Your man, Smiler McGarry."
Whitmore found herself smiling when she sighed, "What's the big man done now?"
"Oh," Gemmill held up her hand, "he's been nothing but of value to the investigation and right now, him and young Barbara McMillan are at Pitt Street following up what *might* prove to be a credible line of inquiry."
"But?"
Gemmill sighed before she continued, "Though it has not been corroborated *nor* might be and can I add, what I'm about to disclose at the minute is strictly between us."
Permitting that to sink in, she sat forward in her chair and said, "Smiler has probably discovered evidence that my predecessor of sixteen years ago, the former DCI John Michael Crawford, quite possibly is responsible for a number of crimes of perverting the course of justice and following on from that, I'd say probable charges of corruption and contravening the Police (Scotland) Act will likely follow too."
Whitmore's eyes narrowed when softly exhaling at the news, she sat back in her chair and sighed, "Go on."
Gemmill related Smiler and McMillan's discovery of the witness, Mrs Rosie Donovan, and her account of the night Donovan's father, Patrick Reagan, was assaulted and robbed.
"So, this woman Donovan, her account completely conflicts what is in the crime report you discovered?"
"It does, yes."
"And is she credible, given the time that has elapsed since she witnessed her father being assaulted?"
"I'm told she's a practising Roman Catholic who works for the local priest and is as straight as a die," her bottom lip pursed when

Gemmill added, "Yes, she's *very* credible. That and when she arrived at the Department just after midday to view our book of photos of the local worthies, I had a word with her too. She's a sharp woman, is Mrs Donovan and when Smiler and Barbara McMillan showed her a photo that they've discovered this afternoon of Moston and a male with him, they reported she identified the male without any hesitation and also identified Moston too."

"And you're sharing this with me why, Laura?"

"Simply put, Lizzie, I don't have the resources to handle what is an investigation now growing arms and eggs. The likelihood is I'm maybe going to have to call in the Serious Crime Squad to lend a hand and while I might be able to keep a lid on it with my own guys, I have no control over the Squad guys so…"

"So, you think that the whole bloody mess will be leaked to the media?"

"That's my concern, yes," Gemmill nodded.

"And I'm guessing you'll want me to have a word with Jimmy Thompson and tell him to expect that albeit it was sixteen years ago, we might be looking at not only a number of charges regarding the perversion of justice coming to light, but possibly corruption by a senior police officer?"

"That's exactly right," Gemmill wryly smiled.

"Well, how does this sound? I'll hold off telling Jimmy till you make your decision whether or not to request the assistance of the Serious Crime mob. That suit you?"

That'll do me, yes," Gemmill grimly smiled.

****

Upon the arrival of the crew of Foxtrot Mike Two at the close in Annette Street, Drew Taylor, carrying the only personal radio for the vehicle simply because of the lack in number of Divisional radios that were operational, heard Mary Wiseman, the civilian controller at Craigie Street, call his shoulder number.

"Go ahead, Mary," he responded as he and Roz alighted from the van.

"Heard the AS call, Drew. Just to give you a heads-up that the call is a regular one of domestic abuse and it's likely a John McDonald on the second floor giving his wife another bleaching, over."

"Roger that," he nodded to Roz as they hurried into the close.

"One other thing, Drew," Wiseman's voice crackled over the air,

"Smiler and Sergeant Devlin gave McDonald the jail last Thursday evening for pummelling his wife, so it's likely if he's not pled guilty at the time, he's out on bail. Oh, and for your information, there's young kids in that house. Over."

"Good to know. Thanks, Mary," Taylor ended the transmission as he and Roz made their way up to the first-floor landing, where they saw a middle-aged woman standing with her arms crossed, who moodily greeted them with, "You took your time. It's probably all over now. She stopped screaming about five minutes ago."

"It was yourself that called?" Roz asked as they passed by the woman, who staring up the stairs after them, confirmed when she raised her voice with, "Aye, it's me all the time, hen, because no other bugger in this close give a damn about him hitting her!"

Reaching the second landing, they saw the unpainted front door with the name 'McDONALD' printed in black coloured, felt pen that was starting to fade into the wood.

Hammering on the door with his fist, Taylor breathlessly shouted, "Police, Mr McDonald. Open the door please."

A further hammering on the door achieved nothing, then pressing the button on the personal radio, he said, "Mary, let Sergeant Devlin know that we've no response to our knocking so, in light of the previously history of calls, we're putting the door in."

He didn't wait for a response, but taking a step back, kicked at the flimsy lock and watched as the wood at the lock shattered and the door swung open.

Seconds later and followed by Roz, Taylor entered the dimly lit hallway.

They had just passed one closed, bedroom door on their right with Taylor now poking his head into the kitchen.

She heard him gasp at the sight of a woman lying face down on the kitchen floor, her hair matted with fresh, bright blood.

When Roz stepped forward to stare over his shoulder, she sensed rather than saw the bedroom door swing open and turning, her eyes widened at the sight of a wild-eyed man, naked other than for a pair of once white football shorts, his torso spotted with blood, exit the room, a wooden handled claw hammer raised in his right, heavily bloodstained hand,

"Drew!" she screamed a warning as wild-eyed, the man lunged at her, the hammer already falling to strike her on the head.

Whether by instinct or some deeply ingrained training, Roz never knew, but as the man reached forward to attack her, in that heartbeat she stepped back, her left arm raised to take the blow and with her body swivelling to her right, used her free hand to shove the man against the wall.

Caught off balance, her attacker stumbled to one side, the hammer descending to strike her a glancing blow on her left forearm as his weight and momentum slammed him against forcibly against the wall, the air suddenly driven from his lungs as he collided heavily with the wall, he loudly exhaled.

Seizing her advantage, Roz raised her right leg up and with her hand continuing to push him against the wall, drove her knee directly into the man's groin.

As her assailant's head stooped and he cried out in pain, she was pulled backwards by Taylor, who stepping forward, snarled when he punched the man in the face.

With an almost gently sigh, his eyes closing, the man slid down in an untidy heap to the floor, the hammer dropping from his grasp.

Roz, her breathing fast and erratic, turned to stare at Taylor before she stuttered, "The woman!"

For those few heartbeats, he didn't respond, his attention taken by the unconscious man, but glanced at her before he slowly shook his head.

****

The supervisory car, driven by Mattie Devlin, pulled up sharply behind Foxtrot Mike Two and before Devlin had switched off the engine, Inspector Iain Cowan was out of the vehicle and racing into the close.

A minute later, with Devlin on his heels, Cowan, his breath coming is rasps from running up the stairs, was about to enter the second floor flat when he was met at the door by Drew Taylor who raised a hand to stop him, then said in a low voice, "There's been a murder, Inspector."

Turning, he nodded into the hallway at the groaning figure who lay face down in the foetal position, his hands handcuffed to the back with Roz Begley, her cap lying on the uncarpeted floor and her hair dishevelled, standing over the prisoner.

Then in the same low voice, Taylor added, "I'm guessing he's John McDonald.

"That's McDonald," Mattie Devlin confirmed from behind the Inspector. "Smiler and me jailed him last week for beating his missus."

"The woman, presumably his wife, she's in the kitchen. He's used a hammer to bludgeon her to death. The hammer's there," he pointed to where it had fallen, "and he's got blood spattering all over his chest and on his right hand and his right forearm."

"You guys okay?" Cowan asked, now catching his breath from racing up the stairs.

"Roz took a belt on her left forearm from what I believe is the murder weapon, the claw hammer, but I don't think she'll suffer anything worse than a bruise."

"Nevertheless, she'll need to be seen by a doctor and her tunic," Cowan was thinking about evidence, "I'm guessing that's been bloodied from the hammer?"

"Aye, sir, likely," Taylor nodded.

"Right," he sighed, "the CID will want that as a production. Mattie," he turned to Devlin, "Knock on some doors and find a telephone to contact the control room. Tell Mary Wiseman to phone upstairs and inform the CID of the circumstances as we know them and suggest we're looking at a domestic gone wrong," he added with a meaningful stare at Devlin.

Cowan had no need to explain, for it was common knowledge in the Force the personal radios were now pretty aged and therefore not encrypted.

He then added, "Tell Mary to inform the CID that at the minute, it's a suspicious death and let her know to keep the death off the air for the time being. Bloody media are usually monitoring the police bands for something like this. Let the CID confirm it's murder."

He paused, then continued, "Tell her as well she's to request Inspector Bruce contact the duty Fiscal and the casualty surgeon and have them attend here. That'll save some time."

"Right then, young Drew," he grimaced when he turned to him, but then Devlin interrupted to say, "The last time I was here, there were a couple of kids. Where are they?"

"Kids? God, yes," Taylor slapped a palm at his forehead. "Mary Wiseman said here was weans in the house."

Turning, he called out to Roz, "There might be kids in the house, Roz."

While Mattie Devlin hurried downstairs to the half landing to call the control room on the radio, Devlin minded McDonald when Roz stepped over the prone man and quickly checked the second bedroom and the front room, returning to the hallway with a shake of her head.

But then seconds later, Cowan and Taylor saw her stop and cock her head to one side, then listening intently, she leaned towards the second bedroom.

The room, decorated many years ago with children's cartoon figures on the wallpaper, was long overdue a make-over. However, she could not help but notice though the sparse furniture was old, the area of the floor was tidy with a cardboard egg-box in one corner, scribbled in bright crayon colours and overflowing with toys, some of which had pieces missing.

Bunk-beds were pushed against the far wall and both had cotton, faded children's quilts neatly pulled tight on the beds. Her eyes narrowed when she saw the lower bed had a number of cuddly toys scattered on the quilt. A worn carpet was on the floor and in general, Roz noted the room to be neat and tidy.

When Taylor quietly moved towards her, she stopped him with a raised hand, then whispered

"I'm hearing something."

Stepping into the room, she heard that the slight shuffling noise seemed to be coming from a cupboard recessed into the wall. Unconsciously holding her breath, Roz slowly pulled open one of the two old-fashioned double doors and startled.

A small boy dressed in faded pyjamas with teddy bears on them, no more than five, she rightly guessed, sat on the floor inside the cupboard with a younger girl, four as it later transpired. The girl sat with her back against the boy's chest with his legs wrapped about her waist and she saw the little girl held a battered looking plastic doll clutched tightly to her.

But what shocked Roz was the boy, who had a fresh red finger marks on his cheek and who undoubtedly had been slapped hard. Fearfully stared at her with wide eyes, the boy held one hand clasped over his sister's eyes and the other over her mouth.

His lips trembling, he stared at Roz when he whispered, "Mummy said I've never to let my wee sister see our daddy hitting mummy or to let her cry. He doesn't like it when Fifi cries and he gets angry."

Tears sprung to Roz's eyes, then pressing her lips tightly together, she held out her hands.
At last she found her voice and whispered back, "Well, mummy is always right, so here, give your wee sister to me and you can both come out now."
A little uncertainly, the boy released his hold on his sister who blinking in the light, smiled at Roz, then asked, "Can I go and see my mummy now?"
****
Sitting in the Pitt Street cafeteria on the fourth floor, Smiler nursed his second coffee as he patiently listened to his neighbour's complaints about her boyfriend's habit of always being late, no matter the occasion.
"He just as no sense of urgency about anything," she shook her head.
"Oh, that's easy solved," he sighed.
"Yeah? How?"
"You're meeting him for dinner at eight, tell him it's a seven-thirty booking. No matter where you're going or who you're meeting with, always give him a thirty-minute window. Believe me, it works."
"And that'll work," she stared sceptically at him.
"My Cheryl, God rest her. All those years married and she never suspected I was lying about the time we'd to be anywhere," he smiled at her, then added, "And before you ask, those were the *only* lies I ever told her. Never lie to a woman unless you have an elephant memory, that's my motto."
The wall phone located by the back exit door rang and was answered by a passing Inspector, who turning his head to stare at the diners, called out, "Is there a Smiler McGarry here?"
"That's me," Smiler rose to his feet then striding towards the Inspector, took the phone from him.
McMillan rose to her feet when he beckoned her over, then said, "That was the photographic. He's ready for us."
Minutes later, returning to the SOCO department, they were treated to a two-minute lecture on how *not* to peel a photo from a sticky page, then shown the detached photo of Moston and his associate. Holding it up to the bright fluorescent light, it was McMillan who asked, "Is that something written on the back?"
Turning the photo over, Smiler held it for them both to see a notation in pencil, that read, *'Me and Cokey, Rothesay, April 1962.'*

His eyes narrowed when in a low voice, he said, "Cokey. Now where have I heard that name recently?"

CHAPTER TWENTY-SEVEN.

Climbing the stairs to the second landing, DCI Laura Gemmill used a low voice when she said to her DI, Sammy Pollock, "Another murder and on top of everything else, just what we need."
"If anything though, boss, it sounds like a domestic, so why not let me deal with it?"
"If you're up for it, Sammy, that would leave me to continue with the other investigation."
"No bother, mark me down as the SIO," he nodded, "and if it's as straight forward as it sounds, I'll need no more than three or four of the team."
"Right then," they arrived at the second landing, to be greeted by Iain Cowan and Mattie Devlin.
"The suspect, John McDonald, he's down in the van being looked after by one of my cops, Ma'am," Cowan nodded at her.
"Roz Begley, his neighbour," he took a deep breath, suddenly feeling the bile rise in his throat, "she's in the second bedroom there on the right with the victim's two small children, a boy and a girl. They were hiding while their father was murdering their mother."
God, kids, Gemmill inwardly thought; I hate it when there's children involved.
"Who have you contacted, Ian?" she asked.
"Casualty surgeon is on his way as is the duty Fiscal. SOCO are due anytime. The victim, Jessie McDonald, she's lying in the kitchen. There," he pointed down into the hallway, "is the claw hammer that is presumably the murder weapon. Apart from poking my nose into the kitchen and confirming the dead body, I haven't left the hallway, so the only contamination will be from the crew of Foxtrot Mike Two. Oh, and Roz Begley, she took a heavy dunt on her left arm when the suspect surprised her and tried to smash her head in with the hammer, so I'm sure you might wish to consider a further charge of attempted murder by the…"
He stopped and took another deep breath.

"Sorry," he shook his head. "No matter how long I've been a police officer, I still can't get used to seeing innocents being murdered like that poor woman lying in there."

"I would suggest, Iain," she forced a smile, "the day you do get used to it is the day you consider chucking this job. Anyway, thank you for your briefing. Sammy here will be the SIO as I'm too involved with the ongoing murder investigations. Your young cop, Roz, is she okay?"

"Bit shaken up, but I intend having her looked at anyway. When you guys take over, I'll have her taken to the Viccy for a check-up and Sammy," he turned to him, "I'll have her tunic with the victim's blood from the hammer he used smeared on it, handed up to your office."

"That and if she's bruised on her arm, I'll want that photographed too, Iain."

The noise of someone breathlessly labouring up the stairs caused them to turn to see the middle-aged doctor, his face beetroot red, who stopping on the landing used a hand on the wall to brace himself when he wheezed, "Why aren't more of these murders committed in bungalows?"

****

Returning to Craigie Street and buoyed by the result of the SOCO's discovery, Smiler and Barbara McMillan were informed by DS Danny Sullivan that both the boss and the DI were out and attending a domestic murder within a flat in Annette Street.

Upon learning the victim was being named as Jessie McDonald, McMillan saw Smiler's face pale, then raising both hands, he quietly said, "Give me a minute."

Leaving the incident room, her curiosity aroused, she turned to Sullivan to ask, "What's with the big man?"

Sullivan's eyebrows rose when he quietly replied, "The bar officer was telling me that last week, Smiler and his neighbour, Sergeant Devlin is it?"

"That's him," she nodded.

"Anyway, they jailed the husband for battering his wife, the victim. That's who's now in custody for her murder."

"Oh, shit," her shoulders slumped as she glanced at the door. "I'd better see that's he's okay."

She found him standing in the corridor with his back to the wall and his head stooped, staring at his feet.

Slowly walking towards him, she softly said, "It's not your fault, Smiler. It's the system."

He took a deep breath, then slowly exhaled before he said, "I know that, hen, but it doesn't make me feel any better. That's two children now without a parent and all because of that shite about women being told, 'you made your bed' and leaving them nowhere to turn to when their husband or partner beats the living hell out of them. Or murders them," he grimly added.

She watched him using the heels of both and as he rubbed furiously at his forehead as though trying to drive the memory of the dead woman from his head.

Scowling, he turned to hiss, "Right now, I'm for visiting the cell and beating *him* to death, I feel that *bloody* angry!"

In the years she had known him, McMillan had never seen him like this and in one frantic thought, wondered if she had the strength to stop him getting past her.

Staring at her and to her relief, he added, "But what's the point, eh? He's going away for murder and his kids, they'll be put into the social system and hopefully, adopted by some caring people, though as I remember her, their mother Jessie was a good woman and loved her weans."

Standing upright from the wall, he wryly smiled at her before he said "You'd think with my service and experience, Barbara, I'd be able to handle bad news a whole lot better than I am right now," then shaking his head, added, "but to be honest, I'm finding this a bit difficult. Look, I'm away for a wee walk to clear my head. I'll be back in a half hour or so, but if the DCI or DI turns up before I return, go ahead and report what we discovered about the photograph."

She stepped to one side and watched him walk off to the stairs, then feeing more deflated than she expected, returned to the incident room.

****

Though the Social Work were informed by the Duty Inspector, Marion Bruce, of the McDonald children's loss, the supervisor apologised that it might be over an hour before she could send someone to collect the children.

In the meantime and with some reluctance, Roz Begley left them both in the care of the female turnkey, a matronly woman with grandchildren of her own who caring for them in her small room, made a huge fuss of them with biscuits and diluting juice.

Making their way upstairs to the CID suite to provide their statements, Taylor asked, "Did the wee lad say how he came by those finger marks on his face?"

She nodded when she replied, "He says his dad slapped him then when his mum tried to pull her husband off her son, she shouted that he run away with his sister and hide. He heard his mummy screaming then…"

She stopped speaking and stood still, her throat unaccountably tight as blinking rapidly, tears once more bit at her eyes.

Taking a slow breath, she was aware of Taylor's hand on her shoulder as he drew her close, then offering her his handkerchief, whispered, "Roz, there's no shame in crying after what you've just seen. Look, away to the ladies and take a few minutes to yourself and when you're ready and no rush," he held up a palm towards her, "I'll see you in the incident room."

Nodding, she hurried off to the toilet on the first floor.

****

The casualty surgeon, now in attendance at Craigie Street cell area, examined John McDonald in the small, brightly lit room laughingly dedicated as the station's 'medical suite,' then turning to Sammy Pollock declared in a flat voice, "I see no reason why Mr McDonald should not be detained overnight."

Sitting on the narrow examination bed, McDonald found his voice he sneered in reply, "What you talking about? I'm injured! I was attacked by them two polis! That wee polis woman, she kneed me in the balls and her pal, the *bastard*! He punched me when I wasn't looking so he did! I'll be complaining about them, so I will! I'll see that pair get sacked!"

Pollock stared hard at him when he softly replied, "That wee polis woman you're referring to. Would that be the same polis woman you tried to murder with the hammer you used to kill your wife?"

They both watched McDonald's eyes widen and his face pale when he stuttered, "You can't pin that on me! I was defending myself against them assaulting me!"

"You can explain that to the judge at your trial," Pollock drily replied, then opening the door, called in the shift's turnkey and said, "Please escort Mr McDonald to a holding cell for the minute while I organise his interview."

Turning to the doctor, he added, "Thank you, Doctor, and I'll await your report for the casefile."

****

In the Inspector's room, Iain Cowan told Mattie Devlin, "No doubt when the CID have finished interviewing McDonald, we'll need to provide someone to attend the observation cell to monitor him while he's in custody."

His brow furrowed when he added, "Short-handed as we are, I'll arrange with Inspector Bruce that her turnkey perform that duty for the time being. However, I'll make an arrangement to have one of the nightshift come out early and that means contacting the nightshift Inspector. So, in the meantime, Mattie, head up to the CID suite and collect Roz Begley. I want her taken to the Viccy to be examined and if there *is* bruising, nip her up to Pitt Street to have it photographed. Remind her too that her jacket will be a production, but I'm sure she'll have spares."

He sighed when he added, "The lassie has been through quite a trauma, particularly finding those poor weans, so use your judgement. If you think she needs to go home, drop her off at her parents, okay?"

"Roger. Want me to take the supervisory motor or persuade the CID to let me have one of their cars?"

"Oh, try and take one of their cars and if they object," he grimly smiled, "remind them we're doing *them* a favour by looking after *their* witness, our Roz."

Devlin smiled when he replied, "Leave it to me, sir."

He was about to leave the room when Cowan quietly said, "Use your judgement, Mattie. No matter what the medics say or what Roz tells you, if *you* don't think she's fit to come back here, take her straight home and no argument."

Devlin nodded in understanding, but inwardly, his mind was already made up.

****

DCI Laura Gemmill, sitting in front of Chief Superintendent Jimmy Thompson, began, "Just a courtesy visit, sir, to let you know that we've landed another murder. But," she held up her hand, "circumstances as they stand indicate it's a straight forward domestic."

Almost immediately, she rubbed at her forehead with the heel of her hand, then added, "Jesus, listen to me. As if there is a such a thing as a straight forward domestic murder."

"It's okay, Laura," he gently said, "I understand and of course, you're right. So, what's the story?"

He listened intently, she unaware of the anger that coursed through his body when she related how John McDonald had beaten his wife, Jessie, to death with a claw hammer and even more so, when McDonald used the same claw hammer to attempt the murder of one of his officers, a young woman.

"Has he admitted the murder?"

"Whether he does or not, to use the old adage, he's done bang to rights, sir, though I should warn you, McDonald intends complaining to his lawyer about the arresting officers…" he paused, then said, "manhandling him at the time of his arrest."

"And Sammy Pollock is the SIO, you say?"

"Yes sir."

"And young Begley? Is she okay?"

"Her sergeant is taking her to the Viccy for a check-up and if there's bruising, he'll take her to Pitt Street to be photographed."

"Hmm. I'll make an arrangement to speak with her."

Staring at him, she could not but think, and that's why you're such a good boss, caring for your people, but instead said, "I'll let Sammy know."

****

In her office upstairs, Chief Inspector Whitmore was at that time on the phone dealing with a complaint.

The Superintendent calling from Pitt Street, the Chief Constable's aide, she now realised from his distinctive Yorkshire accent, related the story of Constable McGarry's confrontation with Donaldson, then added, "For what it's worth, Chief Inspector…" he hesitated, then asked, "Can I call you Lizzie?"

Taken aback, she replied yes without thinking, only to hear him add, "Well, then, call me Trevor."

"Anyway, Lizzie," he continued in a more relaxed voice, "McGarry was, if anything, scrupulously polite, so polite it completely enraged the Chief who, to be frank, couldn't handle your man. So, again for what it's worth and in my humble opinion, your man was absolutely deadpan courteous, but with an undercurrent of condescension that I personally found, well, interesting is one word; funny is another."

And that sound like Smiler, she inwardly sighed, then asked, "And what does the Chief require of me then, Trevor."

"Oh, the Chief? He'd want McGarry hung, drawn and quartered for making him look like the fool…" he almost added, 'he really is,' but stopped short, then said, "Can I suggest that you have a quiet word with McGarry and suggest he watch where he steps, that the Chief has a long memory of those he believed have offended him?"

In a flat voice, she replied, "You mean he's vindictive?"

A slight hesitation followed before he replied, "Sounds like we're on the same page, Lizzie."

She found herself smiling when she said, "Thank you for the heads-up, Trevor, and if you're passing, there's always a coffee here for you."

"Thanks, Lizzie, I'll bear that in mind."

When the call ended and aware that Smiler had returned to duty that morning to assist the CID, Whitmore used the internal number for the CID clerk, then speaking to her former tutor cop from her time on the beat, said, "Bobby, it's Lizzie Whitmore. If Smiler has a moment, can you ask him to pop by my office?"

"Will do, Lizzie," Bobby replied.

****

Returned to the CID suite, his head now a little clearer, Smiler learned from the CID clerk, Bobby Davies that McMillan was in with the DCI and when he'd a minute, he was to attend at the Chief Inspector's office.

He didn't ask if Lizzie Whitmore had said why she wanted to see him, already suspecting his run-in with the Chief Constable was making waves.

Knocking on Gemmill's door, she called out he enter and doing so, saw Barbara McMillan sitting in front of the desk.

Smiler opened the conversation when he said, "Apologies, Ma'am, but hearing Jessie McDonald had been murdered kind of…"

She interrupted with a raised hand and indicating the empty chair by McMillan, said, "No need to explain, Smiler. Anyway, Barbara here has told me of your successful visit to the SOCO and what you've discovered. Cokey? Possibly a nickname, usually short for

Cochrane? Mean anything to you?"

Sitting down, he softly exhaled before he replied, "I'm sure I've heard the name recently, but when or where? I've been wracking my brain, but nothing yet," he shook his head.

He shrugged, then shook his head. "I've been racking my brain trying to recall, but you'll know yourself, Ma'am. The more thought you give it," he sighed with a shake of his head, "the less chance you have of remembering."

"That and you're an old guy," McMillan quipped with a grin.

Even Gemmill smiled at that, then said, "Barbara has been down to the collator's office, but he's nothing recorded for a Cokey."

"As well as the fact," McMillan turned to him, "he's inherited the old City of Glasgow files and was complaining that his predecessor seemed to have no rhyme or reason for his indexing. Apparently he used to tell people he'd an elephant memory so didn't need to index information."

"Aye," Smiler nodded with a frown, "I remember him. Bit of a plonker, actually. Died a few years ago with cirrhosis of the liver after his whisky habit caught up with him. He used to boast anything that was passed to him, he'd decide if it was relevant, so God alone knows what he destroyed that might have been useful."

"So," Gemmill stared at them in turn, "while we cannot unequivocally settle on this individual, Cokey, being the suspect for the two murders, he's our best shot at the minute."

She rubbed a hand across her weary face, feeling older than her thirty-seven years, then said, "Sammy Pollock is the appointed SIO for Jessie McDonald's murder and he's taken four of the team to assist with the post-mortem examination and knocking on doors for witnesses to the previous history of the McDonald's. That said, I expect that Sammy will present the case to Crown Office by Thursday at the latest and his team should be returned to our previous investigation. In the meantime, you two are working well together so I want you to continue to identify this individual Cokey and you, Smiler," she turned to him, "with your knowledge of the area, you're our best hope of finding someone who knows or knew him."

"No pressure then, Ma'am," he wryly smiled.

"No pressure," she smiled back at him.

In the corridor outside, McMillan turned to Smiler, her expression revealing her concern when she asks, "You okay big man?"
He grimly smiles before he nods, then says, "I'm okay, wee pal. I should be used to this job by now, the way the law works and *doesn't* work. If the politicians got it right years ago, we wouldn't need to be arresting spouses time and time again for battering their wives and yes, the occasional husband who takes a beating too."
"That day will come," then smiled as though to reassure him, "but right now, we need to concentrate on where you heard the name, Cokey."
Gently slapping a hand onto her shoulder, he nodded when he replied, "Don't worry, Barbara. I might not be as quick a thinker these days, but it'll come, trust me."
"Now," he stood upright, towering over her, "you away and grab a cuppa or a coffee and I'll see what the Chief Inspector wants me for."
****
The Sister in charge of the casualty department at the Victoria Infirmary saw the young police officer and the sergeant push through the entrance doors and from the expression on the woman's face, recognised she had incurred some kind of injury.
Ignoring the leading looks of those already waiting, she ushered them both through to a cubicle, then asked, "What's the problem?"
It was Roz Begley who replied, "I was struck on the left forearm with a claw hammer by a man I was trying to arrest."
"Sergeant?" the Sister turned to Devlin with her eyebrows raised.
"Eh? Oh, aye, of course," he blushed and left the cubicle.
Helping Roz remove her uniform blouse, the Sister's eyes narrowed when she saw the purple and black bruising of a hammer head, that was imprinted on Roz's skin, then said, "Dear heavens, that must have hurt."
"Probably not as bad as when I kneed him in the balls," Roz smiled.
"Good for you," the Sister grinned, then said, "I'm afraid we'll need to have that x-rayed, eh…"
"Roz," she cringed a little when the Sister gently poked at the bruising, then added, "Roz Begley."
"Well, Roz, I'll fetch the doctor and it's likely he'll authorise the x-ray, just to ensure there's no internal damage, though I suspect the muscle in your arm has protected the ulna and radius bones, so make

yourself comfortable. I'm afraid," she grimaced, "you might be here for a while."

"Could you let my sergeant know that, please. I don't think there's any point in him hanging around."

"I'll do that, dear. Now, how's about a nice cuppa and a biscuit?"

****

The man known to many as Cokey listened to the low mutterings of the crowd at the bar, hearing the rumour that was spreading like wildfire throughout the Govanhill area of the city, that a murder had been committed, that the polis were all over Annette Street like a rash.

Good, he thought with a sigh, if nothing else that will commit the polis to another investigation; maybe they'll even tie it in with the killings of wee Jeannie and that grass Moxy.

If he were honest, it confused him that the cops didn't seem to be doing anything about the two killings and in the paranoia of his mind, brought about the faint hope that they weren't interested in investigating a wee alkies' murder and that of a waster like Moston. Maybe it wasn't worth the effort for them, for who really gave a shit about that pair anyway?

This new murder, so he was hearing, was a supposed to be a woman in a flat somewhere in Annette Street and if the rumour *were* true, it was the wife of that arse John McDonald who was never out of the place. Him that was always cadging drinks and boasting about giving his missus a bleaching.

But rumours being that they were, he sighed, he'd wait and see…and listen.

CHAPTER TWENTY-EIGHT.

Lizzie Whitmore said, "Close the door behind you, Smiler, and take a seat. Now," she stared at him, "it's just me and you, so here's why I've asked you to come and see me."

When she finished recounting the telephone call from the Superintendent regarding the Chief Constable's complaint, she said, "Did you really take the mickey out of the Chief?"

He sighed when he explained, "You know me, Lizzie, I'm not a rude man, but him? Just a bully using his authority to intimidate his staff. You had to be there to see the way he spoke to the SOCO Department's manager. Bad enough if the man had done something wrong, but all he was trying to do was explain how busy his guys were with serious crime and do you know the bollocking he received, it was something just about the Chief wanting some preferential treatment for personal photographs printed and framed? My God," he shook his head, his anger obvious to her, "at his rank, you'd think he at least knew how to speak to people, how to motivate them rather that shout and scream at them. Preferential treatment?" he sneered. "The Chief's obviously never been under pressure like that poor guy is."

He stared at her, his eyes narrowing when he saw her grinning, then asked, "What?"

Sitting back in her chair, her arms folded, she continued grinning, then shook her head when she replied, "Same old Smiler, sticking up for the wee man."

"Someone has to," he grumpily responded.

"Well, for what it's worth, the Superintendent who phoned me totally agrees with you, but he only called really to warn you to watch your p's and q's if you ever encounter the Chief again and you have to know, too," she hurried on, "apparently the story has gone viral around headquarters and beyond."

She fought her laughter when she continued, "Seems someone called Smiler McGarry, a mere constable who works out of Craigie Street took the Chief down a peg or two and in *front* of a whole Department."

"Oh, that's all I need and with me…"

He didn't get to finish for the door was knocked, then pushed open by the Divisional Commander, Chief Superintendent Jimmy Thompson, who stepping into the room, began, "Sorry to interrupt, Lizzie…" then he stopped.

Staring at Smiler, he grinned widely when he said, "What's this I'm hearing about you, big man, telling the Chief Constable off?"

****

The young, floppy haired doctor, examining the returned x-ray, decided to break the good news himself and striding to the cubicle, pulled the curtain aside to inform Roz Begley, "Well, apart from the obvious bruising, Constable, nothing broken, but before you're discharged, Sister will arrange to have you fitted with a sling for the next day or two. Any pain, you can deal with that by the painkillers I'll prescribe and that will be issued by the hospital pharmacy." Liking what he saw, he gave Roz his most winning smile, then asked, "So, how do you spend your free time?"

Recognising the less than subtle approach, her face creased when she sighed, "If I'm not on shift, I usually go and watch my boyfriend practise his martial arts, pummelling other bodybuilders like himself. He's pretty possessive and likes to have me around so he can show off, you know?"

"Ah, right," he grimaced, "then all I can say is take it easy for the next couple of days."

Beating a hasty retreat, he passed the Sister who pokerfaced, entered the cubicle then muttered, "Well done, Roz. Competent enough young fellow, but a pain in the backside the way he mooches around my young nurses. Now then," she continued, "who can I phone to collect you and before you argue, you are *not* to return to work. That sergeant of yours made it very clear you're now off on the sick until your wound is healed, though he did say you have to make an appointment to attend your headquarters and have your injury photographed. He also said to tell you that if you need a lift home, call the station and he'll organise the van to take you home."

"Oh, great, thank you," she nodded, then asked, "Would it be okay if I phoned home myself? I'd rather not have my dad getting a fright when a stranger asks for me to be collected from the hospital."

"No problem," the Sister smiled, then added, "once my nurse has fitted you with a sling, I'll have her bring you to my office."

****

Making their way down the stairs towards the rear exit to the building, McMillan sighed, "Cokey. So, where do we start finding this guy?"

Smiler's brow furrowed when he replied, "I have an idea about that, but if you don't mind we'll have to hunt down someone who might be able to point us in the right direction, but only if I can find him too."

"And who is this guy?" she held open the door for him to step out into the rear yard.

"His name's James Ferguson, Fergie to them that knows him. A number of convictions for breach and minor theft, nothing too serious. I had a word with him previously and he admitted that the locals were talking about Moston as being suspected for killing Jeannie Mason, but it was rumours only; drink fuelled rumours, of course. However, Fergie has lived around here all his life and if there is someone still in the area who goes by the name, Cokey, then it's likely he'll know him or at least, know of him."

"So," she started the engine, "where we will find this man Fergie?"

"He's just started a job labouring at the tile factory over in Dixon Blazes, but I'm reluctant to call him out of his work."

She shrugged when she suggested, "We can always tell his boss we're here to give him some bad news. That way the boss won't suspect why we want to talk to him."

He turned to grin at her, then replied, "The ways a women's mind works never ceases to amaze me, Barbara. Right, let's head over to Dixon Blazes."

****

Mattie Devlin was walking past the charge bar where Drew Taylor and his temporary neighbour, Harry Dawson, were struggling to hold a handcuffed and writhing, but violent male prisoner against the wooden charge bar who was kicking out and yelling blue murder. While the harassed male turnkey tussled with the prisoner to search his pockets and clothing, the out of control twenty-four-years-old screamed abusive threats of vengeance against the arresting officers that included not just them, but their spouses, their children and family members.

Adding his weight to control the prisoner, Devlin grunted, "What's he in for?"

Breathing heavily, Taylor replied, "Broke into a works van parked in Seath Street, Sarge. There were two of them. We had to handcuff this bampot to a lamppost while we chased his pal, but the bugger outrun us."

Dawson, her face bright red with exertion and her hair is disarray, leaned close to the struggling man then hissed, "If you don't calm down I swear, I'm going to sink my teeth into your ear!"

"Aye, right!" he snarled, but then yelped when she bit him on the left ear.

The prisoner screamed, then when she drew her head back, she shrieked, "And *that's* for kicking me on the leg!"

"Seems fair to me," muttered Devlin as finally the three of them, assisted by the turnkey, wrestled the prisoner to the floor from where still wriggling, he was bodily carried to a first-floor cell, then callously dumped into the floor.

"You'll get the cuffs removed when you've calmed down," the turnkey warned him before slamming the door closed.

On the way out of the cell block, a breathless Taylor asked, "What about Roz, Sarge? She okay?"

"I left her at the Viccy waiting for an x-ray, though the Sister didn't think her arm was broken. I told the staff when she's discharged, she's to phone for a lift."

"You can cancel that," the turnkey said from behind them. "Roz phoned in to say her dad's going to collect her."

Trying not to show his disappointment, Taylor nodded, but promised himself when he arrived home, he'd phone her to find out how she was.

****

James Ferguson, known throughout the southside where he'd lived all his life as Fergie, was cheerfully whistling along to the radio blaring out in the warehouse while he operated the hydraulic pallet handler that was stacked with almost a half-ton of boxed tiles. Carefully manoeuvring the handler around a corner to its storage area, his heart sank when he saw his boss approaching and accompanied by a woman and of all people, that big bastard Smiler McGarry.

His eyes narrowed when he saw that McGarry wasn't wearing uniform.

Pulling the handler to a stop, he waited and could feel his stomach churning for this just had to be bad news for him.

"Fergie," his boss's face was grave, "these officers need to speak to your privately. I'm sorry, but it seems to be a very personal issue. Come and see me when you're done."

With that the boss turned away and left them to it.

"You've got me the sack, haven't you?" he angrily accused Smiler, who raised a hand and replied, "Not at all, wee man. We told your boss that your uncle Billy has passed away and we're here to break the news."

Confused, Fergie replied, "What? I've not got an uncle Billy. Well, not any more. He died years ago."

"So," Smiler grinned, "we weren't lying, were we?"

"Why are you really here, then," he stared suspiciously at them in turn.

In a low voice, Smiler replied, "The last time I spoke with you, Fergie, you said that you'd wish we got the person who killed wee Jeannie. Do you recall telling me that?"

"Eh," his face creased, "no, not really. I mean I was pissed. But that said," he shrugged, "aye, I'd like to think you will get whoever it was that did that to her. I mean she was a harmless wee soul when she was sober, was Jeannie."

"Well, between you, me and my neighbour here," Smiler nodded to her, "you might be able to help us, Fergie."

"Me? How?"

"Who's Cokey?"

"Cokey? You mean Cokey from *The Resting Soldier*?"

It was then that like a bolt of lightning, Smiler remembered.

It was the night he and Mattie Devlin had called into the pub to speak with the owner, Cathy McHugh.

The bald barman, someone not previously known to Smiler, who in those few seconds when he'd seen him, had been using a large kitchen knife to slice lemons.

He had called out to his boss and she had replied, calling him Cokey.

Smiling at a puzzled Fergie, he said, "Thanks, wee man, that's all I need to know. I suggest we keep this conversation between the three of us, okay, and for what it's worth, we've suggested to your boss that your family might be wanting you home at this very sad moment, so you might be looking at an early finish," he winked at him.

On their way out of the warehouse, McMillan said, "This guy Cokey, is he known to you?"

"Can't say I ever had any dealings with him, but that said, *The Resting Soldier* has had quite a turnover of staff through the years."

"So, what's our next move?"

"That'll be down to the DCI, wee pal, but I'm thinking that the owner, Cathy McHugh, might soon be looking for a new barman."

****

Feeling a little sorry for herself, though more to do with the thought of the two children she had discovered hiding in the wardrobe, Roz Begley's parents fussed over her when she returned home.

Drawing her a hot bath, her mother insisted on keeping her company in the bathroom and slowly learned of her daughter's attendance at the murder locus, her chest beating rapidly when Roz described how she had dodged the hammer blow intended to strike her on her head. Shocked and more afraid for Roz than she would admit, Nan Begley kept her fears to herself, yet could not deny the pride he felt for her youngest child.

"And you'll rest for the remainder of the week? I mean, you won't be rushing back to work, will you?"

Roz replied, "I'll return when I'm ready, mum. I mean, my arms a bit sore, but I'm not an invalid. Besides, I'm meeting my neighbour tomorrow morning for coffee and we'll probably have a post mortem about what happened."

"A what?" her mother was aghast.

Roz smiled, then explained, "We'll talk over the incident, not keep it bottled up. That's what we'll do. Get it out in the open."

"Ah, okay, yes," Nan nodded with some relief.

The door was knocked and her father's voice called out, "That's Drew Taylor on the phone, Roz. He's asking if you're okay?"

"Yes, dad, tell him I'm fine and I'll see him tomorrow, as arranged."

"Will do."

"Right," her mother rose from the toilet seat, "When you're out of the bath, I'll have some supper ready for you, but take your time. There's no rush."

"Okay," Roz smiled, but when the door was closed, the face of the little boy and his sister returned to her thoughts.

Drawing her legs up, she folded her arms around them, then resting her chin on her knees, the tears finally came.

****

Being the old-fashioned copper, he was, Smiler followed protocol and first spoke with Sammy Pollock, informing him what he and McMillan had learned.

Ushering them through to Laura Gemmill's office, they repeated their information.

"Well," Gemmill sat back in her chair, "when I sent you out to try and identify this man Cokey, I didn't think you'd be back so soon. Your source, Smiler," she addressed him, "are they reliable?"

"We didn't intimate why we wanted to know who Cokey is, Ma'am."

"So, he's fired this guy in without knowing why. Is there any likelihood he'll tip Cokey off about your interest?"

"I'd say no, Ma'am. I've suggested he keep what he told us to himself and if I know him, like I do, any inference that he's grassed Cokey into the police wouldn't sit well with him nor the punters he hangs around with."

"Right, then," she leaned forward, her forearms on her desk. "We know where he works and his nickname, but nothing else about him?"

"Unfortunately not, Ma'am," Smiler shook his head, then explained, "I didn't want to press the source too much for as I said, the less he knows, the less chance of him getting bevvied and letting it slip that Barbara and I had a word with him."

"How do you propose to confirm who this individual is?"

Smiler's brow furrowed when he replied, "*The Restless Soldier's* owner and landlady, Cathy McHugh, and I have what you might call a fractious relationship. We go some way back to the time when she and her former husband bought the pub and while I wouldn't exactly say I can trust her, I know that she suffered Jeannie Mason to be in the pub whereas other pubs would have barred Jeannie. Knowing that, there's a likelihood that with your permission, if I was to have quiet word with Cathy, she might just come across with more info about her barman, Cokey."

"But you can't swear to that?"

"No, I can't," he shook his head, then added, "but what I could tell her is that we're trying to trace an individual called Cokey, that we'd need to eliminate him from our inquiries. Again, though, Cathy's no fool so I won't guarantee she'd fall for that."

"And the hard fact is, Smiler, we don't even know for certain that the Cokey we're after is Albert Moston's accomplice nor even if he is a suspect for the murder."

She slowly shook her head when she added, "What a bloody conundrum this is."

It was Sammy Pollock who interjected with, "Boss, why don't we proceed with identifying Moston's accomplice and if we succeed with that, then treat him as a suspect for Moston's murder?"

"That might work," Gemmill nodded, then turned when McMillan raised a hand to say, "Regarding identifying Cokey that works in the pub, boss. There *might* be another way."

"Go on."

"I've a pal who works in the Inland Revenue in Centre One, in East Kilbride."

She turned to Smiler to ask, "I take it this woman McHugh, she runs a proper business?"

"I would think so, aye," he nodded.

"Then, her employees will be paid and their pay will include their national insurance and tax contributions, so if I can assure my pal that this inquiry is of the utmost urgency and time-critical…" she stared at Gemmill, who with a soft smile, nodded.

"Right then," she returned the nod, "if you excuse me, I'll go and give him a phone."

****

Following the murder of Jessie McDonald and the arrest of the violent man caught breaking into the van, Inspector Iain Cowan's officers had a relatively quiet remainder to their late shift and so, as the night wore on and the world's best police officer, heavy rain and a high wind passed through Glasgow and the West of Scotland, the calls from the public became fewer.

Seated with Mattie Devlin in the Inspector's office, Cowan asked, "What's your plans for the next two days?"

"Phew, with everything that's happened since I appeared in front of the Chief, I haven't had time to catch my breath, but I suppose it'll be the usual round of washing, housework and shopping."

"But at least you can do those chores without worrying about your…" he grimaced, "What was her name again?"

"Other than backstabbing bitch?" Devlin grinned, then added, "Janice Goodwin or I should say, that was the name she gave me, but who really knows," he shrugged.

"Well, I don't think there's any doubt you're well shot of her."

There was a lull in the conversation, broken when Devlin said, "Can I ask you, Inspector, what's my chances of remaining as an acting sergeant until I've kind of served my punishment?"

"How long is a piece of string, Mattie," he shook his head, then added, "But the good news is, you have Jimmy Thompson on your side as well as Lizzie Whitmore, so for as long as you keep doing a good job, which you are," he pointedly nodded, "I'd say keep your head down and fear the worse, but hope for the best."

"So," Devlin smiled, "I'm kind of in limbo?"

"No point in giving you false hope, but just remember who's in your corner."
Pursing his lips, Devlin nodded, inwardly relieved that he'd landed on his feet with Iain Cowan as his shift Inspector.
****
Twenty minutes had passed before Barbara McMillan returned to the incident room where she found Smiler poring over the statement of Rosie Donovan who, according to the detective that noted her statement, was emphatically certain she would recognise Albert Moston's accomplice on the night her father, Patrick Reagan, was assaulted and robbed.
Glancing up as McMillan approached, he had no need to ask if she had been successful for her flushed face, wide grin and the piece of paper she enthusiastically waved betrayed her excitement.
"Got his details," she exhaled.

CHAPTER TWENTY-NINE: 07.10am, Wednesday 14 March 1979.

She'd never been one to tackle pain with prescribed medicine, but once the adrenalin of her experience finally wore off, Roz had little choice but to down the painkillers she'd been given upon her discharge.
However, even those had little effect on the tenderness where she'd been struck by the hammer and sleep had eluded her for several hours before finally, her arm awkwardly tucked between two pillows, she fell over.
Waking that morning, her mouth as dry as a three-day old sock and eyes that felt gritty, she gave in and rose from her bed to find her mother already in the kitchen and preparing breakfast prior to her father departing for work.
"Dad's in the shower," Nan told her.
"If I've had a bad night," Roz smiled at her mother, "it looks like you did too."
She turned as her father, buttoning his shirt, entered the kitchen to tell her, "That's because your mother was up every hour at your door, listening to see if you were okay."

"What your dad's *trying* to say," her mother meaningfully stared at him "is we took turns."

"Oh God, I'm so sorry," Roz began, but stopped when her mother held up her hand and interrupted with, "You think because you're twenty-three and a police officer that we stop worrying about you?"

Roz slumped down into a chair and accepted the mug of tea held out to her before she replied, "Well, for what it's worth, I do appreciate what you do and how you care for me."

"Of course we know that," her father reached down to gently hug at her uninjured right side.

"Now," he sat down opposite, "I'm assuming you'll be going to the doctor today to get a sick line?"

"That's my instruction, yes," she nodded, "then I'll be heading up to headquarters to have my arm photographed."

"Whatever for?" her mother turned from the toaster to glance at her.

"Evidence, mum. The man who attacked me has been charged not just with murdering his wife, but attempting to murder me too. If he pleads not guilty, the jury will need to see evidence of my being hit with the hammer; the bruising and if it should go to trial, by the time it gets to court, my arm will be healed. So, photographic evidence is vital to substantiate the charge."

Her mother's eyes widened and her face paled, her hand instinctively reaching towards her mouth.

"Dear heavens, you never said he tried to kill you."

"Yes, well, you'd enough to contend with, learning that I'd been hit with a hammer."

"And this photo, that will help convict him?"

"It should do," she nodded.

"Then I'll go with you," her mother replied, her anger showing in her eyes while inwardly devising ways she like to hurt the man who attacked her daughter.

"We can catch the subway from Hillhead to the town and while we're there, have some lunch."

"Ah, thanks, mum," her face creased, "but I already have plans like I said. I'm meeting Drew Taylor for coffee?" she reminded her, then added, "And I think it's more than likely he'll want to come to Pitt Street with me."

"Oh, aye?" her mother stared suspiciously at her.

Catching on, Roz defensively sighed, "It's not like that. Drew's my neighbour and it's a neighbour thing, okay?"
Smiling, Nan knowingly replied, "Just keep telling yourself that, dear," yet inwardly pleased it wasn't Roz's ex, that two-timing ratbag, Derek.
****
Smiler arrived at the incident room just minutes after DI Sammy Pollock, who returning form the Sheriff Court with two DC's, greeted him with, "Any more thoughts about this guy Cochrane?"
"Nothing that you guys haven't already considered," he grimaced, "though I'd like to be the one to fetch Mrs Donovan in for the ID parade."
"Not a problem and here's a suggestion. Phone her now to give her some notice and prepare her to come in, but just ensure that she is aware we'll first need to find Cochrane, hopefully at the address we've got for him, then we need to arrange for stand-ins and you know as I do, it's all time consuming."
"Will do, Sammy."
Waiting on the rest of the team arriving, they both greeted Laura Gemmill, who beckoned that Pollock follow her to her office.
Removing her coat and hanging it on the wall hook, she began, "That was good work yesterday by Smiler and young Barbara. Have you organised an arrest team?"
"Already out and away to fetch our suspect in, boss. If you're okay with it, I'll conduct the interview myself."
"What about the report for the murder of Mrs McDonald?"
"All done and dusted, boss. It wasn't exactly a whodunit and there's just a few things to tie-up before I take the case through to the PF's office and I can do that later today."
"And he's away to the court?"
"Aye, he's there now," he nodded. "I was in early and had a couple of the guys accompany me to take him for a private hearing at Ingram Street."
He grimaced when he said, "Turned out we struck lucky. The duty custody Sheriff was in early and took him straight away."
He paused then staring expressively at Gemmill, he added, "It was Sheriff Dean-Baker."
The DCI also grimaced, for Dean-Baker was known throughout the Glasgow Division's as a woman who came down hard on domestic

abusers and many a lawyer had felt her wrath when representing such accused.

"Anyway," he shrugged, "I sat in on the pleading diet, but McDonald's lawyer didn't enter a plea at this time, obviously hoping for a more lenient judge at the formal pleading diet where I'm assuming he'll plead guilty, given the evidence against him. Needless to say, he was remanded to Barlinnie till his trial date, whenever that might be, but you know the thing that *really* annoyed me," his expression darkened.

He didn't wait for a response, but continued, "He was that sorry for himself, right from the time I fetched him from his cell and all through the proceeding, he wept a bucket of tears and not once, not *once*," he repeated with a snarl, "did that bastard ask after his kids; where they were and how were they. Not *once*," he said again with a shake of his head.

Deciding to change the subject and get him out of his black mood, she said, "Right, our suspect Cochrane when he's brought in. I'd have thought you might have let one of the DS's deal with the interview?"

"Simply believe in leading from the front, boss, just as you do," he smiled at her, then tongue in cheek, he added, "Let's not forget who it was that run up the stairs in a tenement fire."

She shook her head and sighed before she replied, "And look what that got me. A lungful of smoke."

"Anyway, digressing completely, some good news for you. Lucy Chalmers was telling me this morning that she and her team have had some success tracking down a number of crime reports that all had attached supplementary forms attached and were written off as unsolvable."

He paused, then savouring the moment, continued, "And *all* signed off by John Michael Crawford, DCI."

She took a quick breath when she asked, "How many crime reports?"

"Eight more, so far."

"Well," he smiled at her as he quickly continued, "you gave her autonomy to deal with it as her inquiry, boss, so she went for it, hell for leather. She tells me that so far she hasn't discovered a living complainer for any of the crime reports; however, what she's done is contact the Personnel Department at Pitt Street for the current addresses and contact numbers of the former, now retired CID officers who were assigned each crime report. To date, her and her team have been in touch with five former detective officers from Craigie Street CID who have provided statements that they did *not* have the opportunity to investigate the muggings, that almost immediately, the DCI took the crime reports from them. Also," he stared at her, "none of the former detectives were aware that a supplementary had been added to the original crime reports to write them off as unsolvable."

Her face displayed her disbelief when she asked, "Didn't any of these former detectives think that was unusual?"

"Apparently Lucy has asked that question of them all, boss, and it seems that Crawford ruthlessly run his Department where anyone who dissented or made waves was quickly transferred either to uniform or elsewhere. So no, heads remained beneath the parapet and not a lot of questions were asked about what he was up to."

"And Lucy has statements from these former officers?"

"Yes, boss," he nodded.

"She's exceeded my expectations," Gemmill grinned, then added, "I'll have a word with her after this morning's briefing."

"Right then, Sammy," she slapped her hands together, "let's speak to the team about Mr Cochrane."

****

The team were fully assembled when Gemmill and Pollock entered the incident room and standing with her back to Danny Sullivan's desk, her arms folded, she began, "Let's get right into it, guys." Staring round the room, she said, "Thanks to some good work yesterday by Barbara McMillan and Smiler McGarry, we have identified a possible suspect for the historical assault and robberies committed by our second victim, Albert Moston, and his then unknown accomplice."

Glancing at a sheet of paper in her hand, she continued, "Patrick Cochrane, known as Cokey, aged thirty-seven years, residing at a flat in one of the high rise buildings up in Myrtle View Road up in Prospecthill, is employed as a barman in *The Resting Soldier* pub in Allison Street where undoubtedly, he'd known Moston and likely, Jeannie Mason too."

She followed this announcement with a short summary of how they had arrived at the suspect's name, but then she paused when the door opened to admit the CID clerk, Bobby Davies and who raised a hand to catch her attention.

"Yes, Bobby?"

"That was the arrest team, Ma'am. They have the suspect in custody. No issues. Said he appeared shocked to see them at the door, but didn't protest why he was being detained nor asked any questions."

"Hmm," her brow furrowed, then replied, "Thanks, Bobby."

Turning back to the team, her eyes sought out Smiler before she said, "Make the arrangement for Mrs Donovan to attend the ID parade," then immediately turning to a stocky built DC, Conor MacLeod, instructed him, "Go ahead and bring in the stand-ins, Conor. You have a description of our suspect?"

"Yes, boss," he nodded.

"Sammy," she turned to him, "might as well inform the Duty Inspector we'll require the cell area for the parade."

"Boss," he too nodded.

"Any questions?" once again, her eyes roamed around the room.

"Whose to run the parade, boss?" Lucy Chalmers asked.

"The Castlemilk DI, Norrie Greene, will be on his way down by now," she replied, then with no more questions, dismissed the team to their respective inquiries or tasks.

A young CID aide, attached to the Department just two weeks previously, asked MacLeod, "Why does it have to be a DI from Castlemilk? Why not have DI Pollock run the parade?"

MacLeod leaned over the slighter man to quietly respond, "Rules of evidence and fair play to a suspect, wee man. Using an officer not connected in any way to the investigation demonstrates fairness to an accused and should deflect any accusation by a defence counsel of bias against an accused. Now," he continued, "let's me and you go out and find our stand-ins."

****

Showering, Roz Begley found her left arm stiff and aching and with some reluctance, decided on two more painkillers that she washed down with a full glass of water.

Dressing was difficult and when attempting to pull on a pink coloured blouse over her head, Roz finally called her mother through to her room to assist her.

At last, her auburn hair combed through and wearing jeans, she slipped on a pair of red coloured, leather zipped ankle boots, then decided against wearing make-up, inwardly reminding herself this was a meeting with her neighbour, not a date.

She turned as her mother knocked on the open door, then smiled when she said, "You look nice, but what about some lippy and I can help applying some blusher, if you like?"

"Thanks, mum, she forced a smile, "but remember, I'm going to police headquarters to have my photograph taken, so I'm not wanting to look glammed up, okay?"

"Oh, right," her mother frowned, then helped her into a hooded, maroon coloured leather bomber jacket. "I hadn't thought about it like that."

"Is Drew collecting you are you wanting me to drop you somewhere?"

"No, I'll be fine. I'm walking to the University Café on Byres Road where I'll meet him there. Now, can you help me put this sling on over my jacket?"

That done, her mother stepped back, then her eyes wet with unshed tears, stepped forward to take Roz's face in both hands and gently kissed her on the cheek.

"What I'd do to that man if I could get my hands on him," she moaned.

"He brutally murdered his wife and left his two children without a parent, Mum. I think you can leave him to a judge and jury."

"Well, you did your job, dear, so let's hope the jury and the judge do *their* job," Nan angrily replied, but her fury was directed at John McDonald, not her daughter.

Minutes later, the sun peeking out from behind a cloud and the air fresh from the previous night's rainfall, Roz was striding down Caird Drive, her left arm in the sling and her handbag strap around her neck and hanging on her right side.

The dull ache had for the moment, subsided and it was then Roz suddenly realised she was looking forward to seeing Drew.

****

Laura Gemmill nodded at Lucy Chalmers when she said. "You and your team have done a grand job, Lucy, and I'll not forget what you've brought to this investigation."

Her face flushed, Chalmers replied, "How far back do you want us to continue searching, boss?"

Gemmill's brow furrowed when she made her decision.

"Give it to midday and after that, we'll go with what you've discovered."

"Do you think it's enough?"

"To bring down a police officer who used his rank and privilege to corrupt the law to further his own career? That and the statements you've obtained? Oh, aye, Lucy," she nodded, "I think it's plenty enough."

Chalmers stared at her DCI when she said in a low voice, "You know you're going to be stirring a hornet's nest, boss. The senior ranks, irrespective of what Force they belong to and no matter you're a DCI, won't take too kindly to a junior police officer and dare I say, a *female* officer, going after someone with the influence and power that an Assistant Chief Constable can wield. You might be harming your own advancement, maybe even find your career coming to a full stop."

Gemmill, resting her backside against the edge of her desk, her arms folded, shook her head and softy exhaled when she responded with, "Yet I can't ignore what went on, Lucy. To do so would make me art and part of him perverting the course of justice, so like it or not, I'm committed to following this through."

Seconds passed before Chalmers's eyes narrowed when she asked, "Hope I'm not speaking out of turn, boss, but does the Div Comm know you're pursuing this line of inquiry?"

She decided not to disclose her conversation with Lizzie Whitmore and her request Whitmore have a discreet word with Jimmy Thompson.

And so she replied, "Not that I'm aware of, but why do you ask?"

She shrugged when she replied, "In my time in the Division, I've come to realise that Jimmy downstairs is a right old-fashioned polis, looks after his people and a good man to have at your back."

Gemmill's eyes narrowed, recalling her conversation with Lizzie Whitmore before she replied, "You might just have given me an idea, so thanks, Lucy."

****

The DS who had led the four man team to detain the suspect, learned the DCI was busy and so reported to Sammy Pollock what was later to become vital information.

"When he opened the door, Sammy," the DS began, "he was bare chested and wearing just a pair of joggers. Right away I could see that he had multiple tattoos on both arms and his chest and it was clear from the tattoos he'd served in the military."

"Anyway," the DS continued, "I had a wee chat with him on the way over and it seems he enlisted in February in nineteen-sixty-six, in the Royal Highland Fusiliers, and was discharged just four months ago, though wouldn't disclose why."

Pollock's eyes narrowed when he said, "Nineteen-sixty-six, that's not too long after he's been involved in the muggings. Sounds like he might have been on his toes. Right," he exhaled, "you've got his personal details, so get onto the Royal Military Police detachment at Edinburgh Castle, tell them it's a time critical request in an ongoing murder inquiry, that we need to know when and where he served and the reason for his dismissal. If they give you any hassle, inform them that we'll obtain a Sheriff's warrant for that information and make sure you get the name of the person you speak to. Ask them to spell it too and their rank as well," he evilly grinned, "because we'll need the info for the warrant. That might change their mind."

****

The suspect for the historical assault and robberies, now identified as Patrick Cochrane, was led to the uniform charge bar where after the Duty Inspector noted his details, then formally cautioned and informed why he was being detained.

He was then requested to provide his lawyers details.

"Don't have a lawyer and I don't need a lawyer. I've not done nothing," Cochrane gruffly replied.

Nevertheless, at the request of the CID, the duty defence lawyer was summoned by the bar officer.

Placed in a detention room while the identification parade was being organised, during that time Smiler had picked up Rosie Donovan from St Albert's chapel house and conveyed her to Craigie Street where leaving her with the CID clerk, Bobby Davies, he went to fetch her a cup of tea.

Popping his head into the incident room, Smiler informed Sammy Pollock that the witness was now present and in turn, learned that DC Conor MacLeod and his neighbour, having visited a well-known corner within Queens Park where the usual layabouts could be found drinking the local cheap wine, had with the promise of the customary five-pound note each, persuaded five of the group to accompany them to participate in the identification parade as stand-ins.

Now the five, loitering in the entrance public foyer of the station, awaited the call through to the cell area where the parade would take place.

DI Nobby Greene, arriving from Castlemilk police station at the same time as the grumpy and unpopular defence counsel who had the misfortune to be next in line for a call-out, reported to DCI Gemmill that he was ready to commence the parade.

Within ten minutes, the five stand-ins were lined up and laughing among themselves that for once, they were in the cell block, but not under arrest.

Their laughter and patter ended when the detention room was opened and the suspect led out.

All five, recognising Cochrane, suddenly found something other than him to take their interest.

DI Greene, accompanied by the defence lawyer, arrived in the cell area where cardboard numbers, one to six, were laid out in a line on the floor.

To one side, the bar officer and the male turnkey stood ready to intervene should Cochrane decide that he would resist the parade.

"Mr Cochrane," Greene politely addressed him, "choose where you'd like to stand, sir."

Wordlessly, Cochrane strode to the position at number four, then hands behind his back, stared at the blank wall in front of him.

The stand-ins were then directed to stand behind the remaining numbers.

Selected to lead the sole witness to the parade, Smiler brought Rosie down to the large metal gate entrance to the cell area and just out of sight of the parade, bade her wait with him to be called forward.

As the reporting officer, DCI Laura Gemmill entered the cell area where for the first time, she set eyes on the man who at the very least, was a street assault and robbery thug and the very best, a possible suspect for the murders of Jeannie Mason and Albert Moston.

At a nod from Gemmill and without naming her, Greene called for, "Witness number one," to enter the cell block.

Pale faced and escorted by Smiler, the five stand-ins turned to stare curiously at Rosie when she confidently strode into the cell block, while Cochrane continued to stare fixedly ahead.

"Gentlemen, please," Greene's sharp voice reminded them of their instruction, to stare ahead and ignore the witness while he beckoned Rosie towards him, then said, "You will be shown a parade comprising of six individuals of similar age, height and appearance. You may ask them to speak, walk or perform any other action that is within reason. Do you have such a request?"

Rosie shook her head, her full attention on Greene.

"I will now ask you to walk along the line of men," he continued, "and if you see the individual that you referred in your statement to the police, please tell me the number that is at his feet. You may proceed," he waved a hand at the men standing in the parade.

Rosie turned and beginning at the man standing at number one, she slowly walked towards him and stared into his face. A tense few seconds passed, then she carried on and did so again with the men standing at numbers two and three, each man scrutinised by her. Turning, she took one more step towards the man stood at number four, then stared the suspect in the eyes.

Seconds passed and the tension in the cell block rose, but then to everyone's surprise, Rosie turned to nod at Greene, then let fly with a right-handed fist to Cochrane's jaw, while screaming, "You evil bastard!"

Taken aback, the blow didn't knock Cochrane down, but certainly caused him to stumble back, his arms rising to block any further punches.

In those few heartbeats, Smiler was sprinting the five yards from the gate across the cell area towards the screaming Rosie, where wrapping his arms around her, he bodily lifted the stocky built woman to the cell block gate, then turning, carried her from the cell area and out of sight of the parade.

Within the cell area, the defence lawyer, a seasoned defender of mostly guilty clients, turned towards Greene where in a laconic voice, he sighed, "I believe we must assume that to be a positive identification against my client, Inspector."

CHAPTER THIRTY.

"Whatever were you thinking?" sitting opposite each other, their knees almost touching, Smiler addressed the shaking woman, the adrenalin no longer coursing through her body.

"I'm so, *so* sorry," she sniffed, the tears running down her cheeks as sitting in the DI's room, she clutched the mug of water with two hands.

Her shoulder's slumped when slowly shaking her head, she continued, "I just saw him and it all came back to me, the sound of my poor old Da screaming when that…that… *bastard* broke Da's arm."

On this occasion, Smiler idly noted she did not make the sign of the cross.

"Well," he sighed, "while I'm glad you picked out the correct man, Rosie, I have to tell you that the DCI won't be pleased you punched him and she might even consider charging you with assaulting him and *that* won't do the case against him any good."

She didn't respond, but seconds later, looked up and stared at him when he softly asked, "Was it worth it?"

A slow smile settled on her face when in the same low voice, she replied, "Aye, Smiler, just to belt him on the jaw. It *was* worth it, but I'm so sorry about my language. I'll need to admit that when I'm at confession," then hurriedly made the sign of the cross.

"Oh," he smiled back when he said, "I think God will allow you that one, Rosie. Now, give me a couple of minutes to speak with the Detective Inspector. I'm thinking he'll want me to add your positive identification to your statement and I'll try to find out if they've made a decision about you when I'm there."

With that he left the room.

****

Drew Tylor, occupying a booth at the rear of the premises, shuffled anxiously on the worn, red leather seat and to his own surprise, realised how unusually nervous he was about meeting Roz Begley. He had slept badly the previous night, swithering about whether or not to disclose that he had feelings for her. The problem, quite apart from the fact she might reject those feelings, was that if she did agree to a relationship with him, then they risked being separated at work. Strathclyde Police did not approve of officers who were romantically involved working in the same Division, let alone the same shift and the reason was quite clear; the perfect example of that policy being John McDonald's assault upon Roz.

For those few seconds witnessing the assault, Taylor's inclination had not been just to save his neighbour's life, but seeing her attacked like that, he'd wanted to tear McDonald apart, hurt him and, he recoiled at the memory of his anger, beat the bastard to death.

Not by nature a violent individual, never had he in all his life wanted to hurt anyone like he had McDonald and all because of his feelings for Roz.

That feeling scared him and now because of it, he truly understood the policy.

He glanced up when he saw the front door to the café pushed open, then Roz entered. Instinctively, he rose to his feet, smiling at how attractive she was and waving at her.

"How's the arm?" he greeted her, resisting the urge to kiss her cheek.

"How are your knuckles?" she responded with a grin.

He lifted his hand to show her the redness and shrugged, "Not as bad as you obviously are."

She slid into the bench seat opposite and for those few seconds, a silence existed, broken when he waved to the waitress, then said, "I've pre-ordered our coffees."

"Looking after me again?" she teased, but surprised when he replied, "Yes, I'd like to do that, Roz."

He was taken aback by his own response, then stuttered, "I'm sorry. That came out all wrong."

She stared at him when she quietly asked, "Did it or are you trying to tell me something?"

His throat felt tight and he could only nod, then found his voice to tell her, "I'm sorry. You've just broken up with Derek and here's me trying to…well, you know," he shrugged again.

"No, actually, I don't," she continued to stare at him, his face reddening and unable to meet her eyes.

She watched him take a deep breath then it all came out in a rush. "Since God alone knows when, I've had these feelings for you and though I tried not to compare you to Sharon, I couldn't help myself and then I had to admit it was you that I really liked, that you were everything she's not and I knew I couldn't fool myself, that Sharon meant nothing to me, that she wasn't real and I can't explain what I mean by that, but working beside you, day after day, I felt more attracted to you than anyone I've ever met and it was absolute agony for me that I couldn't confess how I felt because I know that if word got out the bosses would move one of us and I didn't want to lose you as a neighbour and when that nutter had a go at you yesterday I just wanted to murder him and the very thought of you getting hurt drove me mad and even now I can't explain how crazy I am for you and…" he stopped to draw a breath.

"Jesus, that was quite a mouthful, son," and it was then Taylor realised the middle-aged waitress, a mug of coffee in each hand, was standing over him.

Staring up at her, his mouth fell open and turned to see Roz grinning widely at him.

Oh, shit, he thought, I've really cocked it up.

****

Seated in her office with Sammy Pollock and the incident room manager, DS Danny Sullivan, Gemmill said, "Well, the positive identification gives us enough to charge him with the one assault and robbery, but there's no direct evidence to substantiate charging him with the other eight Lucy Chalmers turned up, albeit we know he was involved with Moston, though we've nothing to tie him in the Moston. However," she drew a breath, "charging him with one assault and robbery gives us enough punch to ask the Fiscal to authorise search warrants for both his flat and his place of work. The pub, the eh…"

"*The Restful Soldier*, boss," he reminded her. "Not a pro-polis pub, so it'll be best to go in mob handed," his brow knitted in thought when he added, "Might be an idea to take Smiler McGarry with us. He's not just big, he knows every bugger who drinks there and as I recall the landlady too."

"Now," she chewed on her lower lip, "at his flat we're looking for footwear that matches the plaster casts the SOCO discovered at both loci and the photographs of Jeannie Mason's injuries. That and any large knives he might have in his kitchen drawer."

"You're thinking of the missing tip, the bit the pathologist discovered in Moston?"

"Exactly," she nodded.

"Wait, what?" Sullivan's head snapped up and he stared at them in turn.

"At Moston's post mortem, Danny," Gemmill explained, "the doctor discovered the broken tip of a large kitchen type knife embedded in Moston's liver; about a quarter of in inch in length, as I recall. I'd decided to keep that info between the DI and me and the production team, so for the meantime...?" she stared at him.

"Sorry, boss, but I can't agree. If you're sending guys out to search for a big knife, they need to know they might be looking for something in particular and finding that, particularly if it's in Cochrane's flat, might just be the evidence that convicts him."

She sighed, the nodded when she added, "Of course, Danny, you're right. I think I just got used to the old mantra for SIO's about keeping something back. Thanks."

"Boss," he acknowledged with a flushed face.

"Sammy," she turned to him, "I've now decided that you and *I* will interview Cochrane, but I want to hold off meantime till the search of his flat and workplace is concluded, just in the event that something of evidential value might turn up; something that will tie him in with the murders."

"Okay, boss," he rose to his feet, "but right now, if you don't mind, I'll hurry along and get those applications for the warrants typed up and maybe add that the warrants are time critical, then I'll go myself to see to them being signed by a Sheriff."

It was then her door was knocked and pushed open by the DS who had been instructed to contact the military at Edinburgh Castle.

"Sorry to intrude," he hurried in, a sheet of paper in his hand, "but I thought you'd want to hear this right away."

Standing facing Gemmill with the DI beside him and Sullivan still seated, he referred to the paper when he began, "Patrick Cochrane, enlisted in February in nineteen-sixty-six at the recruiting office in Sauchiehall Street and was sent to the City of Edinburgh Garrison, where after his basic training, he joined the RHF as an infantryman at Glencourse Barracks. During his service he spent time in Germany, was promoted to Lance-corporal and also served two tours in the Province during the ongoing conflict with the IRA. Described in his annual appraisals as an average soldier, with no real discipline issues. However," he glanced up at Gemmill, "in February last year, he was arrested by the Military Police for assaulting the wife of a fellow soldier, with whom he had been having an affair. Apparently he put her in hospital with a broken jaw and broken ribs. Court-martialled, he was sentenced to military custody, served six months, then in August last year, was dishonourably discharged."

"So, a violent man with women," Gemmell mused.

"That's not the best bit, boss," the DS grinned. "When Cochrane signed up to join the army, he declared he had no family and registered Albert Moston's mother, Irene, as his next of kin."

"And there's the evidential association with our victim," a relieved Gemmill smiled at Pollock.

****

The defence lawyer for Cochrane, having spoken at length with his client, was being escorted by the turnkey through the cell area towards the charge bar and then to foyer of the station, when he saw Smiler McGarry standing there, obviously waiting for him.

"I'll see the gentleman out," Smiler spoke to the turnkey, who glancing at them in turn, nodded and left them there.

When alone and with the turnkey out of earshot, Smiler held out his hand and said, "Long time no see, Freddie."

The lawyer grasped his hand in return and with a wry smile, said, "I'm guessing this is about the witness and her Henry Cooper punch?"

"It would be helpful if your client, so to speak, took it on the chin for what he did to her father."

"And this is just you and I speaking, no one hearing about it and that'll be us square if I convince him?"

"This is nothing to do with that wee issue, Freddie," Smiler quietly replied when he shook his head, then added, "and you know me, that I would never hold that over you."

He continued, "And yes, it's just me asking and this is about a good woman who has suffered for many years after witnessing what your client did to her dad. I'd hate to see her charged with what we might call, justifiable retribution."

Freddie softly smiled when he said, "I was surprised when I saw you at the parade wearing a suit, Smiler. Are you in the CID now?"

"Heavens, no, still pounding the beat for my sins. I'm only helping them out for a few days."

"Well, for what's it's worth," Freddie lowered his voice, "I kind of guess you'd want to speak with me, so I've already told my client that it's not in his interest to make any formal complaint of assault, that if this goes to a jury, your witness will only garner support for

smacking him in the mouth and besides, she never even broke skin."
"Thank you, Freddie. I'm grateful," and again shook his hand.
"No problem."
Freddie turned away, but hesitated, then turning, said in the same low voice, "When you stopped me that night, I could have lost my licence, Smiler, and it would have seriously impacted on my career. You driving me home and what you told me was a right wake-up call and you have to know, I've been sober since then. But I don't take my sobriety for granted. I regularly attend meetings and my wife," he smiled. "Well, she says I'm a better man for it."
With a nod he walked off to the door that would lead him towards the station foyer.
****

Gently stirring her coffee with a teaspoon, Roz saw that Drew Taylor, following his outburst, had calmed down sufficiently for her to ask, "So, these feelings you have. When did they begin?"
Still extremely embarrassed, he took a long breath before he shook his head, then replied, "Honestly? I can't truthfully say."
His face creased when he continued, "I thought I was happy with Sharon, or rather, she told me I was happy with her," he at last smiled, "but then…"
He hesitated, searching for the right words, then finally settled with, "I began to doubt my relationship with her, had these feelings of," his face creased again, "kind of claustrophobia, as though she was completely taking over my life."
"So, you thought you'd transfer your affection to me?" she teased him.
"No," he anxiously waved his hands in front of him, "not at all. I swear, Roz, it wasn't like that. Besides, you were dating Derek and believe me, I would *never* have said anything if that had still been happening."
"Hmm," she pretended to be sceptical, but then smiled and said, "So, again, when did you think you had these feelings?"
He nervously sipped at his cooling coffee, then dabbing at his mouth with the paper napkin to give him those few seconds to collect his thoughts, he said, "Like I said, I was starting to recognise that Sharon as we now know, is manipulative and possessive, so I'd made up my mind to end it with her and, well, I didn't do such a good job of it as you pointed out," he sighed.

"And ending it with her, was that before or after Derek dumped me?"

He stared at her, slightly confused when he said, "I thought you'd said…" he stopped, then starring at her, added, "I didn't realise he'd dumped you. Why would he do that?"

It was Roz who was embarrassed now, when she admitted, "I told you I'd ended it with him, but the truth is, well, he'd cheated on me with someone else and as far as I'm concerned," she shrugged, "that was him leaving me."

She drew a quick breath, then added, "I told you that because I wanted to retain some dignity."

"Man's an idiot," Taylor shook his head.

"So, when exactly did you think about me?"

"If you're asking if I intended swooping in because you were single again, then yes," he smiled at her. "I didn't want to waste any more time being with Sharon when I just knew she wasn't right for me."

"And you think I am right for you?"

His brow knitted when he reached across the table for her hand, conscious she didn't draw away when he gently took hold of it, then quietly replied, "I don't think it, Roz, I believe it."

She continued to meet his gaze for several seconds, then suggested, "Let's see how this plays out for the next week or so, Drew, then we can discuss what we're going to do. Don't forget, if the bosses were to get wind of us seeing each other, one of us will be definitely be moved and me being the junior of the two, it'll be me."

He surprised her when he replied, "I don't care if you or I *are* moved to another Division. I just care that we stay a couple, if that's okay with you."

She smiled, then nodding, said, "First things first. Finish your coffee, then if you've nothing else to do today, you can come on the subway with me to the town," she lifted her left arm, "where I've to have this photographed at headquarters. Then, when that's done, you can buy me lunch."

The waitress rung their bill through the till, then watching them leave the café, smiled as she shook her head.

****

Returned to the DI's room and again seated with an anxious Rosie Donovan, Smiler respectfully rose to his feet when the door was opened to admit DCI Laura Gemmill, who remained standing while she waved him back down into the chair.

"Mrs Donovan," she began, "I'm certain Constable McGarry has already informed you that you were successful identifying the man who you mentioned in your statement to the police. His name is Patrick Cochrane and has been charged with seriously assaulting and robbing your father. However," she grimaced, "whether the Procurator Fiscal will prosecute the case is doubtful and the reason being because you are the sole witness to the incident and there is no other, what we call corroborating evidence to his guilt. If he is to be prosecuted, then it is a decision that will be made by the PF."

She watched the older woman's mouth open almost in disbelief, so raised a hand to continue, "I am aware that will be disappointing news for you, but I will share this with you. Though I'm not at liberty to disclose them, my team and I are actively pursuing other crimes against Cochrane, so it may be he will *not* walk free."

Gemmill took a short breath before she then said, "Now, while I completely understood your motive for assaulting Cochrane..."

"Ma'am!" Smiler quickly raised his hand and glanced at Rosie when he interjected, then asked, "Can I have a private word, please?"

Taken aback, Gemmill's eyes flickered before she replied, "Yes, of course," and beckoned him to follow her into the corridor.

"Yes?" she stared at him as they stood together.

"Eh," his face creased, "just to say I haven't told Mrs Donovan, but Cochrane won't be making a complaint against her. I thought I'd let you break the good news, Ma'am."

"What? Why, I mean, how do you know this?"

He grimaced before he replied, "I'm assured by his lawyer that there will be no complaint."

Eyes narrowing, she suspiciously hissed, "What did you do, Smiler?"

Shrugging, his face the picture of innocence, he replied, "Me? Nothing, Ma'am. I just think that Cochrane accepts an eye for an eye, after what he did to her father."

"And you didn't threaten...I mean," she shook her head to dispel the thought of her suspect flying out of a window, then took a short breath, "you didn't *speak* to Cochrane?"

Eyes widening, he shook his head when, he said, "As God is my witness, I haven't said a word to him, Ma'am."

Still suspicious, she stared at him, his guiltless expression fooling no-one, when she softly said, "But you did do *something*, of that I'm bloody certain. However, in this case I'm happy you somehow sorted that out, so let's go back in and give Mrs Donovan the good news."

****

Just over an hour after instructing Sammy Pollock to obtain the search warrants, the DI was at the Ingram Street courts standing before a Sheriff, coincidentally the same Lady Sheriff who had remanded John McDonald, and swearing to the legitimacy of the information on both warrants.

The warrants now signed and in his possession, he used the car radio to inform the search teams to make their way to both Cochrane's flat and *The Restful Soldier* to commence their searches.

****

Informed by Pollock of the warrants being signed, Laura Gemmill gathered both her search designated teams into the incident room and briefed them on what they were seeking, primarily any footwear that might have been used by Cochrane and, with an approving glance towards DS Danny Sullivan, disclosed the discovery of the quieter-inch tip of a large knife discovered in Albert Moston's liver.

"There's nothing to indicate what type of knife it might be, guys," she glanced around the room, "whether it be a straight forward kitchen implement or now that we know of his military background, some sort of army weapon. As regard the footwear," she continued, "anything you find is to be photographed in situ, then immediately delivered to the SOCO at Pitt Street for comparison with the photos and plaster casts taken at both loci. Any questions?"

"No? Then good luck and those of you going with DS Chalmers to the pub, be careful," she warned.

****

Free of tending Rosie Donovan, who had been returned to St Albert's by the early shift Inspector in his supervisory panda, Smiler found himself neighboured with Barbara McMillan as members of the search team selected to attend *The Restful Soldier*.

DS Lucy Chalmers, the designated search commander, led her six-man team to the old Divisional Transit van in the rear yard, all discreetly armed with their issue wooden batons and handcuffs and were to rendeavous at the pub with four uniformed police officers, who were there to assist if the usual rowdy clientele should object and attempt to intervene during the search.

Conveyed to the pub in the van driven by Smiler, Lucy Chalmers occupied the front passenger seat.

Aware of his knowledge of the area and its residents and in particular, his somewhat fractious relationship with Cathy McHugh, the pub's landlady and owner, she told him, "Leave the search to us, Smiler, while you try to keep her and her punters calm. I'm not wanting us wrestling with some of them bampots instead of being able to conduct the search."

"And knowing her as you do, Lucy, how do you propose I do that?"

"Oh, that's easy," she grinned, "Just charm her like us women know you can."

Blushing, Smiler could only nod, yet a little anxious that this was not going to go well.

Arriving at *The Restful Soldier*, the detectives disembarked to discover that the duty shift's sergeant and three of his larger constables were there outside and waiting for them and without any preamble, all eleven pushed into the noisy pub.

Pre-briefed, one burly uniformed constable stood with his back to the closed entrance door, his eyes surprised at the large number of customers while his right hand casually stroked the hidden pocket of his uniform trousers where therein rested his baton.

A sudden silence settled on the busy pub as the officers entered, broken when from behind the bar, Cathy McHugh's shrill voice called out, "What the hell is going on? Why are you here?"

Her question was answered by Smiler, who not only taller than most of those around him but readily identifiable to most of the customers and who loudly replied, "We've a search warrant for the pub, Cathy, so if everyone remains calm, we'll get done what we're here for and then be on our way."

Almost immediately realising that failing to comply would cause problems for her pub licence, McHugh called for calm from her customers, then added, "Let them get done what they've come for and everyone just settle down, okay?"

Seconds of silence was broken when from the other side of the pub, a youthful male voice shouted, "Fuck that!" and a pint glass, still containing beer, sailed across the heads of the customers to strike one of the detectives on his head and who stunned, crumpled to the floor.

Drawing their batons, the officers as one turned to the crowd, some of whom backed off with their hands raised while a younger element squared up to the police and more glass tumblers came sailing through the air.

Climbing onto a stool behind the bar, McHugh, her hands raised, screamed, "Stop! Everyone just stop!" but to no avail as the officers began battoning anyone who offered or suggested violent behaviour towards them.

As Barbara McMillan was to later relate, "It was a right ongoing rammy."

Hardly a minute had passed when many of the mostly older customers made a determined effort to flee the violence, but were prevented from doing so by the large, burly uniformed cop at the door, who realising the instigator that threw the first glass might be among them, almost cheerfully beat them back with his baton.

"Right, stop!" Smiler bawled at the top of his voice.

Seconds passed before a nerve-wracking silence fell in the pub as Smiler continued, "Either the guy that threw the first glass gives himself up or everyone and I mean *everyone* in here," he bawled, "will be arrested for mobbing and rioting!"

Several of the predominately middle-aged customers gasped, recalling during their lifetimes in a sometimes-troubled Glasgow, a charge of mobbing and rioting carried an indeterminate sentence that could be anything from a heavy fine to life imprisonment, but that if convicted of such a sentence, there was an almost a certainty of the culprits going to prison.

What none of the customers guessed was that Smiler was bluffing, that at best a charge of breach of the peace and assault would be libelled against those arrested.

However, his verbal threat succeeded because an uneasy peace settled in the pub as many customers, their heads down, tried to slide tumblers back onto tables without the officers seeing them do so.

As for detective's assailant who threw the first glass, there was no need for anyone to identify him, for he was soon spotted trying to back into the crowd, his head hung low, then turned to scramble at a high window in a vain attempt to escape the pub.

The crowd of customers parted as unopposed, Smiler quickly strode through them, then grabbed the wrongdoer by the scruff of the neck and snarled, "Come here, you!"

Dragging him back through the now silent crowd, he handed the shaking and compliant prisoner over to Lucy Chalmers, then very loudly suggested, "With this one in custody, Sergeant, should we call it quits?"

Realising the room was still a tinder-box, tight-lipped she nodded as Smiler called out, "Right! We'll get on with our business now and the rest of you," he glanced menacingly around the room, "finish your drinks, if you still have them."

"Mrs McHugh," he called out to her. "The bar's closed till we're away. Agreed?"

Her face pale and her thoughts on how this might affect her future licence applications, it was all she could do to nod.

While Barbara McMillan tended to the dazed, but otherwise uninjured fallen detective and with the uniformed sergeant and his officers maintaining a presence in the now subdued bar area, her colleagues followed McHugh though to the rear room where Lucy Chalmers explained to her that her employee, Patrick Cochrane, was in custody for an assault and robbery, but gave no further details.

"That's nothing to do with me," her arms folded, she huffily protested, then snarled, "So why are you here? He only works for me, nothing else. Why are you here to search my pub?"

"Cathy," Smiler softly addressed her as she turned towards him, "it's a wee bit more complicated than that. There's a suggestion he might have killed Jeannie Mason."

Chalmers was about to rebuke him for disclosing that information, but stopped when she saw McHugh's face pale, then heard her stutter, "What! Wee Jeannie? Oh my God, no!"

Clearly shocked by Smiler's news, she covered her mouth with both hands, then he continued, "We think he might have used one of your knives from the kitchen," he added, while conveniently not disclosing that a knife had *not* been used in the unfortunate woman's murder.

Her head dipping, McHugh staggered back to sit on a tool, then repeated, "Wee Jeannie. Oh no. My God," she rubbed disbelievingly at her forehead, then stuttered, "Pat? Pat Cochrane?"

Smiler solemnly nodded, then seeing her take a breath, she exhaled before she stared him in the eye, then said, "What do you need from me?"

CHAPTER THIRTY-ONE.

Lying on his bed and feeling sorry for himself, Keith Telford heard the phone ringing downstairs, then his mother answering the call. Though he couldn't make out what was being said, he clearly heard her rushing upstairs, then his door opening before she gasped, "That's the phone for you, son. A Chief Inspector, he says he is, from Pitt Street."

"Pitt Street?" he sprung up from the bed, surprising his mother with his agility, particularly as he had previously been hobbling and suggesting maybe a walking stick might be useful.

Rushing past her so quickly, he almost collided with the slightly built woman who stared down the stairs after him.

Lifting the telephone, he cleared his throat then with a feeble sounding voice, said, "Constable Telford, sir."

"Ah, the very man. Chief Inspector McKenna's my name, Constable, and I'm making inquiry into a complaint against you, but I understand you're currently off duty on the sick?"

He could feel his body tense and his knees weaken.

Who the hell would complain against me? What do they think I've done, he inwardly panicked.

"Ah, yes, sir, I've not yet had the opportunity to make appointment with my GP, but I'll do that directly this call has ended."

"Indeed," McKenna's voice did not betray any sympathy. "Well, the fact is I'm contacting you to apprise you of the complaint and naturally, I'd like to have your side of the story, Constable, before I make any decision as to whether or not to proceed with the complaint."

"Sir?" his voice was now even weaker sounding.

"So, are you too unfit to attend here and be interviewed at Pitt Street or would you rather wait till you have returned to duty?"

What Telford couldn't know was that without actually disclosing what the complaint was about or by who, he was relying on Telford's curiosity to want to know as soon as possible.

"We can't do this over the phone, please sir?" he whined.

"Oh, no," McKenna brusquely replied, "Forms to fill, details to note. You understand, of course."

Telford didn't, but took the bait, then suggested, "I could get my father to take me to Pitt Street, I suppose. I'm not really fit to travel by public transport."

"Right, good man," McKenna cheerily replied, then said, "I'll see you here about two o'clock this afternoon."

McKenna ended the call before Telford could protest at the short notice, then angry at his perceived treatment, was about to slam the phone down.

However, he sensed his mother would be listening upstairs and so loudly said, "Yes, sir, well I'll want the three robbers who assaulted me dealt with in the harshest of terms and I will *not* accept anything less. Goodbye."

With a theatrical flourish, he then slammed the phone down into its cradle.

Passing his mother on the stairs, he snapped, "Can you phone dad and ask him to be here at two o'clock this afternoon. I'm wanted at Pitt Street. Something about those robbers I arrested. And I'll need dad to drive me."

She turned to see him heading into the bathroom, then wondered. She had indeed been listening to his side of the call and if memory served her correctly, didn't he previously say that there were *two* robbers, not three?

****

Two papers finished, Crime and General Police Duties and the last, the Traffic paper to sit, then he'd be done.

Sitting on the bench in Kelvin Way, a bottle of water in his hand and a half-eaten sandwich on the bench beside him, Constable Willie Strathmore took advantage of the mid-exam break to get some fresh air.

As they passed, he stared forlornly at what were clearly police officers, all fellow candidates in plain clothes and either chirpy because they believed they had done well in the first two papers or depressed because they instinctively knew they'd failed.

He'd recognised a few faces from F Division, other cops with high hopes, but other than a wave or a smile, did not engage any of them in conversation, preferring instead to suffer in misery alone.
Had he done well with Crime and General Police Duties? He just didn't know, though he had managed to answer all the questions and remained till the final second, checking and re-checking his answers. As for the upcoming Traffic paper; well, that's what he presumed would be the hardest paper of the three because quite frankly, Strathmore accepted he was shite when it came to Traffic Law. That said though, he'd poured heart and soul into studying past papers and in the months preceding the exam, spent much of his beat time looking for Traffic offences to gain some knowledge of the law concerning them.
He had promised his wife, Julie, he'd give her a phone at the lunch break, but the nearby telephone kiosk was smelling like it had been and was being used as a urinal, so would explain when he arrived home. That and there was a queue of fellow cops hanging around to use it.
Glancing at his watch, he finished the last of his sandwich, drunk his water then rose from the bench to return to the Sir Charles Wilson building to resume his seat in the hall.
****
Their warrant cards got them through the Pitt Street entrance to police headquarters, then Roz and Drew Taylor made their way up the stairs to the Scenes of Crime Department on the first floor.
Pushing open the entrance door, they stepped down into the corridor and made their way to the large open, general office where a young, female SOCO officer greeted them.
Explaining they were there for Roz's arm to be photographed, the SOCO officer, who introduced herself as Gayle, first told Taylor, "If you want to take a seat, we won't be too long. I'll be taking the photos, Roz, so if you follow me?"
Led into a photographic studio, the process took no more than ten or eleven minutes, then returning to the general office, Roz was surprised to find Taylor standing with the DI, Sammy Pollock, who greeted her with, "Thanks for getting those photos done, Roz. You'll be aware I'm the reporting officer in the case against McDonald?"
"That's what I heard, sir, yes," she nodded, "but are you here today to collect the photos?"

"Ah, no. You'll be aware of the other murder investigation, Jeannie Mason and the man, Albert Moston. Well, we've searched a suspect's house this morning and I've brought up a number of items, a coat and some footwear actually, that is possibly connected to the murder. I'm just waiting on the SOCO checking them against photos they took of injuries on Mrs Mason body and," he grimaced, "fingers crossed I'm pretty confident that there's bloodstaining on the footwear too, so then I'll be off to the Forensic laboratory on the top floor."

"If the photos and the blood match, sir," Taylor stared at him, "will that be enough to convict your suspect?"

"Again, fingers crossed it'll be the best evidence we have against him."

They all turned when a young SOCO woman, her blonde hair tied back into a ponytail and wearing a white dustcoat with her hands in the pockets, approached, then calmly addressing Pollock, said, "I'll need my supervisor to sign off on it for corroboration purposes, Inspector, but I've examined the footwear you brought in against the photos taken at the mortuary and I'm satisfied that the soles of one pair of brown coloured brogues is a match."

Pollock exhaled through pursed lips, then punched the air when he replied, "You have a phone I can use?"

****

As it happened, just as Begley and Taylor arrived at police headquarters, Constable Keith Telford, had been dropped off at the Pitt Street entrance just twenty minutes earlier.

When he exited the front passenger seat of his father's work's van, it didn't escape his father's notice that the painful limp Telford had exhibited since arriving home on the Monday evening seemed to have healed remarkably well, for his son literally skipped to the front entrance doors of the building.

Now seated at a table in an interview room opposite Chief Inspector Marty McKenna and a sullen faced, female sergeant whose name he didn't catch and who stared with beady eyes at him, he felt not just anxious, but afraid.

His face chalk-white, his legs trembling underneath the table, his hands clasped together so tightly the knuckles were white and inwardly chastising himself for failing to pee before he hurried to the Complaints and Discipline Department, Telford listened as

McKenna related the complaint against him; that while in the rear of a police vehicle, he slapped a handcuffed prisoner to the face.
"But…I…" he stuttered, his throat so dry he could hardly breathe. Then his eyes misted over and the tears began as he hissed, "You don't understand what it's like out there, the thugs we have to deal with. You have no idea," his teeth gritted, "sitting here in your fancy office, picking fault with us out there. Yes," he almost rose from is chair, but when the sergeant did too, he sat heavily back down.
"I defended myself when that bastard had a go at me!"
"When you say the complainer had a go at you, Constable," McKenna calmly repeated, "do you mean the prisoner who was handcuffed to the rear? So, explain to me how he had a go at you?"
"He…" Telford's voice choked and his eyes danced in his head as he fought to formulate some excuse. "He lashed out at me with his feet."
"And this was in the rear of a Transit van with bench seats on both sides, a van that in the rear sitting area can accommodate what," McKenna's eyes narrowed in thought, "maybe eight or at a crush, ten individuals in the rear? Yet you're telling us you chose to sit opposite the prisoner?"
It was McKenna's neighbour, Shona Mulvey, who asked, "And your response to this alleged assault was to slap him on the face?"
"Yes," he quickly replied, then eyes widening, added, "What I mean is, I only slapped him to calm him down."
"Yet according to the witness statements in the case reported by the CID," Mulvey slowly began, "a DC Morris Kerr, your statement indicates that you were assaulted by both the prisoners who I might remind you, were both handcuffed to the rear and makes no mention of you defending yourself, as you now allege."
His body froze and his mind juggled with how to respond to this, then his voice faltering, he muttered, "I must have forgotten to mention that."
"So it would seem," Mulvey turned to glance at McKenna.
Biting at his lower lip as the tears rolled down his cheeks, he sniffed when he asked, "What's going to happen to me? Why am I being picked on like this?"
McKenna sighed before he said, "You are *not* being picked on, Constable, but if you assault a prisoner, particularly one who is handcuffed to the rear and that assault is witnessed by another

individual, whether or not that individual is of good character or another prisoner, you lay yourself open to a charge of assault. Do you understand that?"

Now distraught, his head bowed, it was all that Telford could do to nod.

Glancing at Mulvey, McKenna continued, "While this investigation of the complaint against you is continuing, Constable Telford, consider yourself suspended from duty, so please hand over your warrant card. Now," he sighed again, "I suggest before you leave the building you find a gents and wash your face."

Rising to his feet as did Mulvey, he added, "The sergeant will show you out to the front door and you will hear from us when a decision has been made whether or not to report this complaint to the Procurator Fiscal."

Pushing back his chair, Telford wiped his streaming nose on the sleeve of his jacket, then fumbling in his inner pocket, his hand trembled when he laid his warrant card down onto the table before following Mulvey from the room.

****

Making their way back down the stairs towards the Pitt Street entrance, Roz and Taylor arrived in the foyer as the elevator doors behind them opened and to their mutual surprise, they saw Keith Telford, his face pale, step out.

Both unconsciously greeted him with a smile and it was Taylor who said, "Hello, Keith, what you doing here?"

Telford stopped, his eyes narrowing as he fought back tears when he vehemently screamed back, "It's your fault! Both of you! So…so, just fuck *off*!"

With that, he dashed through the doors and turned right, out of their sight.

Staring at each other, it was a stunned Taylor again who asked, "What the hell was that all about?"

****

DCI Laura Gemmill gently lowered the phone into its cradle, then took a slow breath.

It was suddenly all coming together.

Sammy Pollock's confirmation about Cochrane's footwear being the shoes that stamped down onto Jeannie Mason and now the Forensic laboratory confirming that the blood in the seam of the right brogue shoe is confirmed as that of the victim.

But more so, they had also discovered several, though minute bloodstained splatters on a wax coat taken from Cochrane's wardrobe and were at that time, examining it against both Mason and Albert Moston's blood samples obtained from the victims at the mortuary.

No matter, the evidence of the footwear was, in her mind, sufficient to charge him with at least one murder.

Gotcha, he smiled to herself, but then her eyes narrowed when she inwardly admitted that while one investigation might be resolved, there was still the question of the possible corruption and perverting the course of justice regarding the assaults and robberies.

Lifting her desk phone, she called for DS Danny Sullivan to come to her room to inform him of the news from Pitt Street, just as her door was pushed open by a smiling Lucy Chalmers, who was followed into the room by DC Morris Kerr.

"Good news, boss," Chalmers greeted her, then indicated to Kerr, who she saw was holding a brown coloured paper production bag. Kerr laid the bag onto her desk, then opening it to permit her to glance inside, she saw a large, wide bladed kitchen knife.

"Is this…?" she glanced up at the acting DS.

"It is," Chalmers interrupted with a grin. "Morris here discovered it among the rest of the kitchen knives, boss, and as you can see, the tip is broken off."

The door behind Chalmers opened to admit Danny Sullivan, who stood quietly, listening.

"Any problems at the pub?" Gemmill asked.

She didn't miss the awkward glance between them, before Chalmers replied, "When we got there, the place erupted and we had a right good going barney going on with a tumbler hitting one of my team on the head," but quickly raising a hand, added, "He's okay, though, Just a bit dazed and no skin broken. The culprit responsible is now downstairs being charged. However, it could have been a lot worse, but for our Smiler," she shook her head.

"He threatened them all with a charge of mobbing and rioting and that quickly calmed them down. Anyway," she nodded down at the paper bag, "it was definitely worth it."

"And the knife? Anybody at the pub speaking to Cochrane using it?"

"Curiously, though she's definitely not pro-polis, the landlady, Cathy McHugh, she's given us a statement that Cochrane always insisted nobody use the pub knives but him. Fancies himself as a bit of a chef, apparently, and she paid him extra for cooking the pub grub."

It was Kerr who interjected when he said, "Again, boss, that was down to the big man. He had a quiet word with McHugh and believe me," he shook his head, "I've previously been in that pub trying to speak with her and she wouldn't normally give us the time of day, let alone a statement."

Smiler again, thought Gemmill, then unconsciously shook her head. "Well," she smiled, "as you're here, here's some other good news." However, before she could begin, her desk phone rung and raising her forefinger that they remain, she answered the call.

They watched her expression change, her face light up then she widely smiled before ending the call.

"On top of what I'm about to tell you, that was the Forensic laboratory. It seems that small splatters of blood on a coat taken from Cochrane's wardrobe in his flat is now identified as Albert Moston's blood."

****

Sally Rodgers, working behind the counter at the City Bakeries, was growing a little weary of the mickey-taking by her staff now that word was out about her relationship with the local polis, Smiler McGarry.

Handing change to a regular, her attention was taken when the door to the shop was pushed open and she saw a smiling Elizabeth Cowan enter.

Instructing her deputy to take over, she beckoned Elizabeth to come behind the counter, then led her to the rear shop where to her surprise and delight, Elizabeth hugged her.

"What you doing here?" Sally asked.

"I was at the opticians over in Albert Drive and as I was so close to the shop, I thought I'd pop in to ask you something."

"Yes? Ask me what?" Sally's brow furrowed.

"It's a bit last minute," Elizabeth grimaced, "but are you and Stuart available to come over for dinner this evening? Maybe about seven?"

"Eh, yes, I think so. I mean," she flustered, "I'm sure we are, but depending on when he's finished at work."

"Well, if seven works for you it doesn't matter if you're a little late. Nothing formal, just come as you are. Now, if Stuart *is* held on, that doesn't mean you can't come alone," she bowed her head to rummage in her handbag, then pulling out a piece of paper, added, "Here's our address. He can join us when he's finished work."

She wasn't prepared for the tears in Sally's eyes when the younger woman hugged her tightly, then her voice almost a whisper, said, "Thank you."

"No," Elizabeth drew slightly back and stared into Sally's eyes, "thank *you*. Stuart means a lot to Iain and I, and seeing how happy he is with you in his life, that means more to us both than you can imagine."

Continuing to smile, she added, "Right, I'll away now, but I'm hearing you're a great cook, so don't be expecting anything too fancy, okay?"

Her lips trembling, Sally managed to respond with, "I'm sure no matter what it is, it'll be delicious."

****

Roz Begley and Drew Taylor decided to return to Byres Road for their food, rather than eat in the city centre.

Exiting the Hillhead Underground station, he hesitantly said, "You've never seen inside my flat, have you?"

"No," she peered suspiciously at him when she asked "What you thinking?"

He shrugged, then replied, "I was wondering if maybe we could get a takeaway from that new Thai place in Ruthven Lane off Byres Road. I've heard good things about it. Eh, that's if you like spicy food?"

She stared at him, but couldn't sense any ulterior motive, so smiled when she replied, "Sounds like a plan."

****

Slamming the door to his father's works van, Keith Telford, now more angry than composed, snapped, "Drive!"

Naturally concerned, his father turned to ask, "You okay, son?"

He turned to snarl, "I told you! Just fucking *drive!*"

His father sighed deeply, then took a decision that he knew he should have made many years before when he calmly replied, "Keith, you have no right whatsoever to speak to me in that manner.

Now, please get out of the van."

"Eh, what?"

His father's voice changed when with a low growl, he said, "Either you get out of the van or by *God*, I'll come round to your door and drag you out. Now," his father's voice angrily rose as he turned his head to stare through the windscreen, "get *out!*"

His eyes widening in shock, once more tears rolled down Telford's cheeks as opening the door, he stumbled onto the pavement, then watched in dismay as his father started the engine, then drove off.

CHAPTER THIRTY-TWO.

Seated in Chief Superintendent Jimmy Thompson's office, Chief Inspector Lizzie Whitmore and DCI Laura Gemmill waited for his reaction.

Taking a slow draw of his cigarette, he at last said, "You might not know this, but Mikey Crawford is known to me from way back and to be frank," he shook his head, "what you've disclosed, Laura, doesn't surprise me. Crawford was always a man looking to gain advantage over anyone he saw as a threat to his next promotion. Not a team player, he was shrewd enough to always have a fall guy to take the blame when any of his shenanigans went wrong and many a good officer fell by the wayside after nailing their coat to Crawford's mast."

He slowly shook his head, remembering things long forgotten when he softly muttered, "John Crawford."

Then taking a deep breath, he said, "He was a man who promised much, but delivered very little. What we might call, the consummate politician."

He paused to grind the butt into the ashtray, then withdrawing a new fag from the pack, stopped as though changing his mind and instead, took a sip of his coffee.

Licking at his lips, he laid the mug down, then continued, "As you rightly suggested, Laura, you're about to open a can of worms, particularly as Crawford is till serving, albeit over in Lothian & Borders Police, but the very fact he's now an Assistant Chief Constable? My God, I doubt that this investigation will stay under wraps. We three know there's always someone, somewhere, who no matter the issue, believes either for a backhander or simply for public interest, that this sort of investigation should be leaked to the media."

He paused again and stared at them in turn.

"You say that your team have discovered what, eight or nine assault and robberies that Crawford signed off in the full knowledge that the culprits could be identified?"

"Yes, sir," Gemmill nodded, then added, "but there could be more. What I've done is take the decision to halt the search at those numbers, believing that any more could, well," she frowned, "prove to be even more disastrous to the reputation of the police. Though these crimes were committed during the time of the City of Glasgow Police's watch, we as Strathclyde Police have inherited the inquiries, so it would be us as a Force who suffer the consequences if it all gets out to the media."

Thompson's eyes narrowed when he bent his head and muttered, "Oh, bugger it," then fetched another fag from the packet.

"You know those things are killing you," Whitmore drily reminded him.

Lighting it, he replied with a shrug, "I think I'm past worrying about it now, Lizzie. So," he straightened in his chair and turned towards Gemmill, "Regardless of my thoughts on the matter, Laura, what is *your* intention?"

Her brow knitted thoughtfully before she replied, "Sammy Pollock and I are about to interview Patrick Cochrane, our murder suspect and he is also the man identified for one assault and robbery, sir, though he was obviously working with our murder victim, Albert Moston, so we're satisfied he *is* responsible for the others, too."

"And?"

She drew a short breath, then continued, "If Cochrane should burst and admit that he was Crawford's informant about crime in the F Divisional area and in turn, was protected from being charged for the crimes, then with the signed crime reports writing off the crimes and the witness statements from the former investigating detectives, I will seriously consider making a case against Crawford. However, being in the position he now holds at the L&B Force, I'm almost certain a lot will depend on whether or not the Procurator Fiscal here in Glasgow will support charges of perverting the course of justice and corruption under the Police (Scotland) Act."

"Laura," he stared at her, "let's be frank. I've months to do before I'm gone so I have no qualms about telling you this. I hope you realise that if you do decide to pursue such an action against him, you will piss off a number of high-ranking officers who will no doubt adopt the attitude that as time has passed, the issue should best be left alone. Pursuing Crawford after this length of time?" he shrugged when he shook his head. "It could seriously damage your own career, maybe even finding yourself being moved sideways and certainly killing any hope of a future promotion."

"That has been pointed out to me, sir," she wryly smiled, then added, "even by one of my own DS's, my DI and of course, Lizzie here."

"So, in short, after you've spoken with your suspect, you'll make your decision?" he stared at Gemmill.

"Yes, sir, as I say, that's the plan."

"Well, when you have come to a decision, come and see me. I might have an idea how to resolve your problem."

****

The CID clerk, Bobby Davies, called out to Smiler, "Phone call, big man."

Taking the call, he was surprised to hear it was Sally, who immediately apologised for calling him at work, then related the visit and invite that night to attend at the Cowan's for dinner.

"Do you think you'll be of on time?"

Guessing she was not keen on arriving alone, he truthfully replied, "I'll not be able to promise finishing on time, sweetheart, but honestly, Iain and Elizabeth will be delighted to see you, with or without me. You've no worries there."

"Hmm, okay," she replied with some hesitation, then finished the call.

Placing the phone back down, he turned when Davies grinned, "Sweetheart?"

"Aye very good," he pretended to growl at his old pal.

They both turned when the DCI entered the room and called out, "Anybody seen the DI?"

"I think he's setting up the interview room, boss," replied Lucy Chalmers.

"Right," Gemmill nodded. "You'll know where to find us if anything occurs, then left the room.

****

While Gemmill settled herself into one of the four chairs in the small, windowless and compact interview room, Sammy Pollock left to fetch Patrick Cochrane and his lawyer, Freddie Kirkland, who was also known to Pollock and generally mistrusted by the city CID for his uncooperative attitude towards the police.

Waiting patiently, Gemmill busied herself with her notes that included questions she would put to Cochrane, for many years previously when a rookie DC, her then DS mentor had taught her, "Don't rely on trying to remember what you want to ask, for there's no such thing as an elephant memory, Laura. Always take notes that you can refer to."

She glanced up when Pollock returned with Cochrane and his lawyer, Kirkland, and a uniformed constable, who would remain as security outside the room during the interview.

When the three men were all seated, it was then that Gemmill disclosed the bad news to the prisoner.

"Mr Cochrane," she began, "you have been arrested and charged for an assault and robbery perpetrated on the eighteenth of October, nineteen-sixty-five within the common close in Ascog Street where you seriously assaulted and robbed seventy-two-years-old Patrick Reagan."

"I know that," he sighed with a bored glance at his lawyer.

"As you might also know," she ignored his sarcasm, "having been charged with that crime I will not ask you questions relative to *that* crime."

"Then why are we here, DC Gemmill?" asked Kirkland.

She paused for several seconds to permit them to wonder, then directing her question towards Cochrane, replied, "My information is that you are a former friend of Albert Moston, Mr Cochrane. Moston is known to most people in this area as Moxy."

Though he shook his head and denied knowing Moston well, other than as one of the customers of the pub, but he could not disguise his pale face and sudden intake of breath.

"Yet, not knowing Moston, you provided his mother's details as your next of kin when you joined the army, Mr Cochrane."

His sudden intake of breath escaped no one, least of all his lawyer.

"No comment," his throat visibly tightened and his eyes widened.
She glanced down at the sheet of paper in front of her to give him a few seconds to sweat, then said, "While you were detained here at Craigie Street, my officers conducted a search of both your flat and your place of work, *The Restful Soldier*."
She watched as his eyes tightly closed, then opening them, he repeated, "No comment."
"Might I inquire as to where this line of questioning is heading, DCI Gemmill?" Kirkland quickly asked.
"During the search of your client's flat, sir, my officers discovered footwear that according to our Forensic laboratory and our Scene of Crime Department, were worn by the individual who on Thursday, the eighth of March within the Govanhill Park, murdered Mrs Jeannie Mason. Within the flat they also discovered a coat belonging to your client that had minute blood spattering that matched the blood sample taken from the now deceased, Albert Moston, who was murdered on Saturday, the tenth of March in a close in Annette Street."
She paused for several seconds to let this information sink in in, then continued, "Albert Moston, who your client denied knowing and who was the son of Irene Moston, the woman he provided to the army recruiting office as his next of kin."
"Oh, dear," Kirkland softly sighed, then turned to first frown at his client, then opened his mouth to speak, but Gemmill wasn't finished.
"Earlier today, Mr Cochrane, my officers also searched your place of work where you are employed as a barman and chef and there discovered a knife with a broken tip that the landlady, Mrs McHugh, states is used by you and you alone, to prepare food. This knife has since been examined by the Scene of Crime officers who categorically state it is the knife used to murder Albert Moston."
"At this juncture, DCI Gemmill, and in light of these new accusations," Kirkland wearily interrupted, "I would be most grateful for a private word with my client."
Glancing at Pollock, Gemmill nodded then said, "Five minutes, Mr Kirkland, then might I suggest you and I have a private word before we continue."
****

Barbara McMillan fetched Smiler, her neighbour, Morris Kerr, and herself a coffee, then when all three were seated around Kerr's desk,

she asked, "How do you think it's going at the interview?"
"Anybody's guess," Kerr sighed, "but the boss isn't daft. She'll have her questions prepared and once he's backed into a corner, then bam! He's charged," Kerr confidently nodded.
Kerr stared at Smiler's frown, then asked, "What?"
"I don't know," Smiler exhaled, "I've a feeling there's more going on than we're being told."
"How do you mean?"
"These historical crime reports that the team have been researching, there's more to them than tracing Cochrane, I'm thinking."
"Like what?" McMillan asked.
"That, young Barbara, is what concerns me."
****
Mattie Devlin was catching up with some laundry and ironing when the phone rang.
"Mattie? It's Chief Inspector McLean at Pitt Street. Sorry to call you at home, but I'm informed you've just finished your late shift and on your days off. Is it okay to have a word?"
"Eh, yes sir, of course," he took a breath, expecting bad news.
Guessing Devlin would be worried, McLean cheerily asked, "Firstly, how's the acting rank working out?"
"Oh, ah, same old, same old. To be honest I fell on my feet with the shift Inspector and the cops. Good guys and no issues with me arriving there as a constable, then almost immediately becoming their sergeant."
He licked nervously at his lips when he continued, "So, you're calling me, sir. You have some news about Janice?"
"Yes and no," McLean slowly drawled. "For a start, there's no trace of her at the minute under the name Janice Goodwin; however, I have to inform you that I have been unable to trace a woman born Janice Goodwin with the date of birth you provided. It took a few days, but I made some inquiry at a place down in London called St Catherine's House where all the births, deaths and marriages in England are currently recorded and there's no record of Goodwin there under those details."
"Oh, so you're saying…"
"I'm saying, I don't believe that is her true name."
Devlin heard him sigh when he added, "I'm of the opinion that the woman who purported to be Janice Goodwin was in fact using a

pseudonym. Using the name Goodwin, she seems to have re-invented herself, obtaining not just a driving licence in that name, but a passport too. In short, Mattie, where ever she is, it's likely she's no longer Janice Goodwin, but probably again using another name."

Stunned, his legs feeling weak, Devlin placed his free hand on the hallway wall to support himself when he replied, "But why me? Whatever could someone like me, a sergeant in the police, offer her? I mean, I'm not rich or anything."

"God alone knows what goes through someone's head, Mattie. I mean, she might be a female Walter Mitty or maybe she was hiding out up here for some reason, who knows. Anyway," he took a breath, "the long and sort of it is I've been in touch with the PF and updated my investigation and I regret that without properly identifying her, the PF is reluctant to issue a warrant under the details I provided."

"So, that's it, then?" an angry Devlin asked.

"Regretfully, yes. That's it. However," McLean audibly sighed.

"Sir?"

"Do you still happen to have any of her things, say a hairbrush, maybe?"

"Eh, yes, I haven't cleared everything out yet," Devlin found himself nodding. "Why?"

"I'm thinking, Mattie, if you can stick it into a paper bag and send it to me here at Pitt Street through the dispatches, if there are any hair follicles on the brush, I'm going to have the SOCO retain them in their database under the name Janice Goodwin so that if by any chance, anyone using that name should turn up here in Scotland having committed a crime or offence?"

"Devlin found himself smiling when he replied, "Then we might have her identified. Yes sir, I'll get that done."

Exhaling, Devlin used the heel of his hand to rub at his forehead when he asked, "What now, then sir?"

"Now, Mattie?"

Devlin could not know that the Chief Inspector was smiling.

"Now, you get on with your life. You're officially a single man and albeit there was a hiccup in your career, you seem to have bounced back. From what I'm told by your Chief Inspector, she's expecting good things of you, so good luck and needless to say, if anything *should* turn up regarding the woman calling herself Janice Goodwin,

I'll be in touch."

The call ended, a deflated Devlin staggered through to the kitchen where after setting the kettle to boil, he slumped down into a kitchen chair.

Just a short week ago, his life had seemed to be over, then thanks to a sympathetic boss, he now had another chance.

And this time, he inwardly determined, he'd be a whole lot more circumspect about any women that he'd meet.

****

Standing in the corridor with Sammy Pollock and the uniformed constable, Laura Gemmill turned when the interview door was opened by Cochrane's lawyer, Freddie Kirkland, who closing the door behind him, quietly said, "My client is willing to cooperate, DCI Gemmill, if certain conditions are met."

"And those conditions are?"

"He is aware that there is overwhelming evidence against him for the murders of your two victims and prior to being charged with those murders, will answer any questions you might have."

"Yes, but what are the conditions?"

Kirkland took a breath when he continued, "While my client accepts he has been charged with one assault and robbery, he will also accept *responsibility* for the remaining assaults and robberies, but no charges to be libelled and no court case, for he is well aware that a jury of his peers will be more than sympathetic to a Crown case against him where the victims are members of the elderly community."

Knowing there was no likelihood of being able to prove such charges anyway, Gemmill slowly nodded.

"Further, my client agrees he will plead guilty to both murders and the single charge of assault and robbery, but requests that consideration be given to his full cooperation, that sentencing for the murders and the robbery charge run *concurrently*, rather than consecutively."

Both Gemmill, and Pollock knew, as did Kirkland, that it would suit Crown Office to accept a guilty plea and whether she agreed or not, it was likely Crown Office would accept such a deal, particularly as a guilty plea would also avoid the cost of a lengthy trial.

However, there was a process to follow and so she replied, "We both know, Mr Kirkland, I can't make that promise, but if you are

prepared to give me twenty minutes or so, I'll make a call."
"Then perhaps in the meantime," Kirkland glanced at Pollock, "we might have a coffee brought for my client and I while you attend to your call."
****

Returned home, a dejected Willie Strathmore was surprised to find that his twin daughters were not in the house and that his wife, Julie, was wearing her overcoat. He was even more surprised to see a suitcase sitting in the hallway by the front door.
"What, you leaving me?" he smiled cautiously at her.
She stared at him then shaking her head, replied, "The girls are with my parents for the night and we're off on the train to Ayr, where I've booked us into a B and B."
"Oh," was all he could say.
Julie gently placed a hand on his cheek and continued, "I know how hard you've worked to get this exam, Willie, so I thought you deserved a night away, just me and you. Are you okay with that?"
He grinned when hugging her to him, he said, "More than you can imagine."
****

"Honestly, Drew," Roz Begley told him "I'll enjoy the walk. There's no need to run me home. I'll be fine."
"I'm sure you would be, but if you want to walk, fine by me. We can chat while we're walking."
Helping her on with her jacket, she said once more, "You do have a lovely home, even better than I imagined it to be."
Exiting his close into Chancellor Street and walking together with a discreet distance between them, it occurred to him that Roz had not once mentioned his foolish outburst in the café and it intrigued him, wondering how she felt about his admission of his feelings.
"So, you've been thinking about my flat, then," he lamely smiled at her.
"It's a female thing," she shrugged. "My granny used to tell me the only tidy men she'd ever met where those who were domesticated by their mothers and always advised her daughters and sons to try before they buy."
"What does that mean?" he was genuinely confused.
It was Roz's turn to blush when she replied, "Granny was way ahead of her time and it was her belief that her children live with their

boyfriend or girlfriend before contemplating marriage. That way they'd now what they were getting into before any contract was signed and it was a lot easier to end the relationship than getting stuck in a messy divorce."

"A wise woman," he pretended to agree with the sentiment.

"Aye, she was," Roz smiled at the memory of her progressively minded grandmother, then asked, "What you said in the café."

"What bit?" he felt his face redden.

"About your feelings for me. Are you really *that* certain?"

"Yes, I'm certain, but why do you ask?"

She stopped walking, then turning to him, solemnly replied, "Because I'm guessing you might have had the same feelings for Sharon, but look how that turned out."

He took a slow breath, then shrugged, "I can't explain what I felt for Sharon, but believe me, Roz, it definitely is *not* the same as I feel for you. You have no reason to trust me, so all I ask is the opportunity to show you how I feel, if you give me time."

Staring at him for what was seconds, yet to Taylor felt like forever, she finally nodded, then replied, "Okay. Here's how it is going to work."

****

In fact, it was almost thirty minutes before DCI Laura Gemmill returned during which time she had phoned both the Procurator Fiscal's Office in Glasgow, then been directed to Crown Office in Edinburgh before finally speaking directly with a Crown Advocate Depute.

The Depute, listening to her summarised proposal for a deal with the accused's lawyer, finally agreed that if it negated the cost and burden of a trial, but assured the guilty plea from the accused, she should agree the deal.

Armed with this information, she returned to inform Kirkwood that the deal was acceptable.

Now again with Pollock, Kirkwood and his client and seated within the interview room, she reminded Cochrane of the deal, then once more formally cautioning him at common law, asked, "Why did you murder Jeannie Mason?"

With a glance at Kirkwood, who subtly nodded, he replied, "I had it in my head her and Moxy were talking about me, that he was telling her about me and him when we were doing the muggings."

"You believed they were discussing you, even though those crimes occurred all those years ago."

To her surprise, he blushed and dipped his head when he grunted, "Aye, I thought if she knew about the muggings too, she might grass me in to you people for a half bottle. She just couldn't be trusted where drink was concerned."

"Tell me how you killed her?"

"What?" his expression was one of surprise.

"Talk me through it, please," she stared at him.

He shrugged when he quietly replied, "I told her that night, last week it was, a Thursday I think, that if she gave me a blowjob, I'd give her a bottle of electric soup. Wine, I mean," he corrected himself.

"I told her to wait for me finishing up and I'd agreed to meet her outside a close in Ardbeg Street, number seventeen. She told me it was where she sometimes dossed down," he explained.

He took a deep breath, reliving the moment in his mind, then continued, "I was going to do her there, in the close, but I could hear there was a party going on upstairs and I was worried somebody might come downstairs and find us, so we went from there to the Govanhill Park where she told me she took all her punters."

He stopped, then as if excusing himself, sneered, "You have to know I didn't want sex with her. She was a scabby wee cow, so she was and I wouldn't have touched her with a barge pole, let alone my dick."

Gemmill felt her body tense, her hands bunching beneath the table and an icy cold enveloping her when she experienced an unusual emotion; the urge to reach across the table and batter Cochrane's face with her fists while screaming that Jeannie Mason was once a professional nurse, a wife and a mother and how fucking *dare* he reduce her to some nonentity that did not matter.

However, she forced herself to remain calm, acutely aware that sitting beside her, Sammy Pollock had given her a sideways glance; almost a warning glance as though sensing her emotion.

"So, where in Govanhill Park did you go?"

"Into some bushes, like a wee hiding place she said was safe from anyone seeing us."

"And what happened there?"

"What, you stupid or something?" he snapped back. "I did her, so I did. I fucking killed her, okay? That's what you want to hear, isn't it?" he glanced at his lawyer who raised a calming hand.

Tight-lipped, Gemmill glanced down at her notes, a few precious seconds to compose herself, then in an even voice, she raised her head and staring at Cochrane, asked, "Why did you kill Albert Moston?"

He didn't even hesitate, simply replied in a jeering voice, "Well, for one I was doing the world a favour."

"And the real reason?"

He gave a long, drawn out sigh, then replied, "The night I took the wee harlot to the Park, he saw me with her going in the gate. Of course, he knew me from before and when I left the army, though I dizzied him every time he came into the pub; he was always trying to get my attention. Anyway, after I did Jeannie, he tried to screw money out of me to keep his mouth shut. You know he was a grass, don't you? That and he was always boasting about what he'd done, but when we're were hitting the auld yins for their pensions, it was me that had to do the battering. He was too feart."

Gemmill ignored the question, but then asked, "So, you killed him?"

"For my own protection, aye, I did him too. In a close in Annette Street. With a knife from the pub. Now, you've got it all, is that it," he leaned menacingly forward towards Gemmill, causing Pollock to prepare himself to physically intervene.

However, it was Cochrane's lawyer who quickly said, "But there's more, is there not, DCI Gemmill?"

She sat back in the uncomfortable, upright wooden chair, then pen and paper at the ready, she took a short breath when she stared at Cochrane, then calmly said, "If this deal we've made with you and Mr Kirkland is to work, Mr Cochrane, then tell me about the arrangement you had with Detective Chief Inspector Crawford, back in nineteen-sixty-five."

CHAPTER THIRTY-THREE: Thursday 09.10am 15 March 1979.

The meeting held on the fourth floor of the newly constructed extension to the rear of police headquarters building was chaired by the Deputy Chief Constable, Paula Clarke.

Sitting at the highly polished conference table on Clarke's left was Chief Superintendent Jimmy Thompson and his Divisional DCI, Laura Gemmill.

On Clarke's right, representing the Procurator Fiscal for Glasgow and Strathkelvin, sat an Assistant Procurator Fiscal, Tony Fellowes, who was accompanied by his trainee Depute, Martha Hayes.

"So," Clarke glanced around the table, "from the information and statements that DCI Gemmill has collected, are we agreed that Strathclyde Police will pursue this issue without fear or favour and with all due vigour?"

It was Barclay who responded with, "As far as the PF's office here in Glasgow is concerned, Deputy Chief Constable, and as you are aware, there is no time limitation on the common law crime of perverting the course of justice nor any time limitation on the Police (Scotland) Act, albeit it *is* a statute law. What I will request is that you agree I inform not just my own Procurator Fiscal of this matter, but also apprise the Procurator Fiscal of Edinburgh of your intention. Of course, I will request that he ensures the individual concerned is not alerted."

He paused for a few seconds, then continued, "I assume you will wish to submit an application for a warrant to cover the arrest?"

Clarke glanced at Gemmill, who nodded when she said, "Yes. Given the lengthy passage of time since the crimes were committed, Mr Fellowes, I'd rather that the matter be dealt with by warrant."

Turning to his Depute, Fellowes told her, "See that every courtesy is extended when DCI Gemmill has drawn up the application."

"Sir," she nodded.

"And now," said Clarke, rising to her feet to indicate the meeting was concluded, then turned with a warm smile to Fellowes and Hayes and said, "I'll let you get on."

When both had left the room, Clarke took a deep breath, then sighing, said to Gemmill, "God alone knows how the Chef Constable of L&B will react to this news, though I fear arresting one of his Assistant Chief's will undoubtedly cause ill-feeling between both Forces."

Her eyes narrowed when she asked, "However, that's not for you to concern yourself, DCI Gemmill."

She paused and her brow knitted when she asked, "You are *absolutely* certain of your facts?"

"Certain, yes, Ma'am," confirmed with a confident nod.

It was Thompson who added, "I've known John Crawford for a number of years, Ma'am, and let me assure you, the man is more than capable of what he is about to be charged with. In fact," his face creased, "I fear that this could be the tip of the iceberg, that more of his bullied staff might come forward with tales of his wrongdoing."

"God, I hope not," Clarke sighed with some feeling, then exhaling, smiled and was noticeably a little more relaxed when she said, "I read the Force twenty-four hour bulletin earlier this morning and I understand you had a result for your double murder, Laura."

"Yes, Ma'am. My DI is currently escorting the accused to his initial hearing as we speak."

"This man Cochrane, it's he who provided all the details about Crawford?"

"Yes, Ma'am, and did so in the presence of his lawyer."

"Even better. Well," Clarke shrugged, "I suppose I had better inform the Chief Constable of the shitstorm that is about to descend on our neighbours over in the Lothian area and I fear he will *not* take the news well."

With a forced smile, she was about to leave the room, but stopped, then turning, addressed Thompson when she said, "You will recall that matter we discussed a few days ago, Chief Superintendent."

"Yes, Ma'am, I do," he stared curiously at her.

"You may expect some news tomorrow."

"Ma'am," pokerfaced, he nodded.

Gemmill's curiosity was aroused, but decided it wasn't her place to ask.

****

Iain Cowan, sitting in his conservatory that faced the rear garden and relaxing with a coffee and the early edition of the 'Glasgow News,' lowered the newspaper to address his wife, Elizabeth, sitting in the opposite chair and said, "I thought last night went well."

"Yes," she smiled, "once Stuart, arrived Sally was a lot more at ease."

Seconds passed when he asked, "Are you comfortable with what I told you, Iain? About Sally having been in prison?"

His brow furrowed and he took a deep breath when he replied, "You know my view on men that assault women and from what she's shared with you, I'm in no doubt that the lassie has had a really unfortunate experience, that the judicial system has completely let her down. Ask yourself this, Elizabeth. If it were one of our daughters who had suffered what Sally's been through, would *you* think any less of her? Of course you wouldn't," he sighed, then added, "Besides, Stuart's no fool. He obviously not just believes her, but cares deeply for Sally and trusting him like we both do, that's as fine a benchmark as we'll ever have."

He stared at her with narrowed eyes when he asked, "You think they'll tie the knot?"

"Oh, yes, I do," she nodded. "There's no doubt he's the man for her and he's obviously smitten with her too."

"So," he grinned, "I'm thinking you'll be needing a new frock and I'll need to look out my best suit, eh?"

She smiled before she replied, "I'll never refuse the offer of a new dress, but I think, Iain Cowan, it's about time you threw that rag you call your *best suit* in the bin and we visit Slaters to get you a new three-piece suit, maybe one that fits this time?" she teased him.

****

In the cell area beneath Ingram Street Sheriff Court and after handing his prisoner over to the court staff, Sammy Pollock turned to find Freddie Kirkland striding towards him.

"Morning, DI Pollock," Kirkland greeted him.

Nodding in return, Pollock asked, "You here for Cochrane or are you representing someone else today, Mr Kirkland?"

"Oh, Cochrane is my first job," Kirkland smiled, then added, "after that I'll see who's needing my services."

With a glance around to ensure they were not overheard, he then asked in a low voice, "This statement Cochrane provided to you about the former DCI at Craigie Street. I've recently learned he's still serving as an ACC over in Lothian & Borders Police. Might I assume you guys intend going after him?"

"Depends on a meeting at Pitt Street that's currently going on *and* before you ask," he held up his hand, "I've no way of knowing how that will end. Why do you want to know?"

Kirkland smiled when he replied, "A big fish like an ACC being arrested? Now that would make the news and I'm assuming he would need legal counsel too, so I like to keep my options open." He stared meaningfully at Pollock when he added, "I sometimes hear things, DI Pollock, that as long as they don't interfere with my defence of a client, I might be happy to pass along."

Pollock understood right away and with a grim smile, he said, "You're looking for a heads-up because if Crawford is arrested and brought here to the court, you'd want to be on standby to offer your services as counsel, you mean?"

"A *quid quo pro*, yes," Kirkland stared him in the eye.

Seconds passed, then Pollock, his face twisting, replied, "Let me think about that," before turning and walking off.

****

Drew Taylor, the volume on his record player turned up, was singing along to Donna Summer's *'Hot Stuff'* hit song while ironing his shirt and reflecting on the previous days' time with Roz Begley.

Walking her home the previous evening, she had agreed to come with him on Thursday evening to see the new James Bond film, *'Moonraker,'* at the movies but only after she insisted and he'd agreed they go Dutch.

His attention was distracted by the ringing of the telephone in the hallway and rushing through, found it was his best pal and fellow cop, Ian Parker.

"How's it hanging and what you up to?" Parker greeted him.

"Catching up on some ironing. You?"

"Wondering if you're available for a couple of pints tonight, now that you don't have the lovely Sharon hanging off your arm and leading you where no man doth dare to go."

"Ah, no, sorry. I have plans."

A slight surprised pause ended with, "Anyone I know?"

Taylor smiled at the subtle hint before he probed, "What else you on for, you nosy bugger?"

"Hmm, did I ever mention that lovely wee polis woman I was at Tulliallan with, her that works over in Shettleston? The one I was in the polis cadets with that's got the hots for me?"

"Many, many times, though for some reason not known to me, you never introduced her that makes me think she's probably a five-foot dwarf with warts," Taylor tolerantly smiled. "Anyway, what about her?"

"She's just off the phone to me about Keith Telford."

"Telford," his eyes narrowed. "Does she know him, then? What about him?"

He listened as Parker took a deep breath, then said, "No, she doesn't know him, but last night she was on late shift and during her break, was in the control room talking to her friend when it seems Telford arrived at the public bar and after identifying himself as a cop to the bar officer, he asked for a resignation form."

"He what!"

"Yep!" Parker could not hide the delight in his voice at imparting what he believed to be good news and continued, "Then apparently he filled out the form there and then and left it with his baton and handcuffs on the counter along with two black bin bags full of his uniforms."

"You're at the madam!" a stunned Taylor replied.

"Nope," a gleeful sounding Parker responded. "That's what my wee pal told me and apparently it's all over Shettleston, so likely it'll filter down to Craigie Street too."

"Jesus," Taylor slowly drawled, then unconsciously muttered, "That explains it, then."

"Explains what?" Parker seized upon the comment.

"Ah," he knew he'd slipped up, but carried on anyway, "Roz was away to Pitt Street yesterday getting her injury photographed at the SOCO Department and I went with her. Just to keep her company, you know?"

He could not know that Parker was now grinning when he asked, "So, what happened?"

"We were coming down the stairs to the Pitt Street door when Telford stepped out of the lift. I said, 'hello' and he ranted at us, something about being our fault, then screamed that we were to fuck off. Oh, and I'm sure he'd been crying."

"Well, my wee pal," Parker interjected, "she told me she got a look at his resignation form, not that I've ever seen one myself, but apparently on the form there's a section that asks why the applicant is resigning."

Taylor realised that Parker was enjoying this, so sighed, "And?"

"Telford's written that he was being bullied at work, that his colleagues and by the way, that's me and you and everyone else on the shift, that we were constantly undermining him, refused to accompany him on patrol, that his supervisors picked on him and though he was a hardworking and tenacious…"

"Wait," Taylor interrupted with a shake of his head. "Is this Keith Telford he's writing about or some fictional character?"

"Don't forget, Drew, the man was a legend in his own mind," Parker was grinning now.

"Anyway," he continued again, "apparently he's blamed everyone but himself for him resigning, rather than his own pathetic inadequacies."

"Inadequacies. That's a big word for you, Ian."

"Aye, very good," Parker snorted, then sighed, "Weird or what?"

"No doubt we'll get the full story when we're back on shift," Taylor opined, only to hear Parker ask, "So, you and Roz, eh?"

"Goodbye, Ian, see you tomorrow at work," Taylor cut him off and ended the call.

He stood for several seconds in the hallway, wondering what had motivated Telford to quit the job, but then realised if nothing else, he and his colleagues were a little bit safer knowing that they would not have to depend on the untrustworthy Telford to watch their backs.

****

Cathy McHugh, the owner and landlady of *The Resting Soldier*, was in a real quandary.

Not only had she unwittingly harboured the killer of wee Jeannie Mason, but Cochrane, the *bastard* that he is, had caused the polis to come to the pub where a near riot had followed.

Bad enough that she was now looking for a new chef/barman, it was more than likely that now she'd be looking for a new licensee too, that when the Craigie Street licensing sergeant and whatever minion he brought with him arrived, she'd find herself being reported to the City Licensing Committee and there goes the pub, she inwardly fumed.

Tapping the ash from her cigarette into the glass ashtray on her desk in the rear room, an idea came to her.

Reaching for the phone, she dialled the number for Craigie Street station and when it was answered, took a breath and said, "Can I speak to Constable McGarry, please?"

****

Just as Cathy McHugh was making her phone call, Smiler McGarry, released from assisting the CID and enjoying his day off before resuming early shift on Saturday, was catching up on some domestic duties, when glancing out of the window, he saw old Joe.

Joe, a widower now approaching his seventieth birthday and to supplement his pension, was Smiler's once a fortnight gardener who mowed the lawn and kept the shrubbery neat and tidy.

Knocking on the front room window, Smiler grinned when attracting Joe's attention, he made the motion of drinking from a mug and smiled when Joe returned a thumb's-up.

Ten minutes later and Joe seated at the kitchen table opposite Smiler, his jacket hungover the back of the chair, the two men chewed the fat with their favourite topic; the football season so far.

Twenty idle minutes passed before Joe hesitantly asked, "You work over in the southside, don't you, Stuart?"

"I do. Why do you ask?"

"Do you know anything about cannabis? I mean, who it is that's selling it to the young folk these days?"

Smiler stared for several seconds before he softly said, "That's an odd question coming from you Joe. Have you a reason for asking?" he gently probed.

It was evident the older man was uncomfortable, then nervously licking at his lips, he replied, "You know my lassie, Edith. Her lad, Peter, he's just seventeen. She thinks he's into drugs."

"Well," Smiler drawled, "I don't know your daughter, but of course you've often spoken about her. Why does she think her son is into drugs?"

"Well," he turned to fetch something from his jacket pocket, then opening his hand, showed Smiler a rolled-up piece of kitchen aluminium foil.

"Edith found this in her lad's sock drawer. I don't think it's tobacco," he handed it to Smiler.

With a sigh, he glanced down at the foil, then softly replied, "You're right, Joe. I'm no expert but it's what I think is called crack-cocaine," he sniffed, "and I only know that because I've seen posters in our office warning us to look out for it. Did your daughter ask her son where he got it?"

"No, no," Joe vigorously shook his head. "She's on her own since her man left two years ago and the wee shite, he's been giving her a hard time and though I've tried to talk to him, it's like water off a ducks back. Cheeky young sod, so he is. Thinks he knows more than he does, you know?"

"Am I correct in thinking your daughter is living over in the southside?"

"Aye, that's right. Halbert Street. Do you know it?"

"Oh, aye, I know Halbert Street," Smiler thoughtfully nodded, then asked, "Your grandson. Is he working?"

"He's got a part-time job in a wee café in Minard Road. Should be there now. Why?"

"Just wondering how he's managing to pay for this," Smiler rolled the foil between his fingers.

"So," Joe grimaced when he pointed to the foil, "what should I do about that?"

"You? Nothing," he rubbed thoughtfully at his chin. "But me?" he smiled, "I'm thinking I might be able to do something about it."

****

The CID clerk, Bobby Davies, answered the phone, then said, "Aye, she's here."

Calling out to Barbara McMillan, he told her, "Smiler for you."

"Hello big man," she cheerfully greeted him, "what can I do you for then?"

"You busy?"

"Just winding up some statements relative to the inquiry about you know who," she glanced around her.

"How do you feel about assisting me with some community relations?"

McMillan's eyes narrowed when she suspiciously said, "You're supposed to be on a rest day, Smiler. What's this about?"

"I'm considering gathering some criminal intelligence," he airily replied, then added, "Fancy coming along?"

McMillan sighed, then glancing back at the statement forms on her desk, asked, "When and where?"

****

Worried that her youngest daughter was going through a bad patch following her break-up with her former boyfriend, Derek, and her recent trauma of being struck with a claw-hammer, Nan Begley and most unusually for her, took the day off work to spend time with Roz.

Now settled for lunch in the Italian café in Ingram Street, Nan hesitantly asked, "Your colleague, the young man you work with, Drew. He walked you home last night?"

"Yes, mum, and before you start," Roz raised her hand, "I am *not* diving into a new relationship after breaking up with Derek. It's just that…"

She stopped, uncertain exactly where she was going with her explanation and after Drew had confessed his feelings for her.

In those few seconds Roz asked herself, how exactly do I feel about him?

With a gently sigh, she continued, "Drew came with me yesterday to Pitt Street to have this photographed," she raised her arm in its sling, "then we had lunch at his. It was all very straightforward. Honestly, it's a neighbour thing."

Her mother shrugged when she replied, "It seems a very *caring* neighbour thing then, him wanting to spend the day with you."

"You're reading too much into it," Roz gently rebuked her. "If there was and if there ever will be anything more, you'll be the first to know. Now, lunchtime menu or the *a la carte* or what?"

Nan tightly smiled for it was Roz's throwaway remark, '…if there ever will be anything more…' that struck home, but she decided that conversation was for another day.

****

The manageress of the small café in Minard Road stared from the large, plainclothes police officer to the blonde-haired detective, then said, "Yes, of course. If it's bad news, I'll just fetch him from the kitchen."

A moment later she returned with a pale faced youth, Peter McGowan, who stuttered, "Is this about my papa, Joe?"

"Let's have a wee chat outside, son," Smiler tightly smiled at him.

Leading the way out of the café, Smiler turned into the tenement close entrance next door, followed by the young man and McMillan, then turning sharply, pushed Peter against the close wall.

As if by magic, the wrap of tinfoil appeared in the large man's hand as towering over Peter, he stared into his eyes, but addressed McMillan when he said, "What do you think, Detective. Shall we just give him the jail now?"

Peter was not to know they'd rehearsed everything before entering the café and so she replied, "Let's hear what he has to say first, Constable McGarry."

In a soft, almost seductive voice, she turned to the frightened young man and calmly said, "How you respond to my questions depends on where you spend the night, Peter, whether that be going home to your mother or in a cold cell at Craigie Street awaiting an appearance tomorrow morning at the Sheriff Court. Understand?"

With Smiler looming over the top of the five feet seven-inch teenager and staring menacingly at him, Peter almost wet himself when he stuttered, "Please I don't know anything."

"Aye, you do, son," Smiler growled at him, then added, "We have sufficient evidence to arrest your mother for possession of this crack-cocaine that was discovered in her house. As the tenant, she is responsible for everything in her home. Are you willing to let us give her the jail or what?"

He stared at the tinfoil wrap and tears pricked at his eyes before he shook his head, then admitted, "Mum doesn't know about that. I only bought it to impress a lassie I used to go to school with. I wasn't going to use it, honest, sir."

Neither Smiler nor McMillan were bullies and much as they didn't like the performance they were going through, it was the big man who had convinced her that following on from what Peter's grandfather Joe had told Smiler, the lad needed a sharp lesson in manners and how he treated his mother.

And so it was Smiler who grimly replied, "You impress women with honesty and integrity, son, not pretending to be a junkie."

It was McMillan's turn when she interjected with, "Where did you get the crack, Peter?"

He turned with tears now flowing down his cheeks and sobbing, replied, "In a pub. A pub on Allison Street, the something Soldier it's called."

Smiler's eyes nodded, already confirming his own conclusion when he asked, *"The Resting Soldier?"*

"That's it, yes," Peter eagerly agreed with a nod.

"Who did you buy it from?"

"A guy one of my pals told me about. Jo-Jo somebody."

"And he handed you the crack?" this from McMillan.

He turned to shake his head and now openly weeping, said, "No. He took my money and told me to wait outside and somebody would bring me the crack. A skinny guy. He took me into a close next door to the pub and just gave me that," he nodded down at the tinfoil in Smiler's hand.

"Describe the skinny guy?" Smiler asked.

"I dunno, I'm not good at ages. Maybe your age, Miss," he turned to McMillan. "Forty something?"

He wasn't being cheeky, that was obvious, but McMillan bridled that at twenty-nine, a teenager thought her to be in her forties.

"What else can you tell us about this skinny guy?"

The young man shrugged when he said, He's got long, greasy black hair and, aye," his eyes narrowed in recollection when he nodded, "he's got tattoos across his knuckles on both hands. The one on his right hand says ACAB, whatever that's supposed to mean."

Both Smiler and McMillan recognised the acronym tattoo that stood for 'All Cops Are Bastards.'

Smiler caught her eye and subtly winked when he asked, "Did the skinny guy have anything that would make him easy to pick out in a crowd?"

Choked by tears and unable to speak, it was all that Peter could do to shake his head.

With a sigh, Smiler stood upright and turning to McMillan, asked, "What do you think, Detective. A second chance, maybe?"

Now visibly shaking, Peter's eyes darted from one to the other, then McMillan slowly nodded when she told the teenager, "This is your final warning, young man. We have any reason to come and speak with you again, you *will* go to jail. Is that clearly understood?"

"Yes, Miss," he quietly sobbed.

"Here's what is going to happen, Peter. I'm going to tell your boss in the café that you're too upset to continue working, that you need to go home after the bad news about your auntie who has just died. That your mother needs you but you will return to work for your next shift and you will *not* discuss what happened here in the close to anyone. You got that?"

Just so grateful to be going home, Peter vigorously nodded then when motioned by Smiler that he go, he hurried from the close.

"Well, as we suspected," McMillan stared up at Smiler. "Jo-Jo Donnelly. I'm wondering though, who the skinny guy is that's holding the crack for him when he's dealing?"

"Well, Detective Constable McMillan," he smiled, "that's for you to

find out, but right now I'm away to enjoy the rest of my day off and everything we've learned today, Barbara, that's yours."
"What, you don't want to be part of this?"
"No," he smiled down at her. "If there's kudos to be earned, wee pal, then they are yours. I'm happy enough to have done a favour for a friend and hopefully, set his grandson on the straight and narrow."
She shook her head, then replied, "I'd better go and explain to his boss about him going home. See you tomorrow at work, then."

CHAPTER THIRTY-FOUR: Friday 07.05am 16 March 1979.

By the time the shift had assembled in the muster room, the word had gone around that Keith Telford had handed in his resignation to the public bar at Shettleston police office.
"He'll not be missed anyway, that horrible git," was offered, predictably, by Harry Dawson, who shuddered that the news might just be a rumour.
"Settle down, you lot," Inspector Iain Cowan's voice broke into the conversation, who standing at the lectern with acting Sergeant Mattie Devlin, then turned towards the shift to confirm the news the killer of both Jeannie Mason and Albert Moston had been arrested and was now remanded in custody.
"And not in some small part due to the efforts of our very own, Smiler McGarry," Cowan grinned at the big man.
A cheer and handclapping erupted, with Smiler managing a weak grin and grimacing at the attention.
After reading the daily briefing register, Cowan added, "Smiler, there's a note that you had a telephone call yesterday morning from Cathy McHugh of *The Resting Soldier*. She's looking for you to pop in and see her, but refused to divulge why."
"Sir," he acknowledged with a nod, while thinking it was fortuitous that after speaking with Joe's grandson, there might be an opportunity to make some discreet inquiry about the skinny man running the crack-cocaine for Jo-Jo Donnelly.
After dismissing the shift to their beats, Cowan called Smiler to him then in a low voice, said, "It's early so it should be quiet enough for me to come out for a walk with you, Smiler. Besides," he winked, "I

do fancy a cuppa and a bacon roll."
****

Finished with checking the crime reports from the preceding twenty-four hours, DCI Laura Gemmill turned to the warrant that had been delivered the previous afternoon. The signed Sheriff Warrant that authorised the arrest of Assistant Chief Constable John Michael Crawford.

In agreement with Deputy Chief Constable Paula Clarke, it had been agreed that on the forthcoming Monday morning, both women would travel in a staff car to the Lothian & Borders Police headquarters at Fettes, in Edinburgh, where they would be met by the L&B Deputy Chief Constable who would accompany them to make the arrest.

Thereafter, both women would return with their prisoner to the Sheriff Court at Ingram Street in Glasgow, where after Crawford's appearance to be formally charged in front of a Sheriff and in cognisance of the passage of time since the crimes were committed, it was agreed the Procurator Fiscal would not oppose bail.

Yet still, Gemmill was worried.

All through the following day and continuing to be led by acting DS Lucy Chalmers, the team dedicated to finding further evidence of Crawford's crimes had produced further retired detective officers who were willing to provide statements regarding Crawford's bullying and the suppression of crime reports that those officers were issued.

Indeed, so much evidence was rolling in, Gemmill suspected that being the unlikeable individual Crawford so obviously was, some of those officers were perhaps acting out of spite rather than honesty. Nevertheless, without evidence to the contrary, she and her team was obliged to accept the signed statements, then simply pass them to the Fiscal's Department to judge the veracity of the information they contained.

A conundrum indeed, she wryly thought.

She glanced up when her door was knocked then pushed open by DI Sammy Pollock's shoulder, a mug of coffee in each hand.

"One thing about having a murder or two in the Division," he shook his head, "it tends to keep the crime reports numbers down with the bad guys doing their damnedest to avoid getting a pull from the team," he smiled and laid the mugs down onto her desk, before sitting opposite.

Glancing at the warrant and file in front of her, he asked, "You okay about doing this on Monday, boss? I mean, I'm not questioning your ability, but it's a hell of a thing to go over to Edinburgh and arrest one of their own and a senior boss at that."

"Like it or not, Sammy," she sighed, "It's got to be done and now that I'm the DCI here in F Division, it falls to me to correct the crimes that Crawford committed."

His eyes narrowed when he asked, "Do you think his Chief or his Deputy will tip him the wink to expect you?"

"Honestly? I'd be surprised if they didn't. If they let one of their own be taken from their headquarters without his knowledge, it'll only cause a ripple of suspicion and mistrust among the rest of the Assistant Chief's, so yes; I'm absolutely certain he will be expecting us."

"Well, when you bring him back to the Sheriff Court," he slyly smiled, "let me tell you about a rather interesting conversation I had with Cochrane's lawyer, Freddie Kirkland."

****

Strathclyde Police Chief Constable, Arthur Donaldson, once more inspected himself in the full length mirror screwed to the inside of the door of his private bathroom in his office.

The phone call earlier that morning to Donaldson's secretary from the Chair of the Police and Fire Committee intimating his intention to visit with his Deputy Chair, had caused Donaldson to believe that finally, his budget cuts and savings had been recognised, that the visit was to be a congratulatory handshake and maybe even some form of award; perhaps even being recommended for the prestigious Queen's Police Medal.

In full uniform complete with his cap, he drew himself up to his full five feet eight inches and admired the pose he struck, though once more and other than the obligatory twenty-two years Police Long Service and Good Conduct ribbon, was inwardly conscious of his lack of ribbons that so many of his subordinates sported.

Returning to his office, he sat grandly behind his desk, practising his posture for his visitor's arrival, then startled when his intercom squealed.

"Yes," he snapped.

"Your visitors, sir," the weary voice of his secretary announced.
"Send them in," he sniffed.
He had decided that when the door opened, he would wait for a couple of seconds, permitting them to see him seated at his desk, then would slowly rise to both greet them and command their attention.
Upon their entering the room, the Chair, a stocky built man with collar length greying hair and a former politician of long-standing, well used to dealing with troublesome unions and heckling opponents, nodded to his Deputy, a middle-aged woman whose meek looks belied her tenacious temper, that she close the door.
"I'll get straight to the point," the Chair addressed Donaldson, "the Committee have agreed that your tenure as Chief must end today."
Donaldson, who had convinced himself the unexpected visit was to commend him, was stunned into silence, his eyes widening and his mouth dropping open.
"Eh, what…?" he stuttered, uncertain if he was hearing correctly.
Dropping into one of the two chairs in front of the desk, the Chair waved for him to sit back down, then calmly continued, "It can't come as a surprise, Mr Donaldson, that your past and noticeably, your recent behaviour towards your staff and subordinates has resulted in a large number of complaints alleging bullying and intimidation, as well as a complete lack of respect for those officers and police staff who are themselves in managerial positions within the Force. In fact, the Committee have received so many complaints and I might add, not *only* from the Police Federation representing the rank and file, but the Chief Police Officers Staff Association too as well as a number of the unions representing police staff who are literally beating down our door. It's just not on, Mr Donaldson," he vigorously shook his head, "and we the Committee have decided we have no recourse but to have you step down with immediate effect."
Almost falling back down into his own chair, Donaldson at last found his voice and squeaked, "And if I refuse to stand down?"
Staring at him, the Chair paused before he replied, "I don't think you understand what I'm offering you, Mr Donaldson. You have the opportunity here to tender your resignation for whatever purpose you wish to disclose, whether that be ill-health or family, we really don't care. If you do so, we the Committee will issue a statement regretting your departure and you will depart with some dignity.

However, should you wish to ignore such an opportunity then I am empowered by the Committee to remove you from office right now and that will be witnessed by my Deputy."

"But…" Donaldson, in a voice that was no more than a whisper, swallowed through a throat that suddenly felt like it was lined by broken glass, "…but I thought I was doing a good job."

The Chair took a deep breath, then exhaled and abruptly asked, "Do you wish to resign or face the alternative?"

His head drooping, the reality of his position came like a hammer blow and so Donaldson sniffed, "I'll resign."

Turning to his Deputy, who continued to stand by the door, the Chair nodded to her, then watched as she fetched a sheet of folded paper from her handbag and opening it, laid it on the desk before Donaldson. Then, in a surprisingly deep voice for such a slightly built woman, she said, "Here is a suggested draft of your resignation statement to be issued to the media, Mr Donaldson. You may add to it any reason you see fit for your resigning your post. If you comply with this instruction and as the Chair has said, we the Committee will issue a statement regretting your leaving and wishing you well for your future."

Rising to his feet, the Chair nodded at Donaldson, then with a simple, "Good day, sir," both he and the Deputy left the room.

Still shocked by the sudden turn of events, Donaldson sat at his desk, his body shaking, then gritted his teeth when he felt the tears bite at his eyes.

They would know, he knew. Everyone would know. No matter what statement he put out, they'd know he was being sacked and his dream, his vision of one day being invited to head the Metropolitan Police as their Commissioner, was now gone.

But not only that, he would never again be invited to take up a senior appointment in any police Force.

He was finished.

His shoulders slumped and almost in a daze, he lifted the phone to call his wife.

****

In the small ante-room outside Donaldson's office, the Chair nodded to the secretary, then politely said, "Perhaps you might inform the Deputy Chief Constable that we will be grateful if she might grant us the time to have a few words with her."

****

It didn't escape Smiler's notice that when he and Iain Cowan knocked on the back door of the City Bakeries shop, Sally's staff made some excuse to pop through to the rear room to greet him. When Sally herself grinned, "They know," it explained the smiles and knowing winks.

Two rolls and bacon and two cuppas later and when Sally was helping out at the front counter, Cowan shook his head when he sighed, "No offence, big man, but looking at you and looking at Sally, you're definitely punching above your weight."

"Don't I know it," he agreed with a smile.

"So, digressing completely, why do you think Cathy McHugh wants to see you?"

Smiler's eyes narrowed before he replied, "My guess is that after the debacle in her pub, she'll be looking for some polis support for when she re-applies for her licence. I'm thinking that she'll want me to intercede with the Licensing Sergeant and if she does, she'll be prepared to come across with something that just might be of use to us."

"I thought you told me she was anti-police, that she never touted?"

"Aye, Iain," he nodded, "I did, but given that there was a near riot in her pub with a police officer injured, albeit slightly, her licence is on a sticky wicket and quite possibly, might be revoked."

"And do you have any idea what kind of info she might pass on?"

He smiled when he replied, "Curiously, I do," then related what he and Barbara McMillan had learned the previous day.

"She's the good-looking blonde lassie in the CID upstairs?"

"That's her," Smiler nodded, then added, "But I'll not be dealing with the info myself. Barbara's done a good job and deserves some recognition, so whatever our Cathy has to tell us, it'll go to Barbara."

"Us?"

"Are you not my neighbour this morning?" he grinned.

Reaching for his cap, Cowan replied, "Okay, I know it's not opening time, but I'm guessing there will be someone in *The Resting Soldier* now?"

Glancing at his wristwatch, Smiler nodded, "Aye, it's about this time they have their weekend barrel delivery, so I've no doubt Cathy will be there."

****

Chief Superintendent Jimmy Thompson's desk phone rang and lifting it from its cradle, he was greeted by the Deputy Chief Constable, Paula Clarke, who formally said, "Mr Thompson, how are you this morning?"

"I'm as well as can be expected by a man my age with a pair of useless lungs and arthritis," he tapped the ash from his cigarette into the small tin he used, then smiled into the phone. "And yourself, Ma'am. How are you?"

He wasn't prepared for her response when she replied, "Busy, Mr Thompson. Now, I'm phoning because I require both you and your Chief Inspector, Mrs Whitmore, to attend within the hour at my office here in Pitt Street. Will that be a problem?"

"Eh, no Ma'am. Might I ask why you wish to see us?"

"I'll explain when you arrive. Within the hour, Mr Thompson," she curtly reminded him, then ended the call.

What the hell was that about, he wondered, then dialled the internal number to summon Lizzie Whitmore down to his office.

****

Drew Taylor was a little deflated to learn that his neighbour for the time being Roz Begley was off sick, would be Harry Dawson.

Not that she wasn't a good worker, but impulsive and difficult to control when she got it into her head that someone was a bad yin, seeing everything as black and white with no real sense of any grey area; what Taylor called the good guy, bad guy syndrome.

About to head out to the van, he was called back by Mattie Devlin, who beckoning him into the Inspector's room, said, "I know you'd have preferred someone else to neighbour you, Drew, but Harry's needing a clear head and someone who can calm her when there's something going on. To be honest," he lowered his voice, "she's the makings of a good cop, but just needs a firm lead, someone to rein her in when she's first on the scene, you know?"

Taylor grimly smiled when nodding, he replied, "I know exactly what you mean, Sarge. I've seen her lose it before and it's not a pretty sight."

He sighed, then added, "I'll do my best."

"I know you will, Drew," Devlin clapped him on the shoulder, then almost as afterthought, asked, "How's Roz?"

"Keen to get back to work," Taylor smiled, then was surprised when Devlin added, "I'm hearing one of the Inquiry Department's cops is due to retire soon. Might be an opening there for a young cop with both tickets, Drew. Interested?"

Taken aback, Taylor's eyes widened when he nodded for it was common knowledge that a position in the Inquiry Department could be the first step to promotion; that and it would mean he was off the shift so there would be no need for either him or Roz to move away from the Division.

Turning to leave the room, Devlin stared after him and shaking his head, smiled.

Though he wasn't that much older than Taylor, he thought, young folk these days. They must think we supervisors button up the back. As if it was a secret that he fancied Roz Begley.

****

Cathy McHugh exhaled with annoyance when the front door of the pub was hammered upon.

Pulling open one of the outer shuttered doors, she stood back when she saw it to be Smiler McGarry and a colleague; an Inspector she saw.

"Morning, Cathy," he smiled at her, then added, "I understand you're looking for me?"

"Come through," she abruptly stood to one side to permit them to pass her, then closed the door behind them.

It didn't escape Cowan's notice that even at just gone nine in the morning, McHugh was a hell of a good-looking and glamourous woman.

Leading them through to the rear room, she motioned towards two wooden chairs, then standing with her back to her desk, her arms folded, she sighed, "I'm hearing Pat Cochrane has been charged with Jeannie's murder."

"Aye," Smiler nodded, "Jeannie's murder and the murder of one of your customers, Moxy Moston. Do you know him?"

Her eyes narrowed when she asked, "Skinny, weird looking guy with a funny shaped nose?"

"That's him," Smiler confirmed.

"Fuck!" she shook her head as if in disbelief.

They watched her take a sharp breath when she said, "And the knife you took from the pub. That was the murder weapon?"

"So the Forensics tell us, aye," he nodded again.

Cowan was a little uncertain about Smiler divulging what in reality was evidential information, but knowing him as he did, trusted the big man knew what he was doing and so did not interrupt.

"And you're worried about your licence?" Smiler stared at her.

"Of course I am," she snapped back, then raised a hand to add, "Sorry, but this business as you well know, Smiler, is all I have now. So," she took a soft breath, "what can I do to make amends for what happened in the pub when you and your guys charged in?"

Smiler refrained from laughing for his recollection did *not* include the police charging in, so instead replied, "Jo-Jo Donnelly. He's dealing crack cocaine from here, Cathy. You know it and I know it."

"Listen, Smiler," she took a step forward, then defensively replied, "I know he's a drug-dealing scummy, but believe me, I've had my stewards turn him over a couple of times and he's never had drugs on him. Money, aye, but no drugs."

To her surprise, he nodded when he said, "Aye, you're right. He's not carrying drugs into your pub. His associate is."

"Eh? What associate?"

"Don't have a name, Cathy, but he's skinny, about thirty to forty and has a tattoo across his knuckles; ACAB."

They saw her eyes narrow with recognition, then she slowly nodded and said, "And if I have a name for this man, you'll speak with the Licensing Sergeant on my behalf?"

It was Cowan who replied, "Though I'll not make any promises, I'll personally speak to him myself, Miss McHugh."

She took a few seconds to deliberate on his reply, then nodding, said, "You're describing Frankie Agnew. Shifty wee bastard," her face creased in scorn.

"Funny that," she slowly shook her head, "I always wondered how that wee sod had so much money to spend on the bevy, yet as far as I'm aware, he's never worked a day in his shiftless life. Well, that explains a lot."

"And he's in here every time Donnelly is in the pub?"

"As far as I recall, aye, he is."

Rising to their feet, it was Smiler who said, "Thanks, Cathy. I'll pass on the information and like my Inspector here says, he'll do what he can with the Licensing Sergeant."

She nodded, but didn't respond.

****

Lizzie Whitmore decided that rather than take a patrol car off the street, she'd use her own car to convey her and Jimmy Thompson to Pitt Street where they discovered at the underground car park, a bay had been reserved for them.

"Curiouser and curiouser," Thompson muttered as they headed for the stairwell that led to the front entrance at Pitt Street and door to the Command Suite.

Making themselves known to the Deputy's secretary, the woman smiled, then asking them to wait, used the intercom to alert her boss that they'd arrived.

Almost immediately they heard Clarke's voice instruct that they go straight through.

Seated at her desk, Paula Clarke, on the phone, glanced up as they entered the large office and waved them to sit in the chairs facing her desk.

A minute later, the call ended, she replaced the handset then glancing at them in turn, sighed when she said, "It'll be public knowledge soon enough, but the Chief Constable has resigned."

"Oh," was all that Thompson could muster while Whitmore, refraining from laughing out loud, had to physically force herself from punching the air and loudly shouting, about bloody time.

However, knowing there was more to their being summoned than being imparted this information, it was Thompson who asked, "And you wish to see us why, Ma'am?"

Clarke sat back in her chair and studied them both before she disclosed, "The Police and Fire Committee have chosen me to be the acting Chief Constable in the interim until such time an appointment is made."

Though having been previously alerted to Donaldson's pending dismissal, Thompson did not comment on the news other than to say, "Congratulations, Chief Constable, but again; might I inquire why are we here?"

"Well, as you are aware, Mr Thompson, I am a relatively recent appointment to Strathclyde Police, having arrived just over a year previously from England, and while there are a number of suitable candidates in the Assistant Chief Constable posts at present, I would prefer to appoint a Deputy who is," she paused and smiled, "let's just say, wise to the ways of the Scottish police officer. Someone who can bridge the gap between the rank and file and the Command Suite. God knows," she huffed, "the damage that has been done by my predecessor to relations between the top tier executive and the rank and file, it needs repaired and quickly."

Beside him, he sensed Whitmore turning to stare at him when he burst out, "Jesus, Paula, you can't be serious! I've months left to serve, if I bloody *live* that long, and I've never even contemplated the Command Suite here. In fact, I'm surprised I got this far in the job! That and you'd be promoting me two ranks, Ma'am! That's unheard of!"

"Well actually, Jimmy," she calmly replied, "you're wrong. You're obviously not aware, but a few years ago there was precedent set by the Met in London when it was discovered a Chief Inspector had been overlooked for some years for promotion and was immediately promoted to Chief Superintendent. Her promotion was accepted by the Chief Officers Association representing the English and Welsh Forces and there's also been a recent case of a DS in the RUC being promoted directly to Detective Chief Inspector, so like it or not, I *need* you."

She paused, then said, "Let me explain. Yes," she sighed, "I've every expectation that the Assistant Chief's will be crawling out of the woodwork for the Deputy position and admittedly," she vigorously nodded, "while most of them are good and capable officers, I need someone I can trust who will be forthright, can counsel me and if need be, keep me reined in when I need to be. Someone with your experience and with the time you have left to serve, who will coach me how to be a Chief because I do *not* intend to stay at the acting rank, Jimmy. I'm going after the job full time. So like it or not, *I'm* the acting Chief now and I'm *making* the decision. You will be my Deputy. Got it?"

"Bloody, hell, Paula," he wearily sighed as he slowly shook his head, "I really *do* hope you know what you're doing."

She turned to a smiling Whitmore, then stunned her when Clarke said, "I don't know what you're grinning at Lizzie. Now that you've lost your Divisional Commander, I'm promoting you to Superintendent, so you'll be looking after F Division as the acting Divisional Commander until I appoint a full time Chief Superintendent."

"Now," she turned to stare at them in turn, then with a soft smile, asked, "Are there any more questions before I tell you to bugger off, because I *really* am very busy."

They were at the door when, her brow furrowing, Clarke suddenly remembered, then calling out to Thompson, said, "Oh, one more thing, Deputy Chief Constable."

CHAPTER THIRTY-FIVE.

In the car returning to Craigie Street, Jimmy Thompson still found it hard to believe he was reporting to his new office at Pitt Street on Monday; the office that was today to be vacated by the acting Chief Constable, Paula Clarke, who in turn would now occupy the office of the former Chief, Arthur Donaldson.

"Wish I'd been a fly on the wall when that git Donaldson was informed he was being sacked," he shook his head.

Whitmore, still coming to terms with her new rank, exhaled when she replied, "It'll be all over the Force by now. The rumour mill will be working full time and God alone knows what kind of stories will be getting bandied about him."

"The more lurid the better," Thomson evilly grinned, then said, "I'd like to take my secretary Doris with me, Lizzie, but she knows the running of the office far better than I do, so you've won a watch having her help you settle in."

"Tell me truthfully Jimmy…I mean, sir," she smiled. "How difficult is it running a Division?"

He shrugged when he replied, "When you've got good people working for you, it's not too difficult. As long as they know you have their back, Lizzie, you'll be okay."

He turned to stare at her when he added, "If I was to offer you any advice, then I'd tell you, just be yourself. You're one hell of a police officer, you're experienced and a good administrator and I've been lucky to have you watch my back. Don't think I don't appreciate it, Superintendent."

That was the first formal use of her new rank and unable to explain her feelings, she felt an overwhelming, yet curious urge to cry, for Whitmore had already accepted that her gender preference had stymied her career and she was destined to remain at the Chief Inspector rank. But now?

Now, she realised, with Paula Clarke having shattered the glass ceiling, perhaps anything was possible.

Biting at her lower lip, she stared through the windscreen and took a sharp breath, then exhaled before she said, "You've been a good boss, Jimmy, and if I have learned anything from you, it's stay away from the fags."

He erupted in infectious laughter that lasted almost to the archway leading to the rear yard in Craigie Street.

****

With Iain Cowan gone to speak with the Divisional Licensing Sergeant, Barbara McMillan listened intently as Smiler related the information from Cathy McHugh.

"And this," he handed her a printout, "is what I've found on the PNC and the collator gave me this photo of Agnew."

"Francis Declan Agnew, aged thirty-eight," she muttered as she read, then staring at the photo commented, "My, but he's a right ugly sod, isn't he?"

"Aye, when he fell out the tree, he must've hit every branch on the way down," Smiler sighed.

"Well, he's got a fair number of previous convictions, but only served three months and that was eighteen months ago" she nodded at the printout.

"But it was for dealing cannabis, so another drug conviction for dealing would go badly for him, particularly as its crack-cocaine and the publicity it's getting with the media calling it an epidemic and linking it to a number of deaths in England. Oh," Smiler pointed to the printout, "you'll notice too that Donnelly is listed as an associate."

"So," she glanced about her and lowered her voice, "how do you think I should go about catching these buggers?"

He stared thoughtfully at her, appreciative that she was wise enough to seek his advice and calling on his own experience in the job, then said, "If it were me, wee pal, I'd present the DCI with a game plan, suggesting you bring in one of the plainclothes from Castlemilk, someone who can pass as a punter, then send them in to make a buy from Donnelly. That and have a couple of heavies waiting outside for Agnew to meet with the buyer in whatever close your man is sent to. What I'd further suggest, is, whoever you do send in to make the buy, they need to be really convincing and have a cover story as to why they know he's dealing, because Donnelly's no fool and he'll smell a rat if he isn't certain the buyer is genuine."

His face brow creased when he shook his head, then added, "Wait. Much as I'm sure the DCI would prefer this to be a Divisional capture, it *might* instead be advisable to speak with the Drug Squad at Pitt Street. This kind of operation is their bread and butter and they have detectives specifically trained to be buyers. Perhaps ask the DCI to speak on your behalf to borrow one of them to help with your operation?"

"That's really helpful, Smiler. I'll get the paperwork together and submit a plan to the boss. Thanks, big man," she grinned at him.

They both turned when Iain Cowan opened the door to the general office, then nodding, said, "The Licensing Sergeant is on board, *if* we get a result. And if we *do*, he'll be happy to mention McHugh was instrumental in alerting the police to a drug ring operating in her premises."

"One more thing, Barbara," Smiler stared at her. "Experience has taught me that this being Friday, local drug dealers are busy dealing to the youngsters at the weekends, so if you're sharpish…?"

"I'm right on it," she happily grinned.

****

DCI Laura Gemmill answered her phone to be told by his secretary, if she wasn't busy, Mr Thompson requested she visit him at his office.

Heading downstairs, his secretary Doris nodded that she go straight in and doing so, was surprised to see not the Chief Superintendent, but Lizzie Whitmore seated behind the desk with Thompson sitting in one of the two chairs opposite.

Indicating she take a seat, Gemmill was further taken aback when Thompson disclosed their promotions, then said, "I know it's probably come as a bit of a shock, Laura, but the reason I'm here is not only to clear my desk, but to inform you that it will be me accompanying you on Monday when you travel through to Fettes in Edinburgh, to execute your warrant."

"Now," he sipped at his mug of coffee when he continued, "what's you plan for executing your warrant?"

****

His shift over for the day, Drew Taylor was sitting in the Byres Road café and watching Roz Begley stirring her coffee with her free hand. It had been a relatively trouble-free Friday early shift for Taylor and his temporary neighbour, Harry Dawson, though he shared with Roz, "My heads still buzzing. Not once did she stop nattering. Never even paused for breath other when she was having her break and stuffing doughnuts into her gob," he smiled with a shake of his head.

She smiled before she asked, "Any indication from Willie Strathmore how he did in his elementary exam?"

Taylor grimaced when he related Strathmore's reluctance to even discuss the exam, other than to admit the Traffic paper was a nightmare, but did add Strathmore finished in time to check over all three papers.

"I hope he passes," her brow knitted, for Willie was a popular member of the shift.

"Speaking of exams," Taylor's forehead creased, "you know I've already passed both my elementary and advanced exams?"

"Yes, why?"

"Well," he disclosed the Mattie Devlin's suggestion that there might be an upcoming opening in the Divisional Inquiry Department.

"But that's great news," her face reflected her genuine pleasure, but then she frowned when she asked, "It would mean you leave the shift, though."

"But I'd still be in the Division, Roz," he softly replied.

Her brow knitted when she joked, "And I'd need to train up a new neighbour."

He grinned, knowing that his news had gone down well, then said, "So, you'd miss me."

She stared at him for several seconds before she softly smiled, "If we really intend seeing each other, Drew, why would I miss you?"

****

07.15pm, the same day.

Standing behind the bar of *The Resting Soldier* and in the act of pulling a pint, Cathy McHugh was nudged by her barmaid, who nodded towards the door.

Glancing over, McHugh saw a gaunt faced woman with untidy, shoulder length dark hair pulled back into a loose ponytail, furtively sneak into the busy pub, but her eyes were darting back and forth as if looking for someone. Dressed in an oversized man's long-sleeved, navy coloured blue pullover that had obviously seen better days and a pair of loose fitting once white tracksuit bottoms, the woman's arms were tightly crossed on her chest. As McHugh watched, she appeared to be in her mid to late-twenties as with her head and shoulders both bowed, she shuffled among the customers.

The barmaid, her voice full of derision, sneered, "She's the fourth junkie in the last half hour, boss, and must be in looking for Jo-Jo. Do you want me to get her thrown out?"

McHugh knew that if she interfered in Donnelly's drug business, at best in the dead of night the pub's windows would go in and at worse, a petrol bomb might follow, so sighed, "No, ignore her. Once she's got what she wants, she'll be gone. Now," she faked a smile and turned to the next customer at the busy bar. "What can I get you, darling?"

The junkie woman found who she was looking for and pushed through the customers to a booth where two men sat, each with a half-drunk pint of lager in front of them.

One man in his late forties, heavy set and a thick, untrimmed beard with a shaven head and arms bulging with multiple prison tattoos, wore a short-sleeved Celtic football top and quite obviously Donnelly's minder, stared meanly as the junkie neared the booth. The man sitting opposite, clean shaven and in his late twenties, his short brown hair neatly combed and well-groomed, wearing a light blue coloured polo shirt and sharply creased black trousers, idly tapped his fingers on the table-top as the junkie approached, then turned when her voice low and hesitant, she asked, "You Jo-Jo?"

The minder said, "Fuck off," but said no more when Donnelly raised his hand, then stared at her for several seconds before he replied, "What if I am?"

"My pal, wee Alex. He said you might have something for me, that you would set me up?"

"Who are you and who's wee Alex?"

The junkie woman, her hands twitching, the nails chewed and dirt ridden, shifted nervously from foot to foot, then with a glance around her, she nervously licked at her lips, then whispered, "Me? I'm Dolly. Alex's my pal, you know?"

His eyes narrowed suspiciously and even from three feet away, he could smell her body odour when he leaned forward to hiss at her, "No, *Dolly*, I don't know an Alex."

He watched her eyes flutter as she flinched back, then whined, "Alex told me he was in a wee while ago. He said you would set me up. I can pay, mister, please. Honest. I've got the cash."

It was the minder who leaned across the table to Donnelly, then said, "That wee nyaff who was in half an hour ago, Jo-Jo. Him that paid for…"

An angry Donnelly again raised a hand, then teeth bared, snapped, "I *know* who Alex is, you idiot! It's *her* that I don't know!"

"Oh, aye, right," his face red with embarrassment, the minder sank back into his seat.

"Now," Donnelly turned his attention to the junkie, "who exactly are *you*, Dolly, and where do you come from?"

He watched her swallow and the panic in her eyes when she stuttered, "Please, Mister, I'm hurting. I need something. Please!"

Enjoying watching her plead, he grinned at her pain when he said again. "Where are you from, Dolly? I don't *know* you?"

Her lower lips trembling, tears appeared in her eyes and she seemed to shrink into herself when she stammered, "I'm over in Govan, mister. In a squat in Rathlin Street with my boyfriend. Alex, he used to be, you know…" she shrugged.

"Your junkie ex?" he continued to grin at her, then watched her nod. Seconds passed before he decided there was nothing further to gain from teasing her, so sighed and asked, "What dough you got on you?"

He watched as she hastily scrambled in the pocket of her tracksuit, then offered him two crumpled, five-pound notes.

"Not me, you stupid bitch, him," he gestured towards the minder, who reached across to take the notes from her, then glancing at them to ensure they were genuine, nodded to Donnelly.

The junkie watched as Donnelly beckoned forward a thin, greasy haired man in his late thirties, who hurrying forward at the summons, stared at Donnelly.

"Two fiver bags," Donnelly quietly instructed the man, then told the junkie, "Go with him. He'll see you right."

The man nodded that the junkie follow him through the customers, who seemingly aware what was happening, glanced away, but parted to permit them passage.

Leading her outside into the drizzling rain, he said, "With me," and continued towards a tenement close two doors down from the pub.

Shuffling into the close entrance, the man, his teeth brown and stained, turned to grin at her, then said, "I'm Frankie, hen. You know," he glanced towards the close entrance, "for another bag that Jo-Jo doesn't know about, me and you might have some fun in the back of this close. So, what's your name, hen?"

The junkie softly smiled at him, then unexpectedly slammed him against the tenement wall before she replied, "Me? I'm DC Cairns from Strathclyde Police Drugs Squad and you, ya bozo, you're getting the jail."

****

The two large and extremely intimidating detectives that suddenly appeared from the rear of the tenement close took custody of a shocked Agnew, then used a personal radio to inform DC Barbara McMillan, "That's the courier in custody, Babs. DC Cairns says to mind the big guy with Donnelly who's wearing the Celtic top. Might be a fighter."

Acknowledging the transmission, McMillan, sitting in an enclosed and rusting Transit van with five more detectives that was parked fifty yards along the street from *The Resting Soldier*, opened the rear door and led them towards the pub.

On this occasion, however, their arrival in the pub did not provoke any reaction other than for the customers to again part to permit the detectives to approach Donnelly and his minder.

Stopping at the table, McMillan addressed them both when she said, "You two, you're getting the jail for drug dealing under the Misuse of Drugs Act of 1971. Take them."

She then stepped to one side and the stunned pair found themselves physically dragged from the booth, handcuffed, then wordlessly led from the pub.

Turning, McMillan found Cathy McHugh at her shoulder who in a low voice, said, "I take it this will help me?"

In the same low voice, she replied, "Not my decision, but I will include it in my report that you offered every assistance. And thanks," she added with a nod.

****

Smiler McGarry, sitting comfortably on his couch watching television with Sally Rodgers curled into his arm, turned towards the sound of the phone in the hallway ringing.

Making his way there, he lifted the phone to be greeted by Barbara McMillan who breathlessly told him, "It's a result, big man. Three in custody. Donnelly, his minder and Frankie Agnew, who's squealing like a pig because he knows he's likely to get good time with this conviction."

Smiler grinned into the phone, then asked, "No problems at the pub?"

"None at all, no. And the Drugs Squad DC, a lassie called Deborah Cairns? My God, Smiler, she's *awesome*. When she turned up at Craigie Street for the briefing, I thought she *was* a junkie. Makes me think I might be looking for a career change," she added.

"Debbie," his eyes opened wide. "Sometimes goes by the name Dolly?"

"Aye, that's her. You know her?'

He didn't explain, simply smiled when he replied, "Tell her I said hello. Oh, and well done, wee pal."

There was a second or two pause, then he heard McMillan take a breath before she said, "Thank you, Smiler. For the advice *and* the info."

"As long as the bad guys get the jail, Barbara. That's *all* that matters," he nodded into the phone.

The call ended, Smiler returned to the front room where Sally moved aside to permit him to resume his seat, then returned to her position in his arms.

"I'm thinking," his eyes narrowed when he softly said, "this moving between your flat and here, it's a right kafuffle, so it is. Waste of time all that travelling, so I was thinking, if you were to rent out your flat, why not move in with me?"

He sensed her holding her breath, then she slowly replied, "That's a big step for us both, Stuart. Are you sure you're ready for it?"

His throat felt tight when he slowly said, "What I'm really asking, Sally, is if you're up for it, maybe we could make it official? I mean," she turned to see the doubt in his eyes, "I know there's an age gap, but if you might even consider it, will you marry me?"

Her eyes widened when she softly breathed, "Yes."

EPILOGUE:

Monday 09.15am 19 March 1979.

The Strathclyde Police staff car that arrived in the car park at Fettes Avenue, the headquarters of Lothian & Borders Police, conveyed acting Deputy Chief Constable James Thompson and DCI Laura Gemmill to conduct the arrest of Assistant Chief Constable John Michael Crawford of that Force.

Neither of the Strathclyde officers were under the illusion that Crawford would be unaware of their visit.

After being formally, if a little coldly greeted at the front door by the grim-faced Lothian & Borders Deputy Chief Constable, who escorted them to Crawford's office, this was evident when he stood up from behind his desk, pale faced and dressed in a navy-blue suit and they saw he had with him a black leather travelling bag.

Her mouth dry, it was Gemmill who calmly informed Crawford that a warrant had been issued for his arrest pertaining to historical allegations of corruption and perverting the course of justice.

Then, in the presence of Thompson as the corroborating officer, Gemmill formally cautioned Crawford at common law, but he declined to make any comment.

During the process, it was noted by both Thompson and Gemmill that the Deputy Chief also declined to comment and indeed, apart from his initial greeting, said not a word to them nor Crawford.

The very tense visit to the Lothian & Borders headquarters lasted just under ten minutes before all three returned to the staff car and embarked on the return journey to Glasgow; a journey that was completed in its entirety, in silence.

Upon their arrival in Glasgow city centre, the staff car driver, a retired Traffic sergeant, had been previously instructed and drove directly towards the Sheriff Court in Ingram Street, where the vehicle was expected.

Within twenty minutes of their arrival and in agreement with the Procurator Fiscal, Crawford was escorted by Thompson and Gemmill from a detention room to a closed court where the now accused was presented to a Lady Sheriff.

"Is the prisoner represented?" the Sheriff asked the PF, who nodding to the bewigged and cloaked lawyer across the aisle, replied, "It is my understanding, My Lady, that Mr Kirkland is to represent the accused."

Freddie Kirkland, taking his cue, rose to his feet, then said, "I am charged by the accused to represent him, My Lady, and request the court take note of the fact I have yet to formally interview my client about these scurrilous allegations and therefore have had no opportunity to prepare a defence. I therefore request that at this time, he be released from custody without plea."

A short pause ended when again, in a previous agreement with the PF and to Crawford's surprise, the Sheriff said, "In the case against you, Mr Crawford, I will accede to a Crown request that you be released on your own cognisance till time of trial, a date which will be set and you informed in due course."

Stamping her gavel down onto her desk, the Sheriff rose, indicating the end of the proceedings.

Making their way downstairs to the underground cell area where the staff car awaited them, it was Thompson who sighed, "Well, so far, so good, Laura. Have you an opinion if he'll plead guilty or what?"

"Frankly, sir, the evidence is overwhelming and I think it unlikely he'll want to face a jury, so yes. I'm banking on him pleading guilty."

"If he does, there little doubt he'll be sacked outright and there goes his commutation and his pension too."

She stopped walking, then turning to Thompson, her nostrils flared when she replied, "After the harm he did, sir, and the pensioners who were let down by us the police, I really don't give a shit."

He smiled when he replied, "And for what it's worth, Laura, neither do I."

****

The transition of leadership from former Chief Constable Arthur Donaldson to his Deputy, Paula Clarke, was widely received by the Force with relief, not least by the rank and file who within weeks, benefited from Clarke's sweeping changes that included a review of salaries and overtime payments.

A strong-willed individual, almost immediately and ably backed by her Deputy, Jimmy Thompson, Clarke butted heads with the Police and Fire Committee to argue for more budget financial backing to replace not only the underfunded Force's aging vehicles, but the police stations that were in the main, long past necessary renovations. That and an innovative recruitment drive amongst Britain's armed forces, targeting men and women due to leave the services, was quickly initiated and within six months, resulted in several hundreds of already disciplined and mature, experienced men and women being recruited and passed through Tulliallan Training Centre, thus relieving the hard-pressed rank and file officers.

As the months passed, so did Thompson's tenure as Deputy Chief and in a notable placation to restore harmony between both Forces, he was replaced by a serving and competent Assistant Chief Constable from Lothian & Borders Police, thus mollifying that Force's anger at the arrest of John Michael Crawford.

Settling into retirement, Thompson had but seven weeks before the inoperable cancer that was previously diagnosed, finally took his life.

His funeral service that took place on a wet and windy day within Clydebank's Dalnotter Crematorium and was attended by almost three hundred mourners, mostly police officers who had served with him, past and present.

The eulogy was delivered in part by both Paula Clarke, now confirmed by the Police and Fire Committee as the new and first female Chief Constable of Strathclyde Police, and Superintendent Elizabeth Whitmore, who had the mourners inside and standing outside in the memorial garden, laughing at several anecdotes describing Thompson's comical behaviour and decisions.

It didn't escape most mourner's attention that the individual who was most upset at the widowed Thompson's service was his faithful and loyal secretary, Doris.

****

Almost to the day Jimmy Thompson's death was announced, Lizzie Whitmore competently run F Division, but then received a phone call from the ACC in charge of the Personnel Department to inform her that a Chief Superintendent Wallace, was appointed to be the new Divisional Commander.

Wallace was not a name known to her and therefore she was much surprised when two hours later that same day, her door was knocked and opened by her new boss; a man she instantly recognised.

Trevor Wallace, a former South Yorkshire Constabulary police officer, smiled when he strode into the room to introduce himself, then removing his cap, said, "I'm very pleased to be working with you, Superintendent Whitmore, and I already know how competent and loyal you were to your boss. I hope that I can earn the same support."

With a wide smile and suppressing his laugh, added, "Though I think it's unlikely I'll need you to offer me a phial from a breath kit that's showing negative."

"Now," he removed his cap, then extended his hand, "can we start off on the same page, so if I call you Lizzie then please, when it's just us, I'm Trevor."

****

To his own surprise, Constable Willie Strathmore passed his Police Elementary Examination.

Proud of his cop, Inspector Iain Cowan, now short of a constable with Drew Taylor's transfer to the Divisional Inquiry Department, neighboured Strathmore with Roz Begley in the Foxtrot Mike Two response vehicle.

No longer on the same shift, Taylor and Roz's relationship soon became public knowledge, while among others, Iain Cowan and his long-time friend, Smiler McGarry, pretended surprise.

****

Mr and Mrs Telford finally did sell their home and achieve their dream of moving to a small, one bedroomed flat on the coast in southern Spain.

Their son, Keith, did not accompany them and his whereabouts are currently unknown.

****

Two months after his arrest, John McDonald was sentenced to life imprisonment for the murder of his wife, Jessie McDonald, and nine years for the attempted murder of Constable Begley, both sentences to run concurrently.

Due to the anonymity provided to such children, his son and daughter disappeared into the Social Work foster, then adoption system, but were finally placed together with a family.

As for Patrick Cochrane.

In a deal agreed with the Crown Office, Cochrane pled guilty to the murder of Jeannie Mason and Albert Moston and one charge of the assault and robbery of Patrick Reagan. For these crimes and in recognition of his early plea and assistance in another Crown matter, Cochrane received two life sentences and one sentence of three years, all sentences to run concurrently, but with the caveat he cannot apply for early release until having served twenty-two years. As for the 'other matter,' former Assistant Chief Constable, John Michael Crawford, again in a deal agreed with Crown Office, appeared privately at the Sheriff Court in Glasgow where he pled guilty to a number of charges of corruption and perverting the course of justice.

His Lordship presiding, in previous consultation with the Lord Advocate, admonished Crawford on all charges, deeming that his disgraced dismissal from the Police and loss of both his good name, his sizeable commutation and his equally sizeable pension, was sufficient penalty. That and it would not serve the Scottish Police Service to have his crimes made public.

Her body now returned to her family, on a cold and windy morning, Jeannie Mason was interred within St Conval's Cemetery in Barrhead.

The short service was attended by her former husband, Archie, her son and daughter, Susan and Ian and several former colleagues. Among the mourners too was Constable Stuart McGarry and to his surprise, the landlady of *The Resting Soldier*, Cathy McHugh, who laid a wreath of yellow roses at the grave.

****

On the day acting Sergeant Mathew Devlin's promotion to substantive Sergeant was confirmed, DC Barbara McMillan, supported by DCI Laura Gemmill, submitted her application to join the Force's Drug Squad.

She awaits a date for her interview.

****

On a cold January day in 1980, Stuart McGarry and Sally Rodgers, supported and surrounded by family and friends, tied the knot at Martha Street Registry Office in Glasgow City Centre.

Two weeks later, Sally confirmed her suspicions that she was indeed pregnant.

****

Printed in Great Britain
by Amazon